A BLOOD-S[...]

a last despairing scream, the swirl of a black cloak vanishing in the night. Jack the Ripper has struck again! A faceless creature of nightmare bringing doom to the byways of London, he was a horror more frightening than mere imagination could conjure, as, during his seemingly unstoppable reign of terror in 1888, he sent the denizens of the city scurrying to bar their doors as soon as darkness fell.

Never caught, he continued to haunt the minds of many, speculation about his identity and the reasons for his crimes leading to the creation of many a clever story over the passing years. Now the finest of these many tales—from Sherlock Holmes' investigation of the case as revealed by Ellery Queen to a renewal of Jack-like murders near the London Bridge that was transported to Arizona—have been gathered together in one blood-freezing volume which will leave you looking over your shoulder and walking as fast as you can the next time you hear unknown footsteps following you in the night.

RED JACK

EDITED BY
Martin H. Greenberg,
Charles G. Waugh,
and Frank D. McSherry, Jr.

DAW BOOKS, INC.
DONALD A. WOLLHEIM, PUBLISHER

1633 Broadway, New York, NY 10019

DAW Book Collectors No. 766.

First Printing, December 1988

1 2 3 4 5 6 7 8 9

PRINTED IN THE U.S.A.

ACKNOWLEDGMENTS

"The Prowler in the City at the Edge of the World" by Harlan Ellison originally appeared in *Dangerous Visions;* copyright © 1967 by Harlan Ellison. Reprinted by arrangement with, and permission of, the Author and the Author's agent, Richard Curtis Associates, Inc., New York. All rights reserved. This preferred text from *The Essential Ellison.*

"Sagittarius" by Ray Russell. Copyright © 1962 by Ray Russell. First appeared, in shorter form, in *Playboy*. This complete, definitive version first appeared in *Haunted Castles* (Maclay, 1985). Used by permission of the author.

"The Whitechapel Wantons" by Vincent McConnor. Copyright © 1976 by Vincent McConnor. Reprinted by permission of the author.

A Study in Terror by Ellery Queen. Copyright © 1966 by Ellery Queen. Reprinted by permission of the agents for the author's Estate, the Scott Meredith Literary Agency, Inc., 845 Third Avenue, New York, NY 10022.

"The Final Stone" by William F. Nolan. Copyright © 1986 by William F. Nolan. First printed in *Cutting Edge*. Reprinted by permission of the author.

"Jack's Little Friend" by Ramsey Campbell. Copyright © 1975 by Ramsey Campbell. Reprinted by permission of Kirby McCauley, Ltd.

"Yours Truly, Jack the Ripper" by Robert Bloch. Copyright © 1943 by Weird Tales; renewed © 1971 by Robert Bloch. Reprinted by permission of the Scott Meredith Literary Agency, Inc., 845 Third Avenue, New York, NY 10022.

CONTENTS

SOMEBODY'S FOLLOWING YOU . . .

by Frank D. McSherry, Jr.

The pretty young woman hurried fearfully through the damp white fog billowing along the twisted streets. Her heels clicked over the cobblestones; the whitish mists distorted the sound, made the echoes seem like footsteps following her.

She paused at an intersection.

The echoes took two more steps.

Her heart lurched.

She rushed on, through the long dark tunnels between the ghostly glow of gaslamps. Behind her the steps thudded on, a man's footsteps, heavier, faster now.

She broke into a run. The footsteps did too, pounding now, and looking back she saw his dark bulk emerge from the mists. The yellow gaslight glistened wetly on the knife he held in an upraised hand.

Oh, God, it's him!

Red Jack!

Jack the Ripper!

This opening for many tales of terror was a scene that was real for all too many women in Queen Victoria's London in 1888. Between 31 August and 9 November, five women, all prostitutes, were slashed to death in Whitechapel, a half-mile square tenement area in London's notorious East End. The victims were shockingly mutilated, bodies ripped open and some in-

9

ternal organs removed and missing, horrors done with
surgical skill by someone with a scalpel-sharp knife
who may have been a doctor.

Terror swept over London as the murders continued.
Police and vigilante patrols were intensified. Yet the
killings went on, the murderer striking always in the
dark hours between midnight and dawn and moving,
as if invisible, among the many patrolling police.

After the third murder he began writing letters to the
papers and the police (genuine ones; one mentioned
details of the crime that were known only to the police
and the perpetrator, one contained half a kidney removed from the latest victim). The letters were mocking, one ending "Catch me when you can"; some even
included poems—"Eight little whores, with no hope
of Heaven; one came up to Jack, And now there are
seven"; and one poem was signed with a name that
made him famous: "I'm not a butcher, I'm not a Yid,
Nor yet a foreign skipper; I'm your own, true loving
friend, Yours truly, Jack the Ripper."

He was never caught.

Sinister, shadowy, he seemed to disappear into the
fog he came from. Even today, the one hundredth anniversary of his scarlet career, the guesses about his
true identity remain just that—guesses.

Down through the years, his bloody fame began to
spread. One of the first works of fiction featuring him,
as pointed out by Professor Edward S. Lauterbach,
was a now little-known short story, "The Mysterious
Card Unveiled," by Cleveland Moffett in *The Black
Cat* for August 1889, a sequel to the author's far better
known story, "The Mysterious Card." One of the major works about Red Jack, a short novel by Mrs. Belloc
Lowndes, "The Lodger," appeared in 1911, first
in *McClure's Magazine* and then in 1913 in hardcover.
It has been filmed again and again, most notably in
1926 by a then-unknown director named Alfred Hitchcock. Later versions starred Laird Cregar (1944) and
Jack Palance (1954, re-titled *The Man in the Attic*), as

the brooding, mysterious tenant suspected by his terrified landlady of being the Ripper. (It has even been made into operas, first in 1926 by Alban Berg and in 1960 by Phyllis Tate. The Ripper also appears, disguised as Captain MacHeath, in *The Three Penny Opera* of Bertolt Brecht, and stars as the subject of the hit song, "Mack the Knife.")

But it is only with recent times, in our own generation, that Red Jack has come into his own in fiction, film and fact. Beginning with Robert Bloch's classic short story of terror, "Yours Truly, Jack the Ripper," in 1943, novels, fact studies, films and TV episodes featuring Jack came in a flood. Hardly a year has passed since then without some major publisher, film maker or TV network producing a work about Jack the Ripper. (To list merely a few, there are such factual accounts as *When London Walked in Terror* by Tom Cullen; *The Identity of Jack the Ripper* by Donald McCormick; *The Complete Jack the Ripper* by Donald Rumbelow; films such as *The Final Decree* and a Star Trek episode, "Catspaw"; and novels such as *The Return of Jack the Ripper* by Mark Andrews; *Terror Over London* by Gardner F. Fox; *Jack the Ripper* by Richard Gordon; and Bloch's own *Night of the Ripper*. Nor does this include works based on the case.)

And there's this book you're holding now. It's filled with short stories and novelettes by such writers as Robert Bloch, author of the novel *Psycho* (later filmed by Alfred Hitchcock); Harlan Ellison, multiple Hugo-winner; William F. Nolan, author of the recent (1985) TV movie *Bridge Across Time,* about the Ripper in today's world; and we've even included two books, the already-mentioned *The Lodger,* and a never-before-reprinted Ellery Queen novel, *A Study in Terror,* in which both Ellery and Sherlock Holmes face the problem of the Ripper. And more—

Why is it, that, as the world moves farther and farther away from Victorian times and into the nuclear age, it becomes more and more fascinated by this blood-drenched, shuddery figure of a hundred years ago? A personality that, apparently, could not resist a compulsion to kill?

Psychoanalysts have suggested that this shadowy figure of the Ripper appeals to dark, repressed urges deep inside us; reading about him provides us with a harmless and valuable release for those urges. Correct as this probably is, though, it fails to account for the growing and intense interest felt in Red Jack by our own less repressed age.

Perhaps there is another, hitherto unnoticed reason—

One of the most scary themes of mystery fiction is this: most people cannot tell if one of the seemingly normal-looking people around them is a homicidal maniac.

Between 1953 and 1957 women disappeared in the small town of Plainfield, Wisconsin. Lifelong friends of amiable local handyman Ed Gein jokingly accused him of being responsible and laughed and laughed when Ed replied that yes, he'd hung their bodies up in his shed for butchering and dressing. In November 1957, a lady hardware store owner was found shot to death. Since Gein had been one of her last customers that day, police entered his shed to investigate—and recoiled in horror at what hung from the ceiling. Good old Ed, it seemed, hadn't been kidding. . . .

Robert Bloch based his famous novel, *Psycho*, on newspaper accounts of this case, impressed by the fact that none of the many people who had known Gein for years ever suspected for a moment that he was criminally insane.

Nor is Gein the only homicidal maniac to move, unsuspected, among us. Look at the literally millions of people who failed to recognized the criminal insanity of such monsters as Adolf Hitler or Josef Stalin, people who voted enthusiastically for such killers.

Jack the Ripper, the blood-drenched symbol of the murdering maniac, was never caught. Obviously, none

of the people he lived and worked among ever realized
who and what he was behind his mask of morality.

(Or did they? The Ripper killings ended as abruptly
as they began; perhaps some private citizen instituted
a kind of private justice. Or perhaps, as some authorities have suggested, the Ripper may simply have
moved to another country, to continue his bloody work
elsewhere. There may have been Ripper murders before and after the five officially credited to him (his
poem suggests more), two at the start of 1888, two
more a year later and a third in 1891; the authorities
disagree.)

And perhaps that is why, as our nuclear arsenals
grow, so does our fascination with Jack the Ripper.
Today we have weapons that can kill the whole human
race and destroy all life on this planet; Red Jack is
someone who cannot keep himself from killing; and
the person you vote into power might be, for all you
know, another Jack the Ripper. In the Oval Office, a
red button waits for Red Jack. . . .

Who goes there?

Through the billowing white fog, in the twisted
streets and alleyways of London's Whitechapel, in the
Kremlin . . . or even in the White House. . . .

My God, it's *him!*

Red Jack!

Jack the Ripper!

Someone may be following you tonight . . . or worse
yet he may be leading you.

Turn the pages, and find the lasting legacy of Jack
the Ripper—icy terror, and horror hot as red blood.
Tales that, for all their entertainment value, carry an
extra and horrifying meaning for our time—

THE PROWLER IN THE CITY AT THE EDGE OF THE WORLD

by Harlan Ellison

First there was the City, never night. Tin and reflective, walls of antiseptic metal like an immense autoclave. Pure and dust-free, so silent that even the whirling innards of its heart and mind were sheathed from notice. The city was self-contained, and footfalls echoed up and around—flat slapped notes of an exotic leather-footed instrument. Sounds that reverberated back to the maker like yodels thrown out across mountain valleys. Sounds made by humbled inhabitants whose lives were as ordered, as sanitary, as metallic as the city they had caused to hold them bosom-tight against the years. The city was a complex artery, the people were the blood that flowed icily through the artery. They were a gestalt with one another, forming a unified whole. It was a city shining in permanence, eternal in concept, flinging itself up in a formed and molded statement of exaltation; most modern of all modern structures, conceived as the pluperfect residence for the perfect people. The final end-result of all sociological blueprints aimed at Utopia. Living space, it had been called, and so, doomed to *live* they were, in that Erewhon of graphed respectability and cleanliness.

Never night.

Never shadowed.

. . . a shadow.

A blot moving against the aluminum cleanliness. The movement of rags and bits of clinging earth from graves sealed ages before. A shape.

He touched a gunmetal-gray wall in passing: the imprint of dusty fingers. A twisted shadow moving through antiseptically pure streets, and they become—with his passing—black alleys from another time.

Vaguely, he knew what had happened. Not specifically, not with particulars, but he was strong, and he was able to get away without the eggshell-thin walls of his mind caving in. There was no place in this shining structure to secrete himself, a place to think, but he had to have time. He slowed his walk, seeing no one. Somehow—inexplicably—he felt . . . safe? Yes, safe. For the first time in a very long time.

A few minutes before he had been standing in the narrow passageway outside No. 13 Miller's Court. It had been 6:15 in the morning. London had been quiet as he paused in the passageway of M'Carthy's Rents, in that fetid, urine-redolent corridor where the whores of Spitalfields took their clients. A few minutes before, the foetus in its bath of formaldehyde tightly-stoppered in a glass bottle inside his Gladstone bag, he had paused to drink in the thick fog, before taking the circuitous route back to Toynbee Hall. That had been a few minutes before. Then, suddenly, he was in another place and it was no longer 6:15 of a chill November morning in 1888.

He had looked up as light flooded him in that other place. It had been soot silent in Spitalfields, but suddenly, without any sense of having moved or having *been* moved, he was flooded with light. And when he looked up he was in that other place. Paused now, only a few minutes after the transfer, he leaned against the bright wall of the city, and recalled the light. From a thousand mirrors. In the walls, in the ceiling. A bedroom with a girl in it. A lovely girl. Not like Black Mary Kelly or Dark Annie Chapman or Kate Eddowes

or any of the other pathetic scum he had been forced
to attend . . .

A lovely girl. Blonde, wholesome, until she had
opened her robe and turned into the same sort of slut
he had been compelled to use in his work in Whitechapel . . .

A sybarite, a creature of pleasures, a Juliette she had
said, before he used the big-bladed knife on her. He
had found the knife under the pillow, on the bed to
which she had led him—how shameful, unresisting had
he been, all confused, clutching his black bag with all
the tremors of a child, he who had moved through the
London night like oil, moved where he wished, accomplished his ends unchecked eight times, now led
toward sin by another, merely another of the tarts, taking advantage of him while he tried to distinguish what
had happened to him and where he was, how shameful—
and he had used it on her.

That had only been minutes before, though he had
worked very efficiently on her.

The knife had been rather unusual. The blade had
seemed to be two wafer-thin sheets of metal with a
pulsing, glowing *something* between. A kind of spark-
ing, such as might be produced by a Van de Graaff
generator. But that was patently ridiculous. It had no
wires attached to it, no bus bars, nothing to produce
even the crudest electrical discharge. He had thrust the
knife into the Gladstone bag, where now it lay beside
the scalpels and the spool of catgut and the racked
vials in their leather cases, and the foetus in its bottle.
Mary Jane Kelly's foetus.

He had worked efficiently, but swiftly, and had laid
her out almost exactly in the same fashion as Kate
Eddowes: the throat slashed completely through from
ear-to-ear, the torso laid open down between the
breasts to the vagina, the intestines pulled out and
draped over the right shoulder, a piece of the intestines
being detached and placed between the left arm and
the body. The liver had been punctured with the point

of the knife, with a vertical cut slitting the left lobe of the liver. (He had been surprised to find the liver showed none of the signs of cirrhosis so prevalent in these Spitalfields tarts, who drank incessantly to rid themselves of the burden of living the dreary lives they moved through grotesquely. In fact, this one seemed totally unlike the others, even if she had been more brazen in her sexual overtures. And that knife under the bed pillow . . .) He had severed the vena cava leading to the heart. Then he had gone to work on the face.

He had thought of removing the left kidney again, as he had Kate Eddowes's. He smiled to himself as he conjured up the expression that must have been on the face of Mr. George Lusk, chairman of the Whitechapel Vigilance Committee, when he received the cardboard box in the mail. The box containing Miss Eddowes's kidney, and the letter, impiously misspelled:

> *From hell, Mr. Lusk, sir, I send you half the*
> *kidne I took from one woman, prasarved it*
> *for you, tother piece I fried and ate it; was*
> *very nice. I may send you the bloody knif*
> *that took it out if you only wate while*
> *longer. Catch me when you can, Mr. Lusk.*

He had wanted to sign *that* one "Yours Truly, Jack the Ripper" or even Spring-Heeled Jack or maybe Leather Apron, whichever had tickled his fancy, but a sense of style had stopped him. To go too far was to defeat his own purposes. It may even have been too much to suggest to Mr. Lusk that he had eaten the kidney. How hideous. True, he *had* smelled it . . .

This blonde girl, this Juliette with the knife under her pillow. She was the ninth. He leaned against the smooth steel wall without break or seam, and he rubbed his eyes. When would he be able to stop? When would they realize, when would they get his message, a message so clear, written in blood, that only the blindness of their own cupidity forced them to mis-understand! Would he be compelled to decimate the endless regiments of Spitalfields sluts to make them understand? Would he be forced to run the cobbles ankle-deep in black blood before they sensed what he was saying, and were impelled to make reforms?

But as he took his blood-soaked hands from his eyes, he realized what he must have sensed all along: he was no longer in Whitechapel. This was not Miller's Court, nor anywhere in Spitalfields. It might not even be London. But how could *that* be?

Had God taken him?

Had he died, in a senseless instant between the anatomy lesson of Mary Jane Kelly (that filth, she had actually *kissed* him!) and the bedroom disembowelment of this Juliette? Had Heaven finally called him to his reward for the work he had done?

The Reverend Mr. Barnett would love to know about this. But then, he'd have loved to know about it *all*. But "Bloody Jack" wasn't about to tell. Let the reforms come as the Reverend and his wife wished for them, and let them think their pamphleteering had done it, instead of the scalpels of Jack.

If he was dead, would his work be finished? He smiled to himself. If Heaven had taken him, then it must be that the work *was* finished. Successfully. But if *that* was so, then who was this Juliette who now lay spread out moist and cooling in the bedroom of a thousand mirrors? And in that instant he felt fear.

What if even God misinterpreted what he had done?

As the good folk of Queen Victoria's London had misinterpreted. As Sir Charles Warren had misinterpreted. What if God believed the superficial and ignored the *real* reason? But no! Ludicrous. If anyone would understand, it was the good God who had sent him the message that told him to set things a-right.

God loved him, as he loved God, and God would know.

But he felt fear, in that moment.

Because who was the girl he had just carved?

"She was my granddaughter, Juliette," said a voice immediately beside him.

His head refused to move, to turn that few inches to see who spoke. The Gladstone was beside him, resting on the smooth and reflective surface of the street. He could not get to a knife before he was taken. At last they had caught up with Jack. He began to shiver uncontrollably.

"No need to be afraid," the voice said. It was a warm and succoring voice. An older man. He shook as with an ague. But he turned to look. It was a kindly old man with a gentle smile. Who spoke again, without moving his lips. "No one can hurt you. How do you do?"

The man from 1888 sank slowly to his knees. "Forgive me. Dear God, I did not know." The old man's laughter rose inside the head of the man on his knees. It rose like a beam of sunlight moving across a Whitechapel alleyway, from noon to one o'clock, rising and illuminating the gray bricks of soot-coated walls. It rose, and illuminated his mind.

"I'm not God. Marvelous idea, but no, I'm not God. Would you like to meet God? I'm sure we can find one of the artists who would mold one for you. Is it important? No, I can see it isn't. What a strange mind you have. You neither believe nor doubt. How can you contain both concepts at once . . . would you like me to straighten some of your brain-patterns? No. I see, you're afraid. Well, let it be for the nonce. We'll do it another time."

He grabbed the kneeling man and drew him erect.

"You're covered with blood. Have to get you cleaned up. There's an ablute near here. Incidentally, I was very impressed with the way you handled Juliette. You're the first, you know. No, how could you know? In any case, you *are* the first to deal her as good as she gave. You would have been amused at what she did to Caspar Hauser. Squeezed part of his brain and then sent him back, let him live out part of his life and then—the little twit—she made me bring him back a second time and used a knife on him. Same knife you took, I believe. Then sent him back to his own time. Marvelous mystery. In all the tapes on unsolved phenomena. But she was much sloppier than you. She had a great verve in her amusements, but very little *éclat*. Except with Judge Crater; there she was—'' He paused, and laughed lightly. "I'm an old man and I ramble on like a muskrat. You want to get cleaned up and shown around, I know. And *then* we can talk.

"I just wanted you to know I was satisfied with the way you disposed of her. In a way, I'll miss the little twit. She was such a good fuck.''

The old man picked up the Gladstone bag and, holding the man spattered with blood, he moved off down the clean and shimmering street. "You *wanted* her killed?" the man from 1888 asked, unbelieving.

The old man nodded, but his lips never moved. "Of course. Otherwise why bring her Jack the Ripper?''

Oh my dear God, he thought, *I'm in Hell. And I'm entered as Jack.*

"No, my boy, no no no. You're not in Hell at all. You're in the future. For you the future, for me the world of now. You came from 1888 and you're now in—'' he stopped, silently speaking for an instant, as though computing apples in terms of dollars, then resumed ''—3077. It's a fine world, filled with happy times, and we're glad to have you with us. Come along now, and you'll wash.''

In the ablutatorium, the late Juliette's grandfather changed his head.

"I really despise it,'' he informed the man from 1888, grabbing fingerfuls of his cheeks and stretching the flabby skin like elastic. "But Juliette insisted. I was willing to humor her, if indeed that was what it took to get her to lie down. But what with toys from the past, and changing my head every time I wanted her to fuck me, it was trying; very trying."

He stepped into one of the many identically shaped booths set flush into the walls. The tambour door rolled down and there was a soft *chukk* sound, almost chitinous. The tambour door rolled up and the late Juliette's grandfather, now six years younger than the man from 1888, stepped out, stark naked and wearing a new head. "The body is fine, replaced last year," he said, examining the genitals and a mole on his right shoulder. The man from 1888 looked away. This was Hell and God hated him.

"Well, don't just *stand* there, Jack." Juliette's grandfather smiled. "Hit one of those booths and get your ablutions."

"That isn't my name," said the man from 1888 very softly, as though he had been whipped.

"It'll do, it'll do . . . now go get washed."

Jack approached one of the booths. It was a light green in color, but changed to mauve as he stopped in front of it. "Will it—"

"It will only *clean* you, what are you afraid of?"

"I don't want to be changed."

Juliette's grandfather did not laugh. "That's a mistake," he said cryptically. He made a peremptory motion with his hand and the man from 1888 entered the booth, which promptly revolved in its niche, sank into the floor and made a hearty *zeeeeezzzz* sound. When it rose and revolved and opened, Jack stumbled out, looking terribly confused. His long sideburns had been neatly trimmed, his beard stubble had been removed, his hair was three shades lighter and was now parted on the left side, rather than in the middle. He still wore the same long dark coat trimmed with astrakhan, dark suit with white collar and black necktie (in which was fastened a horseshoe stickpin) but now the garments seemed new, unsoiled of course, possibly synthetics built to look like his former garments.

"Now!" Juliette's grandfather said. "Isn't that

much better? A good cleansing always sets one's mind to rights.'' And he stepped into another booth from which he issued in a moment wearing a soft paper jumper that fitted from neck to feet without a break. He moved toward the door.

"Where are we going?" the man from 1888 asked the younger grandfather beside him. "I want you to meet someone," said Juliette's grandfather, and Jack realized that he was moving his lips now. He decided not to comment on it. There had to be a reason.

"I'll walk you there, if you promise not to make gurgling sounds at the city. It's a nice city, but I live here, and frankly, tourism is boring.'' Jack did not reply. Grandfather took it for acceptance of the terms.

They walked. Jack became overpowered by the sheer *weight* of the city. It was obviously extensive, massive, and terribly clean. It was his dream for Whitechapel come true. He asked about slums, about doss houses. The grandfather shook his head. "Long gone.''

So it had come to pass. The reforms for which he had pledged his immortal soul, they had come to pass. He swung the Gladstone and walked jauntily. But after a few minutes his pace sagged once more: there was no one to be seen in the streets.

Just shining clean buildings and streets that ran off in aimless directions and came to unexpected stops as though the builders had decided people might vanish at one point and reappear someplace else, so why bother making a road from one point to the other.

The ground was metal, the sky seemed metallic, the buildings loomed on all sides, featureless explorations of planed space by insensitive metal. The man from 1888 felt terribly alone, as though every act he had performed had led inevitably to his alienation from the very people he had sought to aid.

When he had come to Toynbee Hall, and the Reverend Mr. Barnett had opened his eyes to the slum horrors of Spitalfields, he had vowed to help in any way he could. It had seemed as simple as faith in the Lord, what to do, after a few months in the sinkholes of Whitechapel. The sluts, of what use were they? No more use than the disease germs that had infected these very same whores. So he had set forth as Jack, to perform the will of God and raise the poor dregs who inhabited the East End of London. That Lord Warren, the Metropolitan Police Commissioner, and His Queen, and all the rest thought him a mad doctor, or an amok butcher, or a beast in human form did not distress him. He knew he would remain anonymous through all time, but that the good works he had set in motion would proceed to their wonderful conclusion.

The destruction of the most hideous slum area the country had ever known, and the opening of Victorian eyes. But all the time *had* passed, and now he was here, in a world where slums apparently did not exist, a sterile Utopia that was the personification of the Reverend Mr. Barnett's dreams—but it didn't seem . . . *right*.

This grandfather, with his young head.

Silence in the empty streets.

The girl, Juliette, and her strange hobby.

The lack of concern at her death.

The grandfather's expectation that he, Jack, *would* kill her. And now his friendliness.

Where were they going?

[Around them, the City. As they walked, the grandfather paid no attention, and Jack watched but did not understand. But this was what they saw as they walked:

[Thirteen hundred beams of light, one foot wide and seven molecules thick, erupted from almost-invisible slits in the metal streets, fanned out and washed the surfaces of the buildings; they altered hue to a vague blue and washed down the surfaces of the buildings; they bent and covered all open surfaces, bent at right angles, then bent again, and again, like origami paper figures; they altered hue a second time, soft gold, and penetrated the surfaces of the buildings, expanding and contracting in solid waves, washing the inner surfaces; they withdrew rapidly into the sidewalks; the entire process had taken twelve seconds.

[Night fell over a sixteen block area of the City. It descended in a solid pillar and was quite sharp-edged, ending at the street corners. From within the area of darkness came the distinct sounds of crickets, marsh frogs belching, night birds, soft breezes in trees, and faint music of unidentifiable instruments.

[Panes of frosted light appeared suspended freely in the air, overhead. A wavery insubstantial quality began to assault the topmost levels of a great structure directly in front of the light-panes. As the panes moved slowly down through the air, the building became indistinct, turned into motes of light, and floated upward. As the panes reached the pavement, the building had been completely dematerialized. The panes shifted color to a deep orange, and began moving upward again. As they moved, a new structure began to form where the previous building had stood, drawing—it seemed—motes of light from the air and forming them into a cohesive whole that became, as the panes ceased their upward movement, a new building. The light-panes winked out of existence.

[The sound of a bumblebee was heard for several seconds. Then it ceased.

[A crowd of people in rubber garments hurried out of a gray pulsing hole in the air, patted the pavement at their feet, then rushed off around a corner, from where emanated the sound of prolonged coughing. Then silence returned.

[A drop of water, thick as quicksilver, plummeted to the pavement, struck, rebounded, rose several inches, then evaporated into a crimson smear in the shape of a whale's tooth, which settled to the pavement and lay still.

[Two blocks of buildings sank into the pavement and the metal covering was smooth and unbroken save for a metal tree whose trunk was silver and slim, topped by a ball of foliage constructed of golden fibers that radiated brightly in a perfect circle. There was no sound.

[The late Juliette's grandfather and the man from 1888 continued walking.]

"Where are we going?"

"To van Cleef's. We don't usually walk; oh, sometimes; but it isn't as much pleasure as it used to be. I'm doing this primarily for you. Are you enjoying yourself?"

"It's . . . unusual."

"Not much like Spitalfields, is it? But I rather like it back there, at that time. I have the only Traveler, did you know? The only one ever made. Juliette's father constructed it, my son. I had to kill him to get it. He was thoroughly unreasonable about it, really. It was a casual thing for him. He was the last of the tinkerers, and he might just as easily have given it to me. But I suppose he was being cranky. That was why I had you carve up my granddaughter. She would have gotten around to me almost any time now. Bored, just silly bored is what she was—"

The gardenia took shape in the air in front of them, and turned into the face of a woman with long white hair. "Hernon, we can't wait much longer!" She was annoyed.

Juliette's grandfather grew livid. "You scum bitch! I *told* you pace. But no, you just couldn't, could you? Jump jump jump, that's all you ever do. Well, now it'll only be feddels less, that's all. Feddels, damn you! I set it for pace, I was *working* pace, and *you* . . . !"

His hand came up and moss grew instantly toward the face. The face vanished, and a moment later the gardenia reappeared a few feet away. The moss shriveled and Hernon, Juliette's grandfather, dropped his hand, as though weary of the woman's stupidity. A rose, a water lily, a hyacinth, a pair of phlox, a wild

celandine, and a bull thistle appeared near the gardenia. As each turned into the face of a different person,
Jack stepped back, frightened.

All the faces turned to the one that had been the bull
thistle. "Cheat! Rotten bastard!" they screamed at the
thin white face that had been the bull thistle. The
gardenia-woman's eyes bulged from her face, the deep
purple eye-shadow that completely surrounded the
eyeball making her look like a deranged animal peering out of a cave. "Turd!" she shrieked at the bull
thistle-man. "We all agreed, we all said and agreed;
you *had* to formz a thistle, didn't you, scut! Well, now
you'll see . . ."

She addressed herself instantly to the others.
"Formz now! To hell with waiting, pace fuck! Now!"

"No, dammit!" Hernon shouted. "We were going
to *paaaaace!*" But it was too late. Centering in on the
bull thistle-man, the air roiled thickly like silt at a
river-bottom, and the air blackened as a spiral began
with the now terrified face of the bull thistle-man and
exploded whirling outward, enveloping Jack and Hernon and all the flower-people and the City and suddenly it was night in Spitalfields and the man from
1888 was *in* 1888, with his Gladstone bag in his hand,
and a woman approaching down the street toward him,
shrouded in the London fog.

(There were eight additional nodules in Jack's
brain.)

The woman was about forty, weary and not too
clean. She wore a dark dress of rough material that
reached down to her boots. Over the skirt was fastened
a white apron that was stained and wrinkled. The
bulbed sleeves ended midway up her wrists and the
bodice of the dress was buttoned close around her
throat. She wore a kerchief tied at the neck, and a hat
that looked like a wide-brimmed skimmer with a raised
crown. There was a pathetic little flower of unidentifiable origin in the band of the hat. She carried a

beaded handbag of capacious size, hanging from a wrist-loop.

Her step slowed as she saw him standing there, deep in the shadows. Saw him was hardly accurate: sensed him.

He stepped out and bowed slightly from the waist. "Fair evenin' to ye, Miss. Care for a pint?"

Her features—sunk in misery of a kind known only to women who have taken in numberless shafts of male blood-gorged flesh—rearranged themselves. "Coo, sir, I thought was 'im for true. Old Leather Apron hisself. Gawdamighty, you give me a scare." She tried to smile. It was a rictus. There were bright spots in her cheeks from sickness and too much gin. Her voice was ragged, a broken-edged instrument barely workable.

"Just a solicitor caught out without comp'ny," Jack assured her. "And pleased to buy a handsome lady a pint of stout for a few hours' companionship."

She stepped toward him and linked arms. "Emily Matthewes, sir, an' pleased to go with you. It's a fearsome chill night, and with Slippery Jack abroad not safe for a respectin' woman such's m'self."

They moved off down Thrawl Street, past the doss houses where this drab might flop later, if she could obtain a few coppers from this neat-dressed stranger with the dark eyes.

He turned right onto Commercial Street, and just abreast of a stinking alley almost to Flower & Dean Street, he nudged her sharply sidewise. She went into the alley, and thinking he meant to steal a smooth hand up under her petticoats, she settled back against the wall and opened her legs, starting to lift the skirt around her waist. But Jack had hold of the kerchief and, locking his fingers tightly, he twisted, cutting off her breath. Her cheeks ballooned, and by a vagary of light from a gas standard in the street he could see her eyes go from hazel to a dead-leaf brown in an instant. Her expression was one of terror, naturally, but commingled with it was a deep sadness, at having lost the

pint, at having not been able to make her doss for the
night, at having had the usual Emily Matthewes bad
luck to run afoul this night of the one man who would
ill-use her favors. It was a consummate sadness at the
inevitability of her fate.

> *I come to you out of the night.*
> *The night that sent me down*
> *all the minutes of our lives*
> *to this instant.*
> *From this time forward, men will*
> *wonder what happened*
> *at this instant. They will silently*
> *hunger to go back, to come to my*
> *instant with you and see my face*
> *and know my name and perhaps*
> *not even try to stop me, for*
> *then I would not be who I am,*
> *but only someone who tried*
> *and failed. Ah.*
> *For you and me it becomes history*
> *that will lure men always;*
> *but they will never understand*
> *why we both suffered, Emily;*
> *they will never truly understand*
> *why each of us died so terribly.*

A film came over her eyes, and as her breath husked
out in wheezing, pleading tremors, his free hand went
into the pocket of the greatcoat. He had known he
would need it, when they were walking, and he had
already invaded the Gladstone bag. Now his hand went
into the pocket and came up with the scalpel.

"Emily . . ." softly.

Then he sliced her.

Neatly, angling the point of the scalpel into the soft
flesh behind and under her left ear. *Sternocleidomas-
toideus.* Driving it in to the gentle crunch of cartilage
giving way. Then, grasping the instrument tightly, tip-

ping it down and drawing it across the width of the throat, following the line of the firm jaw. *Glandula submandibularis.* The blood poured out over his hands, ran thickly at first and then burst spattering past him, reaching the far wall of the alley. Up his sleeves, soaking his white cuffs. She made a watery rattle and sank limply in his grasp, his fingers still twisted tight in her kerchief; black abrasions where he had scored the flesh. He continued the cut up past the point of the jaw's end, and sliced into the lobe of the ear. He lowered her to the filthy paving. She lay crumpled, and he straightened her. Then he cut away the garments laying her naked belly open to the wan and flickering light of the gas standard in the street. Her belly was bloated. He started the primary cut in the hollow of her throat. *Glandula thyreoeidea.* His hand was sure as he drew a thin black line of blood down and down, between the breasts. *Sternum.* Cutting a deep cross in the hole of her navel. Something vaguely yellow oozed up. *Plica umbilicalis medialis.* Down over the rounded hump of the belly, biting more deeply, withdrawing for a neat incision. *Mesenterium dorsale commune.* Down to the matted-with-sweat roundness of her privates. Harder here. *Vesica urinaria.* And finally, to the end, *vagina.*

Filth hole.

Foul-smelling die red lust pit wet hole of sluts.

And in his head, succubi. And in his head, eyes watching. And in his head, minds impinging. And in his head titillation

for a gardenia
  a water lily
  a rose
  a hyacinth
  a pair of phlox
  a wild celandine
and a dark flower with petals of obsidian, a stamen

of onyx, pistils of anthracite, and the mind of Hernon, who was the late Juliette's grandfather.

They watched the entire horror of the mad anatomy lesson. They watched him nick the eyelids. They watched him remove the heart. They watched him slice out the fallopian tubes. They watched him squeeze, till it ruptured, the "ginny" kidney. They watched him slice off the sections of the breast till they were nothing but shapeless mounds of bloody meat, and arrange them, one mound each on a still-staring, wide-open, nicked-eyelid eye. They watched.

They watched and they drank from the deep troubled pool of his mind. They sucked deeply at the moist quivering core of his id. And they delighted:

Oh God how Delicious look at that It looks like the uneaten rind of a Pizza or look at That It looks like lumaconi *oh god IIIIIwonder what it would be like to Tasteit!*

See how smooth the steel.

He hates them all, every one of them, something about a girl, a venereal disease, fear of his God, Christ, the Reverend Mr. Barnett, he . . . he wants to fuck the reverend's wife!

Social reform can only be brought about by concerted effort of a devoted few. Social reform is a justifiable end, condoning any expedient short of decimation of over fifty percent of the people who will be served by the reforms. The best social reformers are the most audacious. He believes it! How lovely!

You pack of vampires, you filth, you scum, you . . .

He senses us!

Damn him! Damn you, Hernon, you drew off too deeply, he knows we're here, that's disgusting, what's the sense now? I'm withdrawing!

Come back, you'll end the formz . . .

. . . back they plunged in the spiral as it spiraled back in upon itself and the darkness of the night of 1888 withdrew. The spiral drew in and in and locked at its most infinitesimal point as the charred and blackened face of the man who had been the bull thistle. He was quite dead. His eyeholes had been burned out; charred wreckage lay where intelligence had lived. They had used him as a focus.

The man from 1888 came back to himself instantly, with a full and eidetic memory of what he had just experienced. It had neither been a vision, nor a dream, nor a delusion, nor a product of his mind. It had happened. They had sent him back, erased his mind of the transfer into the future, of Juliette, of everything after the moment outside No. 13 Miller's Court. And they had set him to work pleasuring them, while they drained off his feelings, his emotions and his unconscious thoughts; while they battened and gorged themselves with the most private sensations. Most of which, till this moment—in a strange feedback—he had not even known he possessed. As his mind plunged on from one revelation to the next, he felt himself growing ill. At one concept his mind tried to pull back and plunge him into darkness rather than confront it. But the barriers were down, they had opened new patterns and he could read it all, remember it all. *Stinking sex hole, sluts, they have to die.* No, that wasn't the way he thought of women, any women, no matter how low or common. He was a gentleman, and women were to be respected. *She had given him the clap. He remembered.* The shame and the endless fear till he had gone to his physician father and confessed it. The look on the man's face. He remembered it all. The way his father had tended him, the way he would have tended a plague victim. It had never been the same between them again. He had tried for the cloth. *Social reform hahahaha.* All delusion. He had been a mountebank, a clown . . . and worse. He had slaughtered for something in which not even he believed. They left his mind wide open, and his thoughts stumbled . . . raced further and further toward the thought of

EXPLOSION!IN!HIS!MIND!

He fell face forward on the smooth and polished metal pavement, but he never touched. Something arrested his fall, and he hung suspended, bent over at the waist like a ridiculous Punch divested of strings or manipulation from above. A whiff of something invisible, and he was in full possession of his senses almost before they had left him. His mind was forced to look at it:

He wants to fuck the Reverend Mr. Barnett's wife.

Henrietta, with her pious petition to Queen Victoria—"Madam, we, the women of East London, feel horror at the dreadful sins that have been lately committed in our midst . . ."—asking for the capture of himself, of Jack, whom she would never, not *ever* suspect was residing right there with her and the Reverend in Toynbee Hall. The thought was laid as naked as her body in the secret dreams he had never remembered upon awakening. All of it, they had left him with opened doors, with unbounded horizons, and he saw himself for what he was.

A psychopath, a butcher, a lecher, a hypocrite, a clown.

"You did this to me! Why did you do this?"

Frenzy cloaked his words. The flower-faces became the solidified hedonists who had taken him back to 1888 on that senseless voyage of slaughter.

van Cleef, the gardenia-woman, sneered. "Why do you think, you ridiculous bumpkin? (Bumpkin, is that the right colloquialism, Hernon? I'm so uncertain in the mid-dialects.) When you'd done in Juliette, Hernon wanted to send you back. But why should he? He owed us at least three formz, and you did passing well for one of them."

Jack shouted at them till the cords stood out in his throat. "Was it necessary, this last one? Was it important to do it, to help my reforms . . . was it?"

Hernon laughed. "Of course not."

Jack sank to his knees. The City let him do it. "Oh God, oh God almighty, I've done what I've done . . .

I'm covered with blood . . . and for *nothing,* for *nothing* . . .''

Cashio, who had been one of the phlox, seemed puzzled. "Why is he concerned about *this* one, if the others don't bother him?"

Nosy Verlag, who had been a wild celandine, said sharply, "They do, all of them do. Probe him, you'll see."

Cashio's eyes rolled up in his head an instant, then rolled down and refocused—Jack felt a quicksilver shudder in his mind and it was gone—and he said lackadaisically, "Mm-hmm."

Jack fumbled with the latch of the Gladstone. He opened the bag and pulled out the foetus in the bottle. Mary Jane Kelly's unborn child, from November 9th, 1888. He held it in front of his face a moment, then dashed it to the metal pavement. It never struck. It vanished a fraction of an inch from the clean, sterile surface of the City's street.

"What marvelous loathing!" exulted Rose, who had been a rose.

"Hernon," said van Cleef, "he's centering on you. He begins to blame you for all of this."

Hernon was laughing (without moving his lips) as Jack pulled Juliette's electrical scalpel from the Gladstone, and lunged. Jack's words were incoherent, but what he was saying, as he struck, was: "I'll show you what filth you are! I'll show you you can't do this kind of thing! I'll teach you! You'll die, all of you!" This is what he was saying, but it came out as one long sustained bray of revenge, frustration, hatred and directed frenzy.

Hernon was still laughing as Jack drove the whisper-thin blade with its shimmering current into his chest. Almost without manipulation on Jack's part, the blade circumscribed a perfect 360° hole that charred and shriveled, exposing Hernon's pulsing heart and wet organs. He had time to shriek with confusion before he received Jack's second thrust, a direct lunge that severed the heart from its attachments. *Vena cava superior. Aorta. Arteria pulmonalis. Bronchus principalis.*

The heart flopped forward and a spreading wedge of blood under tremendous pressure ejaculated, spraying Jack with such force that it knocked his hat from his head and blinded him. His face was now a dripping black-red collage of features and blood.

Hernon followed his heart, and fell forward, into Jack's arms. Then the flower-people screamed as one, vanished, and Hernon's body slipped from Jack's hands to wink out of existence an instant before it struck at Jack's feet. The walls around him were clean, unspotted, sterile, metallic, uncaring.

He stood in the street, holding the bloody knife.

"Now!" he screamed, holding the knife aloft. "Now it begins!"

If the city heard, it made no indication, but

[Pressure accelerated in temporal linkages.]

[A section of shining wall on the building eighty miles away changed from silver to rust.]

[In the freezer chambers, two hundred gelatin caps were fed into a ready trough.]

[The weathermaker spoke softly to itself, accepted data and instantly constructed an intangible mnemonic circuit.]

and in the shining eternal city where night only fell when the inhabitants had need of night and called specifically for night . . .

Night fell. With no warning save: *"Now!"*

In the City of sterile loveliness a creature of filth and decaying flesh prowled. In the last City of the world, a City on the edge of the world, where the ones who had devised their own paradise lived, the prowler made his home in shadows. Slipping from darkness to darkness with eyes that saw only movement, he roamed in search of a partner to dance his deadly rigadoon.

He found the first woman as she materialized beside

a small waterfall that flowed out of empty air and dropped its shimmering, tinkling moisture into an azure cube of nameless material. He found her and drove the living blade into the back of her neck. Then he sliced out the eyeballs and put them into her open hands.

He found the second woman in one of the towers, making love to a very old man who gasped and wheezed and clutched his heart as the young woman forced him to passion. She was killing him as Jack killed her. He drove the living blade into the lower rounded surface of her belly, piercing her sex organs as she rode astride the old man. She decamped blood and viscous fluids over the prostrate body of the old man, who also died, for Jack's blade had severed the penis within the young woman. She fell forward across the old man and Jack left them that way, joined in the final embrace.

He found a man and throttled him with his bare hands, even as the man tried to dematerialize. Then Jack recognized him as one of the phlox, and made neat incisions in the face, into which he inserted the man's genitals.

He found another woman as she was singing a gentle song about eggs to a group of children. He opened her throat and severed the strings hanging inside. He let the vocal cords drop onto her chest. But he did not touch the children, who watched it all avidly. He liked children.

He prowled through the unending night making a grotesque collection of hearts, which he cut out of one, three, nine people. And when he had a dozen, he took them and laid them as road markers on one of the wide boulevards that never were used by vehicles, for the people of this City had no need of vehicles.

Oddly, the City did not clean up the hearts. Nor were the people vanishing any longer. He was able to move with relative impunity, hiding only when he saw large groups that might be searching for him. But *something* was happening in the City. (Once, he heard the peculiar sound of metal grating on metal, the *skrikkk* of plastic cutting into plastic—and he instinctively knew it was the sound of a machine malfunctioning.)

He found a woman bathing, and tied her up with strips of his own garments, and cut off her legs at the knees and left her still sitting up in the swirling crimson bath, screaming as she bled away her life. The legs he took with him.

When he found a man hurrying to get out of the night, he pounced on him, cut his throat and sawed off the arms. He replaced the arms with the bath-woman's legs.

And it went on and on, for a time that had no measure. He was showing them what evil could produce. He was showing them their immorality was silly beside his own.

But one thing finally told him he was winning. As he lurked in an antiseptically pure space between two low aluminum-cubes, he heard a voice that came from above him and around him and even from inside him. It was a public announcement, broadcast by whatever mental communications system the people of the City on the edge of the World used.

OUR CITY IS PART OF US. WE ARE PART OF OUR CITY. IT RESPONDS TO OUR MINDS AND WE WE CONTROL IT. THE GESTALT THAT WE HAVE BECOME IS THREATENED. WE HAVE AN ALIEN FORCE WITHIN THE CITY AND WE ARE GEARING TO LOCATE IT. BUT THE MIND OF THIS MAN IS STRONG. IT IS BREAKING DOWN THE FUNCTIONS OF THE CITY. THIS ENDLESS NIGHT IS AN EXAMPLE. WE MUST ALL CONCENTRATE. WE MUST ALL CONSCIOUSLY FOCUS OUR

THOUGHTS TO MAINTAINING THE CITY. THIS THREAT
IS OF THE FIRST ORDER. IF OUR CITY DIES, WE DIE.

It was not an announcement in those terms, though
that was how Jack interpreted it. The message was
much longer and much more complex, but that was
what it meant, and he knew he was winning. He
was destroying them. Social reform was laughable,
they had said. He would show them.

And so he continued with his lunatic pogrom. He
butchered and slaughtered and carved them wherever
he found them, and they could not vanish and they could
not escape and they could not stop him. The collection
of hearts grew to fifty and seventy and then a hundred.

He grew bored with hearts and began cutting out
their brains. The collection grew.

For numberless days it went on, and from time to
time in the clean, scented autoclave of the City, he
could hear the sounds of screaming. His hands were
always sticky.

Then he found van Cleef, and leaped from hiding in
the darkness to bring her down. He raised the living
blade to drive it into her breast, but she

van   ished

He got to his feet and looked around. van Cleef
reappeared ten feet from him. He lunged for her and
again she was gone. To reappear ten feet away. Finally, when he had struck at her half a dozen times
and she had escaped him each time, he stood panting,
arms at sides, looking at her.

And she looked back at him with disinterest.

"You no longer amuse us," she said, moving her
lips.

Amuse? His mind whirled down into a place far
darker than any he had known before, and through the
murk of his blood-lust he began to realize. It had all
been for their amusement. They had *let* him do it.

They had given him the run of the City and he had capered and gibbered for them.

Evil? He had never even suspected the horizons of that word. He went for her, but she disappeared with finality.

He was left standing there as the daylight returned. As the City cleaned up the mess, took the butchered bodies and did with them what it had to do. In the freezer chambers the gelatin caps were returned to their niches, no more inhabitants of the city need be thawed to provide Jack the Ripper with utensils for his amusement of the sybarites. His work was truly finished.

He stood there in the empty street. A street that would *always* be empty to him. The people of the City had all along been able to escape him, and now they would. He was finally and completely the clown they had shown him to be. He was not evil, he was pathetic.

He tried to use the living blade on himself, but it dissolved into motes of light and wafted away on a breeze that had blown up for just that purpose.

Alone, he stood there staring at the victorious cleanliness of this Utopia. With their talents they would keep him alive, possibly alive forever, immortal in the possible expectation of needing him for amusement again someday. He was stripped to raw essentials in a mind that was no longer anything more than jelly matter. To go madder and madder, and never to know peace or end or sleep.

He stood there, a creature of dirt and alleys, in a world as pure as the first breath of a baby.

"My name isn't Jack," he said softly. But they would never know his real name. Nor would they care. *"My name isn't Jack!"* he said loudly. No one heard.

"MY NAME ISN'T JACK, AND I'VE BEEN BAD, VERY BAD, I'M AN EVIL PERSON BUT MY NAME ISN'T JACK!" he screamed, and screamed, and screamed again, walking aimlessly down an empty street, in plain view, no longer forced to prowl. A stranger in the City.

SAGITTARIUS

by Ray Russell

I
THE CENTURY CLUB

"If Mr. Hyde had sired a son," said Lord Terry, "do
you realize that the loathsome child could be alive at
this moment?"

It was a humid summer evening, but he and his
guest, Rolfe Hunt, were cool and crisp. They were
sitting in the quiet sanctuary of the Century Club (so
named, say wags, because its members all appear to
be close to that age) and, over their drinks, had been
talking about vampires and related, monsters, about
ghost stories and other dark tales of happenings real
and imagined, and had been recounting some of their
favorites. Hunt had been drinking martinis, but Lord
Terry—The Earl Terrence Glencannon, rather—was a
courtly old gentleman who considered the martini one
of the major barbarities of the Twentieth Century. He
would take only the finest, driest sherry before dinner,
and he was now sipping his third glass. The conversation had touched upon the series of mutilation-
killings that were currently shocking the city, and then
upon such classic mutilators as Bluebeard and Jack the
Ripper, and then upon murder and evil in general; upon
certain works of fiction, such as *The Turn of the Screw*
and its alleged ambiguities, *Dracula,* the short play *A
Night at an Inn,* the German silent film, *Nosferatu,*
some stories of Blackwood, Coppard, Machen, Montague James, Le Fanu, Poe, and finally upon *The
Strange Case of Dr. Jekyll and Mr. Hyde,* which had

led the Earl to make his remark about Hyde's hypothetical son.

"How do you arrive at that, sir?" Hunt asked, with perhaps too much deference, but after all, to old Lord Terry, Hunt must have seemed a damp fledgling for all his thirty-five years, and the younger man could not presume too much heartiness simply because the Earl had known Hunt's father in the old days back in London. Lord Terry entertained few guests now, and it was a keen privilege to be sitting with him in his club—"The closest thing to an English club I could find in this beastly New York of yours," he once had granted, grudgingly.

Now, he was deftly evading Hunt's question by tearing a long, narrow ribbon from the evening paper and twisting it into that topological curiosity, the Möbius strip. "Fascinating," he smiled, running his finger along the little toy. "A surface with only one side. We speak of 'split personalities'—schizophrenes, Jekyll-and-Hyde, and whatnot—as if such persons were cleanly divided, marked off, with lines running down their centers. Actually, they're more like this Möbius strip—they *appear* to have two sides, but you soon discover that what you thought was the upper side turns out to be the under side as well. The two sides are one, strangely twisting and merging. You can never be sure which side you're looking at, or exactly where one side becomes the other . . . I'm sorry, did you ask me something?"

"I merely wondered," said Hunt, "how you happened to arrive at that interesting notion of yours: that Mr. Hyde's son—if Hyde had been a real person and if he had fathered a son—might be alive today?"

"Ah," Lord Terry said, putting aside the strip of paper. "Yes. Well, it's simple, really. We must first make a great leap of concession and, for sake of argument, look upon Bobbie Stevenson's story not as a story but as though it were firmly based in *fact.*"

It certainly was a great leap, but Hunt nodded.

"So much for that. Now, the story makes no reference to specific years—it uses that eighteen-followed-by-a-dash business which writers were so fond of in those days, I've never understood why—but we *do* know it was published in 1886. So, still making concessions for sake of argument, mind you, we might say Edward Hyde was 'born' in that year—but born a full-grown man, a creature capable of reproducing himself. We know, from the story, that Hyde spent his time in pursuit of carnal pleasures so gross that the good Dr. Jekyll was pale with shame at the remembrance of them. Surely one result of those pleasures might have been a child, born to some poor Soho wretch, and thrust nameless upon the world? Such a child, born in '86 or '87, would be in his seventies today. So you see it's quite possible."

He drained his glass. "And think of this now: whereas all other human creatures are compounded of both good and evil, Edward Hyde stood alone in the roster of mankind. For he was the first—and, let us hope, the last—human being who was *totally* evil. Consider his son. He is the offspring of one parent who, like all of us, was part good and part evil (the mother) and of one parent who was *all* evil (the father, Hyde). The son, then (to work it out arithmetically, if that is possible in a question of human factors), is three-quarters pure evil, with only a single thin flickering quarter of good in him. We might even weight the dice, as it were, and suggest that his mother, being most likely a drunken drab of extreme moral looseness, was hardly a person to bequeath upon her heir a strong full quarter of good—perhaps only an eighth, or a sixteenth. Not to put too fine a point on it, Hyde's son—if he is alive—is the second most evil person who has ever lived; and—since his father is dead—*the* most evil person on the face of the earth today!" Lord Terry stood up. "Shall we go in to dinner?" he said.

The dining room was inhabited by men in several stages of advanced decrepitude, and still-handsome

Lord Terry seemed, in contrast, rather young. His bearing, his tall, straight body, clear eye, ruddy face, and unruly shock of thick white hair made him a vital figure among a room full of near-ghosts. The heavy concentration of senility acted as a depressant on Hunt's spirits, and Lord Terry seemed to sense this, for he said, as they sat down, "Waiting room. The whole place is one vast waiting room, full of played-out chaps waiting for the last train. They tell you age has its compensations. Don't believe it. It's ghastly."

Lord Terry recommended the red snapper soup with sherry, the Dover sole, the Green Goddess salad. "Named after a play, you know, *The Green Goddess*, George Arliss made quite a success in it, long before your time." He scribbled their choices on the card and handed it to the hovering waiter, also ordering another martini for Hunt and a fourth sherry for himself. "Yes," he said, his eye fixed on some long-ago stage, "used to go to the theatre quite a lot in the old days. They put on jolly good shows then. Not all this rot . . ." He focused on Hunt. "But I mustn't be boor-ish—you're somehow involved in the theatre yourself, I believe you said?"

Hunt told him he was writing a series of theatrical histories, that his histories of the English and Italian theatres had already been published and that currently he was working on the French.

"Ah," the old man said. "Splendid. Will you men-tion Sellig?"

Hunt confessed that the name was new to him.

Lord Terry sighed. "Such is fame. A French actor. All the rage in Paris at one time. His name was spoken in the same breath with Mounet-Sully's, and some even considered him the new Lemaître. Bernhardt nagged Sardou into writing a play for him, they say, though I don't know if he ever did. Rostand left an unfinished play, *Don Juan's Last Night, La Dernière Nuit de Don Juan*, which some say was written expressly for Sel-lig, but Sellig never played it."

"Why not?"

Lord Terry shrugged. "Curious fellow. Very—what would you say—pristine, very dedicated to the highest theatrical art, classic stuff like Corneille and Racine, you know. The very highest. Wouldn't even do Hugo or Dumas. And yet he became a name not even a theatrical historian is familiar with."

"You must make me familiar with it," Hunt said, as the drinks arrived.

Lord Terry swallowed a white lozenge he took from a slim gold box. "Pills," he said. "In our youth we sow wild oats; in our dotage we reap pills." He replaced the box in his weskit pocket. "Yes, I'll tell you about Sellig, if you like. I knew him very well."

II
THE DANGERS OF CHARM

We were both of an age (said Lord Terry), very young, twenty-three or four, and Paris in those days was a grand place to be young in. The Eiffel Tower was a youngster then, too, our age exactly, for this was still the first decade of the century, you see. Gauguin had been dead only six years, Lautrec only eight, and although that Parisian Orpheus, Jacques Offenbach, had died almost thirty years before, his music and his gay spirit still ruled the city, and jolly *parisiennes* still danced the can-can with bare derrières to the rhythm of his *Galop Infernal*. The air was heady with a wonderful mixture of *ancien régime* elegance (the days of which were numbered and which would soon be dispelled forever by the War) combined with a forward-looking curiosity and excitement about the new century. Best of both worlds, you might say. The year, to be exact about it, was 1909.

It's easy to remember because in that very year both Coquelin brothers—the actors, you know—died. The elder, more famous brother, Constant-Benoît, who

created the role of Cyrano, died first, and the younger,
Alexandre Honoré, died scarcely a fortnight later.
Here's a curious tidbit about Coquelin's Cyrano which
you may want to use in your book: he played the first
act wearing a long false nose, the second act with a
shorter nose, and at the end of the play, wore no false
nose at all—the really odd thing being that the audience never noticed it! Sir Cedric told me that just before he died. Hardwicke, you know. Where was I?
Oh, yes. It was through a friend of the Coquelin family—a minor *comédien* named César Baudouin—that I
first came to know Paris and, consequently, Sébastien
Sellig.

He was appearing at the Théâtre Français, in Racine's *Britannicus*. He played the young Nero. And he
played him with such style and fervor and godlike
grace that one could *feel* the audience's sympathies
being drawn toward Nero as to a magnet. I saw him
afterward, in his dressing room, where he was removing his make-up. César introduced us.

He was a man of surpassing beauty: a face like the
Apollo Belvedere, with classic features, a tumble of
black curls, large brown eyes, and sensuous lips. I did
not compliment him on his good looks, of course, for
the world had only recently become unsafe for even
the most innocent admiration between men, Oscar
Wilde having died in Paris just nine years before. I
did compliment him on his performance, and on the
rush of sympathy which I've already remarked.

"Thank you," he said, in English, which he spoke
very well. "It was unfortunate."

"Unfortunate?"

"The audience's sympathies should have remained
with Britannicus. By drawing them to myself—quite
inadvertently, I assure you—I upset the balance, re-
versed Racine's intentions, and thoroughly destroyed
the play."

"But," observed César lightly, "you achieved a
personal triumph."

"Yes," said Selig. "At irreparable cost. It will not happen again, dear César, you may be sure of that. Next time I play Nero, I shall do so without violating Racine."

César, being a professional, took exception. "You can't be blamed for your charm, Sébastien," he insisted.

Sellig wiped off the last streak of paint from his face and began to draw on his street clothes. "An actor who cannot control his charm," he said, "is like an actor who cannot control his voice or his limbs. He is worthless." Then he smiled, charmingly. "But we mustn't talk shop in front of your friend. So very rude. Come, I shall take you to an enchanting little place for supper."

It was a small, dark place called L'Oubliette. The three of us ate an enormous and very good omelette, with crusty bread and a bottle of white wine. Sellig talked of the differences between France's classic poetic dramatist, Racine, and England's, Shakespeare. "Racine is like—" he lifted the bottle and refilled our glasses—"well, he is like a very fine vintage white. Delicate, serene, cool, subtle. So subtle that the excellence is not immediately enjoyed by uninitiated palates. Time is required, familiarity, a return and another return and yet another."

As an Englishman, I was prepared to defend our bard, so I asked, a little belligerently: "And Shakespeare?"

"Ah, Shakespeare!" smiled Sellig. *"Passionel, tumultueux!* He is like a mulled red, hot and bubbling from the fire, dark and rich with biting spices and sweet honey! The senses are smitten, one is overwhelmed, one becomes drunk, one reels, one spins . . . it can be a most agreeable sensation."

He drank from his glass. "Think of tonight's play. It depicts the first atrocity in a life of atrocities. It ends as Nero murders his brother. Later, he was to murder his mother, two wives, a trusted tutor, close friends,

and untold thousands of Christians who died horribly
in his arenas. But we see none of this. If Shakespeare
had written the play, it would have *begun* with the
death of Britannicus. It would then have shown us each
new outrage, the entire chronicle of Nero's decline
and fall and ignoble end. *Enfin,* it would have been
Macbeth.''

I had heard of a little club where the girls danced in
shockingly indecorous costumes, and I was eager to
go. César allowed himself to be persuaded to take me
there, and I invited Sellig to accompany us. He declined, pleading fatigue and a heavy day ahead of him.
''Then perhaps,'' I said, ''you will come with us tomorrow evening? It may not tempt a gentleman of your
lofty theatrical tastes, but I'm determined to see a show
at this Grand Guignol which César has told me of.
Quite bloody and outrageous, I understand—rather like
Shakespeare.'' Sellig laughed at my little joke.
''Will you come? Or perhaps you have a performance . . .''

''I do have a performance,'' he said, ''so I cannot
join you until later. Suppose we plan to meet there, in
the foyer, directly after the last curtain?''

''Will you be there in time?'' I asked. ''The Guignol shows are short, I hear.''

''I will be there,'' said Sellig, and we parted.

III
Stage of Torture

Le Théâtre du Grand Guignol, as you probably know,
had been established just a dozen or so years before,
in 1896, on the Rue Chaptal, in a tiny building that
had once been a chapel. Father Didon, a Dominican,
had preached there, and in the many incarnations the
building was to go through in later years it was to
retain its churchly appearance. Right up to the date of
its demolition in 1962, I'm told, it remained exactly

as it had always been: quaint, small, huddled incon-spicuously in a cobble-stone nook at the end of a Montmartre alley; inside, black-raftered, with gothic tracery writhing along the portals and fleurs-de-lis on the walls, with carved cherubs and a pair of seven-foot angels—dim with the patina of a century—smiling be-nignly down on the less than three hundred seats and loges . . . which, you know, looked not like conven-tional seats and loges but like church pews and confes-sionals. After the good Father Didon was no longer active, his chapel became the shop of a dealer spe-cializing in religious art; still later, it was transformed into a studio for the academic painter, Rochegrosse; and so on, until, in '96, a man named Méténier—who had formerly been secretary to a *commissaire de po-lice*—rechristened it the Théâtre du Grand Guignol and made of it the famous carnival of horror. Méténier died the following year, aptly enough, and Max Maurey took it over. I met Maurey briefly—he was still operating the theatre in 1909, the year of my little story.

The subject matter of the Guignol plays seldom var-ied. Their single acts were filled with girls being thrown into lighthouse lamps . . . faces singed by vit-riol or pressed forcibly down upon red hot stoves . . . naked ladies nailed to crosses and carved up by gyp-sies . . . a variety of surgical operations . . . mad old crones who put out the eyes of young maidens with knitting needles . . . chunks of flesh ripped from vic-tims' necks by men with hooks for hands . . . bodies dissolved in acid baths . . . hands chopped off; also arms, legs, heads . . . women raped and strangled . . . all done in a hyper-realistic manner with ingenious trick props and the Guignol's own secretly formulated blood—a thick, suety, red gruel which was actually capable of congealing before your eyes and which was kept continually hot in a big cauldron backstage.

Some actors—but especially actresses—made spec-tacular careers at the Guignol. You may know of

Maxa? She was after my time, actually, but she was supposed to have been a beautiful woman, generously endowed by Nature, and they say it was impossible to find one square inch of her lovely body that had not received some variety of stage violence in one play or another. The legend is that she died ten thousand times, in sixty separate and distinct ways, each more hideous than the last; and that she writhed in the assaults of brutal rapine on no less than three thousand theatrical occasions. For the remainder of her life she could not speak above a whisper: the years of screaming had torn her throat to shreds.

At any rate, the evening following my first meeting with Sellig, César and I were seated in this unique little theatre with two young ladies we had escorted there; they were uncommonly pretty but uncommonly common—in point of fact, they were barely on the safe side of respectability's border, being inhabitants of that peculiar demimonde, that shadow world where several professions—actress, model, barmaid, bawd—mingle and merge and overlap and often coexist. But we were young, César and I, and this was, after all, Paris. Their names, they told us, were Clothilde and Mathilde— and I was never quite sure which was which. Soon after our arrival, the lights dimmed and the Guignol curtain was raised.

The first offering on the programme was a dull, shrill little boudoir farce that concerned itself with broken corset laces and men hiding under the bed and popping out of closets. It seemed to amuse our feminine companions well enough, but the applause in the house was desultory, I thought, a mere form . . . this fluttering nonsense was not what the patrons had come for, was not the sort of fare on which the Guignol had built its reputation. It was an hors d'oeuvre. The entrée followed.

It was called, if memory serves, *La Septième Porte,* and was nothing more than an opportunity for Blue-beard—played by an actor wearing an elaborately ugly

make-up—to open six of his legendary seven doors for
his new young wife (displaying, among other things,
realistically mouldering cadavers and a torture chamber in full operation). Remaining faithful to the legend, Bluebeard warns his wife never to open the
seventh door. Left alone on stage, she of course cannot resist the tug of curiosity—she opens the door,
letting loose a shackled swarm of shrieking, livid, rag-
bedecked but not entirely unattractive harpies, whose
white bodies, through their shredded clothing, are
crisscrossed with crimson welts. They tell her they are
Bluebeard's ex-wives, kept perpetually in a pitch-dark
dungeon, in a state near to starvation, and periodically
tortured by the vilest means imaginable. Why? the new
wife asks. Bluebeard enters, a black whip in his hand.
For the sin of curiosity, he replies—they, like you,
could not resist the lure of the seventh door! The other
wives chain the girl to them, and cringing under the
crack of Bluebeard's whip, they crawl back into the
darkness of the dungeon. Bluebeard locks the seventh
door and soliloquizes: Diogenes had an easy task, to
find an honest man; but my travail is tenfold—for
where is she, does she live, the wife who does not pry
and snoop, who does not pilfer her husband's pockets,
steam open his letters, and when he is late returning
home, demand to know what wench he has been tum-
bling?

The lights had been dimming slowly until now only
Bluebeard was illuminated, and at this point he turned
to the audience and addressed the women therein.
"Mesdames et Mademoiselles!" he declaimed.
"Écoute! En garde! Voici la septième porte—Hear me!
Beware! Behold the seventh door!" By a stage trick
the door was transformed into a mirror. The curtain
fell to riotous applause.

Recounted badly, *La Septième Porte* seems a trump-
ery entertainment, a mere excuse for scenes of horror—and so it was. But there was a strength, a power
to the portrayal of Bluebeard; that ugly devil up there

on the shabby little stage was like an icy flame, and when he'd turned to the house and delivered that closing line, there had been such force of personality, such demonic zeal, such hatred and scorn, such monumental threat, that I could feel my young companion shrink against me and shudder,

"Come, come, *ma petite,*" I said, "it's only a play."

"*Je le déteste,*" she said.

"You detest him? Who, Bluebeard?"

"Laval."

My French was sketchy at that time, and her English almost nonexistent, but as we made our slow way up the aisle, I managed to glean that the actor's name was Laval, and that she had at one time had some offstage congress with him, congress of an intimate nature, I gathered. I could not help asking *why,* since she disliked him so. (I was naïf then, you see, and knew little of women; it was somewhat later in life I learned that many of them find evil and even ugliness irresistible). In answer to my question, she only shrugged and delivered a platitude: "*Les affaires sont les affaires*—Business is business."

Sellig was waiting for us in the foyer. His height, and his great beauty of face, made him stand out. Our two pretty companions took to him at once, for his attractive exterior was supplemented by waves of charm.

"Did you enjoy the programme?" he asked of me.

I did not know exactly what to reply. "Enjoy? . . . Let us say I found it fascinating, M'sieu' Sellig."

"It did not strike you as tawdry? cheap? vulgar?"

"All those, yes. But at the same time, exciting, as sometimes only the tawdry, the cheap, the vulgar, can be."

"You may be right. I have not watched a Guignol production for several years. Although, surely, the acting . . ."

We were entering a carriage, all five of us. I said,

''The acting was unbelievably bad—with one exception.''

''Really? And the exception?''

''The actor who played Bluebeard in a piece called *La Septième Porte*. His name is—'' I turned to my companion again.

''Laval,'' she said, and the sound became a viscous thing.

''Ah yes,'' said Sellig. ''Laval. The name is not entirely unknown to me. Shall we go to Maxime's?''

We did, and experienced a most enjoyable evening. Sellig's fame and personal magnetism won us the best table and the most efficient service. He told a variety of amusing—but never coarse—anecdotes about theatrical life, and did so without committing that all-too-common actor's offense of dominating the conversation. One anecdote concerned the theatre we had just left:

''I suppose César has told the story of the Guignol doctor. No? Ah then, it seems that at one point it was thought a capital idea to hire a house physician—to tend to swooning patrons and so on, you know. This was done, but it was unsuccessful. On the first night of the physician's tour of duty, a male spectator found one particular bit of stage torture too much for him, and he fainted. The house physician was summoned. He could not be found. Finally, the ushers revived the unconscious man without benefit of medical assistance, and naturally they apologized profusely and explained they had not been able to find the doctor. 'I know,' the man said, rather sheepishly, '*I* am the doctor.' ''

At the end of the evening, César and I escorted our respective (but not precisely respectable) ladies to their dwellings, where more pleasure was found. Sellig went home alone. I felt sorry for him, and there was a moment when it crossed my mind that perhaps he was one of those men who have no need of women—the theatrical profession is thickly inhabited by such men—

but César privately assured me that Sellig had a mistress, a lovely and gracious widow named Lise, for Sellig's tastes were exceedingly refined and his image unblemished by descents into the dimly lit world of the sporting house. My own tastes, though acute, were not so elevated, and thus I enjoyed myself immensely that night.

Ignorance, they say, is bliss. I did not know that my ardent companion's warmth would turn unalterably cold in the space of a single night.

IV
FACE OF EVIL

The *commissaire de police* had never seen anything like it. He spoke poor English, but I was able to glean his meaning without too much difficulty. "It is how you say . . ."

"Horrible?"

"Ah, oui, mais . . . étrange, incroyable . . ."

"Unique?"

"Si! Uniquement monstrueux! Uniquement dégoûtant!

Uniquely disgusting. Yes, it was that. It was that, certainly.

"The manner, M'sieu' . . . the method . . . the—"

"Mutilation."

"Oui, la mutilation . . . est irrégulière, anormale . . ."

We were in the morgue—not that newish Medico-Legal Institute of the University on the banks of the Seine, but the *old* morgue, that wretched, ugly place on the quai de l'Archevêché. She—Clothilde, my *petite amie* of the previous night—had been foully murdered; killed with knives; her prettiness destroyed; her very womanhood destroyed, extracted bloodily but with surgical precision. I stood in the morgue with the *commissaire*, César, Sellig, and the other girl, Mathilde. Covering the corpse with its anonymous sheet, the *commissaire* said, "It resembles, does it not, the work of your English killer . . . Jacques?"

"Jack," I said. "Jack the Ripper."

"Ah oui." He looked down upon the covered body. *"Mais pourquoi?"*

"Yes," I said hoarsely. "Why indeed? . . ."

"La cause . . . la raison . . . le motif," he said; and then delivered himself of a small, eloquent, Gallic shrug. *"Inconnu."*

Motive unknown. He had stated it succinctly. A girl of the streets, a *fille de joie,* struck down, mutilated, her femaleness cancelled out. Who did it? *Inconnu.* And why? *Inconnu.*

"Merci, messieurs, mademoiselle . . ." The *commissaire* thanked us and we left the cold repository of Paris' unclaimed dead. All four of us—it had been "all five of us" just the night before—were strained, silent. The girl Mathilde was weeping. We, the men, felt not grief exactly—how could we, for one we had known so briefly, so imperfectly?—but a kind of embarrassment. Perhaps that is the most common reaction produced by the presence of death: embarrassment. Death is a kind of nakedness, a kind of indecency, a kind of *faux pas.* Unless we have known the dead person well enough to experience true loss, or unless we have wronged the dead person enough to experience guilt, the only emotion we can experience is embarrassment. I must confess my own embarrassment was tinged with guilt. It was I, you see, who had used her, such a short time before. And now she would never be used again. Her warm lips were cold; her knowing fingers, still; her cajoling voice, silent; the very stronghold and temple of her treasure was destroyed.

In the street, I felt I had to make some utterance. "To think," I said, "that her last evening was spent at the Guignol!"

Sellig smiled sympathetically. "My friend," he said, "the Grand Guignol is not only a shabby little theatre in Montmartre alley. This—'' his gesture took in the world ''—this is the Grandest Guignol of all.''

I nodded. He placed a hand on my shoulder. "Do not be too much alone," he advised me. "Come to the Théâtre tonight. We are playing *Cinna.*''

"Thank you," I said. "But I have a strange urge to revisit the Guignol . . .''

César seemed shocked or puzzled, but Sellig understood. "Yes," he said, "that is perhaps a good thought." We parted—Sellig to his rooms, César with the weeping girl, I to my hotel.

I have an odd infirmity—perhaps it is not so odd, and perhaps it is no infirmity at all—but great shock or disappointment or despair do not rob me of sleep as they rob the sleep of others. On the contrary, they rob me of energy, they drug me, they send me into the merciful solace of sleep like a powerful anodyne. And so, that afternoon, I slept. But it was a sleep invaded by dreams . . . dreams of gross torture and mutilation, of blood, and of the dead Clothilde—alive again for the duration of a nap—repeating over and over again a single statement.

I awoke covered with perspiration, and with that statement gone just beyond the reach of my mind. Try as I did, I could not recall it. I dashed cold water in my face to clear my head, and although I had no appetite, I rang for service and had some food brought me in my suite. Then, the theatre hour approaching, I dressed and made my way toward Montmartre and the Rue Chaptal.

The Guignol's *chef-d'oeuvre* that evening was a bit of white supremacy propaganda called *Chinoiserie.* ("The yellow menace" was just beginning to become a popular prejudice.) A white girl played by a buxom but ungifted actress, was sold as a slave to a lecherous Chinese mandarin, and after being duly ravished by him and established as his most favored concubine, fell into the clutches of the beautiful but jealous Chinese woman who had hitherto occupied that honored

post. The Woman Scorned, taking advantage of the
temporary absence of her lord, seized the opportunity
to strip her rival naked and subject her to the first in-
stallment of The Death of a Thousand Slices, when
her plans were thwarted by the appearance of a handsome French lieutenant who freed the white girl and
offered her the chance to turn the tables on the Asian
witch. The liberated victim, after first frightening her
tormentress with threats of the Thousand Slices,
proved a credit to her race by contenting herself with
a plume. Although I had been told that *l'épisode du
chatouillement*—the tickling scene''—was famed far
and wide, going on for several minutes of shrieking
hysterics until the tickled lady writhed herself out of
her clothing, I left before its conclusion. The piece
was unbearably boring, though it was no worse than
the previous evening's offering. The reason for its te-
diousness was simple: Laval did not appear in the play.
On my way out of the theatre, I inquired of an usher
about the actor's absence. "Ah, the great Laval," he
said, with shuddering admiration. "It is his—do you
say 'night away'?"

"Night off . . ."

"Oui. His night off. He appears on alternate nights,
M'sieu'. . ."

Feeling somehow cheated, I decided to return the
following night. I did so; in fact, I made it a point to
visit the Guignol every night that week on which Laval
was playing. I saw him in several little plays—shockers
in which he starred as the monsters of history and
legend—and in each, his art was lit by black fire and
was the more admirable since he did not rely upon a
succession of fantastic make-ups—in each, he wore the
same grotesque make-up (save for the false facial hair)
he had worn as Bluebeard; I assumed it was his trade-
mark. The plays—which were of his own authorship,
I discovered—included *L'Inquisiteur,* in which he
played Torquemada, the merciless heretic-burner
(convincing flames on the stage) and *L'Empoisonneur,*

in which he played the insane, incestuous Cesare Borgia. There were many more, among them, a contemporary story, *L'Éventreur,* in which he played the currently notorious Jack the Ripper, knifing pretty young harlots with extreme realism until the stage was scarlet with sham blood. In this, there was one of those typically Lavalesque flashes, an infernally inspired *cri de coeur,* when The Ripper, remorseful, sunken in shame, enraged at his destiny, surfeited with killings but unable to stop, tore a rhymed couplet from the bottom of his soul and flung it like a live thing into the house:

> *La vie est un corridor noir*
> *D'impuissance et de désespoir!*

That's not very much in English—"Life is a black corridor of impotence and despair"—but in the original, and when hurled with the ferocity of Laval, it was Kean's Hamlet, Irving's Macbeth, Salvini's Othello, all fused into a single theatrical moment.

And, in that moment, there was another fusion—a fusion, in my own mind, of two voices. One was that of the *commissaire de police*—"It resembles, does it not, the work of your English killer . . . Jacques?" The other was the voice of the dead Clothilde, repeating a phrase she had first uttered in life, and then, after her death, in that fugitive dream—*"Je le déteste."*

As the curtain fell, to tumultuous applause, I sent my card backstage, thus informing Laval that *"un admirateur"* wished to buy him a drink. Might we meet at L'Oubliette? The response was long in coming, insultingly long, but at last it did come and it was affirmative. I left at once for L'Oubliette.

Forty minutes later, after I had consumed half a bottle of red wine, Laval entered. The waitress brought him to my table and we shook hands.

I was shocked, for, as I looked into his face, I immediately realized that Laval never wore evil make-up on the Guignol stage.

He had no need of it.

V

AN INTIMATE KNOWLEDGE OF HORRORS

Looking about, Laval said, "L'Oubliette," and sat down. "The filthy place is aptly named. Do you know what an *oubliette* is, M'sieu'?"

"No," I said; "I wish my French were as excellent as your English."

"But surely you know our word, *oublier?*"

"My French-English lexicon," I replied, "says it means 'to forget, to omit, to leave.' "

He nodded. "That is correct. In the old days, a variety of secret dungeon was called an *oubliette*. It was subterranean. It had no door, no window. It could be entered only by way of a trap door at the top. The trap door was too high to reach, even by climbing, since the walls sloped in the wrong direction and were eternally thick with slime. There was no bed, no chair, no table, no light, and very little air. Prisoners were dropped down into such dungeons to be—literally— forgotten. They seldom left alive. Infrequently, when a prisoner was fortunate enough to be freed by a change in administration, he was found to have become blind—from years in the dark. And almost always, of course, insane."

"You have an intimate knowledge of horrors, Monsieur Laval," I said.

He shrugged. *"C'est mon métier."*

"Will you drink red wine?"

"Since you are paying, I will drink whisky," he said; adding, "if they have it here."

They did, an excellent Scotch and quite expensive. I decided to join him. He downed the first portion as soon as it was poured—not waiting for even a perfunctory toast—and instantly demanded another. This, too, he flung down his throat in one movement, smacking his bestial lips. I could not help thinking how much more graphic than our "he drinks like a fish" or "like a drainpipe" is the equivalent French figure of speech: "he drinks like a hole."

"Now then, M'sieu' . . . Pendragon? . . ."

"Glencannon."

"Yes. You wished to speak with me."

I nodded.

"Speak," he said, gesturing to the barmaid for another drink.

"Why," I began, "I'm afraid I have nothing in particular to say, except that I admire your acting . . ."

"Many people do."

What a graceless boor, I told myself, but I continued: "Rightfully so, Monsieur Laval. I am new to Paris, but I have seen much theatre here these past few weeks, and to my mind yours is a towering talent, in the front rank of contemporary *artistes,* perhaps second only to—"

"Eh? Second?" He swallowed the fresh drink and looked up at me, his unwholesome eyes flaming. "Second to—whom, would you say?"

"I was going to say, Sellig."

Laval laughed. It was not a warming sound. His face grew uglier. "Sellig! Indeed. Sellig, the handsome. Sellig, the classicist. Sellig, the noble. *Bah!*"

I was growing uncomfortable. "Come, sir," I said, "surely you are not being fair . . ."

"Fair. That is oh so important to you English, is it not? Well, let me tell you, M'sieu' Whatever-your-name-is—the lofty strutting of the mountebank Sellig makes me sick! What he can do, fools can do. Who cannot pompously declaim the cold, measured alexandrines of Racine and Corneille and Molière? Stop any schoolboy on the street and ask him to recite a bit of *Phèdre* or *Tartuffe* and he will oblige you, in that same stately classroom drone Sellig employs. Do not speak to me of this Sellig. He is a fraud; *worse*—he is a bore.''

''He is also,'' I said, ''my friend.''

''A sorry comment on your taste.''

''And yet it is a taste that can also appreciate you.''

''To some, champagne and seltzer water taste the same.''

''You know, sir, you are really quite rude.''

''True.''

''You must have few friends.''

''Wrong. I have none.''

''But that is distressing! Surely—''

He interrupted. ''There is a verse of the late Rostand's. Perhaps you know it. *'A force de vous voir vous faire des amis . . . '* et cetera?''

''My French is poor.''

''You need not remind me. I will give you a rough translation. 'Seeing the sort of friends you others have in tow, I cry with joy: send me another foe!' ''

''And yet,'' I said, persisting, ''all men need friends . . .''

Laval's eyes glittered like dark gems. ''I am no ordinary man,'' he said. ''I was born under the sign of Sagittarius. Perhaps you know nothing of astrology? Or, if you do, perhaps you think of Sagittarius as merely the innocuous sign of the Archer? Remember, then, just who that archer is—not a simple bear or bull or crab or pair of fish, not a man, not a creature at all, but a very unnatural creature half human, half bestial. Sagittarius: the Man-Beast. And I tell you this, M'sieu' . . .'' He dispatched the whisky in one gulp and banged the empty glass on the table to attract the attention of the barmaid. ''I tell you this,'' he repeated. ''So potent was the star under which I was born, that I have done what no one in the world has done—nor ever *can* do!''

The sentence was like a hot iron, searing my brain. I was to meet it once again before I left Paris. But now, sitting across the table from the mad—for he indeed seemed mad—Laval, I said, softly, "And what is it you have done, Monsieur?"

He chuckled nastily. "That," he said, "is a professional secret."

I tried another approach. "Monsieur Laval . . ."

"Yes?"

"I believe we have a mutual friend."

"Who may that be?"

"A lady."

"Oh? And her name?"

"She calls herself Clothilde. I do not know her last name."

"Then I gather she is not, after all, a lady."

I shrugged. "Do you know her?"

"I know many women," he said; and his face clouding with bitterness, he added, "Do you find that surprising—with this face?"

"Not at all. But you have not answered my question."

"I may know your Mam'selle Clothilde; I cannot be certain. May I have another drink?"

"To be sure." I signalled the waitress, and turned again to Laval. "She told me she knew you in her—professional capacity."

"It may be so. I do not clot my mind with memories of such women." The waitress poured out another portion of Scotch and Laval downed it. "Why do you ask?"

"For two reasons. First, because she told me she detested you."

"It is a common complaint. And the second reason?"

"Because she is dead."

"Ah?"

"Murdered. Mutilated. Obscenely disfigured."

"Quel dommage."

"It is not a situation to be met with a platitude, Monsieur!"

Laval smiled. It made him look like a lizard. "Is it

not? How must I meet it, then? With tears? With a clucking of the tongue? With a beating of my breast and a rending of my garments? Come, M'sieu' . . . she was a woman of the streets . . . I scarcely knew her, if indeed I knew her at all . . .''

"Why did she detest you?" I suddenly demanded.

"Oh, my dear sir! If I knew the answers to such questions, I would be *clairvoyant*. Because I have the face of a Notre Dame gargoyle, perhaps. Because she did not like the way I combed my hair. Because I left her too small a fee. Who knows? I assure you, her detestation does not perturb me in the slightest.''

"To speak plainly, you relish it."

"Yes. Yes, I relish it."

"Do you also relish—" I toyed with my glass. "—blood, freshly spilt?"

He looked at me blankly for a moment. Then he threw back his head and roared with amusement. "I see," he said at last. "I understand now. You suspect I murdered this trollop?"

"She is dead, sir. It ill becomes you to malign her."

"This *lady,* then. You really think I killed her?"

"I accuse you of nothing, Monsieur Laval. But . . . .''

"But?"

"But it strikes me as a distinct possibility."

He smiled again. "How interesting. How very, very interesting. Because she detested me?"

"That is one reason."

He pushed his glass to one side. "I will be frank with you, M'sieu'. Yes, I knew Clothilde, briefly. Yes, it is true she loathed me. She found me digusting. But can you not guess why?''

I shook my head. Laval leaned forward and spoke more softly. "You and I, M'sieu', we are men of the world . . . and surely you can understand that there are things . . . certain little things . . . that an imaginative man might require of such a woman? Things which—if she were overly fastidious—she might find objectionable?'' Still again, he smiled. ''I assure you, her detestation of me had no other ground than that. She was a silly little *bourgeoise*. She had no flair for her profession. She was easily shocked.'' Conspiratorially, he added: ''Shall I be more specific?''

''That will not be necessary.'' I caught the eye of the waitress and paid her. To Laval, I said, ''I must not detain you further, Monsieur.''

''Oh, am I being sent off?'' he said, mockingly, rising. ''Thank you for the whisky, M'sieu'. It was excellent.'' And, laughing hideously, he left.

VI
The Monster

I felt shaken, almost faint, and experienced a sudden desire to talk to someone. Hoping Sellig was playing that night at the Théâtre Français, I took a carriage there and was told he could probably be found at his rooms. My informant mentioned an address to my driver, and before long, Sébastien seemed pleasantly surprised at the appearance of his announced guest.

Sellig's rooms were tastefully appointed. The drapes were tall, classic folds of deep blue. A few good pictures hung on the walls, the chairs were roomy and comfortable, and the mingled fragrances of tobacco and book leather gave the air a decidedly masculine musk. Over a small spirit lamp, Sellig was preparing a simple ragout. As he stood in his shirt sleeves, stirring the food, I talked.

''You said, the other evening, that the name Laval was not unknown to you.''

''That gentleman seems to hold you fascinated,'' he observed.

''Is it an unhealthy fascination, would you say?'' I asked, candidly.

Sellig laughed. ''Well, he is not exactly an appealing personage.''

"Then you do know him?"

"In a sense. I have never seen him perform, however."

"He is enormously talented. He dominates the stage. There are only two actors in Paris who can transfix an audience in that manner."

"The other is . . . ?"

"You."

"Ah. Thank you. And yet, you do not equate me with Laval?"

Quickly, I assured him: "No, not at all. In everything but that one quality you and he are utterly different. Diametrically opposed."

"I am glad of that."

"Have you known him long?" I asked.

"Laval? Yes. For quite some time."

"He is not 'an appealing personage,' you said just now. Would you say he is . . . morally reprehensible?"

Sellig turned to me. "I would be violating a strict confidence if I told you any more than this: if he is morally corrupt (and I am not saying that he is), he is not reprehensible. If he is evil, then he was evil even in his mother's womb."

A popular song came to my mind, and I said, lightly, "More to be pitied than censured?"

Sellig received this remark seriously. "Yes," he said. "Yes, that is the point precisely. 'The sins of the father . . .' " But then he broke off and served the ragout.

As he ate, I—who had no appetite—spoke of my troubled mind and general depression.

"Perhaps it is not good for you to stay alone tonight," he said. "Would you like to sleep here? There is an extra bedroom."

"It would inconvenience you . . ."

"Not at all. I should be glad of the company."

I agreed to stay, for I was not looking forward to my lonely hotel suite, and not long after that we retired to our rooms. I fell asleep almost at once, but woke in a sweat about three in the morning. I arose, wrapped myself in one of Sellig's robes, and walked into the library for a book that might send me off to sleep again.

Sellig's collection of books was extensive, although heavily overbalanced by plays, volumes of theatrical criticism, biographies of actors, and so forth, a high percentage of them in English. I chose none of these: instead, I took down a weighty tome of French history. Its pedantic style and small type, as well as my imperfect command of the language, would combine to form the needed sedative. I took the book to bed with me.

My grasp of written French being somewhat firmer than my grasp of the conversational variety, I managed to labor through most of the first chapter before I began to turn the leaves in search of a more interesting section. It was quite by accident that my eyes fell upon a passage that seemed to thrust itself up from the page and stamp itself upon my brain. Though but a single sentence, I felt stunned by it. In a fever of curiosity, I read the other matter on that page, then turned back and read from an earlier point. I read in that volume for about ten minutes, or so I thought, but when I finished and looked up at the clock, I realized that I had read for over an hour. What I had read had numbed and shaken me.

I have never been a superstitious man. I have never believed in the existence of ghosts, or vampires, or other undead creatures out of lurid legend. They make excellent entertainment, but never before that shattering hour had I accepted them as anything more than entertainment. But as I sat in that bed, the book in my hands, the city outside silent, I had reason to feel as if a hand from some sub-zero hell had reached up and laid itself—oh, very gently—upon my heart. A shudder ran through my body. I looked down again at the book.

The pages I had read told of a monster—a real monster who had lived in France centuries before. The

Marquis de Sade, in comparison, was a mischievous schoolboy. This was a man of high birth and high aspirations, a marshal of France who at the peak of his power had been the richest noble in all of Europe and who had fought side by side with Joan of Arc, but who had later fallen into such depths of degeneracy that he had been tried and sentenced to the stake by a shocked legislature. In a search for immortality, a yearning to avoid death, he had carried out disgusting experiments on the living bodies of youths and maidens and little children. Seven or eight hundred had died in the laboratory of his castle, died howling in pain and insanity, the victims of a "science" that was more like the unholy rites of the Black Mass. "The accused," read one of the charges at his trial, "has taken innocent boys and girls, and inhumanly butchered, killed, dismembered, burned and otherwise tortured them, and the said accused has immolated the bodies of the said innocents to devils, invoked and sacrificed to evil spirits, and has foully committed sin with young boys and in other ways lusted against nature after young girls, while they were alive or sometimes dead or even sometimes during their death throes." Another charge spoke of "the hand, the eyes, and the heart of one of these said children, with its blood in a glass vase . . ." And yet this madman, this miscreant monster, had offered no resistance when arrested, had felt justified for his actions, had said proudly and defiantly under the legislated torture: *"So potent was the star under which I was born that I have done what no one in the world has done nor ever can do."*

His name was Gilles de Laval, Baron de Rais, and he became known for all time and to all the world, of course, as Bluebeard.

I was out of bed in an instant, and found myself pounding like a madman on the door of Sellig's bedroom. When there was no response, I opened the door and went in. He was not in his bed. Behind me, I heard another door open. I turned.

Sellig was coming out of yet another room, hardly more than a closet: behind him, just before he closed the door and locked it, I caught a glimpse of bottles and glass trays—I remember surmising, in that instant, that perhaps he was a devotee of the new art of photography, but I had no wish to dwell further on this, for I was bursting with what I wanted to say. "Sébastien!" I cried. "I must tell you something . . ."

"What are you doing up at this hour, my friend?"

". . . Something incredible . . . terrifying . . ." (It did not occur to me to echo his question.)

"But you are distraught. Here, sit down . . . let me fetch you some cognac . . ."

The words tumbled out of me pell-mell, and I could see they made very little sense to Sellig. He wore the expression of one confronted by a lunatic. His eyes remained fixed on my face, as if he were alert for the first sign of total disintegration and the cognac he had placed in my hand.

Sellig spoke. "Let me see if I understand you," he began. "You met Laval this evening . . . and he said something about his star, and the accomplishment of something no other man has ever accomplished . . . and just now, in this book, you find the same statement attributed to Bluebeard . . . and, from this, you are trying to tell me that Laval . . ."

I nodded. "I know it sounds mad . . ."

"It does."

". . . But consider, Sébastien: the names, first of all, are identical—Bluebeard's name was Gilles de *Laval*. In the shadow of the stake, he boasted of doing what no man had ever done, of succeeding at his ambition . . . and are you aware of the nature of his ambition? To live forever! It was to that end that he butchered hundred of innocents, trying to wrest the very riddle of life from their bodies!"

"But you say he was burned at the stake . . ."

"No! *Sentenced* to be burned! In return for not revoking the confessions he made under torture, he

was granted the mercy of strangulation before burning . . ."

"Even so—"

"Listen to me! His relatives were allowed to remove
his strangled body from the pyre before the flames
reached it! That is a historical fact! They took it
away—so they *said!*—to inter it in a Carmelite church
in the vicinity. But don't you see what they really
did?"

"No . . ."

"Don't you see, Sébastien, that this monster had
found the key to eternal life, and had instructed his
helots to revive his strangled body by use of those
same loathsome arts he had practised? Don't you see
that he went on living? That he lives still? That he
tortures and murders still? That even when his hands
are not drenched in human blood, they are drenched
in the mock blood of the Guignol? That the actor Laval
and the Laval of old are one and the same?"

Sellig looked at me strangely. It infuriated me. "I
am not mad!" I said. I rose and screamed at him:
"Don't you understand?"

And then—what with the lack of food, and the wine
I had drunk with Laval, and the cognac, and the tremulous state of my nerves—the room began to tilt, then
shrink, then spin, then burst into a star-shower, and I
dimly saw Sellig reach out for me as I fell forward
into blackness.

VII
A TRANSPARENT CRYPTOGRAM

The bedroom was full of noonday sunlight when I
awoke. It lacerated my eyes. I turned away from it and
saw someone sitting next to the bed. My eyes focussed, not without difficulty, and I realized it was a
woman—a woman of exceptional beauty. Before I
could speak, she said, "My name is Madame Pelle-

tier. I am Sébastien's friend. He has asked me to care for you. You were ill last night.''

"You must be . . . Lise . . ."

She nodded. "Can you sit up now?"

"I think so."

"Then you must take a little bouillon."

At the mention of food, I was instantly very hungry. Madame Pelletier helped me sit up, propped pillows at my back and began to feed me broth with a spoon. At first, I resisted this, but upon discovering that my trembling hand would not support the weight of the spoon, I surrendered to her ministrations.

Soon, I asked, "And where is Sébastien now?"

"At the Théâtre. A rehearsal of *Oedipe.*" With a faintly deprecatory inflection, she added, "Voltaire's."

I smiled at this, and said, "Your theatrical tastes are as pristine as Sébastien's."

She smiled in return. "It was not always so, perhaps. But when one knows a man like Sébastien, a man dedicated, noble, with impeccable taste and living a life beyond reproach . . . one climbs up to his level, or tries to."

"You esteem him highly."

"I love him, M'sieu'."

I had not forgotten my revelation of the night before. True, it seemed less credible in daylight, but it continued to stick in my mind like a burr. I asked myself what I should do with my fantastic theory. Blurt it out to this charming lady and have her think me demented? Take it to the *commissaire* and have him think me the same? Try to place it again before Sébastien, in more orderly fashion, and solicit his aid? I decided on the last course, and informed my lovely nurse that I felt well enough to leave. She protested; I assured her my strength was restored; and at last she left the bedroom and allowed me to dress. I did so quickly, and left the Sellig rooms immediately thereafter.

By this time, they knew me at the Théâtre Français, and I was allowed to stand in the wings while the Voltaire tragedy was being rehearsed. When the scene was finished, I sought out Sellig, drew him aside, and spoke to him, phrasing my suspicions with more calm than I had before.

"My dear friend," he said, "I flatter myself that my imagination is broad and ranging, that my mind is open, that I can give credence to many wonders at which other men might scoff. But *this*—"

"I know, I know," I said hastily, "and I do not profess to believe it entirely myself—but it is a clue, if nothing more, to Laval's character; a solution, perhaps, to a living puzzle . . ."

Sellig was a patient man. "Very well. I will have a bit of time after this rehearsal and before tonight's performance. Come back later and we will . . ." His voice trailed off. "And we will talk, at least. I do not know what else we can do."

I agreed to leave. I went directly to the Guignol, even though I knew that, being midafternoon, it would not be open. Arriving there, I found an elderly functionary, asked if Monsieur Laval was inside, perhaps rehearsing, and was told there was no one in the theatre. Then, after pressing a bank note into the old man's hand, I persuaded him to give me Laval's address. He did, and I immediately hailed a passing carriage.

As it carried me away from Montmartre, I tried to govern my thoughts. Why was I seeking out Laval? What would I say to him once I had found him? Would I point a finger at him and dramatically accuse him of being Gilles de Laval, Baron de Rais, a man of the Fifteenth Century? He would laugh at me, and have me committed as a madman. I still had not decided on a plan of attack when the carriage stopped, and the driver opened the door and said, "We are here, M'sieu'."

I stepped out, paid him, and looked at the place to

which I had been taken. Dumbfounded, I turned to the driver and said, "But this is not—"

"It is the address M'sieu' gave me." He was correct. It was. I thanked him and the carriage drove off. My mind churning, I entered the building.

It was the same one which contained Sellig's rooms. Summoning the concierge, I asked the number of Laval's apartments. He told me no such person lived there. I described Laval. He nodded and said, "Ah. The ugly one. Yes, he lives here, but his name is not Laval. It is De Retz."

Rayx, Rays, Retz, Rais—according to the history book, they were different spellings of the same name. "And the number of his suite?" I asked, impatiently.

"Oh, he shares a suite," he said. "He shares a suite with M'sieu' Sellig . . ."

I masked my astonishment and ran up the stairs, growing more angry with each step. To think that Sébastien had concealed this from me! Why? For what reason? And yet Laval had not shared the apartment the night before . . . What did it mean?

Etiquette discarded, I did not knock but threw open the door and burst in. "Laval!" I shouted. "Laval, I know you are here! You cannot hide from me!"

There was no answer. I stalked furiously through the rooms. They were empty. "Madame?" I called. "Madame Pelletier?" And then, standing in Sellig's bedroom, I saw that the place had been ransacked. Drawers of chiffoniers had been pulled out and relieved of their contents. It appeared very much as if the occupant had taken sudden flight.

Then I remembered the little room or closet I had seen Sellig leaving in the small hours. Going to it, I turned the knob and found it locked. Desperation and anger flooded my arms with strength, and yelling unseemly oaths, I broke into the room.

It was chaos.

The glass phials and demijohns had been smashed into shards, as if someone had flailed methodically among them with a cane. What purpose they had served was now a mystery. Perhaps a chemist could have analyzed certain residues among the debris, but I could not. Yet, somehow, these ruins did not seem, as I had first assumed, equipment for the development of photographic plates.

Again, supernatural awe turned me cold. Was this the dread laboratory of Bluebeard? Had these bottles and jars contained human blood and vital organs? In this Paris apartment, with Sellig as his conscripted assistant, had Laval distilled, out of death itself, the inmost secrets of life?

Quaking, I backed out of the little room, and in so doing, displaced a corner of one of the blue draperies. Odd things flicker through one's mind in the direst of circumstances—for some reason, I remembered having once heard that blue is sometimes a mortuary color used in covering the coffins of young persons . . . and also that it is a symbol of eternity and human immortality . . . blue coffins . . . blue drapes . . . Bluebeard . . .

I looked down at the displaced drape and saw something that was to delay my return to London, to involve me with the police for many days until they would finally judge me innocent and release me. On the floor at my feet, only half hidden by the blue drapes, was the naked, butchered, dead body of Madame Pelletier.

I think I screamed. I know I must have dashed from those rooms like a possessed thing. I cannot remember my flight, nor the hailing of any carriage, but I do know I returned to the Théâtre Français, a babbling, incoherent maniac who demanded that the rehearsal be stopped, who insisted upon seeing Sébastien Sellig.

The manager finally succeeded in breaking through the wall of my hysteria. He said only one thing, but that one thing served as the cohesive substance that made everything fall into place in an instant.

"He is not here, M'sieu'," he said. "It is very odd

. . . he has never missed a rehearsal or a performance before today . . . he was here earlier, but now . . . an understudy has taken his place . . . I hope nothing has happened to him . . . but M'sieu' Sellig, believe me, is not to be found.''

I stumbled out into the street, my brain a kaleidoscope. I thought of that little laboratory . . . and of those two utterly opposite men, the sublime Sellig and the depraved Laval, living in the same suite . . . I thought of Sagittarius, the Man-Beast . . . I thought of the phrase ''The sins of the fathers,'' and of a banal tune, ''More to be Pitied than Censured.'' . . . I realized now why Laval was absent from the Guignol on certain nights, the very nights Sellig appeared at the Théâtre Français . . . I heard my own voice, on that first night, inviting Sellig to accompany us to the Guignol: ''Will you come? Or perhaps you have a performance?'' And Sellig's answer: ''I do have a performance'' (yes, but *where?*) . . . I heard Sellig's voice in other scraps: *I have not watched a Guignol performance for several years; I have never seen Laval perform* . . .

Of course not! How could he, when he and Laval . . .

I accosted a gendarme, seized his lapels, and roared into his astonished face: ''Don't you see? How is it possible I overlooked it? It is so absurdly simple! It is the crudest . . . the most childish . . . the most transparent of cryptograms!''

''*What* is, M'sieu'?'' he demanded.

I laughed—or wept. ''*Sellig!*'' I cried. ''One has only to spell it backward!''

VIII
OVER THE PRECIPICE

The dining room of the Century Club was now almost deserted. Lord Terry was sipping a brandy with his coffee. He had refused dessert, but Hunt had not, and he was dispatching the last forkful of a particularly rich *baba au rhum*. His host produced from his pocket a massive, ornate case—of the same design as his pill box—and offered Hunt a cigar. It was deep brown, slender, fragrant, marvelously fresh. "The wizard has his wand," said Lord Terry, "the priest his censer, the king his sceptre, the soldier his sword, the policeman his nightstick, the orchestra conductor his baton. I have these. I suppose your generation would speak of phallic symbolism."

"We might," Hunt answered, smiling; "but we would also accept a cigar." He did, and a waiter appeared from nowhere to light them for the two men.

Through the first festoons of smoke, Hunt said, "You tell a grand story, sir."

"Story," the Earl repeated. "By that, you imply I have told a—whopper?"

"An extremely entertaining whopper."

He shrugged. "Very well. Let it stand as that and nothing more." He drew reflectively on his cigar.

"Come, Lord Terry," Hunt said. "Laval and Sellig were one man? The son of Edward Hyde? Starring at the Guignol in his evil personality and then, after a drink of his father's famous potion in that little laboratory, transforming himself into the blameless classicist of the Théâtre Français?"

"Exactly, my boy. And a murderer, besides, at least the Laval part of him; a murderer who felt I was drawing too close to the truth, and so fled Paris, never to be heard from again."

"Fled where?"

"Who knows? To New York, perhaps, where he still lives the double life of a respectable man in constant fear of involuntarily becoming a monster in public (Jekyll came to that pass in the story), and who must periodically imbibe his father's formula simply to remain a man . . . and who sometimes fails. Think of it! Even now, somewhere, in this very city, this very *club*, the inhuman Man-Beast, blood still steaming on his hands, may be drinking off the draught that will transform him into a gentleman of spotless reputation! A gentleman who, when dominant, loathes the dormant evil half of his personality—just as that evil half, when *it* is dominant, loathes the respectable gentleman! I am not insisting he is still alive, you understand, but that is precisely the way it was in Paris, back in the early Nineteen Hundreds."

Hunt smiled. "You don't expect me to believe you, sir, surely?"

"If I have given you a pleasant hour," Lord Terry replied, "I am content. I do not ask you to accept my story as truth. But I do inquire of you: why *not* accept it? Why couldn't it be the truth?"

"He is teasing me, of course," Hunt told himself, "luring me on to another precipice of the plot, like any seasoned storyteller. And part of his art is the dead seriousness of his tone and face."

"Why couldn't it?" Lord Terry repeated.

Hunt was determined not to be led into pitfalls, so he did not trot out lengthy rebuttals and protestations about the fantastic and antinatural "facts" of the tale— he was sure the Earl had arguments woven of the best casuistry to meet and vanquish anything he might have said. So he simply conceded: "It could be true, I suppose."

But a second later, not able to resist, he added, "The—story—does have one very large flaw."

"Flaw? Rubbish. What flaw?"

"It seems to me you've tried to have the best of both worlds, sir, tried to tell two stories in one, and they don't really meld. Let's say, for the sake of argument, that I am prepared to accept as fact the notion that Gilles de Rais was not burned at the stake, that he not only escaped death but managed to live for centuries, thanks to his unholy experiments. All well and good. Let's say that he was indeed the Guignol actor known as Laval. Still well, still good. But you've made him something else—something he could not possibly be. The son of Dr. Henry Jekyll, or rather, of Jekyll's alter ego, Edward Hyde. In my trade, we would say your story 'needs work.' We would ask you to make up your mind—was Laval the son of Edward Hyde, or was he a person centuries older than his own father? He could not be both.''

Lord Terry nodded. ''Oh, I see,'' he said. ''Yes, I should have made myself clearer. No, I do not doubt for a moment that Laval and Sellig were one and the same person and that person the natural son of Edward Hyde. I think the facts support that. The Bluebeard business is, as you say, quite impossible. It was a figment of my disturbed mind, nothing more. Sellig could not have been Gilles.''

''Then—''

''You or I might take a saint as our idol, might we not, or a great statesman—Churchill, Roosevelt—or possibly a literary or musical or scientific genius. At any rate, some lofty benefactor of immaculate prestige. But the son of Hyde? Would he not be drawn to and fascinated by history's great figures of evil? Might he not liken himself to Bluebeard? Might he not assume his name? Might he not envelop himself in symbolic blue draperies? Might he not delight in portraying his idol upon the Guignol stage? Might it not please his fiendish irony to saddle even his 'good' self with a disguised form of Gilles's name, and to exert such influence over that good self that even as the noble Sellig he could wallow in the personality of, say, a Nero? Of *course* he was not actually Bluebeard. It was adulation and aping, my dear sir, identification and a touch of madness. In short, it was hero worship, pure and simple.''

He had led Hunt to the precipice, after all, and the younger man had neatly tumbled over the edge.

''There is something else,'' Lord Terry said presently. ''Something I have been saving for the last. I did not wish to inundate you with too much all at once. You say I've tried to tell two stories. But it may be—it just possibly may be—that I have not two but three stories here.''

''Three?''

''Yes, in a way. It's just supposition, of course, a theory, and I have no evidence at all, other than circumstantial evidence, a certain remarkable juxtaposition of time and events that is a bit too pat to be coincidence . . .''

He treated himself to an abnormally long draw on his cigar, letting Hunt and the syntax hang in the air; then he started a new sentence: ''Laval's father, Edward Hyde, may have left his mark on history in a manner much more real than the pages of a supposedly fictional work by Stevenson. Certain criminal deeds that are matters of police record may have been his doing. I think they were. Killings that took place between 1885 and 1891 in London, Paris, Moscow, Texas, New York, Nicaragua, and perhaps a few other places, by an unknown, unapprehended monster about whom speculation varies greatly but generally agrees on one point: the high probability that he was a medical man. Hyde, of course, was a medical man; or rather, Jekyll was; the same thing, really.

''What I'm suggesting, you see, is that Laval was—is?—not only the son of Hyde but the son of the fiend who has been supposed an Englishman, a Frenchman, an Algerian, a Polish Jew, a Russian, and an American; whose supposed true names include George Chapman, Severin Klosowski, Neill Cream, Sir William Gull, Aleksandr Pedachenko, Ameer Ben Ali, and even Queen Victoria's grandson, Eddy, Prince Albert

Victor Christian Edward. His sobriquets are also legion: Frenchy, El Destripador, L'Éventreur, The Whitechapel Butcher, and, most popularly—"

Hunt snatched the words from his mouth: "Jack the Ripper."

IX
THE SUSPENSION OF DISBELIEF

"Exactly," said Lord Terry. "The Ripper's killings, without exception, resembled the later Paris murders, and also the earlier massacres of Bluebeard's, in that they were obsessively sexual and resulted in 'wounds of a nature too shocking to be described,' as the London *Times* put it. The Bluebeard comparison is not exclusive with me—a Chicago doctor named Kiernan arrived at it independently and put it forth at the time of the Whitechapel murders. And the current series of perverted butcheries here in New York are, of course, of that same stripe. Incidently, may I call your attention to the sound of Jekyll's name? Trivial, of course, but it would have been characteristic of that scoundrel Hyde to tell one of his victims his name was Jekyll, which she might have taken as 'jackal' and later gasped out in her last fits, you know. We've placed Hyde's 'birth' at 1886 for no better reason than because the Stevenson story was published in that year . . . but if the story is based in truth, then it is a telling of events that took place before the publication date, perhaps very shortly before. Yes, there is a distinct possibility that Jack the Ripper was Mr. Hyde."

Hunt toyed with the dregs of his coffee. "Excuse me, Lord Terry," he said, "but another flaw has opened up."

"Truth cannot be flawed, my boy."

"Truth cannot, no." This time, it was Hunt who stalled. He signalled the waiter for hot coffee, elaborately added sugar and cream, stirred longly and thoughtfully. Then he said, "Jack the Ripper's crimes were committed, you say, between the years 1885 and 1891?"

"According to the best authorities, yes."

"But sir," Hunt said, smiling deferentially all the while, "in Stevenson's story, published in 1886, Hyde *died*. He therefore could not have committed those crimes that took place after 1886."

Lord Terry spread his arms expansively. "Oh, my dear boy," he said, "when I suggest that the story was based in truth, I do not mean to imply that it was a newspaper report, a dreary list of dates and statistics. For one thing, many small items, such as names and addresses, were surely changed for obvious reasons (Soho for Whitechapel, perhaps). For another thing, Stevenson was a consummate craftsman, not a police blotter. The unfinished, so-called realistic story is stylish today, but in Stevenson's time a teller of tales had to bring a story to a satisfying and definite conclusion, like a symphony. No, no, I'm afraid I can't allow you even a technical point."

"If names were fabricated, what about that Jekyll-jackal business?"

"Quite right—I retract the Jekyll-jackal business. Trivial anyway."

Hunt persisted. "Was Hyde's nationality a fabrication of Stevenson's, too, then?"

"No, I'm inclined to believe he was actually English . . ."

"Ah! But Laval and Sellig—"

"Were French? Oh, I rather think not. Both spoke English like natives, you know. And Laval drank Scotch whisky like water—which I've never seen a Frenchman do. Also, he mistook my name for Pendragon—a grand old English name out of Arthurian legend, not the sort of name that would spring readily to French lips, I shouldn't think. No, I'm sure they—he—were compatriots of mine."

"What was he—they—doing in France?"

"For the matter of that, what was I? But if you really need reasons over and above the mundane, you might consider the remote possibility that he was using an assumed nationality as a disguise, a shield from the police. That's not *too* fanciful for you, I hope? Although this may be: might not a man obsessed with worship of Gilles de Rais, a man who tried to emulate his evil idol in all things, also put on his idol's nation and language like a magic cloak? But I shan't defend the story any further." He looked at his gold pocket watch, the size of a small potato and nearly as thick. "Too late, for one thing. Time for long-winded old codgers to be in their beds."

It was dismissal. He was, after all, an earl, and accustomed to calling the tune. Hunt hoped, however, that he hadn't offended him. As they walked slowly to the cloakroom to redeem Hunt's hat, the Earl's guest thought about truth and fiction and Byron's remark that the first was stranger than the second. He thought, too, about that element so essential to the reception of a strange tale whether it be true or false—the element of believability, at least the suspension of disbelief. Lord Terry had held him spellbound with his story, then had covered his tracks and filled in the chinks in his armor pretty well. If Hunt were disposed to be indulgent and generous, he could believe—or suspend disbelief—in the notion that Hyde was an actual person, that he was the maniac killer known as Jack the Ripper, even that he had sired a son who'd lived and died under the names of Laval and Sellig around the turn of the century, in a glamorous Paris that exists now only in memories and stories. All that was comfortably remote. But it was the other idea of Lord Terry's—that Hyde's son might still be alive today—that strained Hunt's credulity, shattered the pleasant spell, and somewhat spoiled the story for him. By any logical standard, it was the easiest of all to believe, granted the other premise; but belief does not depend upon logic, it is a delicate and fragile flower that draws nourishment from intuition and instinct and hunch. There was something about this latter half of the Twentieth Century—with its sports cars and television and nuclear bombs and cold wars—that just did not jibe with the flamboyant alchemy, the mysterious powders, the exotic elixirs, the bubbling, old-fashioned retorts and demijohns of Dr. Jekyll's and Mr. Hyde's. The thought of Laval, a monster "three-quarters pure evil, with only a single thin flickering quarter of good in him," alive now, perhaps in New York, perhaps the perpetrator of the current revolting crimes; the thought of him rushing desperately through crowded Manhattan streets to some secret laboratory, mixing his arcane chemicals and drinking off the churning, smoking draught that would transform him into the eminently acceptable Sellig—no, that was the last straw. It was the one silly thing that destroyed the whole story for Hunt. He expressed these feelings, cordially and respectfully, to Lord Terry.

The Earl chuckled good naturedly. "My story still— needs work?"

Hunt's hat was on and he stood at the door, ready to leave his host and allow him to go upstairs to bed. "Yes," he said, "just a little."

"I will take that under advisement," Lord Terry said. Then, his eyes glinting with mischief, he added, "As for those old-fashioned demijohns and other outmoded paraphernalia, however—modern science has made many bulky pieces of apparatus remarkably compact. The transistor radio and whatnot, you know. To keep my amateur standing as a raconteur, I must continue to insist that my story is true—except for one necessary alteration. Good night, my boy. It was pleasant to see you."

"Good night, sir. And thanks again for your kindness."

Outside, the humidity had been dispelled, and the air, though warm, was dry and clear. The sky was cloudless and dense with the stars of summer. From among them, Hunt picked out the eleven stars that form the constellation Sagittarius. The newspapers were announcing the appearance of another mutilated corpse, discovered in an alley only a few hours before. Reading the headlines, Hunt recalled a certain utterance— *"This* . . . is the Grandest Guignol of all." And another— *"La vie est un corridor noir/D'impuissance et de désespoir."* He bought a paper and hailed a taxi.

It was in the taxi, three blocks away from the club, that he suddenly "saw" the trivial, habitual action that had accompanied Lord Terry's closing remark about modern compactness. The old man had reached into his pocket for that little gold case and had casually taken a pill.

THE WHITECHAPEL WANTONS

by Vincent McConnor

A door opened, the angry sound of rusty hinges echoing through the empty street, but no one heard.

And nobody saw the figure of a girl, briefly visible against a blur of candlelight that revealed a narrow hall with steep wooden stairs.

The girl closed the door and, fumbling with her key in the dark, locked it again. You couldn't be too careful, although, up to now, the Ripper had always killed in the streets. Mostly in dark alleys—some of them not far from here.

She had known all of the girls, Polly Nichols and the others.

The newspaper said that Polly was the second to die.

Hesitating on the top step, peering up and down the silent street, she returned the key to her purse and slipped it into the pocket of her jacket. Now both hands were free for any emergency she might have to face.

The ground-floor shop next door, which did a brisk trade in pickled eels during the day, was shuttered for the night.

Nobody ventured out after dark any more unless it was urgent business. It was the women who were in danger, but men stayed off the streets at night because the police were stopping them to ask who they were and where they were going. If their answers sounded suspicious they were taken in for questioning.

The pubs were suffering. There were still a few regulars every night, but a girl was afraid to speak to a stranger because he might be the Ripper. Nobody knew what he looked like.

She was probably the only one in all of London who had seen his face and she wasn't going to tell the police!

Shivering under her thin summer dress, she clutched the short velvet jacket more securely around her. The air was as sharp as a knife and it was only early October. Another week and she would need to find herself a winter coat from a pushcart in Petticoat Lane.

She glanced at the sky above the low rooftops and chimneys and saw that clouds were shoving across the stars. There was no moon.

As she came down the two splintered steps to the cobbled street, she wondered what name she ought to use tonight.

This week she had been calling herself Annie but somehow that always seemed a bit common. Maybe tonight she would use Violette again. That nice young toff last week had said it suited her when she told him her name was Violette. He had been ever so kind, paid her two whole shillings . . .

Passing a row of dark shops, heading toward the street lamp at the corner, she kept close to the buildings, hurrying her steps as she skirted the mouth of each alley.

London had been choking with smoke and fog each time the Ripper killed. Tonight, at least, there was no fog.

She had decided to tell Cora what she knew and explain about her plan. It couldn't work unless somebody helped her and Cora was her dearest friend now that Polly was dead.

Her plan. She shivered again. She had never thought she would plan to kill anybody. But Polly had been her friend since the first week she had arrived in London. They had met that rainy night near the Haymar-

ket. What a silly innocent she was in those days, fresh
from Liverpool. Only three years ago . . .

She had never seen Whitechapel until Polly brought
her here, insisting she move in and share her lodgings.

That night last month when the two constables had
pounded on the door waking her from a sound sleep,
she couldn't believe what they told her. She had
thought Polly was asleep in the other bed. Their questions had frightened her, and when they took her to
identify the body she had fainted.

She still lived in Polly's room, but it was getting
harder to pay the rent each week. Business was terrible
because of the Ripper and it wouldn't get much better
as long as he prowled the streets. She never had so
much as two shillings in her purse any more—barely
enough to buy a scrap of food each day. Something
had to be done and the police weren't doing anything.

She reached the street lamp and turned down another
dark street.

Last night in the Black Swan one of the girls said
the Ripper must be a constable or he would've been
caught long ago. Everybody laughed but at the same
time they had wondered if the Ripper could be a policeman. Some of them were terribly nasty to a girl,
cruel and insulting. Although there was a new one—
Constable Divall—who was ever so nice. In his twenties and not at all bad-looking.

There were so many extra constables on night duty
in Whitechapel now that nobody could slip out to do
an honest job of burglary any more, afraid they'd be
picked up by the police searching the streets for the
Ripper. What made it even worse was that some of
the constables were not in uniform and those who were
traveled in pairs. Though you couldn't blame them,
the whole city of London was in a fair panic.

And she was the only one who knew for certain that
the Ripper wasn't a policeman!

Now she could make out a blur of gaslight at the far
end of the narrow street.

Cora should be in the Black Swan by now. It must be past midnight. The empty streets were frightening. At any moment he could appear out of the dark and come lurching toward her.

She had seen his blond hair under a black bowler, his face pale against the high collar of his black coat. She'd glimpsed his eyes when Polly took his arm and, giggling as usual, disappeared into the fog with him. Never to be seen again, at least not alive . . .

Reaching the protective circle of light from the gaslight on the corner, she paused to look in every direction, then darted across the cobbles toward the Black Swan.

A dark shape moved near her feet.

She gasped with fright, then realized it was only Old Cobbie, drunk as a lord, sprawled on the paving stones.

Grasping the wrought-iron handle, she pushed against the heavy oak door and entered the pub.

A candle in a brass lantern guttered above the bar.

Three faces turned to stare. The owner, Tom, behind the bar and two of the regulars, all three with drinks in their fists.

"Evenin', miss!"

"Seen Cora t'night, Tom?"

"Showed up ten minutes ago. She's in the back."

Violette crossed to the bar, sawdust crunching under her thin slippers. "Nobody on the street t'night."

"You girls come rushin' in like the Ripper's after ye."

"Maybe he is! He got Polly, didn' he?" She never stood close to the bar when she ordered a drink because it wasn't ladylike to lean against the polished wood the way men did. "I'll have a mild, please." She brought out her purse, selected a coin from the few she owned, and put it on the bar. "A girl can't make a livin' on these empty streets."

"If Scotland Yard don't soon catch the blighter we'll all be out of business, every bloomin' pub in Whitechapel. Here y'are, me girl." Tom handed her the half-pint and turned back to his cronies.

Violette carried her beer around the corner toward the back, noticing that there was no fire on the hearth to send a flicker of warmth across the smoke-blackened beams of the ceiling. The only light came from a wax-encrusted candle in the mouth of a wine bottle on the table where Cora sat—the only person in the room.

Cora waved, pushing a scarlet feather away from her eye and adjusting her velvet hat more firmly on her black curls. "I thought maybe you wouldn' be comin' out t'night, Annie."

"I had to." She set her beer on the scrubbed wood table and sank onto a bench, facing her friend. "Rent's due t'morrow, so I've got t' earn a bit of money. An' I'm not Annie t'night—I'm Violette."

"Whatever you say, Vi. As I came here I saw nothin' but constables in the streets, strips of rubber nailed t' their boots so the Ripper wouldn' hear 'em comin'."

"I didn't see nobody." She took a first gulp of beer, observing that Cora, as usual, was drinking gin and had been reading something on a crumpled sheet of paper. "I have t' talk to you, luv. About Polly."

"Oh?" Cora held the sheet of paper across the table. "Did you see this?"

As Violette took the slip of paper she saw that it was a printed leaflet.

"Police 'ave spread these all over Whitechapel!"

Violette held the leaflet close to the candle so that she could read the words.

POLICE NOTICE.
TO THE OCCUPIER.

On the mornings of Friday, 31st, August, Saturday 8th, and Sunday, 30th of September, 1888, Women were murdered in or near Whitechapel, supposed by some one residing in the immediate neighbourhood. Should you know of any person to whom suspicion is attached, you are earnestly requested to communicate at once with the nearest Police Station.

Metropolitan Police Office,
30th September, 1888

"Someone in the neighborhood?" She looked at Cora. "They're bonkers! He's a toff from the West End." Handing the leaflet back across the table, she asked, "Where'd you get this?"

"Found it under me door this afternoon."

"My landlady must've gotten one but I didn' see the old girl before I came out. Been avoidin' her." She took another gulp of beer.

"Ivy tol' me last night they're sayin' the Ripper's a famous surgeon from Harley Street! That's why he slices all his victims up so neat!"

"Ivy's a fool. Nobody knows for certain who he is—or, for that matter, how many girls he's done in."

"They're also sayin' the Ripper's a woman."

"The Ripper's a *man!* A real toff."

"Oh?" Cora folded the sheet of paper and tucked it into her purse. "How d' you know what he looks like?"

"That's what I wanted t' tell you."

"What?"

"I've seen him."

"The Ripper?"

"With me own two eyes."

"When?"

"The night he killed Polly. We was in a doorway near Swallow Court, Polly an' me, keepin' out of the cold. She seen him first, comin' down the street, an' went t' meet him—hopin' for a bit of luck, of course! I watched while they talked, standin' close t'gether in the fog, then he offered her his arm like a regular gent an' they turned back, same way he'd come. I thought, of course, they was goin' to a hotel. I had no idea it was the Ripper.''

"Did he see you?"

"I never moved out of the doorway."

"But you had a good look at him?"

"I'd recognize him anywhere!"

"Have you told the police?"

"Wouldn' I be the fool t' do that! I ain't told nobody 'til this minute, not even you! An' I'm only tellin' you t'night 'cause I need your help.''

Cora stared at her suspiciously. "What sort of help?"

"Well, Polly was my best friend in London. Now you're the only friend I got." She glanced toward the front door of the pub to be sure the men at the bar couldn't hear what she was about to say. "The police ain't goin' t' catch the Ripper 'cause they don't know what he looks like. But I do! I've seen him! An' I'm goin' t' get rid of the blighter!''

"Get rid of him?"

"For Polly's sake! Put an end to him—once and for all. That's what I'm goin' t' do. So a girl can be safe on the streets again . . .''

"Then you *are* goin' t' tell the police what he looks like?''

"I wouldn' dare! If the Ripper found out I'd seen him—that I know what he looks like—my life wouldn't be worth a ha'penny! He'd come after me with his bloody knife! You've got t' help me, Cora. I can't do it without you. It'll take the two of us!''

"Do what, Vi? What the devil are you talkin' about?''

"I'm goin' t' kill the Ripper."

"*Kill* him?"

"Of course I have t' find him first, but . . .''

She explained her plan in a rush of words, and then arranged to meet Cora the following afternoon, to search through the nearby docks for a crate. A wooden crate large enough to hold a man's body.

Walking toward the docks late the next afternoon, they discussed the plan over and over, working out exactly what each would have to do.

Cora was dubious at first, but then she was caught up in the excitement of the idea and began to make suggestions of her own.

They located a discarded wooden crate outside one of the warehouses, which they lugged between them back to Violette's lodging. Mrs. Paddick, her landlady, watched them ease their awkward burden through the narrow hall, past her open kitchen door, with suspicious eyes. " 'Ere now! Wot's this?''

Violette winked at Cora as they set the crate down with a hollow thud. "Cora's helpin' me put this in the alley, Mrs. Paddick.''

"Wotever for?''

"Had t' find a large box for Polly's belongin's.''

"The poor girl!''

"I'm sendin' her clothes an' things to her family in Birmingham. You won't mind if I leave this out in the back for a few days, will you? It's much too heavy t' carry upstairs.''

"Leave it there as long as you want. Nobody'll touch it.''

"It could be a week or more before I can pack everything.''

"Take y'r time, luv. Let me know if there's any way I can 'elp.'' She moved back into the dark hole of her kitchen. "Stop by when ye finish there an' I'll 'ave a nice hot cup of tea for ye.''

"That's ever so kind, Mrs. Paddick!'' Cora called after her.

"She's in a right good humor t'day,'' Violette whispered. "I paid me rent this mornin' so she'll leave us alone. Anyway, the ol' girl's so deaf she never hears nothin' no matter how many times I come in an' out at night.''

They carried their wooden box through the open back door and set it down next to the dustbin in the grimy back alley.

Violette raised the hinged lid and let it fall back down the side, then turned the crate over, with Cora's help, so that the open side, out of sight from the door, faced the dustbin.

She demonstrated how Cora could hide inside the crate until she was needed and showed her the barrow that was always propped against the wall next door, behind the eel shop. They would load the crate onto the barrow, push it down the alley to the next street, and in a matter of minutes reach the river. She also pointed to a small ax resting near a stack of firewood that was used in the eel-shop kitchen and showed her where to place the ax beside the back door so she, Vi, would be able to find it in the dark when she brought the Ripper here . . .

They went over the plan several more times in Violette's room after their tea in Mrs. Paddick's kitchen. They stretched out on the two lumpy beds and continued to discuss the plan until they fell asleep.

Later, just before midnight, they went out together.

And for the first time in many weeks they felt safer in the empty streets.

The next day they decided it would be much more practical, as well as cheaper, for both of them if Cora moved in and shared her room.

Mrs. Paddick didn't suspect that she had a new tenant. She was, as Violette had said, extremely deaf and seldom came upstairs unless there was trouble with one of the lodgers.

The two girls saw to it that there was nothing to arouse her suspicions. Even when they brought visitors to their room Mrs. Paddick heard nothing and, from long experience, probably wouldn't have complained if she had.

Violette and Cora went out together each night around midnight and walked through the dark streets and alleys of Whitechapel. But Violette saw no sign of the Ripper.

The entire city of London was in a state of hysteria because any night now the Ripper was expected to kill again. It had been more than a week since the last body was found.

The newspapers printed fresh stories every day.

And strangely, a deluge of toffs from the West End began to swarm through Whitechapel every night to see the place where Jack had slashed his victims. The pubs began to flourish again and a girl could make several shillings a night. Most of them, like Violette and Cora, took to walking in pairs—like the police—for their own protection.

The two girls went to the Black Swan every night to have a drink and catch up with the day's gossip. With the increase in business even Violette was drinking gin now.

It was crowded and noisy, every table occupied in the back room, where a new barmaid darted back and forth with trays of drinks.

Violette watched the activity, seated at her usual table with Cora, sipping at her glass of gin.

"You think he'll show up t'night?" Cora asked in a whisper.

"T'night or t'morrow night," Violette answered, feeling the warmth from the gin flowing through her body. "Whenever he shows up, we'll be ready for him."

"S'pose he never does come back?"

"He will."

"S'pose all these people keep him away. He might go to another part of London—Chelsea or Soho."

"I think, t'night, we should keep away from the busy streets—stay in the alleys, around Swallow Court, where Polly met him."

"Whatever you say."

"More gin, ladies?"

They looked up to see the blonde barmaid, smiling and eager, her apron splashed with beer.

"Not just now," Violette answered. "We'll be havin' drinks later, with some gents."

"Watch out for the Ripper." The tousled barmaid leaned closer, lowering her voice. "I heard just now, he's left-handed."

"Fancy that!" Cora exclaimed, glancing at her friend. "Left-handed."

"Who said he was?" Violette asked. "I thought nobody ain't ever seen the bloke."

"Gentleman told me it's in the newspaper t'day. Scotland Yard found out from the knife wounds in the last girl's body. Cut her up somethin' 'orrible!"

"A likely story!" Violette scoffed. "How could they tell he's left-handed from that?"

"I wouldn' know, luv. They say the Queen gave orders t' the 'ome Secretary t'day t' catch the Ripper in a hurry so the ladies of London can walk the streets in safety again." She darted away, in response to a summons from another table.

"Ladies?" Cora laughed, the feathers quivering on her hat. "That's us!"

Violette frowned. "Left-handed, is he?" She shivered suddenly.

"Drink up, luv!" Cora raised her glass. "We'd better be on our way."

Violette noticed, as they came from the Black Swan, that mist was rising between the damp cobbles and a dirty grey fog was pressing down from overhead. "The Ripper will be out t'night, I know he will . . ."

"If you say so." Cora peered up and down the narrow street but there was nobody in sight.

They turned into the first alley, choking and coughing as their lungs filled with the acrid coal smoke the fog was pushing down from nearby chimneys.

There were lanterns on the stone walls, but their light was so dim that they had to feel their way along them. The rough surface dripped with moisture and, within seconds, their fingers were cold and wet. "What a filthy night!" Violette grasped Cora's arm with her hand so they wouldn't become separated. "I almost wish I was home in Liverpool."

"Do you ever think of goin' back, Vi?"

"Not really. I s'pose I could get me old job again, workin' as housemaid."

"You liked that?"

"Cleanin' an' pickin' up? I hated it!" She glimpsed a misty circle of light from a street lamp at the end of the alley. "Here's Swallow Court."

"I don't know this part of Whitechapel."

Violette wiped her damp fingers on her coat. "There's a doorway over there. We can stand out of the fog an' still see the street."

"Where you an' Polly stood that night?"

"That's right." Violette kept close to a building, looking for the remembered doorway. "We knew this street well, Polly an' me. Came here many a night." She glimpsed the dark entrance with its recessed doors through drifting veils of fog. "Here we are!" She led the way under the shallow arch and leaned back against one of the heavy oak doors.

Cora huddled beside her. "The fog's gettin' heavier."

"He'll be here t'night, I know he will." Vi motioned across the street. "You can't see it now but there's another alley over there."

"You really think he'll be out?"

"I'm sure of it!"

"Maybe we shouldn't wait . . ."

Vi turned to face Cora. "You backin' out?"

"No!"

"Do you remember what you have t' do?"

"I remember, Vi. Everything . . ."

"When I see him I'll go straight t' meet him, catch him before he can slip away. You hurry back t' Mrs. Paddick's an' through the downstairs hall t' the alley.

Be sure t' put that ax where I showed you, next to the door so I can find it in the dark. Then hide inside the box until I bring him. You'll hear us but don't make a sound. An' don't show y'r face 'til I call you."

"I'm scared, Vi."

"So am I."

"He could kill us."

"We have t' do this. For Polly—for what he did t' her an' all them other poor girls."

"I know we do."

Violette froze. "Here he is!"

"You're sure?"

"It's him. You know what t' do!"

Violette stepped down from the doorway onto the wet cobblestones.

"Be careful, Vi," Cora whispered.

She hurried toward him through the swirling fog. It was the same pale face and the same blond hair under the black bowler. The same coat with the high collar. Tonight he was wearing grey gloves.

He saw her coming toward him and began to smile.

Violette slowed her steps.

"Good evening, miss . . ."

"Evenin' . . ." She listened for Cora's footsteps behind her, but there was no sound of any kind.

"Miserable evening, what?" He continued to smile.

"Yes." He wasn't a bad-looking sort. Nice smile. White teeth under a small moustache. She mustn't let him force her into Swallow Court where he had taken Polly.

"It would be much more pleasant inside somewhere, don't you think?"

"I—I've a place near here."

"Could we possibly go there, do you suppose?"

"Why not?"

"Splendid! Can you find your way in this fog?"

"Oh, yes." She trembled as she felt his gloved hand under her arm. The same hand that had killed Polly.

"It's nearby, you say?" He walked beside her, back the way she had come.

"It's a nice room where nobody will bother us. Ever so cozy . . ."

"You're not London-born, are you?"

"How'd you guess?"

"Your accent sounds like Liverpool."

"I'm not sayin' where I'm from."

He laughed. "It doesn't matter."

"We go through here." She turned with him into the side street, avoiding the alley Cora would have taken. This should give Cora time to reach the house ahead of them.

What would happen if Cora got lost in the fog? She had said she didn't know this part of Whitechapel.

Dear God! Don't let that happen . . .

"Have you been in London long?" he asked.

"Long enough t' know my way round."

"I shouldn't wonder!" He laughed again.

They saw only one person, an ancient Chinese, slinking close to the dark shopfronts.

Violette found the house without difficulty, unlocked the door, and motioned for her escort to enter. "We mustn't talk," she whispered. "The landlady lives on this floor an' she's a holy terror." She closed the door behind them and saw that he seemed taller when he removed his bowler. The only light came from a flickering candle in a niche near the stairs. "We go through the back."

"Oh? Why's that?"

"There's another house in the rear. Where I live . . ." She moved ahead of him through the narrow hall, into the shadows. The floor-boards creaked underfoot but there was no other sound in the house.

Violette saw that the rear door was closed.

Had Cora gotten here ahead of them? It would be terrible if the street door flew open behind them and Cora came rushing in.

Would she be there in the back, crouched in that crate?

Violette reached the door and saw that the bolt had been pulled back.

Cora was here!

She opened the door and raised her voice as she spoke to warn Cora they had arrived. "Here we are. You go first."

"As you wish." He stepped outside, into the fog again. "I say! It's dark out here."

"Stand still for a minute. 'Til you can see where you are."

"Good idea . . . By the way, you haven't told me your name."

"Violette."

"Violette? I rather like that."

She could see his bare head now, dark against the grey fog. Bending quickly, she felt beside the step until she touched the cold wooden handle of the ax. Lifting it slowly with both hands, she had a sudden aversion to what she was about to do. Never in her life had she done anything like this before. But she had to do it!

"Well, now! Which way do we go?"

The sound of his voice released her.

Violette raised the ax above her head and, with all her strength, crashed the metal head against his skull. Incredibly, as she watched, he dropped out of sight without a sound.

She had done it!

The ax slipped from her hands.

For a moment she didn't move.

The distant moan of a foghorn sounded a warning from the river.

Violette stepped down onto the hard ground and cautiously thrust her right foot out until she touched his body. She gave it a tentative kick. There was no reaction.

Only then did she find her voice. "Cora . . ."

* * *

The two girls didn't speak as, side by side, they pushed the awkward barrow through the dark streets.

Everything had worked out as they had planned.

The Ripper was dead and Violette felt no remorse. She had only paid him back for Polly and those other poor girls.

She remembered her grandmother back in Liverpool reading from the Bible. "Eye for eye, tooth for tooth, hand for hand, foot for foot . . ." Her grandmother said what it really meant was a life for a life.

Jack the Ripper's life for Polly's life! And for all the others.

The only noise was the creaking of the barrow as its wooden wheels bumped over the damp cobbles. No sound came from the crate, which they had covered with an old blanket, or from the silent thing that was stuffed inside.

Jack was in the box! Violette smiled at the thought . . .

She was surprised that he had died so quickly. It took so little to kill a person. She'd had no idea it was that easy.

Cora, beside her, was gasping from the effort it took to push the clumsy barrow through the fog.

Her own breathing, she realized, was becoming more difficult. Each time a wheel stuck, refused to bump over a large cobblestone, they had to lift the barrow clear before they could push on.

The foghorn sounded much louder. They must be getting close to the river. Soon they would reach the old warehouses. After that, and they would see the wharves.

She could smell the river now.

The police would fish his body out of the water, but they would find nothing to tell them who he was. They wouldn't even know he was the Ripper. She had taken all the money from his pockets and stuffed it, uncounted, into her purse. There had been no wallet.

And not much money, a few pound notes and some coins.

Also, to her surprise, there had been very little blood. Early tomorrow, before Mrs. Paddick was awake, she must go down to the backyard and clean away any spots.

The barrow struck another cobblestone and wouldn't budge.

"Damn!" Cora exclaimed. "Is it much farther?"

"We're almost at the river. I can smell it." Vi released the wooden handle and circled the barrow to see what was hindering their progress.

Cora followed and bent beside her to peer underneath.

"Wot's all this?"

Cora screamed at the sound of the ominous masculine voice.

Both girls straightened as two uniformed figures appeared out of the fog.

Violette recognized one of the faces. "Constable Divall!"

"Somethin' wrong here, miss?" Divall moved closer, followed by the other constable.

"I'm helpin' me friend move," Violette answered quickly. "An' the bloomin' barrow got stuck."

"Let's see if we can help. Give me a hand, Thompson."

The girls held their breath as the other constable joined Divall to ease the wheel over the obstruction, then watched apprehensively as they lifted the barrow between them and carried it several paces before they set it down again.

"You've got somethin' right heavy here!" Divall turned to look at them again.

"It's me friend's trunk," Violette explained.

"That's right!" Cora managed to say. "Me trunk."

"All her belongin's. She's movin' t' a new lodgin' house. Thanks ever so much, Constable."

"My pleasure, miss." Divall touched his helmet as

he continued on with the other constable. "Watch out for the Ripper! He could be out on a night like this."

"We'll be careful!"

Cora giggled nervously.

Violette saw now why she hadn't heard the approach of the two constables. They had thin strips of rubber—probably cut from bicycle tires—nailed to their boots. She didn't move until they had faded into the fog.

Cora sighed. "That was awful close."

"He's not a bad lookin' sort, for a constable. C'mon, luv! Before we're caught again."

They grasped the handle of the barrow and, pushing harder than before, continued on their way. The fear of meeting other policemen strengthened their arms and quickened their steps. And they remained silent, saving their breath, until they found themselves on a wooden dock with the Thames lapping among the pilings underneath.

There were several lighted lanterns at irregular intervals along the side of the large warehouse.

They pushed the barrow to an open space at the edge of the rotting wharf.

Violette pulled the blanket away and, with Cora's help, managed to tip the crate onto the wooden planks of the wharf. Then, grasping the handle together again, they used the barrow as a ram and, pushing with all their might, shoved the crate to the edge. One final violent push and the crate scraped over the side.

It struck the water with a tremendous splash.

The two girls hurried to the edge of the wharf and looked down. In a spill of light from the nearest lantern, they saw circles of waves spreading out from the spot where the crate had entered the water.

They waited, peering down, but it didn't come to the surface again.

Without a word they turned the barrow around and, hurrying now, headed back the way they had come.

* * *

The door opened but the sound of rusty hinges was muffled by the fog.

Violette came out, closing the door and locking it.

She saw that the fog was much heavier. The street lamp at the distant corner was completely blotted out.

As she came down the steps to the cobbled street she decided that it was a bit late to go back to the Black Swan. Instead she turned toward Swallow Court again. There was nothing to be afraid of there now that the Ripper was dead.

Cora was getting ready for bed when she left. It would have been impossible for her to sleep for another two or three hours—she was much too excited by what she had done . . .

Maybe she would meet a nice young toff from the West End. She couldn't take him back to her lodging because Cora would be asleep there but at least she didn't need to worry about the Ripper any more. He was at the bottom of the Thames.

When she and Cora had reached the back alley at Mrs. Paddick's, the first thing they had done was put the barrow back where it belonged behind the eel shop. Then, in the dark, she had wiped the ax clean and set it in place beside the stack of firewood.

Early tomorrow she would go down and make sure there were no other bloodstains anywhere . . .

When they went upstairs to their room, she had found several dried bloodstains on her skirt. Cold water got rid of them, but she would have to wash the skirt tomorrow . . .

The sound of her heels echoed sharply against the cobbles but that didn't matter now. She didn't care who heard them.

She had taken his money from her purse and, spreading it out on the bed, divided the pound notes and coins equally with Cora. Each of them had ended up with more than three pounds. Three whole pounds!

Apparently he had left his wallet and personal pa-

pers at home in case the police picked him up. There
was nothing in his pockets that told you who he was . . .

Cora, stretched out on the other bed, had laughed.
"Maybe he wasn't the Ripper!"

"Why do you say that?"

"Polly could've gone with another man first—the
one you saw—then met the Ripper later."

She had continued folding the pound notes into her
purse. "No, he was the Ripper all right. But we'll
never know who he was—his name or nothin'."

Of course he was the Ripper! That's why his pockets
were empty . . .

She sensed rather than heard that someone was following her.

As she reached the alley that led to Swallow Court
she touched the damp plaster wall so she wouldn't lose
her way.

The lanterns, hanging from spikes, were like small
holes in the fog.

Now she could hear footsteps behind her on the cobblestones. Maybe this would be a nice gent. Young
and pleasant . . .

He was much closer now, almost at her heels.

Violette smiled as she turned to greet him.

A dark figure loomed out of the fog.

She was unable to see his face, only that he was
raising an arm as though he was about to lift his hat.
His left arm.

Something in his gloved hand caught a glint of light
from the nearest lantern.

A knife! In his left hand!

The Ripper was left-handed . . .

Violette tried to scream, but his other gloved hand
grasped her throat. She saw the arm swing down and
felt the first hard thrust of the knife into her flesh.

A STUDY IN TERROR

by Ellery Queen

Ellery Begins

Ellery brooded.

For a reasonable time.

After which he got up from his typewriter, seized ten pages of doomed copy and tore them into four ragged sections.

He scowled at the silent typewriter. The machine leered back.

The phone rang, and he jumped for it as if it were a life-preserver.

"Don't snarl at *me*," said a hurt voice with undertones of anguish. "I'm having fun, per orders."

"Dad! Did I snap at you? I'm in a plot bind. How's Bermuda?"

"Sunshine, blue water, and more damn sand than you can shake a billy at. I want to come *home*."

"No," Ellery said firmly. "The trip cost me a bundle and I'm going to get my money's worth."

Inspector Queen's sigh was eloquent. "You always were a dictator where I'm concerned. What am I, a basket case?"

"You're overworked."

"Maybe I could arrange a rebate?" Inspector Queen suggested hopefully.

"Your orders are to rest and relax—forget everything."

"Okay, okay. There's a hot horseshoe game going on across from my cabana. Maybe I can horn in."

"Do that, dad. I'll phone tomorrow for the score."

Ellery hung up and glared at the typewriter. The problem remained. He circled the table warily and began to pace.

Providentially, the doorbell rang.

"Leave them on the table," Ellery called. "Take the money."

The visitor disobeyed. Feet crossed the foyer and entered the scene of the great man's agony. Ellery grunted. "You? I thought it was the boy with the delicatessen."

Grant Ames, III, with the aplomb of the privileged bore—a bore with millions—aimed his perfect Brooks Brothers toward the bar. There he exchanged the large manilla envelope he was carrying for a bottle of scotch and a glass. "I came to make a delivery, too," Ames announced. "Something a hell of a lot more important than pastrami," and sat down on the sofa. "You stock pretty good scotch, Ellery."

"I'm glad you like it. Take the bottle with you. I'm working."

"But I claim the prerogative of a fan. I devour every one of your stories."

"Borrowed from unscrupulous friends," Ellery growled.

"That," Grant said, pouring, "is unkind. You'll apologize when you know my mission."

"What mission?"

"A delivery. Weren't you listening?"

"Of what?"

"That envelope. By the gin."

Ellery turned in that direction. Grant waved him back. "I insist on filling you in first, Maestro."

The doorbell rang again. This time it was the sandwiches. Ellery stamped into the foyer and returned with his mouth full.

"Why don't you go to work, Grant? Get a job in one of your father's frozen-food plants. Or become a pea-picker. Anything, but get out of my hair. I've got work to do, I tell you."

"Don't change the subject," Grant III said. "You wouldn't have a kosher pickle there, would you? I'm crazy about kosher pickles."

Ellery offered him a slice of pickle and collapsed in his chair. "All right, damn it. Let's get it over with. Fill me in on what?"

"The background. Yesterday afternoon there was a do up in Westchester. I attended."

"A do," Ellery said, looking envious.

"Swimming. A little tennis. That sort of thing. Not many on the scene."

"Most people have the bad habit of working on weekday afternoons."

"You can't make me feel guilty with that kind of drivel," said the playboy. "I'm doing you a service. I acquired the envelope mysteriously, and I bring it to your door as instructed."

"As instructed by whom?" Ellery had still not glanced at the envelope.

"I haven't any idea. When I made my escape, I found it lying on the seat of my Jag. Someone had written on the envelope, 'Please deliver to Ellery Queen.' The way I figure it, it's someone who holds you in too much awe to make the personal approach. And who's aware of our deathless friendship."

"Sounds dreary. Look, Grant, is this something you've made up? I'm damned if I'm going to play games with you at a time like this. I've got that demon deadline breathing down my neck. Go diddle around with one of your playgirls, will you?"

"The envelope." Grant came up like an athlete and went and got it and brought it back. "Here. Duly delivered. From hand to hand. Do with it what you will."

"What am I supposed to do with it?" asked Ellery sourly.

"No idea. It's a manuscript. Handwritten. Looks quite old. Read it, I suppose."

"Then you've examined it?"

"I felt it my duty. It might have been poison-pen stuff. Even pornography. Your sensibilities, old buddy. I had to consider them."

Ellery was studying the inscription with grudging curiosity. "Written by a woman."

"I found the contents quite harmless, however," Grant went on, nursing his glass. "Harmless, but remarkable."

"A standard envelope," Ellery muttered. "Sized to accommodate eight-and-a-half by eleven sheets."

"I swear, Ellery, you have the soul of a book-keeper. Aren't you going to open it?"

Ellery undid the clasp and pulled out a cardboard-backed notebook with the word *Journal* printed on it in a large, old-fashioned script.

"Well," he said. "It does look old."

Grant regarded him with a sly smile as Ellery opened the ledger, or notebook, studied the first page with widening eyes, turned over, read, turned over again, read again.

"My God," he said. "This purports to be an adventure of Sherlock Holmes in the original manuscript, handwritten by Dr. Watson!"

"Would you say it's authentic!"

Ellery's silvery eyes glittered. "You've read it, you say?"

"I couldn't resist."

"Are you familiar with Watson's style?"

"I," Grant said, admiring the color of the scotch in his glass, "am an *aficionado*. Sherlock Holmes, Ellery Queen, Eddie Poe. Yes, I'd say it's authentic."

"You authenticate easily, my friend." Ellery glanced at his typewriter with a frown; it seemed far away.

"I thought you'd be excited."

"I would if this were on the level. But an unknown Holmes story!" He riffled through the pages. "And, what's more, from the look of it, a novel. A lost novel!'' He shook his head.

"You don't believe it."

"I stopped believing in Santa Claus at the age of three, Grant. You, you were born with Santa Claus in your mouth.''

"Then you think it's a forgery."

"I don't think anything yet. But the odds that it is are astronomical.''

"Why would anyone go to all this trouble?"

"For the same reason people climb mountains. For the hell of it.''

"The least you can do is read the first chapter.''

"Grant, I don't have the time!''

"For a new Sherlock Holmes novel?'' Back at the bar Ames poured himself another scotch. "I'll sit here quietly guzzling and wait.'' He went back to the sofa and crossed his long legs comfortably.

"Damn you.'' For a long moment Ellery glared at the notebook. Then he sighed, sounding remarkably like his father, and settled back and began to read.

From the Journal of John Watson, M.D.

CHAPTER I

THE SURGEON'S-KIT

"You are quite right, Watson. The Ripper may well be a woman."

It was a crisp morning in the fall of the year 1888. I was no longer residing permanently at No. 221B, Baker Street. Having married, and thus become weighted with the responsibility of providing for a wife—a most delightful responsibility—I had gone into practise. Thus, the intimate relationship with my friend, Mr. Sherlock Holmes had dwindled to occasional encounters.

On Holmes's side, these consisted of what he mistakenly termed "impositions upon your hospitality," when he required my services as an assistant or a confidant. "You have such a patient ear, my dear fellow," he would say, a preamble which always brought me pleasure, because it meant that I might again be privileged to share in the danger and excitement of another chase. Thus, the thread of my friendship with the great detective remained intact.

My wife, the most understanding of women, accepted this situation like Griselda. Those who have been so constant to my inadequate accounts of Mr. Sherlock Holmes's cases of detection will remember her as Mary Morstan, whom I providentially met while I was involved, with Holmes, in the case I have entitled *The Sign of Four*. As devoted a wife as any man could boast, she had patiently left me to my own devices on too many long evenings, whilst I perused my notes on Holmes's old cases.

One morning at breakfast, Mary said, "This letter is from Aunt Agatha."

I laid down my newspaper. "From Cornwall?"

"Yes, the poor dear. Spinsterhood has made her life a lonely one. Now her doctor has ordered her to bed."

"Nothing serious, I trust."

"She gave no such indication. But she is in her late seventies, and one never knows."

"Is she completely alone?"

"No. She has Beth, my old nanny, with her, and a man to tend the premises."

"A visit from her favourite niece would certainly do her more good than all the medicine in the world."

"The letter does include an invitation—a plea, really—but I hesitated . . ."

"I think you should go, Mary. A fortnight in Cornwall would benefit you also. You have been a little pale lately."

This statement of mine was entirely sincere; but another thought, a far darker one, coloured it. I venture to say that, upon that morning in 1888, every responsible man in London would have sent his wife, or sister, or sweetheart, away, had the opportunity presented itself. This, for a single, all-encompassing reason. Jack the Ripper prowled the night-streets and dark alleys of the city.

Although our quiet home in Paddington was distant in many ways from the Whitechapel haunts of the maniac, who could be certain? Logic went by the boards where the dreadful monster was concerned.

Mary was thoughtfully folding the envelope. "I don't like to leave you here alone, John."

"I assure you I'll be quite all right."

"But a change would do you good, too, and there seems to be a lull in your practise."

"Are you suggesting that I accompany you?"

Mary laughed. "Good heavens, no! Cornwall would bore you to tears. Rather that you pack a bag and visit your friend Sherlock Holmes. You have a standing invitation at Baker Street, as well I know.''

I am afraid my objections were feeble. Her suggestion was a most alluring one. So, with Mary off to Cornwall and arrangements relative to my practise quickly made, the transition was achieved; to Holmes's satisfaction, I flatter myself in saying, as well as to my own.

It was surprising how easily we fell in to the well-remembered routine. Even though I knew I could never again be satisfied with the old life, my renewed proximity to Holmes was delightful. Which brings me, in somewhat circuitous fashion, back to Holmes's remark out of the blue. He went on, ''The possibility of a female monster cannot by any means be ignored.''

It was the same old cryptic business, and I must confess that I was slightly annoyed. ''Holmes! In the name of all that's holy, I gave no indication whatever that such a thought was passing through my mind.''

Holmes smiled, enjoying the game. ''Ah, but confess, Watson. It was.''

''Very well. But——''

''And you are quite wrong in saying that you gave no indication of your trend of thought.''

''But I was sitting here quietly—motionless, in fact!—reading my *Times*.''

''Your eyes and your head were far from motionless, Watson. As you read, your eyes were trained on the extreme left-hand column of the newspaper, that which contains an account of Jack the Ripper's latest atrocity. After a time, you turned your gaze away from the story, frowning in anger. The thought that such a monster should be able to roam London's streets with impunity was clearly evident.''

''That is quite true.''

''Then, my dear fellow, your eyes, seeking a resting-place, fell upon that copy of the *Strand Magazine* lying beside your chair. It happens to be open to an advertisement in which Beldell's is offering ladies' evening gowns at what they purport to be a bargain-price. One of the gowns in the advertisement is displayed upon a model. Instantly, your expression changed; it became reflective. An idea had dawned upon you. The expression persisted as you raised your head and re-directed your gaze toward the portrait of her Majesty which hangs beside the fireplace. After a moment, your expression cleared, and you nodded to yourself. You had become satisfied with the idea that had come to you. At which point, I agreed. The Ripper could well be a female.

"But, Holmes——"

"Come, now, Watson. Your retirement from the lists has dulled your perceptions."

"But when I glanced at the *Strand* advertisement, I could have had any of a dozen thoughts!"

"I disagree. Your mind was totally occupied with the story of the Ripper, and surely the advertisement concerning ladies' evening gowns was too far afield from your ordinary interests to divert your thoughts. Therefore, the idea that came to you had to be adjunct to your ponderings upon the monster. You verified this by raising your eyes to the Queen's portrait upon the wall."

"May I ask how that indicated my thought?" asked I, tartly.

"Watson! You certainly saw neither the model nor our gracious Queen as suspects. Therefore, you were scrutinising them as women."

"Granted," I retorted, "but would I not have been more likely to regard them as victims?"

"In that case, your expression would have reflected compassion, rather than that of a bloodhound come suddenly upon the scent."

I was forced to confess defeat. "Holmes, again you destroy yourself by your own volubility."

Holmes's heavy brows drew together. "I do not follow."

"Imagine what an image you would create were you to refuse all explanation of your amazing deductions!"

"But at what expense," said he, drily, "to your melodramatic accounts of my trifling adventures."

I threw up my hands in surrender; and Holmes, who rarely indulged in more than a smile, on this occasion echoed my hearty laughter.

"So long as the subject of Jack the Ripper has arisen," said I, "allow me a further question. Why have you not interested yourself in the grisly affair, Holmes? If for no other reason, it would be a signal service to the people of London."

Holmes's long, thin fingers made an impatient gesture. "I have been busy. As you know, I returned from the Continent only recently, where the mayor of a certain city retained me to solve a most curious riddle. Knowing your turn of mind, I presume you would call it *The Case of the Legless Cyclist*. One day I shall give you the details for your files."

"I shall be delighted to get them! But you *are* back in London, Holmes, and this monster is terrorising the city. I should think you would feel obligated——"

Holmes scowled. "I am obligated to no one."

"Pray do not misunderstand me——"

"I'm sorry, my dear Watson, but you should know me well enough to assume my total indifference towards such a case."

"At the risk of appearing more dense than most of my neighbours——"

"Consider! When given a choice, have I not always sought out problems of an intellectual character? Have I not always been drawn to adversaries of stature? Jack the Ripper, indeed! What possible challenge could this demented oaf present? A slavering cretin roaming the streets after dark, striking at random."

"He has baffled the London Police."

"I venture to suggest that that may reflect the shortcomings of Scotland Yard rather than any particular cleverness on the part of the Ripper."

"But still——"

"The thing will end soon enough. I daresay that one of these nights Lestrade will trip over the Ripper while the maniac is in the process of committing a murder, and thus bring him triumphantly to book."

Holmes was chronically annoyed with Scotland Yard for not measuring up to his own stern efficiency; for all his genius, he could be childishly obstinate on such occasions. But further comment from me was cut off by the ringing of the downstairs bell. There was a slight delay; then we heard Mrs. Hudson ascending, and it was with astonishment that I observed her entrance. She was carrying a brown parcel and a pail of water, and she wore an expression of sheer fright.

Holmes burst out laughing for the second time that morning. "It's quite all right, Mrs. Hudson. The package appears harmless enough. I'm sure we shall not need the water."

Mrs. Hudson breathed a sigh of relief. "If you say so, Mr. Holmes. But since that last experience, I was taking no chances."

"And your alertness is to be commended," said Holmes, as he took the parcel. After his long-suffering landlady left, he added, "Just recently, Mrs. Hudson brought me a parcel. It was in connection with an unpleasant little affair I brought to a satisfactory conclusion, and it was sent by a vengeful gentleman who under-estimated the keenness of my hearing. The ticking of the mechanism was quite audible to me, and I called for a pail of water. The incident gave Mrs. Hudson a turn from which she has still not recovered."

"I don't wonder!"

"But what have we here? Hmmm. Approximately fifteen inches by six. Four inches thick. Neatly wrapped in ordinary brown paper. Post-mark, Whitechapel. The name and address written by a woman, I should hazard, who seldom puts pen to paper."

"That seems quite likely, from the clumsy scrawl. And that is certainly done in a woman's hand."

"Then we agree, Watson. Excellent! Shall we delve deeper?"

"By all means!"

The arrival of the parcel had aroused his interest, not to mention mine; his deep-set grey eyes grew bright when he removed the wrappings and drew forth a flat leather case. He held it up for my inspection. "Well, now. What do you make of this, Watson?"

"It is a surgeon's instrument-case."

"And who would be better qualified to know? Would you not say also that it is expensive?"

"Yes. The leather is of superb quality. And the workmanship is exquisite.'

Holmes set the case upon the table. He opened it, and we fell silent. It was a standard set of instruments, each fitting snugly into its appropriate niche in the crimson-velvet lining of the case. One niche was empty.

"Which instrument is missing, Watson?"

"The large scalpel."

"The post-mortem knife," said Holmes, nodding and whipping out his lens. "And now, what does this case tell us?" As he examined the case and its contents closely, he went on. "To begin with the obvious, these instruments belonged to a medical man who came upon hard times."

Obliged, as usual, to confess my blindness, I said, "I am afraid that is more obvious to you than to me."

Preoccupied with his inspection, Holmes replied absently, "If you should fall victim to misfortune, Watson, which would be the last of your possessions to reach the pawn-broker's shop?"

"My medical instruments, of course. But——"

"Precisely."

"Wherein do you perceive that this case was pledged?"

"There is double proof. Observe, just there, through my lens."

I peered at the spot he indicated. "A white smudge."

"Silver-polish. No surgeon would cleanse his instruments with such a substance. These have been treated like common cutlery by someone concerned only with their appearance."

"Now that you point it out, Holmes, I must agree. And what is your second proof?"

"These chalk-marks along the spine of the case. They are almost worn away, but if you will examine them closely, you will see that they constitute a number. Such a number as a pawn-broker would chalk upon a pledged article. Obviously, the counterpart of the number upon the pawn-ticket."

I felt the choler rising to my face. It was all too evident to me now.

"Then the kit was stolen!" I exclaimed. "Stolen from some surgeon, and disposed of, for a pittance, in a pawn-shop!" My readers will forgive my indignation, I am sure; it was difficult for me to accept the alternative—that the practitioner would have parted with the instruments of a noble calling under even the most grievous circumstances.

Holmes, however, soon disillusioned me. "I fear, my dear Watson," said he, quite cheerfully, "that you do not perceive the finer aspects of the evidence. Pawnbrokers are a canny breed. It is part of their stock-in-trade not only to appraise the articles brought to them for pledge, but the persons offering them as well. Had the broker who dispensed his *largesse* for this surgical-case entertained the slightest suspicion that it had been stolen, he would not have displayed it in his shop-window, as of course you observe he has done."

"As of course I do not!" said I, testily. "How can you possibly know that the case has been displayed in a window?"

"Look closely," said Holmes. "The case lay open in a place exposed to the sun; does not the faded velvet on the inner surface of the lid tell us that? Moreover, the pronounced character of the fading marks the time-span as an appreciable one. Surely this adds up to a shop-window?"

I could only nod. As always, when Holmes explained his astonishing observations, they appeared child's-play.

"It is a pity," said I, "that we do not know where the pawn-shop lies. This curious gift might merit a visit to its source."

"Perhaps in good time, Watson," said Holmes, with a dry chuckle. "The pawn-shop in question is well off the beaten track. It faces south, on a narrow street. The broker's business is not flourishing. Also, he is of foreign extraction. Surely you see that?"

"I see nothing of the sort!" said I, nettled again.

"To the contrary," said he, placing his finger-tips together and regarding me kindly, "you see everything, my dear Watson; what you fail to do is to observe. Let us take my conclusions in order. These instruments were not snatched up by any of the numerous medical students in the City of London, which would assuredly have been the case had the shop lain on a well-travelled thoroughfare. Hence my remark that it lies off the beaten track."

"But must it lie on the south side of a narrow street?"

"Note the location of the bleached area. It runs neatly along the uppermost edge of the velvet lining, not elsewhere. Therefore, the sun touched the open case only at its zenith, when its rays were not obstructed by the buildings on the opposite side of the street. Thus the pawn-shop stands on the south side of a narrow street."

"And your identification of the pawn-broker as of foreign extraction?"

"Observe the numeral *seven* in the chalked pledge-mark on the spine. There is a short cross-mark on the ascender. Only a foreigner crosses his sevens in such a fashion."

I felt, as usual, like the fifth-form school-boy who had forgotten the words to the national anthem. "Holmes, Holmes," said I, shaking my head, "I shall never cease to marvel——"

But he was not listening. Again, he had stooped over the case, inserting his tweezers beneath the velvet lining. It gave way, and he peeled it off.

"Aha! What have we here? An attempt at concealment?"

"Concealment? Of what? Stains? Scratches?"

He pointed a long, thin finger. "That."

"Why, it's a coat of arms!"

"One with which I confess I am not familiar. Therefore, Watson, be kind enough to hand down my copy of *Burke's Peerage*."

He continued to study the crest as I moved dutifully towards the book-shelves, murmuring to himself. "Stamped into the leather of the case. The surface is still in excellent condition." He came erect. "A clew to the character of the man who owned the case."

"He was careful with his possessions, perhaps?"

"Perhaps. But I was referring to——"

He broke off. I had handed him the Burke, and he leafed swiftly through the pages. "Ah, here we have it!" After a quick scrutiny, Holmes closed the book, laid it on the table, and dropped into a chair. He stared intently into space with his piercing eyes.

I could contain my patience no longer. "The crest, Holmes! Whose is it?"

"I beg your pardon, Watson," said Holmes, coming to with a start. "Shires. Kenneth Osbourne, the Duke of Shires."

The name was well-known to me, as indeed to all England. "An illustrious line."

Holmes nodded absently. "The estates, unless I mistake, lie in Devonshire, hard by the moors, among hunting-lands well-regarded by noble sportsmen. The manor house—it is more of a feudal castle in appearance—is some four hundred years old, a classic example of Gothic architecture. I know little of the Shires history, beyond the patent act that the name has never been connected with the world of crime.''

''So, Holmes,'' said I, ''we are back to the original question.''

''Indeed we are.''

''Which is: this surgeon's-case—why was it sent to you?''

''A provocative question.''

''Perhaps an explanatory letter was delayed.''

''You may well have hit upon the answer, Watson,'' said Holmes. ''Therefore, I suggest we give the sender a little time, let us say until—'' he paused to reach for his well-worn Bradshaw's, that admirable guide to British rail movements ''—until ten-thirty to-morrow morning. If an explanation is not then forthcoming, we shall repair to Paddington Station and board the Devonshire express.''

''For what reason, Holmes?''

''For two reasons. A short journey across the English countryside, with its changing colours at this time of year, should greatly refresh two stodgy Londoners.''

''And the other?''

The austere face broke into the most curious smile. ''In all justice,'' said my friend Holmes, ''the Duke of Shires should have his property returned to him, should he not?'' And he sprang to his feet and seized his violin.

''Wait, Holmes!'' said I. ''There is something in this you have not told me.''

''No, no, my dear Watson,'' said he, drawing his bow briskly across the strings. ''It is simply a feeling I have, that we are about to embark upon deep waters.''

Ellery Continues

Ellery raised his eyes from the manuscript. Grant Ames, III, was at the scotch again.

"You will be cut down eventually," Ellery said, "by a pickled liver."

"Killjoy," Ames said. "But at the moment I feel myself a part of history, son. An actor under the Great Proscenium."

"Drinking himself to death?"

"Bluenose. I'm talking of the manuscript. In the year 1888 Sherlock Holmes received a mysterious surgeon's kit. He trained his marvelous talents on it and began one of his marvelous adventures. Three-quarters of a century later, another package is delivered to another famous detective."

"What's your point?" grumbled Ellery, visibly torn between Dr. Watson's manuscript and the empty typewriter.

"All that remains to complete the historic re-run is to train the modern talent on the modern adventure. Proceed, my dear Ellery. I'll function as Watson."

Ellery squirmed.

"Of course, you may challenge my *bona fides*. In substantiation, I point out that I have followed the Master's career faithfully."

That pierced the fog. Ellery studied his guest distastefully. "Really? All right, wise guy. Quote: 'It was in the spring of the year 1894 and all London was interested, and the fashionable world dismayed, by the murder of the—'?"

" '—Honourable Ronald Adair.' Unquote," said Ames promptly. *"The Adventure of the Empty House, from The Return of Sherlock Holmes."*

"Quote: 'She had drawn a little gleaming revolver and emptied barrel after barrel into—'"

" '—Milverton's body, the muzzle within two feet of his shirt-front.' Unquote. *The Adventure of Charles Augustus Milverton.*"

"You scintillate, Watson! Quote: 'These are the trodden, but not the downtrodden. These are the lowly, but never the low.'"

"Unquote." The playboy yawned. "Your efforts to trap me are childish, my dear Ellery. You quote yourself, from *The Player on the Other Side.*"

Ellery scowled at him. The fellow was not all overstuffed blondes and expensive scotch. *"Touché, touché.* Now let's see—I'm sure I can stick you—"

"I'm sure you can if you stall long enough, but that's exactly what I'm not going to let you do. Go into your act, Mr. Queen. You've read the first chapter of the manuscript. If you don't come up with some Queenian deductions, I'll never borrow a book of yours again."

"All I can tell you at the moment is that the handwriting purporting to be Watson's is precise, firm, and a little crabbed."

"You don't sound like Holmes to me, old buddy. The question is, *is* it Watson's? Is the manuscript the McCoy? Come, come, Queen! Apply your powers."

"Oh, shut up," Ellery said, and he went on reading.

Chapter II

The Castle on the Moor

In his latter life, as I have recorded elsewhere, my friend Sherlock Holmes retired from the feverish pace of London to keep bees, of all things, on the South Downs. He thus terminated his career with no regret whatever, turning to that husbandman's activity with the same single-mindedness that had enabled him to track down so many of the world's cleverest criminals.

But at the time Jack the Ripper stalked London's streets and by-ways, Holmes was a whole-hearted creature of urban life. His every faculty was keyed to the uncertainties of London's dawns and dusks. The sinister stench of a Soho alley could set his nostrils aquiver, whilst the scent of spring stirring a rural countryside might well put him a-dozing.

It was therefore with surprise and pleasure that I witnessed his interest in the passing scene as the express hurtled us towards Devonshire that morning. He gazed through the window with a concentrated air, then suddenly straightened his thin shoulders.

"Ah, Watson! The sharp air of approaching winter. It is invigorating."

I for one found it not so at the moment, an atrocious cigar between the teeth of a dour old Scot, who had boarded with us, befouling the compartment. But Holmes seemed not to notice the reek. Outside, the leaves were turning, and flashes of autumnal colour streamed past.

"This England, Watson. This other Eden, demi-Paradise."

I recognised the near-quotation and was doubly surprised. I knew, certainly, of the sentimental streak in my friend, but he rarely allowed it to show through the fabric of his scientific nature. Yet, pride of birthright in the Briton is a national trait, and Holmes had not escaped it.

As our journey neared its destination, his cheerful mien vanished; he became pensive. We were on the moors, those broad stretches of mire and morass that cling like a great scab to England's face. As if nature insisted upon a proper setting, the sun had vanished behind thick cloud-banks, and we seemed to have been plunged into a place of eternal twilight.

We soon found ourselves upon the platform of a small country station, where Holmes thrust his hands deep into his pockets, his deep-set eyes kindled, as they so often did when he was beset by a problem.

"Do you recall the affair of the Baskervilles, Watson, and the curse that darkened their lives?"

"Well do I!"

"We are not far from their holdings. But of course we go in the opposite direction."

"And just as well. That hound of Hell still haunts my dreams."

I was puzzled. Ordinarily, when Holmes was involved in a case, he viewed his surroundings singlemindedly, sharply aware of a bruised twig while remaining oblivious of the landscape in which it lay. At such times, reminiscence was no part of it. Now he stirred restlessly, as though he regretted having allowed impulse to send him upon our journey.

"Watson," said he, "let us arrange for the rental of a dog-cart, and get this business over with."

The pony we procured no doubt had relations among the ones that ran wild on the moors, but the little beast was tractable enough, and it clipped steadily away at the road between the village and the Shires land-hold.

After a time, the turrets of Shires Castle came into view, adding their tone of melancholy to the scene.

"The game-preserves are beyond," said Holmes. "The Duke has a variegated terrain." He scanned the country before us and added, "I doubt, Watson, that we shall find a jolly, red-cheeked host in that forbidding pile."

"Why do you say that?"

"People of long blood-lines tend to reflect the colour of their surroundings. You will recall that there was not a single cheerful face at Baskerville Hall."

I did not dispute this, my attention being fixed upon the scowling grey of Shires Castle. It had once been complete with moat and draw-bridge. However, more modern generations had come to depend for defence of life and limb upon the local constabulary. The moat had been filled in, and the bridge-chains had not creaked for many a year.

We were ushered into a cold and cavernous drawing-room by a butler who took our names like Charon checking our passage across the Styx. I soon learned that Holmes's prediction had been accurate. The Duke of Shires was as icily forbidding a man as ever I had met.

He was of slight stature and gave the impression of being phthisical. It was an illusion. Upon closer inspection I saw a well-blooded face, and I sensed a wiry strength in his frail-appearing body.

The Duke did not invite us to be seated. Instead, he stated abruptly, "You were fortunate in finding me here. Another hour, and I should have been on my way to London. I spend little time here in the country. What is your business?"

Holmes's tone in no way reflected the ill-manners of the nobleman. "We will intrude upon your time no longer than necessary, your Grace. We came merely to bring you this."

He proffered the surgeon's-kit, which we had wrapped in plain brown paper and secured with sealing-wax.

"What is it?" said the Duke, not stirring.

"I suggest, your Grace," replied Holmes, "that you open it and discover for yourself."

With a frown, the Duke of Shires stripped off the wrappings. "Where did you get this?"

"I regret that I must first ask your Grace to identify it as your property."

"I have never seen it before. What earthly reason had you for bringing it to me?" The Duke had raised the lid and was staring at the instruments with what certainly appeared to be genuine bewilderment.

"If you will draw down the lining, you will find our reason imprinted upon the leather underneath."

The Duke followed Holmes's suggestion, still frowning. I was watching closely as he stared at the coat of arms, and it was my turn to feel bewilderment. His expression changed. The palest of smiles touched his thin lips, his eyes brightened, and he regarded the case with a look I can only describe as one of intense satisfaction, almost of triumph. Then, as quickly, the look vanished.

I glanced at Holmes in search of some explanation, knowing that he would not have missed the nobleman's reaction. But the sharp eyes were hooded, the familiar face a mask. "I am sure your Grace's question is now answered," said Holmes.

"Of course," replied the Duke in casual tones, as though brushing the matter aside as of no consequence. "The case does not belong to me."

"Then perhaps your Grace could direct us to the owner?"

"My son, I presume. It no doubt belonged to Michael."

"It came from a London pawn-shop."

The Duke's lips curled in a cruel sneer. "I do not doubt it."

"Then if you will give us your son's address——"

"The son I refer to, Mr. Holmes, is *dead*. My younger, sir."

Holmes spoke gently. "I am indeed sorry to hear that, your Grace. Did he succumb to an illness?"

"A very great illness. He has been *dead* for six months."

The emphasis put by the nobleman upon the word "dead" struck me as odd. "Was your son a physician?" I inquired.

"He studied for the profession, but he failed at it, as he failed at everything. Then he *died.*"

Again that strange emphasis. I glanced at Holmes, but he seemed more interested in the ponderous furnishings of the vaulted room, his glance darting here and there, his thin, muscular hands clasped behind his back.

The Duke of Shires held forth the case. "As this is not my property, sir, I return it to you. And now, if you will excuse me, I must prepare for my journey."

I was puzzled by Holmes's behaviour. He had accepted the Duke's cavalier treatment without rancour. Holmes was not in the habit of allowing people to walk over him with hob-nail boots. His bow was deferential as he said, "We shall detain you no longer, your Grace."

The Duke's rude behaviour was consistent. He made no move to reach for the bell-rope that would have summoned the butler. Thus, we were compelled to find our way out as best we could, under his stare.

This proved a stroke of good fortune. We were crossing the baronial hall towards the outer portal, when two persons appeared through a side-entrance, a man and a child.

In contrast to the Duke, they did not seem at all hostile.

The child, a girl of nine or ten years of age, smiled as brightly as her little pallid face would permit. The man, like the Duke, was of slender build. His quick, liquid eyes, although they questioned, were merely curious. His dark resemblance to the Duke of Shires left room for but one conclusion. This was the other son.

It did not seem to me that their arrival was particularly startling, but it appeared to disconcert my friend Holmes. He came to a jerky halt, and the surgeon's-kit that he was carrying fell to the floor with a clatter of steel against stone that echoed through the great hall.

"How clumsy of me!" he exclaimed, and then proceeded to be even clumsier by blocking me off as I attempted to retrieve the instruments.

The man, with a smile, sprang into the breach. "Allow me, sir," said he, and went to his knees.

The child reacted almost as quickly. "Let me help you, Papa."

The man's smile glowed. "So you shall, my dear. We'll help the gentleman together. You may hand me the instruments. But carefully, lest you cut yourself."

We watched in silence as the little girl handed the shining instruments to her father, one by one. His affection for her was touchingly apparent, his dark eyes hardly bearing to leave her as he swiftly returned the instruments to their proper niches.

When the business was finished, the man arose. But the little girl continued to scan the flag-stones upon which we stood. "The last one, Papa. Where did it go?"

"It appears to have been missing, dearest. I don't think it fell from the case." He glanced questioningly at Holmes, who came out of the brown study into which he contrived to have fallen.

"Indeed it was missing, sir. Thank you, and pardon my clumsiness."

"No harm done. I trust the instruments were not damaged." He handed the case to Holmes, who took it with a smile.

"Have I, perchance, the honour of addressing Lord Carfax?"

"Yes," the dark man said, pleasantly. "This is my daughter, Deborah."

"Allow me to present my colleague, Dr. Watson; I am Sherlock Holmes."

The name seemed to impress Lord Carfax; his eyes widened in surprise. "Dr. Watson," he murmured in acknowledgement, but his eyes remained on Holmes. "And you, sir—I am honoured indeed. I have read of your exploits."

"Your Lordship is too kind," replied Holmes.

Deborah's eyes sparkled. She curtsied and said, "I am honoured to meet you, too, sirs." She spoke with a sweetness that was touching. Lord Carfax looked on proudly. Yet I sensed a sadness in his manner.

"Deborah," said he, gravely, "you must mark this as an event in your life, the day you met two famous gentlemen."

"Indeed I shall, Papa," replied the little girl, solemnly dutiful. She had heard of neither of us, I was quite certain.

Holmes concluded the amenities by saying, "We called, your Lordship, to return this case to the Duke of Shires, whom I believed to be its rightful owner."

"And you discovered that you were in error."

"Quite. His Grace thought that it had possibly belonged to your deceased brother, Michael Osbourne."

"Deceased?" It was more a tired comment than a question.

"That was what we were given to understand."

Sadness appeared clearly in Lord Carfax's face. "That may or may not be true. My father, Mr. Holmes, is a stern and unforgiving man, which you no doubt surmised. To him, the good name of Osbourne stands above all else. Keeping the Shires escutcheon free of blemish is a passion with him. When he disowned my younger brother some six months ago, he pronounced Michael dead." He paused to sigh. "I fear Michael will remain dead, so far as Father is concerned, even though he may still live."

"Are you yourself aware," asked Holmes, "whether your brother is alive or dead?"

Lord Carfax frowned, looking remarkably like the Duke. When he spoke, I thought I detected evasiveness in his voice. "Let me say, sir, that I have no actual proof of his death."

"I see," replied Holmes. Then he looked down at Deborah Osbourne and smiled. The little girl came forward and put her hand into his.

"I like you very much, sir," said she, gravely.

It was a charming moment. Holmes appeared embarrassed by this open-hearted confession. Her small hand remained in his as he said, "Granted, Lord Carfax, that your father is an unbending man. Still, to disown a son! A decision such as that is not made lightly. Your brother's transgression must indeed have been a serious one."

"Michael married against my father's wishes." Lord Carfax shrugged his shoulders. "I am not in the habit, Mr. Holmes, of discussing my family's affairs with strangers, but—" and he touched his daughter's shining head "—Deborah is my barometer of character." I thought his Lordship was going to ask what Holmes's interest in Michael Osbourne was based upon, but he did not.

Holmes, too, appeared to have expected such a question. When it did not come, he extended the surgical-case. "Perhaps you would like to have this, your Lordship."

Lord Carfax took the case with a silent bow.

"And now—our train will not wait, I fear—we must be off." Holmes looked down from his great height. "Good-bye, Deborah. Meeting you is the most agreeable thing that has happened to Dr. Watson and me in a very long time."

"I hope you will come again, sir," replied the child. "It gets so lonely here when Papa is away."

Holmes said little as we drove back to the village. He scarcely replied to my comments, and it was not until we were flying back towards London that he invited conversation. His lean features set in that abstracted look I knew so well, he said, "An interesting man, Watson."

"Perhaps," I replied, tartly. "But also as repulsive a one as ever I care to meet. It is men of his calibre—they are few, thank heaven!—who stain the reputation of the British nobility."

My indignation amused Holmes. "I was referring to *filius* rather than *pater.*"

"The son? I was touched by Lord Carfax's evident love for his daughter, of course——"

"But you felt he was too informative?"

"That was exactly my impression, Holmes, although I don't see how you became aware of it. I did not enter into the conversation."

"Your face is like a mirror, my dear Watson," said he.

"Even he admitted that he talked too freely about his family's personal affairs."

"But did he? Let us assume him, first, to be a stupid man. In that case he becomes a loving father with an overly-large oral cavity."

"But if we assume him, with more difficulty, to be not stupid at all?"

"Then he created precisely the image he wished to, which I incline to believe. He knew me by name and reputation, and you, Watson. I strongly doubt that he accepted us as mere Good Samaritans, come all this way to restore an old surgeon's-kit to its rightful owner."

"Should that necessarily loose his tongue?"

"My dear fellow, he told us nothing that I did not already know, or could not have discovered with ease in the files of any London daily."

"Then what was it that he did not reveal?"

"Whether his brother Michael is dead or alive. Whether he is in contact with his brother."

"I assumed, from what he said, that he does not know."

"That, Watson, may have been what he wished you

to assume." Before I could reply, Holmes went on. "As it happens, I did not go to Shires uninformed. Kenneth Osbourne, the lineal Duke, had two sons. Michael, the younger, of course inherited no title. Whether or not this instilled jealousy in him I do not know, but he so conducted himself thenceforward as to earn the sobriquet, from the journalists of London, of The Wild One. You spoke of his father's brutal sternness, Watson. To the contrary, the record reveals the Duke as having been amazingly lenient with his younger son. The boy finally tried his father's patience too far when he married a woman of the oldest profession; in fine, a prostitute."

"I begin to see," muttered I. "Out of spite, or hatred, to besmirch the title he could not inherit."

"Perhaps," said Holmes. "In any case, it would have been difficult for the duke to assume otherwise."

"I did not know," said I, humbly.

"It is human, my dear Watson, to side with the under-dog. But it is wise to discover beforehand exactly who the under-dog is. In the case of the Duke, I grant that he is a difficult man, but he bears a cross."

I replied, with some despair, "Then I suppose my evaluation of Lord Carfax is faulty, also."

"I do not know, Watson. We have very little data. However, he did fail on two counts."

"I was not aware of it."

"Nor was he."

My mind was centred upon a broader prospect. "Holmes," said I, "this whole affair is curiously unsatisfactory. Surely this journey was not motivated by a simple desire on your part to restore lost property?"

He gazed out of the carriage-window. "The surgeon's-kit was delivered to our door. I doubt we were mistaken for a lost-and-found bureau."

"But by whom was it sent?"

"By someone who wished us to have it."

"Then we can only wait."

"Watson, to say that I smell a devious purpose here

is no doubt fanciful. But the stench is strong. Perhaps you will get your wish.''

''My wish?''

''I believe you recently suggested that I give the Yard some assistance in the case of Jack the Ripper.''

''Holmes——!''

''Of course there is no evidence to connect the Ripper with the surgeon's-kit. But the post-mortem knife is missing.''

''The implication has not escaped me. Why, this very night it may be plunged into the body of some unfortunate!''

''A possibility, Watson. The removal of the scalpel may have been symbolical, a subtle allusion to the fiendish stalker.''

''Why did the sender not come forward?''

''There could be any number of reasons. I should put fear high on the list. In time, I think, we shall know the truth.''

Holmes lapsed into the preoccupation I knew so well. Further probing on my part, I knew, would have been useless. I sat back and stared gloomily out the window as the train sped towards Paddington.

Ellery Tries

Ellery looked up from the notebook.

Grant Ames, finishing his nth drink, asked eagerly, ''Well?''

Ellery got up and went to a bookshelf, frowning. He took a book down and searched for something while Grant waited. He returned the book to the shelf and came back.

''Christianson's.''

Grant looked blank.

''According to the reference there, Christianson's was a well-known stationery manufacturer of the period. Their watermark is on the paper of the note-book.''

''That does it, then!''

''Not necessarily. Anyway, there's no point in try-ing to authenticate the manuscript. If someone's trying to sell it to me, I'm not buying. If it's genuine, I can't afford it. If it's a phony—''

''I don't think that was the idea, old boy.''

''Then what was the idea?''

''How should I know? I suppose someone wants you to read it.''

Ellery pulled his nose fretfully. ''You're sure it was put into your car at that party?''

''Had to be.''

''And it was addressed by a woman. How many women were there?''

Grant counted on his fingers. ''Four.''

''Any bookworms? Collectors? Librarians? Little old ladies smelling of lavender sachet and must?''

''Hell, no. Four slick young chicks trying to look seductive. After a husband. Frankly, Ellery, I can't conceive one of them knowing Sherlock Holmes from Aristophanes. But with your kooky talents, you could stalk the culprit in an afternoon.''

''Look, Grant, any other time and I'd play the game. But I told you. I'm in one of my periodic binds. I simply haven't the time.''

''Then it ends here, Maestro? For God's sake, man, what are you, a hack? Here I toss a delicious mystery into your lap—''

''And I,'' said Ellery, firmly placing the notebook in Grant Ames's lap, ''toss it right back to you. I have a suggestion. *You* rush out, glass in hand, and track down your lady joker.''

''I might at that,'' whined the millionaire.

''Fine. Let me know.'

''The manuscript didn't grip you?''

''Of course it does.'' Reluctantly, Ellery picked up the journal and riffled through it.

"That's my old buddy!" Ames rose. "Why don't I leave it here? After all, it is addressed to you. I could report back at intervals—"

"Make it long intervals."

"Mine host. All right, I'll bother you as little as I can."

"Less, if possible. And now will you beat it, Grant? I'm serious."

"What you are, friend, is grim. No fun at all." Ames turned in the doorway. "Oh, by the way, order some more scotch. You've run out."

When he was alone again, Ellery stood indecisively. Finally he put the notebook down on the sofa and went to his desk. He stared at the keys. The keys stared back. He shifted in his swivel chair; his bottom was itching. He pulled the chair closer. He pulled his nose again.

The notebook lay quietly on the sofa.

Ellery ran a sheet of blank paper into the machine. He raised his hands, flexed his fingers, thought, and began to type.

He typed rapidly, stopped, and read what he had written:

"The Lord," said Nikki, *"choves a leerful giver."*

"All *right!*" said Ellery. "Just one more chapter!"

He jumped up and ran over to the sofa and grabbed the notebook and opened it and began to devour Chapter III.

CHAPTER III

WHITECHAPEL

"By the way, Holmes, whatever became of Wiggins?" I asked the question late the following morning in the rooms at Baker Street.

We had had a buffet supper the previous evening at the station after our return from Shires Castle, whereupon Holmes had said, "The young American pianist, Benton, plays at Albert Hall tonight. I recommend him highly, Watson."

"I was not aware that the States had produced any great pianoforte talents."

Holmes had laughed. "Come, come, my dear fellow! Let the Americans go. It has been more than a century now, and they have been doing quite well over there."

"You wish me to accompany you? I should be delighted."

"I was suggesting the concert for your evening. I have a few investigations in mind which are better made at night."

"In that case, I prefer the easy-chair by the fire and one of your fascinating books."

"I recommend one I recently acquired, *Uncle Tom's Cabin,* by an American lady named Stowe. A lugubrious work, meant to stir the nation to correct a great injustice. It was, I believe, one of the causes of the War Between the States. Well, I must be off. Perhaps I shall join you in a night-cap later."

Holmes, however, returned very late, after I was abed. He did not awaken me, so that our next meeting was at breakfast. I hoped for an account of his night's work, but none was forthcoming. Nor did he appear to be in haste to get on with things, lounging lazily in his mouse-coloured dressing-gown over his tea and clouding the room with heavy exhalations from his beloved clay pipe.

Came a sudden clatter upon the stairs, and there rushed into the room a dozen of the dirtiest, most ragged urchins in all London. They were Holmes's incredible band of street Arabs, whom he called variously "the Baker Street division of the detective police force," his "unofficial force," and "the Baker Street irregulars."

" 'Tention!" snapped Holmes; and the urchins struggled into a ragged line and presented their begrimed little faces in what they evidently took to be a military posture.

"Now, have you found it?"

"Yes, sir, we 'ave," replied one of the band.

"It was me, sir!" cut in another eagerly as he grinned, showing gaps where three teeth were wanting.

"Very good," said Holmes, sternly, "but we work as a unit. No individual glory, men. One for all and all for one."

"Yes, *sir*," came the chorus.

"The report?"

"It's in Whitechapel."

"Ah!"

"On Great Heapton Street, near the pass-over. The street is narrow there, sir."

"Very good," said Holmes again. "Here is your pay. Now be off with you."

He gave each urchin a shining shilling. They clattered happily away, as they had come, and we soon heard their shrill young voices from below.

Now Holmes knocked the dottle from his pipe. "Wiggins? Oh, he did very well. Joined her Majesty's forces. My last note from him was post-marked Africa.''

''He was a sharp youngster, as I recall.''

''So are they all. And London's supply of the little beggars never diminishes. But I have an inquiry to make. Let us be off.''

It took no feat of intellect to predict our destination. So I was not surprised when we stood before a pawnshop window on Great Heapton, in Whitechapel. The street, as Holmes had deduced and the urchins confirmed, was narrow, with high buildings on the side opposite the shop. When we arrived, the sun was just cutting a line across the glass, the inscription upon which read: *Joseph Beck—Loans*.

Holmes pointed to the display in the window. ''The kit sat there, Watson. Do you see where the sun strikes?''

I could only nod my head. Accustomed though I was to the unerring keenness of his judgements, the proof never ceased to amaze me.

Inside the shop, we were greeted by a pudgy man of middle-age whose moustaches were heavily waxed and drilled into military points. Joseph Beck was the archetype of German tradesmen, and his efforts to produce a Prussian effect were ludicrous.

''May I be of service, sirs?'' His English was thickly accented.

I presume, in that neighbourhood, we were a cut above his usual run of clients; possibly he hoped to acquire a pledge of high value. He actually clicked his heels and came to attention.

''A friend,'' said Holmes, ''recently made me a gift, a surgeon's-case purchased in your shop.''

Herr Beck's protuberant little eyes turned sly. ''Yes?''

''But one of the instruments was missing from the case. I should like to complete the set. Do you have some surgical instruments from which I might select the missing one?''

"I am afraid, sir, I cannot help you." The pawn-broker was clearly disappointed.

"Do you recall the set I refer to, the transaction?"

"*Ach*, yes, sir. It took place a week ago, and I get very few such articles. But the set was complete when the woman redeemed it and carried it away. Did she tell you one instrument was missing?"

"I do not recall," Holmes said, in an off-hand manner. "The point is that you cannot help me now."

"I am sorry, sir. I have no surgical instruments of any description."

Holmes pretended petulance. "All the way down here for nothing! You have caused me great inconvenience, Beck."

The man looked astonished. "You are being unreasonable, sir. I do not see how I am responsible for what occurred after the case left my shop."

Holmes shrugged his shoulders. "I suppose not," said he, carelessly. "But it is a nuisance. I came a long distance."

"But, sir, if you had inquired of the poor creature who redeemed the set——"

"The poor creature? I don't understand."

The severity of Holmes's tone frightened the man. With the tradesman's instinct to please, he hastened to apologise. "Forgive me, sir. My heart went out to the woman. In fact, I let her have the case at a too generous price. Her terribly disfigured face has haunted me."

"Ah," murmured Holmes. "I see." He was turning away in clever disappointment when his hawk's-face brightened. "A thought occurs to me. The man who originally pledged the case—if I could get in touch with him . . ."

"I doubt it, sir. It was some time ago."

"How long?"

"I would have to consult my ledger."

Frowning, he produced a ledger from underneath the

counter and thumbed through it. "Here it is. Why, it has been almost four months. How time flies!"

"Quite," agreed Holmes, drily. "You have the name and address of the man?"

"It was not a man, sir. It was a lady."

Holmes and I glanced at each other. "I see," said Holmes. "Well, even after four months, it might still be worth an effort. What is her name, pray?"

The pawn-broker peered at his ledger. "Young. Miss Sally Young."

"Her address?"

"The Montague Street Hostel."

"Odd place of residence," I ventured.

"Yes, *mein Herr*. It is in the heart of Whitechapel. A dangerous place these days."

"Indeed it is. Good-day to you," said Holmes, civilly. "You have been most accommodating."

As we walked away from the pawn-shop, Holmes laughed softly. "A type who must be adroitly handled, this Joseph Beck. One can lead him great distances, but he cannot be pushed an inch."

"I thought he coöperated handsomely."

"Indeed he did. But the least odour of officialdom in our inquiry and we should not have pried the time of day out of him."

"Your theory that the scalpel was removed as a symbolical gesture, Holmes, has been proved correct."

"Perhaps, though the fact is of no great value. But now, a visit to the Montague Street Hostel and Miss Sally Young seems in order. I'm sure you have formed opinions as to the stations of the two females we are seeking?"

"Of course. The one who pawned the set was clearly in straitened financial circumstances."

"A possibility, Watson, though far from a certainty."

"If not, why did she pledge the set?"

"I am inclined to think it was a service she rendered

a second party. Some-one who was unable or did not
care to appear personally at the pawn-shop. A surgeon's-
kit is hardly an article one would expect to find a lady
owning. And as to the woman who redeemed the
pledge?''

''We know nothing of her except that she sustained
some injury to the face. Perhaps she is a victim of the
Ripper, who escaped death at his hands?''

''Capital, Watson! An admirable hypothesis. However, the point that struck me involves something a
little different. You will remember that *Herr* Beck re-
ferred to the one who redeemed the case as a *woman,*
while he spoke in a more respectful tone of the pledger
as a *lady.* Hence, we are safe in assuming that Miss
Sally Young is a person to command some respect.''

''Of course, Holmes. The implications, I am frank
to admit, escaped me.''

''The redeemer is no doubt of a lower order. She
could well be a prostitute. Certainly this neighbourhood abounds with such unfortunates.''

Montague Street lay at no great distance; it was less
than a twenty-minute walk from the pawn-shop. It
proved to be a short thoroughfare connecting Purdy
Court and Olmstead Circus, the latter being well-
known as a refuge for London's swarms of beggars.
We turned into Montague Street and had progressed
only a few steps when Holmes halted. ''Aha! What
have we here?''

My glance followed his to a sign over an archway
of ancient stone, displaying a single word, *Mortuary.*
I do not see myself as especially sensitive, but as I
gazed into the murky depths of the tunnel-like entrance, the same depression of spirit came over me that
I had experienced at first sight of the Shires castle.

''This is no hostel, Holmes,'' said I. ''Unless a
sanctuary for the dead can be called such!''

''Let us suspend judgement until we investigate,''
replied he; and he pushed open a creaking door that
led into a cobbled courtyard.

"There is the smell of death here, without a doubt," said I.

"And very recent death, Watson. Else why should our friend Lestrade be on the premises?"

Two men stood in conversation at the far side of the courtyard, and Holmes had identified the one of them more quickly than I. It was indeed Inspector Lestrade of Scotland Yard, even leaner and more ferret-like than I recalled him.

Lestrade turned at the tramp of our footsteps. An expression of surprise came over his face. "Mr. 'Olmes! What are you doing here?"

"How good to see you, Lestrade!" exclaimed Holmes, with a warm smile. "It is heartening to find Scotland Yard dutifully following where crime leads."

"You needn't be sarcastic," grumbled Lestrade.

"Nerves, man? Something seems to have you by the short hairs."

"If you don't know what it is, you didn't read the paper this morning," said Lestrade, shortly.

"As a matter of fact, I did not."

The police officer turned to acknowledge my presence. "Dr. Watson. It has been a long time since our paths crossed."

"Far too long, Inspector Lestrade. You are well, I trust?"

"A bit of lumbago now and again. I'll survive." Then he added darkly, "At least until I see this Whitechapel maniac dragged to the gallows."

"The Ripper again?" Holmes asked, sharply.

"The very same. The fifth attack, Mr. 'Olmes. You have, of course, read about him, although I haven't heard of you coming 'round to offer your services."

Holmes did not parry the thrust. Instead, his eyes flicked in my direction. "We draw closer, Watson."

"What was that?" exclaimed Lestrade.

"The fifth, you said? No doubt you mean the fifth *official* murder?"

"Official or not, 'Olmes——"

"What I meant was that you cannot be sure. You have found the bodies of five of the Ripper's victims. But others may have been dismembered and thoroughly disposed of."

"A cheerful thought," muttered Lestrade.

"This 'fifth' victim. I should like to view the body."

"Inside. Oh, this is Dr. Murray. He is in charge here."

Dr. Murray was a cadaverous man, with a death-like complection, and a poised manner which impressed me favourably. His attitude reflected the inner resignations one often finds in those who deal intimately with the dead. He acknowledged Lestrade's introduction with a bow, and said, "I do officiate here, but I had rather posterity remembered me as director of the hostel next door. It affords greater opportunity for service. The poor wretches who come here are beyond aid."

"Let's get on with it," interrupted Lestrade, and conducted us through a door. A strong carbolic-acid odour greeted us, an odour I had grown to know too well in her Majesty's Indian service.

The room into which we were shown demonstrated how little is ever done to confer dignity upon the dead. It was less a room than a long, wide passage-way, each inch of whose walls and ceiling was tastelessly whitewashed. One entire side consisted of a raised platform, upon which rude wooden tables jutted out at intervals. Fully half the tables were occupied by sheeted, still figures; but Lestrade led us to the far end.

There, another platform stood, with its table and sheeted morsel of humanity. This platform was slightly higher, and so placed that a sign, *The Corpse for Today,* might well have seemed appropriate.

"Annie Chapman," said Lestrade, morosely. "The latest victim of our butcher." With that, he drew back the sheet.

Holmes was the most objective of men where crime

was concerned, but a grim pity invaded his face. And I must confess that I—accustomed to death both in the bed and upon the battlefield—was sickened. The girl had been slaughtered like an animal.

To my amazement, I saw what appeared to be disappointment supplant the pity upon Holmes's face. ''The face is not scarred,'' he murmured, as if in complaint.

''The Ripper does not mutilate the faces of his victims,'' said Lestrade. ''He confines his attentions to the more private parts of the body.''

Holmes had turned cold and analytical. He could now have been regarding a specimen in a dissection-room. He touched my arm. ''Note the skill of this unholy work, Watson. It verifies what we have read in the journals. The fiend does not cut at random.''

Inspector Lestrade was scowling. ''There is certainly nothing skilful in that slash across the abdomen, 'Olmes. The Ripper used a butcher's cleaver for that one.''

''Before the abdomen was dissected, possibly with a surgeon's scalpel,'' muttered Holmes.

Lestrade shrugged his shoulders. ''That second blow, the one to the heart. It was done by a cleaver, also.''

''The left breast was removed with consummate skill, Lestrade,'' said I, with a shudder.

''The Ripper's surgery varies. Its skill seems to depend upon the time that is available to him. In some cases there has been scarcely any, cases in which he was interrupted in his devil's work.''

''I am compelled to alter certain superficial ideas I had formed.'' Holmes appeared to speaking to himself rather than to us. ''A madman, certainly. But a clever one. Perhaps a brilliant one.''

''Then you admit, Mr. 'Olmes, that the Yard is contending with no blundering idiot?''

''Most assuredly, Lestrade. And I shall be happy to give you whatever aid my limited powers allow.''

This widened Lestrade's eyes. He had never before heard Holmes deprecate his own talents. The policeman searched for a suitable rejoinder, but apparently such was his astonishment that he could find none.

He recovered sufficiently, however, to voice his standard plaint. "And if you are lucky enough to apprehend the fiend——"

"I seek no credit, Lestrade," said Holmes. "Rest assured, the Yard shall reap the glory." He paused, then added, gloomily, "If there is any." He turned to Dr. Murray. "I wonder if we may be permitted to inspect your hostel, Doctor?"

Dr. Murray bowed. "I should be honoured, Mr. Holmes."

At that moment a door opened, and a pathetic figure appeared. There was much about the shuffling creature to pity, but I was struck first by the total vacancy in his eyes. The expressionless features, the sagging, partially-open mouth, bespoke an idiot. The man shuffled forward and stepped upon the platform. He cast a look of empty inquiry at Dr. Murray, who smiled as one smiles at a child.

"Ah, Pierre. You may cover the body."

A spark of eagerness appeared on that vacuous countenance. I could not help thinking of a faithful dog given a chore by a kindly master. Then Dr. Murray gestured, and we moved away from the platform.

"I'll be off," said Lestrade, sniffing wrinkle-nosed at the carbolic. "If there is any information you require, Mr. 'Olmes," said he, politely, "do not hesitate to call upon me."

"Thank you, Lestrade," said Holmes, with equal courtesy. The two detectives had evidently decided to call a truce until the morbid affair could be resolved— the first such truce between them, I might add, that ever I was aware of.

As we quitted the charnel-house, I glanced back and

saw Pierre smoothing the sheet carefully over the body of Annie Chapman. Holmes, I noted, also glanced in the simpleton's direction, and something kindled in his grey eyes.

CHAPTER IV

DR. MURRAY'S HOSTEL

"One does what one can," said Dr. Murray, a few moments later, "but, in a city of the size of London, it is a little like trying to sweep back the sea with a broom. A sea of destitution and despair."

We had left the morgue, and crossed a flag-stoned inner courtyard. He ushered us through another door, and into a shabby but more cheerful atmosphere. The hostel was very old. It had been built originally as a stable, a long, low, stone building with the places for the stalls still clearly marked. Again, buckets of white-wash had been used, but the eternal odour of the carbolic was here mingled with a slightly less disagreeable effluvium of medicines, steaming vegetable stew, and unbathed bodies. As the building extended onward in railway fashion, the stalls had been fashioned into larger units, double and sometimes triple their original size, and put to appropriate uses. Black-lettered cards identified them variously as dormitories for women and for men. There was a dispensary, and a clinical waiting-room with stone benches. Ahead of us, a sign read: *This Way to Chapel and Dining-Hall.*

Curtains had been drawn across the entrance to the women's dormitory, but that of the men stood open, and several sorry-looking derelicts slept upon the iron cots.

In the clinical area, three patients awaited attention, while the dispensary was occupied by a huge, brutish man who looked freshly come from sweeping a chimney. He was seated, a sullen scowl upon his face. His

144

eyes were fastened upon a pretty young lady ministering to him. One of his vast feet rested upon a low stool; the young lady had just finished bandaging it. She came up from her knees and brushed a lock of dark hair back from her forehead.

"He cut it badly upon a shard of broken glass," she told Dr. Murray. The doctor stooped to inspect the bandage, giving the brute's foot no less attention than it would have received in any Harley Street surgery. He straightened and spoke kindly.

"You must come back to-morrow and have the dressing changed, my friend. Be sure, now."

The oaf was entirely without gratitude. "I can't put my boot on. 'Ow am I goin' to get about?"

He spoke as though the doctor were responsible, with such surliness that I could not restrain myself. "If you had stayed sober, my good man, perhaps you could have avoided the broken glass."

" 'Ere now, guv'ner!" says he, bold as brass. "A man's got to 'ave a pint once in a while!"

"I doubt if you've ever held yourself to a pint."

"Please wait here a few moments," interposed Dr. Murray, "I'll have Pierre bring you a stick. We keep a small stock for emergencies."

Turning to the young lady, he went on, "Sally, these gentlemen are Mr. Sherlock Holmes and his colleague, Dr. Watson. Gentlemen, this is Miss Sally Young, my niece and good right arm. I don't know what the hostel would be without her."

Sally Young extended a slim hand to each of us in turn. "I am honoured," said she, cool and self-possessed. "I have heard both names before. But I never expected to meet such famous personages."

"You are too kind," murmured Holmes.

Her tact in including me, a mere shadow to Sherlock Holmes, was gracious, and I bowed.

Said Dr. Murray, "I'll get the stick myself, Sally. Will you conduct Mr. Holmes and Dr. Watson the rest of the way? Perhaps they would like to see the chapel and the kitchen.''

''Certainly. This way, please.''

Dr. Murray hurried away in the direction of the morgue, and we followed Miss Young. But only for a short distance. Before we reached the door, Holmes said abruptly, ''Our time is limited, Miss Young. Perhaps the tour can be finished during another visit. We are here to-day for professional reasons.''

The girl seemed not to be surprised. ''I understand, Mr. Holmes. Is there something I can do?''

''Perhaps there is. Some time ago you pledged a certain article in a pawn-shop on Great Heapton Street. Do you recall?''

With no hesitation whatever, she replied, ''Of course. It was not so long ago as that.''

''Would you object to telling us how you came by the case, and why you pledged it?''

''Not at all. It belonged to Pierre.''

I thought this startling news, but Holmes did not move a muscle. ''The poor fellow who has lost his wits.''

''A pitiful case,'' said the girl.

''A hopeless one, I venture to say,'' said Holmes. ''We met him a few minutes ago. Could you enlighten us as to his background?''

''We know nothing about him prior to his arrival here. But that arrival, I must say, was dramatic. I came through the morgue late one night, and found him standing beside one of the corpses.''

''Doing what, Miss Young?''

''He was doing nothing whatever, merely standing by the body in the confused state you must surely have noticed. I approached him and brought him to my uncle. He has been here ever since. The police were evidently not seeking him, for Inspector Lestrade has shown no interest in him whatever.''

My opinion of Miss Sally Young went higher. Here was courage indeed. A girl who could walk at night

about a charnel-house, see a gargoyle figure such as
Pierre's standing over one of the corpses, and not flee
in terror!

"That's hardly a criterion," began Holmes, and
stopped.

"I beg your pardon, sir?"

"A random thought, Miss Young. Please proceed."

"We came to the opinion that some-one had guided
Pierre to the hostel and left him, as unwed mothers
leave their infants at the door of a sanctuary. Dr. Murray examined him, and found that he had once sustained a terrible injury, as if he had been brutally
beaten. The wounds about his head had healed, but
nothing could be done to dispel the mists that had permanently settled over his brain. He has proved to be
harmless, and he is so pathetically eager to help about
the place that he has made his own berth. We of course
would not dream of sending him back into a world
with which he cannot cope."

"And the surgeon's-kit?"

"He had a bundle with him, containing wearing ap-
parel. The kit was buried in their midst, the only thing
of value he possessed."

"What did he tell you of himself?"

"Nothing. He speaks only with effort, single words
which are hardly intelligible."

"But his name—Pierre?"

She laughed, an attractive touch of colour coming
into her cheeks. "I took the liberty of baptising him.
What clothing he carried bore French labels. And there
was a coloured handkerchief with French script inter-
woven in the cloth. Thus, and for no other reason, I
began calling him Pierre, although I feel sure he is not
French."

"How did you happen to pawn the case?" asked
Holmes.

"That came about quite simply. As I have told you,
Pierre brought virtually nothing with him, and our
funds at the hostel are severely allocated. We were in

no position to outfit Pierre properly. So I thought of the surgical-case. It was clearly of value, and he could have no need of it. I explained to him what I proposed, and to my surprise he nodded violently.'' She paused here to laugh. ''The only difficulty was in getting him to accept the proceeds. He wanted to put it into the general fund of the hostel.''

''Then he is still capable of emotion. At least of gratitude.''

''Indeed he is,'' replied Sally Young, warmly. ''And now perhaps, sir, you will answer a question of mine. Why are you interested in the surgeon's-kit?''

''It was sent to me by an unknown person.''

Her eyes widened. ''Then someone redeemed it!''

''Yes. Have you any idea who that person might have been?''

''Not in the least.'' After a thoughtful pause, she said, ''There does not necessarily have to be a connection. I mean, some-one could have come upon the case and redeemed it as a bargain.''

''One of the instruments was missing when it reached me.''

''That is odd! I wonder what could have happened to it.''

''The set was complete when you pledged it?''

''Indeed it was.''

''Thank you, Miss Young.''

At that moment the door before us opened; a man came through. And, although Lord Carfax was perhaps not the last person I expected to see, he was certainly not the first.

''Your Lordship,'' exclaimed Holmes. ''Our paths cross again.''

Lord Carfax was as surprised as I. Indeed, he seemed utterly discomposed. It was Sally Young who broke the silence. ''Your Lordship has met these gentlemen?''

''We had that privilege only yesterday,'' said Holmes. ''At the Duke of Shires's residence.''

Lord Carfax found his voice. "Mr. Holmes refers to my father's country-home." Then, turning back to Holmes, he said, "This is a far more likely place for me to be than for you gentlemen. I spend a good deal of my time here."

"Lord Carfax is our angel from Heaven," said Sally Young, rapturously. "He has given of his money and of his time so generously, that the hostel is as much his as ours. It could hardly exist without him."

Lord Carfax flushed. "You make too much of it, my dear."

She laid an affectionate hand upon his arm; her eyes were very bright. Then the glow faded; her whole manner changed. "Lord Carfax. There is another one. Have you heard?"

He nodded, somberly. "I wonder if it will ever end! Mr. Holmes, are you by any chance applying your talents to the hunt for the Ripper?"

"We shall see what develops," said Holmes, abruptly. "We have taken up enough of your time, Miss Young. I trust that we shall meet again."

With that we bowed and departed, going out through the silent morgue, that was now deserted except for the dead.

Night had fallen, and the street-lamps of Whitechapel dotted the lonely thoroughfares, deepening rather than banishing the shadows.

I drew up my collar. "I don't mind saying, Holmes, that a good fire and a cup of hot tea——"

"On guard, Watson!" cried Holmes, his reactions far sharper than my own; and an instant later we were fighting for our lives. Three toughs had leapt out of the darkness of a courtyard and were upon us.

I saw the flash of a knife-blade as one of them shouted, "You two take the big cove!" Thus I was left with the third thug, but he was quite enough, armed as he was with a glittering weapon. The savagery of his attack left no doubt as to his intentions. I whirled to meet his attack not an instant too soon. But my stick slipped from my grasp, and I would have gone down with the brute's blade in my flesh if he had not slipped in his eagerness to get at me. He fell forward, pawing the air, and I acted from instinct, bringing my knee upwards. A welcome bolt of pain shot up my thigh as my knee-cap connected with my assailant's face. He bellowed in pain and staggered back, blood spouting from his nose.

Holmes had retained his stick and his wits. From the corner of my eye I witnessed his first defensive move. Using the stick as a sword, he thrust straight and true at the nearest man's abdomen. The ferrule sank deep, bringing a scream of agony from the man and sending him down, clutching at his belly.

That was all I saw, because my assailant was up and at me again. I got my fingers around the wrist of his knife-arm and veered the blade off its course towards my throat. Then we were locked together, struggling desperately. We went to the cobble-stones in a frantic sprawl. He was a big man, strongly-muscled, and even though I strained against his arm with every ounce of my strength, the blade moved closer to my throat.

I was in the act of consigning my soul to its Maker when a thud of Holmes's stick glazed the eyes of my would-be murderer and pitched him over my head. With an effort I heaved off the weight of the man's body, and struggled to my knees. At that moment there was a cry of rage and pain from one of Holmes's assailants. One of them cried, "Come on, Butch! These blokes are a bit thick!" and, with that, my attacker was snatched to his feet, the trio ran off into the shadows, and disappeared.

Holmes was kneeling beside me. "Watson! Are you all right? Did that knife get into you?"

"Not so much as a scratch, Holmes," I assured him.

"If you'd been hurt, I should never have forgiven myself."

"Are *you* all right, old chap?"

"Except for a bruised shin." Helping me to my feet,

Holmes added grimly, "I am an idiot. An attack was the last thing I anticipated. The aspects of this case change swiftly."

"Don't blame yourself. How could you possibly have known?"

"It is my business to know."

"You were alert enough to beat them at their own game, when every advantage was on their side."

But Holmes would not be comforted. "I am slow, slow, Watson," said he. "Come, we shall find a hansom and get you home to that fire and a hot tea."

A cab hove in sight and picked us up. When we were rattling back toward Baker Street, Holmes said, "It would be interesting to know who sent them."

"Obviously, someone who wishes us dead," was my retort.

"But our ill-wisher, whoever he is, appears to have used poor judgement in selecting his emissaries. He should have chosen cooler heads. Their enthusiasm for the job impaired their efficiency."

"Our good fortune, Holmes."

"They achieved one goal, at least. If there was any doubt before, they have wedded me irrevocably to this case." Holmes's tone was grim indeed, and we rode the remainder of the journey in silence. It was not until we were seated before the fire with steaming cups of Mrs. Hudson's tea that he spoke again.

"After I left you yesterday, Watson, I corroborated a few small points. Did you know that a nude—a quite good work, by the way—by one Kenneth Osbourne, hangs in the National Gallery?"

"Kenneth Osbourne, did you say?" I exclaimed.

"The Duke of Shires."

Ellery Succeeds

He had typed steadily through the night; dawn found him blinking, stubbled, and famished.

Ellery went into the kitchen and opened the refrigerator and brought out a bottle of milk and the three sandwiches he had failed to eat the previous afternoon. He wolfed them down, drained what was left of the milk, wiped his mouth, yawned, stretched, and went to the phone.

"Morning, dad. Who won?"

"Who won what?" Inspector Queen asked querulously, from Bermuda.

"The horseshoe game."

"Oh, that. They rang in some stacked shoes on me. How's the weather in New York? Lousy, I hope."

"The weather?" Ellery glanced at the window, but the Venetian blinds were closed. "To tell you the truth, dad, I don't know. I worked all night."

"And you sent me down here for a rest! Son, why don't you join me?"

"I can't. It's not only this book I've got to finish, but Grant Ames dropped in yesterday. He drank me dry and left a package."

"Oh?" said the Inspector, coming to life. "What kind of package?"

Ellery told him.

The old man snorted. "Of all the baloney. Somebody's pulling a funny on you. Did you read it?"

"A few chapters. I must say it's pretty well done. Fascinating, in fact. But then—out of nowhere— lightning struck, and I got back to my typewriter. How do you plan to spend your day, dad?"

"Frying myself on that damned beach. Ellery, I'm so bored I'm beginning to chew my nails. Son, *won't* you let me come home?"

"Not a chance," said Ellery. "You fry. Tell you what. How would you like to read an unpublished Sherlock Holmes?"

Inspector Queen's voice took on a cunning note. "Say, that's an idea. I'll call the airline and book a stray seat—I can be in New York in no time—"

"Nothing doing. I'll mail the manuscript down to you."

"To hell with the manuscript!" howled his father.

"So long, daddy," said Ellery. "Don't forget to wear your dark glasses on the beach. And you eat everything they put on your plate."

He hung up hastily, not a second too soon.

He peered at the clock. It had the same bloodshot look as the typewriter.

He went into his bathroom, took a shower, and came back in his pajamas. The first thing he did in his study was to yank the telephone jack out of the wall socket. The second thing he did was to seize Dr. Watson's journal.

It will put me to sleep, he said to himself cunningly.

CHAPTER V

THE DIOGENES CLUB

The following morning I awoke to find Holmes up and pacing. Making no reference whatever to the previous night's misadventure, he said, "Watson, I wonder if you would inscribe a few notes for me."

"I should be happy to."

"I apologise for demeaning you to the role of amanuensis, but I have a special reason for wishing the details of this case to be put down in orderly fashion."

"A special reason?"

"Very. If your time is free, we shall call this afternoon upon my brother Mycroft, at his club. A consultation may bear us fruit. In certain ways, you know, Mycroft's analytical talents are superior to mine."

"I am aware of the high respect in which you hold him."

"Of course, his is what you might call a sedentary ability, in that he detests moving about. If a streetchair were ever invented to transport one from office to home and back again, Mycroft would be its first purchaser."

"I do recall that he is a man of rigid routine."

"Thus, he tends to reduce all riddles, human or otherwise, to chess-board dimensions. This is far too restrictive for my taste, but his methods are often quite stimulating, in the broader analysis."

Holmes rubbed his hands together. "And now, let us list our actors. Not necessarily in the order of their importance, we have, first, the Duke of Shires . . ."

Holmes re-capitulated for an hour, whilst I took

notes. Then he prowled the rooms whilst I re-arranged my notes into some semblance of order. When I had finished, I handed him the following *résumé*. It contained information of which I had no previous knowledge, data that Holmes had gathered over-night.

The Duke of Shires (Kenneth Osbourne)

Present holder of title and lands dating back to 1420. The twentieth descendant of the line. The Duke lives quietly, dividing his time between his estates and a town-house on Berkeley Square, where he pursues a painter's career. He sired two sons by a wife now ten years deceased. He has never re-married.

Lord Carfax (Richard Osbourne)

Elder son of Kenneth. Lineal inheritor of the dukedom. He sired one daughter, Deborah. But tragedy struck when his wife perished upon the delivery-table. The child is cared for by a governess at the Devonshire estate. The bond of affection between father and daughter is strong. Lord Carfax exhibits deep humanitarian tendencies. He gives generously of both his money and his time to the Montague Street Hostel in London, a sanctuary for indigents.

Michael Osbourne

Second son of Kenneth. A source of shame and sorrow to his father. Michael, according to testimony, bitterly resented his inferior position as a second son and non-inheritor, and embarked upon a profligate life. Bent, it is said, upon disgracing the title beyond his reach, he is also reported to have married a woman of the streets, apparently for no other reason than to further that misguided end. This reprehensible act is purported to have taken place while he was a medical student in Paris. He was expelled from the Sorbonne shortly thereafter. His fate thence forward, and his present address, are un-known.

Joseph Beck

A pawn-broker with a shop on Great Heapton Street. Of doubtful importance, on the basis of data at hand.

Dr. Murray

A dedicated M.D. who superintends the Montague Street morgue, and devotes himself to the adjoining hostel he himself created.

Sally Young

The niece of Dr. Murray. She gives her full time to the hostel. A devoted nurse and social-worker, it was she who pledged the surgeon's-kit at Beck's pawn-shop. When questioned, she gave information freely, and appeared to hold nothing in reserve.

Pierre

A seemingly harmless imbecile taken in at the hostel, where he performs menial tasks. The surgeon's-case was found among his possessions, and pledged by Miss Young for his benefit. He appears to have come from France.

The Scar-faced Woman

Unidentified.

Holmes ran through the *résumé* with a dissatisfied frown. "If this accomplishes nothing else," said he, "it shows us what a little way we have come, and how far we have still to go. It does not list the victims, who under-score our need for haste. There have been five known butcheries, and any delay on our part will no doubt add to the list. So if you will clothe yourself, Watson, we shall flag a hansom and be off to the Diogenes Club."

Holmes sat deep in thought as we rattled over the cobble-stones, but I risked disturbing him for something that came suddenly to mind.

"Holmes," said I, "as we were leaving the Duke of Shires's estate, you mentioned that Lord Carfax had failed on two counts. I think I have become aware of one of them."

"Indeed?"

"It occurs to me that he made no inquiry as to how you had come by the surgical-case. It therefore seems logical that he already knew."

"Excellent, Watson."

"In the light of the omission, are we justified in assuming that it was he who sent it to you?"

"We have at least a right to suspect that he knows who did."

"Then perhaps Lord Carfax is our key to the identity of the scar-faced woman."

"Entirely possible, Watson. However, recognising a key as such, and turning it, can be two different matters entirely."

"I must confess that his Lordship's second lapse has escaped me."

"You will recall that, in Lord Carfax's presence, I dropped the case and spilled its contents onto the floor? And that he courteously picked up the instruments?"

"Yes?"

"But perhaps you failed to note the practised skill with which he replaced them, each to its proper niche, with no hesitation whatever."

"Why, of course!"

"And, now that you recall this, what additional information does it give you concerning his Lordship?"

"That, even though he professes no surgical knowledge or experience, he is quite familiar with the tools of surgery."

"Precisely. A fact that we must place in our mental

file for future reference. But here we are, Watson, and Mycroft awaits us.''

The Diogenes Club! I remembered it well, even though I had entered its hushed precincts but once. That had been upon the occasion when Mycroft had shifted to his more active brother's shoulders the curious affair of the Greek Interpreter, which case I had the honour and satisfaction of recording for the pleasure of Holmes's not inconsiderable body of admirers.

The Diogenes Club was formed by, and for the benefit of, men who chose to seek solitude in the heart of the clamorous city. It is a luxurious place, with easy-chairs, excellent food, and all the other appurtenances of creature-comfort. The rules are geared to the Club's basic purpose, and are strictly enforced; rules devised to discourage, nay, to forbid, all sociability. Talking, save in the Stranger's Room—into which we were soundlessly ushered—is forbidden. In fact, it is forbidden any member to take the slightest notice of any other. A tale is told—apocryphal, I am sure—of a member succumbing to a heart-attack in his chair and being found to have expired only when a fellow-member noticed that the *Times* propped before the poor man was three days old.

Mycroft Holmes awaited us in the Stranger's Room, having taken time off, I was later informed, from his government post, around the corner in Whitehall. This, I might add, was an unheard-of interruption of his fixed habits.

Still, neither of the brothers, upon meeting, seemed in any haste to get to the business at hand. Mycroft, a large, comfortable man with thick grey hair and heavy features, bore little resemblance to his younger brother. He extended his hand, and exclaimed, ''Sherlock! You're looking fit. Bouncing all over England and the Continent appears to agree with you.'' Shifting the meaty hand to me, Mycroft said, ''Dr. Watson. I had heard that you escaped from Sherlock's clutch into matrimony. Surely Sherlock has not re-captured you?''

"I am most happily married," I assured him. "My wife is visiting an aunt at the moment."

"And Sherlock's long arm reaches out instantly!"

Mycroft's smile was warm. For an unsocial man, he had a curious talent for making one feel at ease. He had met us at the door, and now he moved towards the bow-window looking out upon one of London's busiest streets. We followed, and the brothers stood side by side, surveying the passing scene.

"Sherlock," said Mycroft, "I have not been in this room since your last visit, but the faces outside never change. From the look of that street, it could have been yesterday."

"Yet," murmured Sherlock, "it has changed. Old intrigues have died, new ones have been born."

Mycroft pointed. "Those two fellows at the kerb. Are they involved in some dire plot?"

"Do you mean the lamp-lighter and the book-keeper?"

"The very men."

"I'd say not. The lamp-lighter is consoling the book-keeper for being recently sacked."

"I agree. The book-keeper will no doubt find a berth, but he will lose it speedily and find himself again out on the street."

I was compelled to interrupt. "Come, come," said I, and heard myself repeating my old objections. "This is too much!"

"Watson, Watson," chided Mycroft, "after all these years with Sherlock, I should not expect such myopia from you. Even from this distance, surely you observe the smears of ink, both black and red, upon the first man's fingers? Just as surely, the occupational mark of the book-keeper?"

"Observe also," added Holmes the younger, "the ink-blot upon his collar, where he touched pen to linen, and the unpressed condition of his otherwise quite respectable suit."

"From which is it too difficult, my dear Watson,"

interposed Mycroft, with a kindliness that irritated me, "to project the man's slovenliness to his work, and thus conjure up an irate employer?"

"An employer not only irate but unforgiving," said Sherlock, "as evidenced by the newspaper in the book-keeper's jacket-pocket, opened to the *Situations* column. Hence, he is unemployed."

"But you said he would find a berth!" said I, testily, to Mycroft. "If the fellow is so inefficient, why should a new employer consider him?"

"Most would not, but many of the entries in the newspaper are marked, clearly for investigation. Such energy in seeking a new situation must eventually be rewarded."

I threw up my hands. "I concede, as usual! But the other man's being a lamp-lighter—surely that is sheer surmise on your part?"

"A little more technical," my friend Holmes admitted. "But observe the spot that is shiny on his inner right sleeve, extending upwards above the cuff."

"An unfailing mark of the lamp-lighter," said Mycroft.

"In extending his pole to reach the gas-globe with his flame," explained Sherlock, "he rubs the lower end of the pole against that portion of his sleeve again and again. Really elementary, Watson."

Before I could retort, Holmes's mood changed, and he turned from the window with a frown. "I wish our present problem were as easily solved. That is why we are here, Mycroft."

"Give me the details," replied his brother, with a smile. "My afternoon must not be entirely lost."

Twenty minutes later, ensconced in easy-chairs in the Stranger's Room, we sat in silence. It was broken by Mycroft. "Your picture is well-delineated, Sherlock, so far as it goes. But surely you are capable of solving the riddle yourself."

"I have no doubt of that, but there is little time. Preventing further outrages is urgent. Two minds are better than one. You might well discern a point that would save me a precious day or two of searching.''

''Then let us see precisely what you have. Or, rather, precisely what you do not have. Your pieces are far from complete.''

''Of course.''

''Yet you have touched a sensitive spot somewhere, as witness the swift and murderous attack upon you and Watson. Unless you wish to ascribe it to coincidence?''

''I do not!''

''Nor I.'' Mycroft tugged at an ear. ''Of course, it is no cerebral feat to identify the mysterious Pierre by his true name.''

''Certainly not,'' replied Holmes. ''He is the Duke of Shires' second son, Michael.''

''As to Michael's grievous injuries, the father may be unaware of them. But Lord Carfax certainly knows of Michael's presence at the hostel, and beyond doubt recognised his younger brother.''

''I am quite aware,'' said Holmes, ''that Lord Carfax has not been entirely candid.''

''He interests me. The philanthropic cloak is an admirable disguise for devilry. Lord Carfax could well have been responsible for Michael's delivery into Dr. Murray's care.''

''Also,'' said Holmes, grimly, ''for his injuries.''

''Possibly. But you must find the other pieces, Sherlock.''

''Time, Mycroft, time! That is my problem. I must identify, quickly, the right thread in this skein, and seize upon it.''

''I think you must somehow force Carfax's hand.''

I broke in. ''May I ask a question?''

''By all means, Watson. We had no intention of excluding you.''

''I can be of little help, but certainly identifying Jack the Ripper is our first concern. Therefore I ask, do you believe we have met the murderer? Is the Ripper one of the people with whom we have come in contact?''

Sherlock Holmes smiled. ''Do you have a candidate for that dubious honour, Watson?''

''If I were compelled to make a decision, I should name the imbecile. But I must confess that I missed badly in not postulating him as Michael Osbourne.'

''On which grounds do you condemn him?''

''Nothing tangible, I fear. But I cannot forget the *tableau* I witnessed as we were leaving the Montague Street morgue. Dr. Murray, you will recall, commanded 'Pierre' to cover the unfortunate's corpse. There was nothing conclusive in his action, but his manner made my flesh fairly crawl. He seemed entranced by the mutilated cadaver. In smoothing out the sheet, his hands ran lovingly over the cold flesh. He appeared to be enamoured of the butchery.''

There was a pause during which the brothers evaluated my contribution. Then Mycroft said, gravely, ''You have made a most pertinent point, Watson. I would only say that it is difficult, as you are aware, to interpret the actions generated by a damaged mentality. However, your instinctive revulsion may be worth more than all the logic we can muster.''

''The observation is certainly to be considered,'' remarked Sherlock.

I gathered the impression, however, that neither put any great stock in my statement; that they were merely being kind.

Mycroft came ponderously to his feet. ''You must gather more facts, Sherlock.''

His brother clenched his hands.

It had occurred to me that this entire episode with Mycroft was not at all like the sure-footed, self-confident Sherlock Holmes I had known. I was puzzling the matter when Mycroft, speaking quietly, said, ''I believe I know the source of your confusion, Sherlock. You must banish it. You have become subjective in regard to this case.''

"I fail to comprehend," Holmes said, a trifle coldly.

"Five of the most heinous murders of the century, and perhaps more to come. If you had entered the case sooner, you might have prevented some of these. That is what gnaws at you. The acid of guilt can dull the keenest intellect."

Holmes had no rebuttal. He shook his head impatiently, and said, "Come, Watson, the game is afoot. We stalk a savage beast."

"And a cunning one," said Mycroft, in clear warning. Then he said, "Sherlock, you seek a scar-faced woman. Also, one of the key-pieces that is missing, the ill-reputed wife of Michael Osbourne. What does that suggest?"

Holmes fixed his brother with an angry eye. "You must indeed feel that I have lost my faculties, Mycroft! It of course suggests that they are one and the same."

On that note, we left the Diogenes Club.

Ellery's Nemesis Investigates

The apartment bell was a carved rosebud set in ivory leaves. Grant Ames jabbed it, and the result was a girl wearing poisonous-green lounging pajamas.

"Hello, Madge. I happened to be in the neighborhood, so here I am."

She glowed. That thinly patrician male face reminded her of a very big dollar sign. "And so you thought you'd drop in?" she said, making it sound like Einstein's first formulation of the Theory; and she threw the door so wide it cracked against the wall.

Grant moved warily forward. "Nice little nest you've got here."

"It's just an ordinary career gal's efficiency apartment. I combed the East Side, absolutely combed it. And finally found this. It's sickeningly expensive, but of course one wouldn't dare live anywhere but Upper East.''

''I didn't know you'd gone in for a career.''

''Oh, definitely. I'm a consultant. You drink scotch, don't you?''

It behooved a legman to follow through, Grant thought. He asked brightly, ''And with whom do you consult?''

''The public relations people at the factory.''

''The one your father owns, of course.''

''Of course.''

Madge Short was a daughter of Short's Shapely Shoes, but with three brothers and two sisters to share the eventual loot. She wagged her pert red head as she extended a scotch-and.

''And the factory is located—?''

''In Iowa.''

''You commute?''

''Silly! There's a Park Avenue office.''

''You surprise me, dear heart. I see you in a different role.''

''As a bride?'' Two outstanding young breasts lifted the poisonous green like votive offerings.

''God, no,'' Grant said hurriedly. ''I visualize you somewhere in the literary field.''

''You've got to be kidding!''

Grant had checked the room. There were no books in sight—no magazines, either—but that wasn't necessarily conclusive.

''I see you as reading a great deal, chickie. A bit of a bookworm, so to speak.''

''In this day and age? Wherever would one get the *time?*''

''Oh, one wedges it in here and there.''

''I do read some. *Sex and the Single—*''

''I'm a detective bug myself. Father Brown. Bishop Cushing.'' He watched narrowly for her reaction. It was like watching for a pink piglet to react.

''I like them, too.''

"With a smattering," Grant went on cunningly, "of the philosophers—Burton, Sherlock Holmes."

"One of the men at that party, he's an expert on Zen." Doubt was beginning to creep in. Grant quickly changed his tactics.

"That blue bikini you wore. Was it ever sharp."

"I'm so glad you liked it, dahling. How about another scotch?"

"No, thanks," Grant said, getting up. "Time goes bucketing by, and—well, there you are." She was hopeless.

He collapsed behind the wheel of the Jag.

How did those fellows do it? Holmes? Even Queen?

While something was pressing against Ellery's nose, smothering him. He awoke and discovered that it was the journal with which he had gone to bed. He yawned, dropped it on the floor, and sat up groggily, elbows on knees. The journal now lay between his feet, so he doubled up, head between his hands.

And began to read, southward.

CHAPTER VI

I STALK THE RIPPER

The following morning, I must say, Holmes infuriated me.

When I awoke, he was up and clothed. I instantly saw, from the reddened condition of his eyes, that he had slept little; indeed, I suspected that he had been out all night. But I made no inquiry.

To my gratification, he was of a mind to talk, rather than to sink into one of his reticent moods, out of which little more than cryptic sounds ever emerged.

"Watson," said he, without preliminary, "there is a notorious public-house in Whitechapel."

"There are many."

"True, but the one to which I refer, The Angel and Crown, abuses even the riotous pleasures tendered by that district. It is situated in the heart of the Ripper's prowling-grounds, and three of the murdered prostitutes were seen on the premises shortly before their deaths. I mean to give sharp attention to The Angel and Crown. To-night I shall indulge in a little carousing there."

"Capital, Holmes! If I may confine myself to ale——"

"Not you, my dear Watson. I still shudder at how close to death I have already led you."

"See here, Holmes——"

"My mind is made up," replied he, firmly. "I have no intention of confronting your good wife, upon her return, with the dismal news that her husband's body may be found in the morgue."

166

"I thought I gave a good account of myself!" said I, heatedly.

"You did, certainly. Without you I might myself well be occupying a pallet in Dr. Murray's establishment. That is no justification, however, for risking your safety a second time. Perhaps whilst I am absent to-day—I have much to do—your practise could do with a little attention."

"It is going along quite nicely, thank you. I have a working arrangement with a most able locum tenens."

"Then might I suggest a concert, or a good book?"

"I am quite capable of occupying my time fruitfully," said I, coldly.

"Indeed you are, Watson," said he. "Well, I must be off! Expect me when you see me. I promise I shall put you abreast of affairs upon my return."

With that he darted out, leaving me to steam at a temperature only a little below that of Mrs. Hudson's tea.

My determination to defy Holmes did not form at once; but, before my morning repast was finished, it was clearly shaped. I passed the day reading a curious monograph from Holmes's book-shelf on the possible use of bees in murder-intrigues, both by causing them to contaminate their honey, and by training them to attack a victim in a swarm. The work was anonymous, but I recognised the concise style of Holmes in the writing. Then, as darkness fell, I planned my night's foray.

I would arrive at The Angel and Crown in the guise of a lecherous man-about-town, sure that I would not stand out, as many of London's more hardened *habitués* made a practise of frequenting such places. I therefore hurried home and donned evening attire. Capping my regalia with top-hat and opera cape, I surveyed myself in the glass, and found that I cut a more dashing figure than I had dared hope. Slipping a loaded revolver into my pocket, I went out into the street, hailed a hansom, and gave The Angel and Crown as my destination.

Holmes had not yet arrived.

It was a horrible place. The long, low-ceilinged public-room was thick with eye-smarting fumes from the many oil-lamps. Clouds of tobacco smoke hung in the air, like storm-warnings. And the crude tables were crowded by as motley a collection of humanity as ever I had encountered. Evil-faced Lascars on leave from the freighters that choke the Thames; inscrutable Orientals; Swedes, and Africans, and seedy-looking Europeans; not to mention the many varieties of native Britons—all bent upon supping off the flesh-pots of the world's largest city.

The flesh-pots were dubiously spiced with females of all ages and conditions. Most were pitiful in their physical deterioration. Only a few were attractive, younger ones who had just set foot upon the downward path.

It was one of these latter who approached me after I had found a table, had ordered a pint of stout, and sat surveying the reckless scene. She was a pretty little thing, but the wicked light in her eye, and her hard manner, indelibly marked her.

" 'Ullo, luv. Buy a gel a gin-an'-bitters?"

I was about to decline the honour, but a brutish-looking waiter standing by cried, "Gin-an'-bitters for the lady!" and ploughed towards the bar. The man was no doubt paid on the basis of the liquor the girls wheedled from their marks.

The wench dropped into the chair opposite me and laid her rather dirty hand upon mine. I withdrew mine quickly. This brought an uncertain smile to her painted lips, but her voice was cajoling as she said, "Shy, ducks? No need to be."

"I merely dropped in for a quick pint," said I. The adventure no longer seemed so alluring.

"Sure, luv. All the toffs drop in for quick pints.

Then they just 'appen to find out what else we 'ave for sale.''

The waiter returned, slopped down the gin-and-tonic, and fumbled among the coins I had laid upon the table. I was sure he appropriated several pence too many, but I did not make an issue of it.

"Me name's Polly, luv. What's yers?''

"Hawkins,'' said I, quickly. "Sam Hawkins.''

" 'Awkins, is it?'' she laughed. "Well it's a bit of a change from Smythe. Yer 'eart'd bleed at 'ow many bloody Smythes come 'round.'

My reply, if indeed I had any, was cut down by an outburst in another part of the room. A dark-visaged sailor of gorilla proportions gave out a roar of rage and upset a table in his zeal to get at another patron who appeared to have offended him, a Chinese of insignificant stature. For a moment it seemed likely that the Oriental would be killed, so ferocious was the sailor's aspect.

But then another man interposed himself. He was thick-browed, with a heavy neck, and shoulders and arms like trees, although he did not match the angry sailor's proportions. The Oriental's unexpected defender smashed his fist into the sailor's solar plexus. It was a mighty blow, and the sailor's gasp could be heard all over the room as he doubled over in agony. Again the smaller man measured the giant, and again he delivered a blow, this time to the brute's jaw. The sailor's head snapped back; his eyes glazed; and, as he collapsed, his assailant was ready with a hunched shoulder, and caught the man's body like a sack of meal. His load balanced, the victor made calmly for the door, lugging the unconscious mariner as though he weighed no more than a child. He opened the door and hurled the man into the street.

"That's Max Klein,'' said my doxy in awe. "Strong as a bloody ox, 'e is. Max just bought this place. 'E's owned it for about a four-month, an' 'e don't allow no bloke to get kilt in it, 'e don't.''

The performance had been impressive indeed; but, at that moment, something else drew my attention. The door through which Klein had flung the sailor had scarcely closed when it was put to use by a new customer, one whom I thought I recognised. I peered through the haze to make sure my identification was correct. There was no doubt. It was Joseph Beck, the pawn-broker, moving towards a table. I made a mental note to report this fact to Holmes, and then I turned back to Polly.

"I got a nice room, luv," said she, in a seductive tone.

"I fear I'm not interested, Madam," said I, as kindly as I could.

"Madam, 'e says!" cried she, with indignation. "I ain't *that* old, guv'ner. I'm young enough, I promise yer. Young *an'* clean. You 'ave nothin' to fear from me."

"But there must be someone *you* fear, Polly," said I, observing her closely.

"Me? I don't go ter 'urt nobody."

"I mean the Ripper."

A whining note leaped into her voice. "Yer just tryin' to scare me! Well, I ain't afraid." She took a gulp of her drink, eyes darting here and there. They came to focus on a point over my shoulder, and I realised that they had been directed that way during most of our conversation. I turned my head, and beheld as vicious-looking a creature as the imagination could have conjured.

He was incredibly filthy, and he had a hideous knife-scar across one cheek. This twisted his mouth in a permanent leer, and the damaged flesh around his left eye added further to his frightful aspect. I have never seen such malevolence in a human face.

" 'E got Annie, the Ripper did," Polly whispered. " 'E gouged the poor thing up good—Annie wot never 'urt a soul."

I turned back to her. "That brute there, with the knife-scar?"

" 'Oo knows?" Then she cried, "Wot's he 'ave to go and do those things for? Wot's the fun in shovin' a blade into a poor gel's belly, an' cuttin' off 'er breast an' all?"

He was the man.

Explaining my absolute certainty is difficult. In earlier life I indulged for a time in gambling, as a young man will, and there is a feeling that comes over one on certain occasions that is not founded in reason. Instinct, a sixth sense—call it what you will—it comes, and it is impossible to ignore it.

Such a feeling came over me as I studied the creature behind us; his gaze was fixed upon the girl who sat with me, and I could see the foul slaver at the corners of his contorted mouth.

But what to do?

"Polly," I asked, quietly, "did you ever see that man before?"

"Me, ducks? Not ever! Narsty-lookin' cove, ain't 'e?" Then, with the instability that characterises the loose woman, Polly's mood changed. Her natural recklessness, possibly re-inforced by too many drinks, came to the fore. She suddenly raised her glass.

" 'Ere's luck, luv. If yer don't want me lily-white body, yer don't. But yer a good bloke, and I wish yer the best."

"Thank you."

"A gel's got t'make a livin', so I'll be off. Another night, maybe?"

"Perhaps."

She arose from the table, and moved away, flaunting her hips. I watched her, anticipating that she would approach another table for another solicitation. But she did not. Instead, she scanned the room, and then moved swiftly to the door. She had found the pickings poor that night in The Angel and Crown, I thought, and was going to resort to the streets. I had scarcely

begun to feel relief when the repulsive creature beyond
my shoulder jumped up and set out after her. My alarm
may be imagined. I could think of no other course than
to touch the weapon in my pocket for reassurance, and
follow the man to the street.

I was beset by a momentary blindness, having to
adjust my eyesight to the darkness after the glare of
the public-room. When my eyes focussed, fortunately,
the man was still within my view. He was skulking
along, close by the wall, at the end of the street.

I was now certain that I was embarked upon a perilous course. He was the Ripper, and he was stalking
the girl who had endeavoured to entice me to her room,
and there was only I between her and a hideous death.
I gripped my revolver convulsively.

I followed, treading on the balls of my feet like a
Red Indian of the American plains. He turned the corner; and, fearful both of losing him and of finding
him, I hurried after.

I rounded the corner, panting, and peered cautiously
ahead. There was only one gas-lamp, which made my
survey doubly difficult. I strained my eyes. But my
quarry had disappeared.

Apprehension seized me. Perhaps the fiend had already dragged the poor girl into an areaway and was
slashing the life from her young body. If only I had
had the foresight to bring a pocket lantern! I ran forward into darkness, the profound silence of the street
broken only by the sounds of my footsteps.

There was enough light to warn me that the street
narrowed at the other end, coming down to a passage-
way. It was into this that I plunged, my heart in my
mouth at what I might find.

Suddenly I heard a choked cry. I had collided with
something soft. A fear-stricken voice babbled,
"Mercy! Oh, pray, 'ave mercy!"

It was Polly, who had been pressed against the wall
in the darkness. In fear that her cries might frighten

the Ripper away, I clapped my hand over her mouth and whispered into her ear.

"It's all right, Polly. You are in no danger. I am the gentleman you sat with. I followed you——"

I was struck from behind by a sudden, enormous weight, and knocked back, staggering, along the passage. But my brain still functioned. I had been outwitted by the cunning devil I had followed from The Angel and Crown. He had crept into some shadow and allowed me to pass him. Now, enraged at the prospect of being deprived of his prey, he was attacking like a jungle beast.

I answered in kind, fighting desperately, trying to pull the revolver from my pocket. It should have been in my hand; but, during my stint in her Majesty's Indian service, I had served as a surgeon, not a soldier; I had no training in hand-to-hand fighting.

I was therefore no match for the monster with whom I had come to grips. I went down under his onslaught, gratefully aware that the girl had fled. I felt his powerful hands upon my throat, and I flailed out desperately with my free arm as I struggled still to clear the weapon from my pocket.

To my stupefaction, a familiar voice growled, "Now let us see what manner of beast I have flushed!" Even before a bull's eye lantern flashed, I became aware of my blunder. The evil-appearing creature seated behind me in the pub had been Holmes—in disguise!

"Watson!" He was as astonished as I.

"Holmes! Good heavens, man! Had I managed to get my revolver out, I might have shot you!"

"And a good thing, too," grumbled he. "Watson, you can write me down an ass." He lifted his lithe body from me and grasped my hand to help me to my feet. Even then, knowing he was my old friend, I could only marvel at the cleverness of his disguise, so different did he appear.

We had no time for further recriminations. As Holmes was pulling me erect, a scream rent the night.

His hand released me instantly, and down I tumbled again. An oath erupted from his throat, one of the very few outbursts of profanity I have ever heard from him.

"I've been outdone!" he cried; and he went streaking away into the night.

As I scrambled to my feet, the female cries of terror and pain increased in volume. Suddenly they were cut off; and the sounds of a second pair of running feet were added to those of Holmes.

I must confess that I showed to little advantage in the affair. I had once been the middle-weight boxing champion of my regiment, but those days were in the long-ago, and I leaned against the brick wall, fighting nausea and dizziness. At that moment, I should not have been able to respond had our gracious Queen herself been screaming for aid.

The vertigo passed; the world righted itself; I moved shakily back, as I had come, groping my way along through the silence that had ominously fallen. I had re-traced my steps some two hundred paces, when a quiet voice stopped me.

"Here, Watson."

I turned to my left and discovered a break in the wall.

Again, Holmes's voice: "I dropped my lantern. Will you be so kind as to search for it, Watson?"

His quiet tone was doubly chilling, in that it concealed an agonised inner struggle. I knew Holmes; he was shaken to the core.

Good fortune attended my search for the lantern. I took a single step, and bumped it with my foot. I re-lighted it, and staggered back from one of the most horrible scenes that has ever met my eyes.

Holmes was on his knees, back bowed, head lowered, a picture of despair.

"I have failed, Watson. I should be brought to the dock for criminal stupidity."

I scarcely heard him, stunned as I was by the bloody sight that confronted me. Jack the Ripper had vented his obscene madness upon poor Polly. Her clothing had been torn from her body, baring fully half of it to view. A great, ragged slash had opened her abdomen, and its torn and mutilated contents were exposed like those of a butchered animal. A second savage thrust had severed her left breast almost from her body. The terrible scene swam before my eyes.

"But he had so little time! How—?"

But Holmes came alive; he sprang to his feet. "Come, Watson! Follow me!"

So abruptly did he launch himself from the area-way towards the street that I was left behind. I called upon the reserve of strength each man possesses in moments of emergency, and ran, pell-mell, after him. He was well in the forefront all the way, but I did not lose him; and, when I again came close, I found him thundering upon the door of Joseph Beck's pawn-shop.

"Beck!" Holmes shouted. "Come out! I demand that you come out this instant!" His fists smote again and again upon the panel. "Open this door, or I shall smash it in!"

A rectangle of light appeared overhead. A window opened; a head was thrust out. Joseph Beck cried, "Are you mad? Who are you?"

The light from the lamp in his hand revealed a red-tasselled night-cap and a high-necked night-dress.

Holmes stood back and bellowed up at him. "Sir, I am Sherlock Holmes, and if you do not come down immediately I shall climb this wall and drag you out by your hair!"

Beck was, understandably, shaken. Holmes was still in his disguise; and to be roused out of sleep, and find such a hideous figure banging at his door in the dead of night, was certainly not an experience for which the life of a tradesman had prepared the pawn-broker.

I sought to help. "*Herr* Beck! You remember me, do you not?"

He gaped down at me. "You are one of the two gentlemen—?"

"And, despite his appearance, this is the other, Mr. Sherlock Holmes, I promise you."

The pawn-broker hesitated; but then he said, "Very well; I shall come down."

Holmes paced with impatient strides until the light appeared in the shop, and the street-door opened.

"Step out here, Beck!" commanded Holmes, in a deadly voice; and, fearfully, the German obeyed. My friend's powerful hand darted out, and the man shrank back, but he was too slow. Holmes tore open the front of his night-dress, revealing a bare chest pimpled with the chill.

"What are you doing, sir?" quavered the tradesman. "I do not understand."

"Be silent!" said Holmes, harshly; and in the light of Beck's lamp he examined the pawn-broker's chest minutely. "Where did you go, Joseph Beck, after you left The Angel and Crown?" asked Holmes, releasing his grasp.

"Where did I go? I came home to bed!" Reassured by Holmes's milder tone, Beck was now hostile.

"Yes," replied Holmes, thoughtfully, "it appears that you did. Go back to bed, sir. I am sorry if I have frightened you."

With this, Holmes turned unceremoniously away, and I followed. I looked back as we reached the corner, to see *Herr* Beck still standing before his shop. Holding the lamp high above his head, he appeared for all the world like a night-shirted caricature of that noble statue, Liberty Enlightening the World, presented to the United States by the people of France, the great, hollow, bronze figure that now stands in the harbour at New York City.

We returned to the scene of the butchery, to find that the body of poor Polly had been discovered. An army of the morbidly curious choked the entrance to the street, whilst the lanterns of officialdom illuminated the darkness beyond.

Holmes gazed grimly at the scene, hands thrust deep

into his pockets. "There is no point in identifying ourselves, Watson," said he, in a mutter. "It would only
make for profitless conversation with Lestrade."

It did not surprise me that Holmes preferred not to
reveal our part in that night's terrible affair. It was not
merely that he had his methods; in this circumstance,
his self-esteem was involved, and it had suffered a
grievous blow.

"Let's slip away, Watson," said he, bitterly, "like
the addle-brained idiots we have become."

CHAPTER VII

THE SLAYER OF HOGS

"What you failed to see, Watson, was the cloaked figure of Joseph Beck leaving the pub, just as the girl gave evidence of her intention to go elsewhere. You had eyes only for me."

It was dismally evident to me that I had been the culprit, not he, but there was no hint of this in his voice. I attempted to assess the blame, but he cut short my apologies. "No, no," said he, "it was my stupidity that let the monster slip through our fingers, not yours."

Chin on breast, Holmes went on. "When I emerged from the pub, the girl was just turning the corner. Beck was nowhere in sight, and I could only assume either that he had made off in the other direction, or was crouched in one of the dark doorways nearby. I chose the latter assumption. I followed the girl around the corner and heard approaching footsteps, catching a glimpse of a caped man entering behind us. Not dreaming that it was you—your figure and Beck's do not greatly differ, I fear, Watson—I took the skulker to be our pawnbroker. I hid myself in turn, and you passed me. Then I heard the cries, and I thought I had stalked the Ripper successfully. Whereupon I attacked, and discovered my unforgiveable error."

We had finished our morning tea, and Holmes was pacing his quarters at Baker Street in a fury. I followed his movements sadly, wishing I possessed the power to erase the whole incident from the slate, not only for Polly's sake, but for my friend's peace of mind.

"Then," continued Holmes, savagely, "whilst we were preoccupied with our blunders, the Ripper struck. The arrogance of this fiend!" cried he. "The contempt, the utter self-confidence, with which he perpetrates his outrages! Believe me, Watson, I shall lay the monster by the heels if it is the last act of my life!"

"It would appear," said I, trying to divert his bitter thoughts, "That Joseph Beck has been exonerated, at least of last night's murder."

"Quite so. Beck could not possibly have reached his quarters, cleansed himself of the blood, undressed, and donned night-clothes before we were upon him." Holmes seized his cherry-wood, and his Persian slipper, then cast them down in disgust. "Watson," said he, "all we accomplished last night was to eliminate one suspect from amongst London's millions. At such a rate, we shall succeed in spotting our quarry some time during the next century!"

I could find nothing to say in refutation. But then Holmes suddenly threw back his spare shoulders and directed a steely glance at me. "But enough of this, Watson! We shall imitate the Phoenix. Get dressed. We are going to pay another visit to Dr. Murray's mortuary."

Within the hour, we stood before the Montague Street portal to that gloomy establishment. Holmes glanced up and down the shabby thoroughfare.

"Watson," said he, "I should like a more detailed picture of this neighborhood. Whilst I venture inside, will you be good enough to scout the near streets?"

Eager to atone for my bungling of the previous night, I readily agreed.

"When you have finished, you will no doubt find me in the hostel." Holmes disappeared through the morgue gate.

I found that the vicinity of Montague Street possessed no common commercial establishments. The further side was occupied by a row of warehouses that presented locked entrances and no signs of life.

But when I turned the corner, I came upon a more active scene. I saw a green-grocer's stall, where a house-wife haggled with the proprietor over the price of a cabbage. The shop next door housed a tobacconist's. Just beyond, there stood a small, evil-looking public-house with a weathered replica of a hansom cab above the door.

My attention was soon drawn to an open entranceway on the street's near side. A great squealing emanated therefrom. It sounded as if a battalion of pigs was being slaughtered. As it turned out, this was precisely the case. I entered through an ancient stone archway, came out into a courtyard, and found myself in an abattoir. Four lean, live hogs were penned in one corner; the butcher, a grossly-muscled youth in a bloody leather apron, was in the act of dragging a fifth toward a suspended hook. In a callous manner, he hoisted the animal, and chained its hind legs to the hook. A rusted pulley creaked as he hauled on the rope. He tied a swift knot, and the hog squealed and thrashed as if it knew its fate.

As I watched in disgust, the butcher's boy took up a long knife and, without a qualm, plunged it into the hog's throat. The sounds gurgled away, and the boy stepped back to avoid the gout of dark blood. Then, he walked carelessly into the red pool, and slashed the animal's throat open. Whereupon the knife swept down, opening the animal from tail to jowls.

It was not the butchery, however, that made me look away. My glance was drawn to what appeared to me even more horrible—the sight of the idiot, the creature whom both Sherlock Holmes and his brother Mycroft had identified as Michael Osbourne. He was crouched in one corner of the abattoir, oblivious of all else but the butcher's work. The operation seemed to fascinate him. His eyes drank in the bloody carcase of the animal in a manner that I can only describe as obscene.

His preliminary work done, the butcher's boy stepped back and favoured me with a smile.

"Lookin' for a bit o' pork, guv'ner?"

"No, thank you! I was strolling by——"

"An' you heard the squealin'. Yer has to be a stranger, guv'ner, else you would not o' bothered. The neighbourhood's used to their ruddy noise." He turned cheerfully to Michael Osbourne. "Ain't that right, dummy?"

The imbecile smiled, and nodded.

"The dummy's the on'y one that keeps me comp'ny. I'd be fair lonesome 'thout him."

"Your work is certainly not carried on under the most cleanly condition," said I, distastefully.

"Clean-ly, says 'e," chuckled the boy. "Guv'ner, folk 'ereabouts 've got a fat lot more to turn their stomachs than a little dirt on their pork—bloody right they 'ave!" He winked. "The gels, 'specially. They're too busy o' nights keepin' their own 'ides in one piece.'

"You refer to the Ripper?"

"That I do, guv, that I do. 'E's keepin' the tarts nervy o' late."

"Did you know the girl who was murdered last night?"

"I did. Passed 'er two-and-six t'other night for a quick whack, I did. Poor little tart didn't 'ave'er rent, and I'm that gen'rous, I 'ates to see a gel trampin' the ruddy streets in the fog fer want o' a bed."

Some instinct made me pursue the tasteless conversation. "Have you any idea as to the identity of the Ripper?"

"Lord love yer, guv. 'E might just be yer own lordship, now, mightn't 'e? Yer got to admit, 'e's prob'ly a toff, don't yer?"

"Why do you say that?"

"Well, now, let's look at it this way. I'm at 'ome with blood in my perfession, cozy with it, yer might say, and so I 'ave to think that way, right?"

"What are you driving at?"

"Guv, the way that Ripper carves 'em up, 'e's just

got to get smeary. But nobody's never seen a smeared-up bloke runnin' from one o' those murders, now, 'ave they?''

"I believe not," said I, rather startled.

"An' why not, guv'ner? 'Cause a toff wearin' a opry cloak over 'is duds could cover up the bloody res-ee-doo, so ter speak! Wouldn' yer say? Well, I 'ave ter get back to this carcase.''

I fled the stench and gore of the place. But I took an image with me, that of Michael Osbourne squatting in his corner, laving the slaughter with watering eyes. No matter what Holmes had said, the misshapen wreck of humanity remained my principal suspect.

I circumnavigated the square and made my entrance into the morgue through the Montague Street gate, the adjacent premises fixed in mind. The morgue was untenanted, save for the dead. Traversing its narrow length, I paused near the raised table that was reserved for unwilling guests. A white-sheeted form lay there. I contemplated it for a few moments; then, moved by pity, I drew the sheet back from the face.

Her sufferings past, Polly's marble features reflected acceptance of whatever she had found beyond the pale. I do not rate myself a sentimental man, but I do believe that there is a dignity in death, however it comes. Nor am I deeply religious. Still, I breathed a small prayer for the salvation of this unhappy child's spirit. Then I went away.

I found Homes in the dining-hall of the hostel, in company with Lord Carfax and Miss Sally Young. The latter gave me a smile of welcome. "Dr. Watson, may I fetch you a cup of tea?''

I declined with thanks, and Holmes spoke crisply. "You arrive fortuitously, Watson. Lord Carfax is about to tender some information.'' His Lordship looked a trifle dubious. "You may speak before my colleague in complete confidence, your Lordship.''

"Very well. As I was about to relate, Mr. Holmes, Michael left London for Paris some two years ago. I expected him to live a licentious life in that most licentious of cities, but I strove to keep in touch with him, nonetheless; and I was both surprised and gratified to learn that he had entered the Sorbonne to study medicine. We maintained a correspondence, and I became optimistic as to his future. He appeared to have turned a new leaf.'' At this point, his Lordship's eyes lowered, and a great sadness came over his sensitive face. "But then, disaster struck. I was stunned to learn that Michael had married a woman of the streets."

"Did you meet her, my lord?"

"Never, Mr. Holmes! I frankly admit that I had little stomach for a face-to-face encounter. It is true, however, that I would have confronted the woman, had the opportunity arisen."

"How, then, do you know she was a prostitute? Your brother would hardly have included such an item in his bill of particulars when he informed you of his marriage."

"My brother did not inform me. I received the information in a letter from one of his fellow-students, a person I had never met, but whose written word reflected an earnest interest in Michael's welfare. This gentleman acquainted me with Angela Osbourne's calling, and suggested that, if I had my brother's future at heart, I should leave for Paris immediately and try to repair his fortunes before they were irretrievably destroyed."

"You informed your father of this communication?"

"Indeed I did not!" said Lord Carfax, sharply. "Unhappily, my correspondent saw to that. He had dispatched two letters, in the event one should be ignored, I suppose."

"How did your father react?"

"You need hardly ask that question, Mr. Holmes."

"The Duke did not reserve judgement until proof was forthcoming?"

"He did not. The letter was too patently truthful; I

did not doubt it myself. As for my father, it was in perfect consonance with what he had always expected of Michael.'' Lord Carfax paused, pain invading his face. ''I shall not soon forget the renunciation. I suspected that Father had also received a letter, and I rushed to his town-house. He was at his easel when I arrived; as I entered the studio, his model drew a robe over her nudity, and my father laid down his brush and surveyed me calmly. He said, 'Richard, what brings you here at this time of day?'

''I saw the tell-tale envelope with the French stamp lying by his palette, and I pointed to it. ''That, your Grace. I presume it is from Paris.'

'' 'You are correct.' He picked up the envelope, but did not remove its contents. 'It is inappropriate. It should have been edged in black.'

'' 'I do not understand you,' I replied.

''He laid the letter down, coldly. 'Should not all announcements of death be thus marked? So far as I am concerned, Richard, this letter informs me of Michael's demise. In my heart, the service has already been read, and the body is in the earth.'

''His terrible words stunned me. But, knowing that argument was futile, I left.''

''You made no effort to reach Michael?'' asked Holmes.

''I did not, sir. To me, he was beyond salvation. Some two months later, however, I received an anonymous note saying that I would find something of interest if I made a visit to this hostel. I did so. I do not have to tell you what I found.''

''The note. Did you preserve it, your Lordship?''

''No.''

''A pity.''

Lord Carfax appeared to be struggling with a natural reticence. Finally, he burst out, ''Mr. Holmes, I cannot express to you my shock at finding Michael in his present condition, the victim of an attack so savage that it had turned him into what you have seen—a misshapen creature with but the merest fragment of his reason left.''

''How did you proceed, if I may ask?''

Lord Carfax shrugged his shoulders. ''The hostel seemed as good a place as any for him. So that part of the problem was solved.''

Miss Sally Young had been sitting in amazed silence, her eyes never leaving his Lordship's face. Lord Carfax took cognizance of this. With a sad smile, he said. ''I trust you will forgive me, my dear, for not setting the case before you earlier. But it seemed unnecessary—indeed, imprudent. I wished Michael to remain here; and, in truth, I was not eager to confess his identity to you and your uncle.''

''I understand,'' said the girl, quietly. ''You were entitled to keep your secret, my lord, if for no other reason than that your support of the hostel has been so generous.''

The nobleman seemed embarrassed. ''I should have contributed to the maintenance of the hostel in any event, my dear. However, I do not deny that Michael's refuge here enhanced my interest. So perhaps my motives have been as selfish as they have been eleemosynary.''

Holmes had been studying Lord Carfax keenly as the story unfolded.

''You made no further efforts in your brother's behalf?''

''One,'' replied his Lordship. ''I communicated with the Paris police, as well as with Scotland Yard, inquiring if their records bore any report of an attack such as my brother had suffered. Their records did not reveal one.''

''So you left it there?''

''Yes!'' cried the harassed noblemen. ''And why not?''

''The felons might have been brought to justice.''

''By what method? Michael had become a hopeless idiot. I doubt if he would have been able to recognise his assailants. Even could he have done so, his testimony in a criminal proceeding would have been valueless.''

"I see," said Holmes, gravely; but I perceived that he was far from satisfied. "And as to his wife, Angela Osbourne?"

"I never found her."

"Did you not suspect that she wrote the anonymous note?"

"I assumed that she did."

Holmes came to his feet. "I wish to thank your Lordship for being so candid under the difficult circumstances."

This brought a bleak smile. "I assure you, sir, that it has not been through choice. I have no doubt that you would have come by the information through other channels. Now, perhaps, you can let the matter rest."

"Hardly, I fear."

Lord Carfax's face became intense. "I tell you, upon my honour, sir, that Michael has had nothing to do with the horrible murders that have convulsed London!

"You reassure me," replied Holmes, "and I promise your Lordship that I will do my utmost to spare you further suffering."

Lord Carfax bowed, and said nothing more.

With that, we took our leave. But as we went out of the hostel, I could see only Michael Osbourne, crouched in that filthy abattoir, enchanted by the blood.

Ellery's Legman Reports

Grant Ames III lay on Ellery's sofa balancing the glass on his chest, exhausted. "I went forth an eager beaver. I return a wreck."

"From only two interviews?"

"A party is one thing—you can escape behind a patio plant. But alone, trapped inside four walls . . ."

Ellery, still in pajamas, crouched over his typewriter and scratched the foundations of a magnificent beard. He typed four more words and stopped.

"The interviews bore no fruit?"

"Two gardensful, one decked in spring green, the other in autumnal purple. But with price tags on the goodies."

"Marriage might be your salvation."

The idler shuddered. "If masochism is one of your vices, old buddy, we'll discuss it. But later, when I get my strength back."

"You're sure neither put the journal in your car?"

"Madge Short thinks Sherlock is some kind of new hair-do. And Katherine Lambert—Kat's not a bad kitten from the neck down. She paints, you know. Redid a loft in the Village. Very intense. The coiled-spring type. You sit there waiting to get the broken end in your eye."

"They may have put you on," Ellery said brutally. "You wouldn't be hard to fool."

"I satisfied myself," Grant said with dignity. "I asked subtle questions. Deep. Searching."

"Such as?"

"Such as, 'Kat, did you put a manuscript addressed to Ellery Queen into the seat of my car at Lita's bash the other day?' "

"And she replied?"

Grant shrugged. "It came in the form of a counter-question—'Who's Ellery Queen?' "

"Have I asked you to leave lately?"

"Let's be kind to each other, friend." Grant paused to drink deeply. "I'm not reporting total failure. I've merely cut the field in half. I shall go doggedly forward. Beyond the Bronx lies New Rochelle.

"Who lives there?"

"Rachel Hager. Third on my list. And then there's Pagan Kelly, a Bennington chick whom you can find in almost any picket line whose protest is silly."

"Two suspects," Ellery said. "But don't rush into it. Go off somewhere and ponder your attack."

"You mean you want me to dawdle?"

"Isn't that what you do best? But not in my apartment. I've got to get this story finished."

"Did you finish the journal?" the playboy asked, not stirring.

"I'm busy with my own mystery."

"Have you gone far enough to spot the killer?"

"Brother," Ellery said, "I haven't spotted the murderer in my own story yet."

"Then I'll leave you to your labors. Oh. Suppose we never find out who sent you the manuscript?"

"I think I'd manage to survive."

"Where did you get your reputation?" the young man asked nastily. He left.

Ellery's brain dangled, like a foot that has fallen asleep. The typewriter keys looked a thousand yards away. Vagrant thoughts began to creep into the vacuum. How was dad getting along in Bermuda? What were the latest sales figures on his last book? He did not have to ask himself who had sent the manuscript by way of Grant Ames III. He already knew the answer to that. So, by a natural process, he began to wonder about the identity of Sherlock Holmes's visitor from Paris (he had peeked ahead).

After a short battle, which he lost, he went into the bedroom. He plucked Dr. Watson's journal from the floor, where he had left it, and stretched out on his bed to read on.

Chapter VIII

A Visitor from Paris

The ensuing days were most trying. In all our association, I had never seen Holmes so restless, and so difficult to get along with.

After our interview with Lord Carfax, Holmes ceased to communicate with me. My overtures were ignored. It then occurred to me that I had intruded further into this case than into any of the investigations I had shared with him. In the light of the chaos I had managed to create, my chastisement seemed just. So I retreated into my customary rôle of by-stander, and awaited developments.

They were slow in coming. Holmes had turned, like the Ripper, into a creature of the night. He vanished from Baker Street each evening to return at dawn and spend the day in brooding silence. I kept to my own room, knowing that solitude was essential to him at such times. His violin wailed at intervals. When I could stand its scratching no longer, I took myself off into the welcome hubbub of London's streets.

On the third morning, however, I was appalled at his appearance.

"Holmes! In God's name!" I cried. "What has happened to you?"

There was an ugly purple contusion below his right temple. The left sleeve of his jacket had been ripped away, and a gashed wrist had no doubt bled copiously. He walked with a limp, and he was as begrimed as any of the street Arabs he so often sent on mysterious missions.

"A dispute in a dark by-way, Watson."

"Let me attend to those wounds!"

I snatched my satchel from my room and returned. Grimly he displayed the bloody knuckles of his right fist. "I attempted to lure our enemy into the open, Watson. I succeeded." Pressing Holmes into a chair, I began my examination. "I succeeded, but I failed."

"You take perilous risks."

"The assassins, two of them, rose to my bait."

"The same ones who attacked us?"

"Yes. My purpose was to lay one of them by the heels, but my revolver jammed—of all the accursed luck!—and both got away."

"Pray relax, Holmes. Lie back. Close your eyes. Perhaps I should give you a sedative."

He made an impatient gesture. "These scratches are nothing. It is my failure that pains me. So near and yet so far. Had I been able to hold one of those scoundrels, I should have gotten the name of his employer soon enough, I warrant you."

"Is it your feeling that these brutes are perpetrating the butcheries?"

"Good heavens, no! They are wholesome, healthy bruisers beside the depraved creature we seek." Holmes stirred nervously. "Another, Watson, a blood-thirsty tiger loose in the jungle of London."

The dread name came into my head. "Professor Moriarty?"

"Moriarty is not involved in this. I have checked his activities, and his whereabouts. He is occupied elsewhere. No, it is not the Professor. I am certain our man is one of four."

"To which four do you refer?"

Holmes shrugged his shoulders. "What does it matter so long as I am unable to put my hands upon him?"

The physical strain had begun to wear on him. Holmes lay back in the chair and gazed, heavy-lidded, at the ceiling. But the fatigue did not extend to his mental faculties.

"This 'tiger' you refer to," said I. "What does it profit him to go about killing luckless prostitutes?"

"The affair is far more tangled than that, Watson. There are several dark threads that twist and turn in this maze."

"That repulsive simpleton at the hostel," I muttered.

Holmes's smile was humourless. "I fear, my dear Watson, that you have your finger upon the wrong thread."

"I cannot believe that Michael Osbourne is in no way involved!"

"Involved, yes. But——"

He did not finish, because at that moment the bell sounded below. Mrs. Hudson was soon opening the door. Holmes said, "I have been expecting a visitor; he is prompt. Pray remain, Watson. My jacket, if you please. I must not look like a street-brawler who has dropped in for medical treatment."

By the time he had gotten into the garment and lighted his pipe, Mrs. Hudson was ushering a tall, blond, good-looking chap into our parlour. I estimated him to be in his mid-thirties. He was assuredly a man of breeding; except for a single startled glance, he made no reference to Holmes's battered appearance.

"Ah," said Holmes. "Mr. Timothy Wentworth, I believe. You are welcome, sir. Take the seat by the fire. The air is damp and chill this morning. This is my friend and colleague, Dr. Watson."

Mr. Timothy Wentworth bowed acknowledgement, and took the proffered chair. "Your name is famous, sir," said he, "as is that of Dr. Watson. I am honoured to make your acquaintance. But I have a busy schedule in Paris, and I tore myself away only because of my regard for a friend, Michael Osbourne. I have been utterly mystified by his unheralded disappearance from Paris. If I can do anything to help Michael, I shall consider the Channel crossing well worth the inconvenience."

"A most admirable loyalty," said Holmes. "Perhaps we can enlighten each other, Mr. Wentworth. If you will tell us what you know about Michael's sojourn in Paris, I shall pick up for you the end of his story."

"Very well. I met Michael some two years ago, when we enrolled together at the Sorbonne. I think I was attracted to him because we were opposites. I am myself somewhat retiring; indeed, my friends consider me shy. On the other hand, Michael was possessed of a fiery spirit, sometimes gay, sometimes bordering upon the violent, when he felt that he had been put upon. He never left the least doubt as to his opinion on any subject; however, by making allowances for each other's short-comings, we got on well together. Michael was very good for me."

"And you for him, sir, I've no doubt," said Holmes. "But, tell me. What did you learn of his personal life?"

"We were candid with each other. I quickly learned that he was second son to a British nobleman."

"Was he embittered by the misfortune of second birth?"

Mr. Timothy Wentworth frowned as he considered his answer. "I should have to say yes, and yet no. Michael had a tendency to break out, one might say, to go wild. His breeding and background forbade such behaviour, and caused a guilt to arise within him. He needed to palliate that guilt, and his position as second son was something against which to revolt, and thus justify his wildness." Our young guest stopped self-consciously. "I'm putting it badly, I fear."

"To the contrary," Holmes assured him, "you express yourself with admirable clarity. And I may assume, may I not, that Michael harboured no bitterness against either his father or his elder brother?"

"I am sure he did not. But I can also understand the contrary opinion of the Duke of Shires. I see the Duke as a man of proud, even haughty, spirit, preoccupied with the honour of his name.''

''You see him exactly as he is. But pray go on.''

''Well, then there came Michael's alliance with that woman.'' Timothy Wentworth's distaste was apparent in his tone. ''Michael met her in some Pigalle rat's-nest. He told me about her the following day. I thought nothing of it, considering it a mere dalliance. But I now see Michael's withdrawal from our friendship as dating from that time. It was slow when measured in hours and days, but swift enough as I look back upon it—from the time he told me of the meeting, to the morning he packed his clothes in our digs, and told me that he had married the woman.''

I interjected a comment. ''You must have been shocked, sir.''

''Shocked is hardly the term. I was stunned. When I found words with which to remonstrate, he snarled at me to mind my own affairs, and left.'' Here, a deep regret appeared in the young man's honest, blue eyes. ''It was the termination of our friendship.''

''You did not see him again?'' murmured Holmes.

''I tried, and did see him briefly on two other occasions. Word of that sort of thing, of course, cannot be kept secret—a short time later, Michael was dropped from the Sorbonne. When I heard this, I made a point of seeking him out. I found him living in an unspeakable sty on the Left Bank. He was alone, but I presume his wife was living there with him. He was half-drunk, and received me with hostility—a different man by far from the one I had known. I could not even begin to reach him, so I placed some money upon the table and left. A fortnight later, I met him in the street, near the Sorbonne. His appearance cut me to the quick. It was as if a lost soul had returned to gaze wistfully upon the opportunities he had thrown away. His defiance remained, however. When I attempted to accost him, he snarled at me and slunk away.''

"I gather, then, that you have never laid eyes upon his wife?"

"No, but there were rumours concerning her. It was whispered about that the woman had a confederate, a man with whom she had consorted both before and after her marriage. I have no certain knowledge of that, however." He paused, as though pondering the tragic fate of his friend. Then he raised his head and spoke with more spirit. "I believe that Michael was somehow put upon in that disastrous marriage, that in no way did he deliberately seek to bring shame upon his illustrious name."

"And I believe," said Holmes, "that I can reassure you on that point. Michael's kit of surgical instruments has recently come into my possession, and I discovered upon examining it that he had carefully covered the emblazoned coat of arms it bore with a piece of velvet cloth."

Timothy Wentworth's eyes widened. "He was forced to dispose of his instruments?"

"The point I wish to make," continued Holmes, "is that this very act of concealing the insignia indicates, not only shame, but an effort to protect the name he has been accused of seeking to disgrace."

"It is intolerable that his father will not believe that. But now, sir, I have told you all I know, and I am eager to hear what you have to tell me."

Holmes was markedly reluctant to reply. He arose from his chair and took a quick turn across the room. Then he stopped. "There is nothing you can do for Michael, sir," said he.

Wentworth seemed ready to spring up. "But we made a bargain!"

"Michael, some time after you last saw him, suffered an accident. At present he is little more than mindless flesh, Mr. Wentworth. He remembers nothing of his past, and his memory will probably never return. But he is being well cared-for. As I have said, there is nothing you can do for him, and in suggesting that you do not see him I am attempting to spare you further distress.''

Timothy Wentworth turned his frown upon the floor, considering Holmes's advice. I was glad when he sighed, and said, ''Very well, Mr. Holmes, then it is over.'' Wentworth came to his feet and extended his hand. ''But if there is anything I can ever do, sir, please get in touch with me.'

''You may depend upon it.''

After the young man left, Holmes stood in silence, gazing from the window at our departing visitor. When he spoke, it was in so low a voice that I could scarcely catch his words. ''The more grievous our faults, Watson, the closer a true friend clings.''

''What was that, Holmes?''

''A passing thought.''

''Well, I must say that young Wentworth's account changes my opinion of Michael Osbourne.''

Holmes returned to the fire to stab a restless poker at the log. ''But I am sure you realise that his hearsay was of far more significance than his fact.''

''I confess I do not follow you.''

''The rumour that the woman, Michael's wife, had a male accomplice throws additional light upon the problem. Now, who could this man be, Watson, other than our elusive missing link? Our tiger who set assassins upon us?''

''But how did he know?''

''Ah, yes. How did he discover that I was on his trail before I knew it myself? I think we shall make another call upon the Duke of Shires, at his town-house in Berkeley Square.''

We were not destined, however, to make that visit. At that moment the bell again rang downstairs, and we heard Mrs. Hudson again answer the door. A great clatter followed; the caller had rushed past our land-lady and was taking the stairs two at a time. Our door burst open, and there he stood, a thin and pimple-faced youth with a great air of defiance about him. His manner was such that my hand moved automatically toward a fire-iron.

"W'ich o' you gents is Mr. Sherlock 'Olmes?"

"I, my lad," answered Holmes; and the youth extended a parcel wrapped in brown paper. "This 'ere's to be given to yer, then."

Holmes took the parcel and opened it with no ceremony.

"The missing scalpel!" cried I.

Holmes had no chance to reply. The messenger had bolted, and Holmes whirled about. "Wait!" he shouted. "I must speak with you! You shall not be harmed!"

But the boy was gone. Holmes rushed from the room. I hastened to the window, and beheld the youth fleeing down the street as though all the devils of Hell were after him, Sherlock Holmes swiftly in his wake.

Ellery's Legman Legs It Again

"Rachel?"

She looked back over her shoulder. "Grant! Grant Ames!"

"Just thought I'd drop in," said the playboy.

"So sweet of you!"

Rachel Hager wore a pair of blue jeans and a tight sweater. She had long legs and a slim body, but there were plenty of curves. Her mouth was full and wide, and her eyes were an odd off-brown, and her nose was pugged. She looked like a madonna who had run into a door.

This pleasing paradox did not escape Grant Ames III. She didn't look like this the other day, he thought, and pointed to what she had been doing in the backyard.

"I didn't know you grew roses."

Her laugh revealed the most beautiful buck teeth.

"I try. Heavens, how I try. But my thumb stays its natural color. What brings you into the wilds of New Rochelle?" She slipped off her gloves and lifted a strand of hair off her forehead. The shade was mouse brown, but Grant was sure that, bottled, it would have lined them up at the cosmetic counters.

"Just driving by. Hardly got a chance to say hello at Lita's the other day.'

"I was there by accident. I couldn't stay around."

"I noticed you didn't swim."

"Why, Grant! Such a nice compliment. Most girls are noticed when they do. How about the patio? I'll bring you a drink. Scotch, isn't it?"

"At times, but at the moment I could do with a frosty iced tea."

"Really? I'll be right back."

When she returned, Grant watched her cross her long legs in a lawn chair too low to be comfortable. For some reason he was stirred. "Lovely garden."

That enchanting buck-toothed laugh again. "You should see it after the kids leave."

"The kids?"

"From the orphanage. We bring a group over once a week, and it's *wild*. They do respect the roses, though. One little girl just sits and stares. Yesterday I gave her an ice cream cone and it melted all over her hand. It was that Mammoth Tropicana over there. She tried to kiss it."

"I didn't know you worked with children." As a matter of cold fact, Grant had not had the least idea what Rachel did, and until now had not cared a whit.

"I'm sure I get more out of it than they do. I'm working on my Master's now, and I have time to spare. I was thinking of the Peace Corps. But there's so much to do right here in the U.S.—in town, in fact."

"You're gorgeous," Grant unbelievingly heard himself mutter.

The girl looked up quickly, not sure she had heard him right. "What on earth are you talking about?"

"I was trying to remember how many times I've seen you. The first was at Snow Mountain, wasn't it?"

"I think it was."

"Jilly Hart introduced us."

"I remember because I broke my ankle that trip. But how can *you* possibly remember? With your harem?"

"I'm not entirely irresponsible," said Grant stuffily.

"I mean, why should you? Me? You've never shown—"

"Would you do me a favor, Rachel?"

"What?" asked Rachel suspiciously.

"Go back and do what you were doing when I got here. Dig at your roses. I want to sit here and look at you."

"Is this your latest line?"

"It's very strange," he mumbled.

"Grant. What did you come here for?"

"Damned if I can remember.'

"I'll bet you can," the girl said, a little grimly. "Try."

"Let me see. Oh! To ask if you'd put a brown manila envelope on the seat of my Jag at Lita's. But the hell with that. What kind of fertilizer do you use?"

Rachel squatted. Grant had visions of *Vogue*. "I have no formula. I just keep mixing. Grant, what's the matter with you?"

He looked down at the lovely brown hand on his arm.

My God! It's happened!

"If I come back at seven, will you have a frock on?" he asked.

She looked at him with a dawning light. "Of course, Grant," she said softly.

"And you won't mind my showing you off here and there?"

The hand squeezed. "You darling."

"Ellery, I've found her, I've found her!" Grant Ames III babbled over the telephone.

"Found whom?'

"THE Woman!"

"Who put the envelope in your car?" Ellery said in a peculiar voice.

"Who put what?" said Grant.

"The envelope. The journal."

"Oh." There was a silence. "You know what, Ellery?"

"No. What?"

"I didn't find out."

Ellery went back to Dr. Watson, shrugging.

CHAPTER IX

THE LAIR OF THE RIPPER

I could do nothing but wait. Infected by Holmes's fever of impatience, trying to occupy the hours, I assessed the situation, endeavouring to apply the methods I had so long witnessed Holmes employ.

His identification of the Ripper as one of four men came in for its share of my ponderings, you may be sure, but I was confused by other elements of the puzzle—Mycroft's assertion that, as yet, his brother did not have all the pieces, and Holmes's yearning to come to grips with the "tiger" prowling London's byways. If the Ripper was one of four persons whom Holmes had already met, where did the "tiger" fit in? And why was it necessary to locate him before the Ripper could be brought to book?

Elation would have been mine, had I known that at the moment I myself held the key. But I was blind to both the key and its significance; and, when this knowledge did come to me, it brought only humiliation.

Thus I fretted away the hours with but a single break in the monotony. This occurred when a note was delivered to Baker Street by a smartly-uniformed pageboy. "Sir, a message from Mr. Mycroft Holmes to Mr. Sherlock Holmes."

"Mr. Holmes is absent at the moment," said I. "You may leave the note."

After I had dismissed the page, I examined the note. It was in a sealed envelope, from the Foreign Office. The Foreign Office was where Mycroft had his being.

My fingers were itching to tear the flap, but of course I did not. I pocketed the missive and went on with my pacing. The hours passed, with no sign of Holmes. At times, I went to the window and watched the fog that was settling in over London. As twilight fell, I remarked to myself what a fortuitous night this would be for the Ripper.

This had evidently occurred to the maniac also. Quite dramatically, upon the heels of my thought, there came a message from Holmes, delivered by an urchin. I tore it open with trembling fingers as the boy waited.

> *My dear Watson:*
>   *You will give this boy a half-crown for his trouble, and meet me post-haste at the Montague Street morgue.*
>   *Sherlock Holmes.*

The urchin, a bright-faced lad, had never before received such a handsome *pourboire*, I am certain. In my relief, I gave him a crown.

In no time at all I was in a hansom, urging the cabman on through the thickening pea-soup that befogged the streets. Fortunately, the jehu had the instincts of a homing-pigeon. In a remarkably short time he said, "The right-'and door, guv'ner. Walk strite on and watch yer nose, or yer'll bang into the ruddy gite."

I found the gate with some groping, went in, and through the court, and found Holmes by the raised table in the mortuary.

"Still another, Watson," was his portentous greeting.

Dr. Murray and the imbecile were also present. Murray stood silently by the table, but Michael-Pierre cringed by the wall, naked fear upon his face.

As Murray remained motionless, Holmes frowned. Said he, sharply, "Dr. Murray, you do not question Dr. Watson's stomach for it?"

"No, no," replied Murray, and drew back the sheet.

But my stomach was tested, nonetheless. It was the most incredible job of butchery on a human body that the sane mind could conceive. With demented skill the Ripper had gone berserk. In decency, I refrain from setting down the details, save for my gasp, "The missing breast, Holmes!"

"This time," responded Holmes, grimly, "our madman took away a trophy."

I could endure it no longer; I stepped down from the platform. Holmes followed. "In God's name, Holmes," cried I, "the beast must be stopped!"

"You are in good company with that prayer, Watson."

"Has Scotland Yard been of any aid to you?"

"Rather, Watson," replied he, sombrely, "have I been of any aid to Scotland Yard? Very little, I fear."

We took our leave of Murray and the imbecile. In the swirling fog of the street, I shuddered. "That wreck who was once Michael Osbourne . . . Is it my fancy, Holmes, or did he crouch there for all the world like Murray's faithful hound, expecting a kick for some transgression?"

"Or," replied Holmes, "like a faithful hound sensing his master's horror and seeking to share it. You are obsessed with Michael Osbourne, Watson."

"Perhaps I am." I forced my mind to turn back. "Holmes, were you able to apprehend the messenger who took to his heels?"

"I clung to his trail for several blocks, but he knew London's labyrinths as well as I. I lost him."

"And you spent the rest of the day how, may I ask?"

"A portion of it in the Bow Street Library, attempting to devise a pattern from a hypothetical projection of the madman's brain."

He began walking slowly through the fog-bank, I by his side. "Where are we going, Holmes?"

"To a particular section of Whitechapel. I laid out the pattern, Watson, a positioning of all the known Ripper murders, super-imposed upon a map of the area which they cover. I spent several hours studying it. I am convinced that the Ripper works from a central location, a room, or a flat, a sanctuary from which he ventures forth and to which he returns."

"You propose to search?"

"Yes. We shall see if shoe-leather will reward us where the arm-chair has failed."

"In this fog it will take leg-work indeed."

"True, but we have certain advantages on our side. For example, I have made it a point to question the witnesses."

This startled me. "Holmes! I did not know there were any."

"Of a sort, Watson, of a sort. On several occasions, the Ripper has worked perilously close to detection. In fact, I suspect that he deliberately arranges his murders in that fashion, out of contempt and bravado. You will recall our brush with him."

"Well do I!"

"At any rate, I have decided, from the sounds of his retreating footsteps, that he moves from the perimeter of a circle toward its centre. It is within the centre of that circle that we shall search."

Thus we plunged, that fog-choked night, towards the cesspools of Whitechapel into which the human sewage from the great city drained. Holmes moved with a sure-footedness that bespoke his familiarity with those malodorous depths. We were silent, save when Holmes paused to inquire, "By the way, Watson I trust you thought to drop a revolver into your pocket."

"It was the last thing I did before I left to join you."

"I, too, am armed."

We ventured first into what proved to be an opium-den. Struggling for breath in the foul fumes, I followed as Holmes moved down the line of bunks, where the addicted victims lay wrapped in their shabby dreams. Holmes paused here and there for a closer inspection. To some he spoke a word; at times, he received a word in return. When we left, he appeared to have garnered nothing of value.

From there we invaded a series of low public-houses, where we were greeted for the most part by sullen silence. Here, also, Holmes spoke *sotto voce* with certain of the individuals we came upon, in such a manner that I was sure he was acquainted with some of them. On occasion, a coin or two passed from his hand into a filthy palm. But always we moved on.

We had left the third dive, more evil than the others, when I could contain myself no longer.

"Holmes, the Ripper is not a cause. He is a result."

"A result, Watson?"

"Of such corrupt places as these."

Holmes shrugged his shoulders.

"Does it not stir you to indignation?"

"I would of course welcome a sweeping change, Watson. Perchance in some future, enlightened time, it will come about. In the meanwhile, I am a realist. Utopia is a luxury upon which I have no time to dream."

Before I could reply, he pushed open another door, and we found ourselves in a brothel. The reek of cheap scent almost staggered me. The room into which we entered was a parlour, with half a dozen partially-naked females seated about in lewd poses as they awaited whoever might emerge from the fog.

Quite candidly, I kept shifting my eyes from the inviting smiles and lascivious gestures that greeted us on all sides. Holmes rose to the occasion with his usual equanimity. Giving his attention to one of the girls, a pale, pretty little thing who sat clad in nothing but a carelessly open robe, he said, "Good-evening, Jenny."

"Evenin', Mr.'Olmes."

"That address I gave you, of the doctor. Did you visit him?"

"That I did, sir. 'E gave me a clean bill o' 'ealth, 'e did."

A beaded curtain parted and a fat *madame* with eyes like raisins stood regarding us. "What brings you out on a night like this, Mr. Holmes?"

"I am sure you know, Leona."

Her face turned sulky. "Why do you think my girls are off the streets? I don't want to lose any of them!"

A plump, over-painted creature spoke angrily. "H'it's a bloody shyme, h'it is—a poor gel gettin' pushed by bobbies all the time."

Another commented, "Better than a bloody blade in yer gut, dearie."

"Almost 'ad me a gent, h'I did, wot lives at the Pacquin. 'E was a-goin' up the stairs, all w'ite tie an' cape, 'e was, an 'e stops w'en 'e sees me. Then this bobby shoves 'is dish outa the fog. 'Ere now, dearie,' says 'e. 'Off to yer crib. This is no night to be about.' " The girl spat viciously upon the floor.

Holmes's voice was even as he said, "The gentleman fled, I presume?"

"Up t' 'is room, w'ere else? But not a-takin' me with 'im!"

"An odd place for a gentleman to live, would you not say?"

The girl wiped her mouth with the back of her hand. " 'E can live w'ere 'e pleases, blarst 'is eyes!"

Holmes was already moving towards the door. As he passed me, he whispered, "Come, Watson. Hurry, hurry!"

Back in the fog, he gripped my hand and pulled me recklessly forward. "We have him, Watson! I'm certain of it! Visits—questions—a dropped comment—and we come upon the trail of a fiend who can do many things. But making himself invisible is not one of them!"

Sheer exultancy rang out from every word as Holmes dragged me after him. A few moments later I found myself stumbling up a flight of narrow stairs against a wooden wall.

The exertion of the chase had taxed even Holmes's superb stamina; and, as we climbed, he gasped out his words. "This Pacquin is a sordid rooming-house, Watson. Whitechapel abounds with them. Fortunately, I was familiar with the name."

I glanced upwards, and saw that we were approaching a partly-open door. We reached the top of the stairs, and Holmes hurled himself inside. I staggered after him.

"What accursed luck!" cried he. "Some-one has been here before us!"

Not in all our days together had I seen Holmes present such an image of bitter frustration. He loomed in the middle of a small, shabbily-furnished room, revolver in hand, grey eyes a-blaze.

"If this was the lair of the Ripper," cried I, "he has fled."

"And for good, no doubt of that!"

"Perhaps Lestrade was also on his trial."

"I wager not! Lestrade is off bumbling through some alley."

The room had been well-torn up in the Ripper's haste to get away. As I sought words to ease Holmes's disappointment, he grimly took my arm. "If you doubt that the maniac operates from this den, Watson, look there."

I followed his pointing finger, and saw it. The grisly trophy—the breast missing from the corpse in the Montague Street morgue.

I have seen violence and death enough, but this was worse. There was no heat here, no anger; only dank horror, and my stomach revolted against it.

"I must leave, Holmes. I shall wait for you below."

"There is no point in my remaining, either. What is to be seen here is to be seen quickly. Our quarry is far too cunning to leave the slightest clew behind."

At that moment, possibly because my mind sought a diversion, I remembered the message. "By the way, Holmes, a messenger brought a note to Baker Street this afternoon from your brother Mycroft. In the excitement, I forgot." I handed him the envelope forthwith, and he tore it open.

If I expected his thanks, I was disappointed. After reading the missive, Holmes raised cold eyes. "Would you care to hear what Mycroft writes?"

"Indeed I would."

"The note reads: 'Dear Sherlock: A bit of information has come to me, in a way I shall explain later, which will be of value to you. A man named Max Klein is the proprietor of a Whitechapel sink named The Angel and Crown. Klein, however, purchased the place only recently; some four months ago, in fact, Your brother, Mycroft.'"

I was too confounded to suspect which way the wind lay. I give myself that grace, at least, because so much more can be explained only by admitting to an abysmal stupidity. At any rate, I blurted forth, "Oh, yes, Holmes. I was aware of that. I got the information from the girl with whom I talked during my visit to The Angel and Crown."

"Did you indeed?" asked Holmes, dangerously.

"A redoubtable fellow, this Klein. It occurred to me that it had not taken him long to impress his personality upon the place."

Holmes exploded, raising his fists. "Great God in Heaven! I wade knee-deep in idiots!"

The wind I had not suspected struck me with its blast. My mouth dropped open. I managed feebly to say, "Holmes, I do not understand!"

"Then there is no hope for you, Watson! First, you garner the exact information that would have enabled me to solve this case, and you blithely keep it to yourself. Then, you forget to give me the note containing that same vital fact. Watson! Watson! Whose side are you on?"

If I had been confused before, I was now completely at sea. No protest was possible; and defiance, defence of my self-esteem, was out of the question.

But Holmes was never a man to belabour a point. "The Angel and Crown, Watson!" cried he, leaping toward the door. "No, to the morgue first! We shall present that devil with a sample of his own handi-work!"

Ellery Hears from the Past

The doorbell rang.

Ellery slammed down the journal. It was undoubt-edly that alcoholic blotter again. He debated answer-ing, glanced guiltily at his typewriter, and went out into the foyer and opened the door.

It was not Grant Ames, but a Western Union mes-senger. Ellery scribbled his name and read the un-signed telegram.

WILL YOU FOR BLANK'S SAKE PLUG IN YOUR TELEPHONE QUESTION MARK AM GOING STIR CRAZY EXCLAMATION POINT

"No answer," Ellery said. He tipped the messenger and went straightway to obey the Inspector's order.

Muttering to himself, he also plugged in his shaver and plowed its snarling head through his beard. As long as he keeps phoning, he thought, he's still in Bermuda. If I can browbeat him into just one more week . . .

The revitalized phone rang. Ellery snapped the shaver off and answered. Good old dad.

But it was not good old dad. It was the quavering voice of an old lady. A very old lady.

"Mr. Queen?"

"Yes?"

"I have been expecting to hear from you."

"I must apologize," Ellery said, "I planned to call on you, but Dr. Watson's manuscript caught me at a most awkward time. I'm up to my ears in a manuscript of my own."

"I'm so sorry."

"I'm the one who's sorry, believe me."

"Then you have not had the time to read it?"

"On the contrary, it was a temptation I couldn't resist, deadline or not. I've had to ration myself, though. I still have two chapters to go."

"Perhaps, Mr. Queen, with your time so limited, I'd best wait until you have completed your own work."

"No—please. My problems there are solved. And I've looked forward to this chat."

The cultured old voice chuckled. "I needn't mention that my advance order for your new mystery has been placed, as always. Or would you consider that deliberate flattery? I hope not!"

"You're very kind."

There was something under the quiet, precise diction, the restraint, the discipline, something Ellery felt sure of, possibly because he had been expecting it—a tension, as if the old lady were almost to the snapping point.

"Were you at all troubled as to the authenticity of the manuscript, Mr. Queen?"

"At first, frankly, when Grant brought me the manuscript, I thought it a forgery. I soon changed my mind."

"You must have thought my mode of delivery eccentric."

"Not after reading the opening chapter," Ellery said. "I understood completely."

The old voice trembled. "Mr. Queen, *he did not do it. He was not the Ripper!*"

Ellery tried to soothe her distress. "It's been so many years. Does it really matter any longer?"

"It does, it does! Injustice always matters. Time changes many things, but not that."

Ellery reminded her that he had not yet finished the manuscript.

"But you know, I feel that you know."

"I'm aware in which direction the finger's pointing."

"And keeps pointing, to the end. But it is not true, Mr. Queen! Sherlock Holmes was wrong for once. Dr. Watson was not to blame. He merely recorded the case as it unfolded—as Mr. Holmes dictated. But Mr. Holmes failed, and did a great injustice."

"But the manuscript was never published—"

"That makes no genuine difference, Mr. Queen. The verdict was known, the stain indelibly imprinted."

"But what can I do? No one can change yesterday."

"The manuscript is all I have, sir! The manuscript and that abominable lie! Sherlock Holmes was not infallible. Who is? God reserves infallibility for Himself alone. The truth must be hidden in the manuscript somewhere, Mr. Queen. I am pleading with you to find it."

"I'll do my best."

"Thank you, young man. Thank you so very much."

With the connection safely broken, Ellery slammed down the phone and glared at it. It was a miserable invention. He was a nice guy who did good works and was kind to his father, and now this.

He was inclined to wish a pox on the head of John Watson, M.D., and all adoring Boswells (where was his?); but then he sighed, remembering the old lady's trembling voice, and sat down with Watson's manuscript again.

CHAPTER X

THE TIGER OF THE ANGEL
AND CROWN

"I earnestly hope, my dear fellow, that you will accept my apology."

These words from Holmes were the most welcome I had ever received. We were back in the street, pushing along through the fog, as there were no hansoms cruising Whitechapel that night.

"You were totally justified, Holmes."

"To the contrary. I displayed a childish petulance that ill becomes a grown man. Blaming others for one's own mistakes is indefensible. The information, which you so readily extracted from the girl Polly, I should have had the intelligence to come by long ago. You actually proved an ability to do my work far better than I have done it myself."

All of which was specious; but Holmes's praise salved my pride, nonetheless.

"I cannot accept the accolade, Holmes," I protested. "It did not occur to me that Klein was indicated as your missing link."

"That," said Holmes, still over-generous, "was because you neglected to turn your perceptions in the proper direction. We were looking for a strong man, a man brutal and remorseless. Klein, from what you told me, filled that bill; also, from what I myself observed in the pub. Others in Whitechapel would qualify as equally vicious, although it is true that the other bit of information points directly to Klein."

"His recent purchase of the pub? When you explain, it becomes quite simple."

"What happened is now predictable, with only the smallest percentage in favour of error. Klein saw an opportunity in the person of Michael Osbourne. Both Michael and, beyond all doubt, the prostitute Angela, of whom Michael became enamoured, were weak individuals, easily controlled by this cruelly dominating man. It was Klein who engineered the infamous marriage that ruined Michael Osbourne."

"But to what purpose?"

"Blackmail, Watson! The plan failed when Michael stood upon his better nature and refused his coöperation. The plot was saved by Klein only through sheer luck, I am certain. Thus he was able to extort enough money to buy The Angel and Crown, and has no doubt further feathered his noisome nest since."

"But so much is still unanswered, Holmes. Michael—reduced to a state of imbecility. His wife Angela—whom, I remind you, we have yet to locate—hideously scarred."

"In good time, Watson, in good time."

My confusion was the more compounded by Holmes's tone of confidence.

"Their present plight, you may be sure, is the result of Klein's rage at being thwarted by Michael's refusal to be a party to the blackmail scheme. No doubt it was Klein who administered that brutal beating to Michael which brought on his imbecility. How Angela became disfigured is not so evident, but I suggest that she went to Michael's defence."

At this moment, we walked out of the fog into a pocket of visibility, and saw the gate to the mortuary. I shuddered. "And now, Holmes, you plan to transport the body of that poor girl to The Angel and Crown?"

"Hardly, Watson," said he, absently.

"But you mentioned confronting Klein with his handiwork."

"That we shall do, I promise you."

Shaking my head, I followed Holmes through the

mortuary into the hostel, where we found Dr. Murray ministering to the blackened eye of a man who had probably imbibed violence with his pint in some pub.

"Is Michael Osbourne on the premises?" demanded Holmes.

Dr. Murray was haggard. Over-work, and the thankless task of caring for the uncared-for, were taking their toll. Said he, "A short time ago, I would not have recognized that name——"

"Please," interrupted Holmes. "Time is paramount, Dr. Murray. I must take him away with us."

"To-night? Now?"

"There have been certain developments, Doctor. Before dawn, the Ripper will have been run to earth. The account must be settled with the beast responsible for Whitechapel's blood-bath."

Dr. Murray was as bewildered as I. "I do not understand. Do you mean, sir, that the Ripper is a creature of an even greater villain?"

"In a sense. Have you seen Inspector Lestrade lately?"

"He was here an hour ago. He is undoubtedly out in the fog somewhere."

"Tell him, should he return, to follow me to The Angel and Crown."

"But why are you taking Michael Osbourne with you?"

"To confront his wife," said Holmes, impatiently. "Where is he, man? We waste precious time!"

"You will find him in the small room off this end of the mortuary. That is where he sleeps."

We found the imbecile there, and Holmes shook him gently awake. "Angela is waiting for you," said he.

There was no flicker of understanding in the vacant eyes; but, with the trust of a child, he accompanied us into the fog. It was now so thick that we depended completely upon Holmes's hound-like senses to keep us on our course. And, so sinister was the atmosphere

of London that night, I half-expected to feel the bite
of a blade between my ribs at any moment.

But my curiosity was strong. I ventured a query.
"Holmes, I assume that you expect to find Angela
Osbourne at The Angel and Crown."

"I am certain of it."

"But what purpose is served by facing her with Michael?"

"The woman may be reluctant to speak. There will
be a certain shock-value in suddenly confronting her
with her husband."

"I see," said I, although I did not, quite; and lapsed
back into silence.

At last there was the sound of a hand tapping upon
wood, and I heard Holmes say, "This is it, Watson.
Now we search."

A faintly-glowing window indicated that it was a
domicile of some sort. Said I, "Was that the front
door you tapped upon?"

"It was, but we must find another. I wish to reach
the upper rooms unseen."

We pawed along the wall and around a corner. Then
a breeze stirred the fog, thinning it.

Holmes had thought to borrow a dark lantern during
our visit to the hostel, although he had not used it
during our journey. It might well have brought us to
the unwelcome attention of foot-pads. It now served
us in good stead, outlining a rear door, apparently used
for the delivery of beer-kegs and spirits. Holmes
pushed the panel open and reached inside. "The hasp
has been recently broken," said he; and we went
through stealthily.

We were in a store-room. I could hear the muffled
noise from the public-room, but it appeared that our
presence had gone undetected. Holmes quickly found
a laddered ascent to the upper storey. We climbed it
with caution, crept through a trap-door, and found ourselves at the end of a dimly-lit corridor.

''Wait here with Michael,'' whispered Holmes. He soon returned. ''Come!''

We followed him to a closed door; a line of light shone upon our boot-tips. Holmes pressed us back against the wall and tapped upon the panel. There was quick movement inside. The door opened, and a female voice queried, ''Tommy?''

Holmes's hand was in like a snake and locked over a shadowed face. ''Do not scream, Madam,'' said he, in a commanding whisper. ''We mean you no harm. But we must speak to you.''

Holmes warily relaxed the pressure of his hand. The woman's voice asked, ''Who are you?'' in understandable fear.

''I am Sherlock Holmes. I have brought your husband.''

I heard a gasp. ''You have brought Michael—here? In God's name, why?''

''It was the prudent thing to do.''

Holmes entered the room and nodded to me to follow. Grasping Michael's arm, I did so.

Two oil-lamps were burning, and in their light I saw a woman, wearing a veil whose gauzy texture did not quite conceal a hideous scar. It was undoubtedly Angela Osbourne.

At the sight of the imbecile—her husband—she grasped the arms of the chair in which she sat, and half-arose. But then she sank back and sat with the rigidity of a corpse, her hands gripped together.

''He does not recognise me,'' she murmured in despair.

Michael Osbourne stood silently by me, regarding her with his empty eyes.

''As well you know, Madam,'' said Holmes. ''But the time is short. You must speak. We know that Klein is responsible for both your husband's condition and your disfigurement. Tell me about the interlude in Paris.''

The woman wrung her hands. ''I will not waste time

making excuses for myself, sir. There are none. As
you can perhaps see, I am not like those poor girls
downstairs who fell into their shameful calling through
poverty and ignorance. I am what I have become because of that beast, Max Klein.

"You wish to know about Paris. I went there because Max had arranged an assignation for me with a
wealthy French merchant. Whilst this was taking
place, I met Michael Osbourne, and he was taken with
me. Believe me, sir, I had no intention of shaming
him; but when Max Klein arrived in Paris, he saw an
opportunity to use the smitten youth for his own ends.
Our marriage was the first step in his plan, and he
compelled me to use my wiles. Michael and I were
married, despite my tearful protestations to Max.

"Then, with Michael safely in his clutch, Max
sprang his trap. It was the most blatant blackmail, Mr.
Holmes. He would acquaint the Duke of Shires with
the facts, said he, and threaten to reveal his son's wife
for what I was, parading me before all the world, unless his Grace paid."

"But this never came about," said Holmes, eyes
gleaming.

"No. Michael had more spine than Max had anticipated. He threatened to kill Max, even made the attempt. It was a dreadful scene! Michael stood no
chance before Max's brute strength. He felled Michael
with a blow. But then Max's temper, his sheer savagery of nature, seized him, and he administered the
terrible beating that resulted in Michael's present condition. Indeed, the beating would have ended in Michael's death, had I not intervened. Whereupon Max
plucked a knife from the table, and rendered me as
you see. His rage left him in the nick of time, averting
a double murder."

"His beating of Michael and mutilation of you did
not make him abandon his plan?"

"No, Mr. Holmes. Had it done so, I am sure Max
would have left us in Paris. Instead, using the consid-

erable sum of money he took from Michael, he brought us back to Whitechapel and purchased this public-house."

"That money was not gained through blackmail, then?"

"No. The Duke of Shires was generous with Michael until he disowned him. Max stripped Michael of every penny he had. Then he imprisoned us here, in The Angel and Crown, plotting, no doubt, to go on with whatever infamous plan he had in mind."

"You said he brought you *back* to Whitechapel, Mrs. Osbourne," said Holmes. "Is this Klein's habitat?"

"Oh, yes, he was born here. He knows its every street and alley. He is greatly feared in this district. There are few who dare cross him."

"What was his plan? Do you know?"

"Blackmail, I am sure. But something happened to balk him; I never discovered what it was. Then Max came to me one morning, fiercely elated. He said that his fortune was made, that he needed Michael no longer, and planned to murder him. I pleaded with him. Perhaps I was able to touch off a spark of humanity in his heart; in any case, he humoured me, as he put it, and delivered Michael to Dr. Murray's hostel, knowing his memory was gone."

"The good fortune that elated Klein, Mrs. Osbourne. What was its nature?"

"I never learned. I did ask him if the Duke of Shires had agreed to pay him a large sum of money. He slapped me and told me to mind my affairs."

"Since that time you have been a prisoner in this place?"

"A willing one, Mr. Holmes. Max has forbidden me to leave this room, it is true, but my mutilated face is my true gaoler." The woman bowed her veiled head. "That is all I can tell you, sir."

"Not quite, Madam!"

"What else?" said she, head rising.

"There is the matter of the surgeon's-case. Also, of an unsigned note informing Lord Carfax of his brother Michael's whereabouts."

"I have no idea, sir——" she began.

"Pray do not evade me, Madam. I must know everything."

"There seems to be no way of keeping a secret from you!" cried Angela Osbourne. "What are you, man or devil? If Max were to get wind of this, he would surely kill me!"

"We are your friends, Madam. He will not hear it from us. How did you discover that the case had been pledged with Joseph Beck?"

"I have a friend. He comes here at the risk of his life, to talk to me and do my errands."

"No doubt the 'Tommy' you expected when I knocked upon your door?"

"Please do not involve him, Mr. Holmes, I beg of you!"

"I see no reason to involve him. But I wish to know more about him."

"Tommy helps out at times at the Montague Street Hostel."

"You sent him there originally?"

"Yes, for news of Michael. After Max delivered him to the hostel, I slipped out one night, at great risk to myself, and posted the note you refer to. I felt I owed Michael at least that. I was sure Max would never find out, because I could see no way in which Lord Carfax might trace us, with Michael's memory gone."

"And the surgeon's-case?"

"Tommy overheard Sally Young discuss with Dr. Murray the possibility of pawning it. It occurred to me that it might be a means of interesting you to turn your talents, Mr. Holmes, to the apprehension of Jack the Ripper. Again I slipped out, redeemed the case, and posted it to you."

"Removing the post-mortem scalpel was deliberate?"

"Yes. I was sure you would understand. Then, when I heard no word of your entrance into the case, I became desperate, and I sent the missing scalpel to you."

Holmes leaned forward, his hawk's-face keen. *"Madam, when did you decide that Max Klein is the Ripper?"*

Angela Osbourne put her hands to her veil, and moaned. "Oh, I don't know, I don't know!"

"What made you decide he was the monster?" asked Holmes, inexorably.

"The nature of the crimes! I can conceive of no one save Max as being capable of such atrocities. His maniacal temper. His dreadful rages . . ."

We were not destined to hear any more from Angela Osbourne. The door burst open, and Max Klein sprang into the room. His face was contorted by an unholy passion that he was just able, it appeared, to hold in leash. He had a cocked pistol in his hand.

"If either of you moves so much as a finger," cried he, "I'll blow you both to Hell!"

There could be little doubt that he meant it.

Ellery's Legman's Last Bow

The doorbell rang.

Ellery ignored it.

It rang again.

He kept reading.

A third time.

He finished the chapter.

When he finally got there, his caller had given up and left. But he had slipped a telegram under the foyer door.

BOSOM FRIEND DASH WHILE HUNTING A THORN YOUR LEGMAN FOUND A ROSE STOP HE WILL HUNT NO MORE STOP HER NAME IS

RACHEL HAGER BUT A NAME CANNOT DO
JUSTICE TO HER STOP SHE WENT TO THAT
PARTY ONLY BECAUSE I WAS THERE COMMA
A FACT THAT POPS MY BUTTONS STOP LAW-
FUL WEDLOCK IS NEXT STOP STOP WE PLAN
CHILDREN STOP OUR JOINT LOVE TO YOU
STOP
GRANT

"Thank God I'm shed of *him*," said Ellery, aloud,
and went back to Sherlock Holmes.

CHAPTER XI

HOLOCAUST

I think that Holmes would have braved Klein's pistol, were it not that the proprietor of The Angel and Crown was immediately followed into Mrs. Osbourne's room by a man whom I recognised as one of the thugs who had attacked Holmes and me. Under the muzzles of two weapons, Holmes perforce held himself in check.

Max Klein's rage became evil satisfaction.

"Tie them up," snarled he, to his confederate. "And the man who tries to resist gets a bullet through his head."

The thug tore the cords from the window-drapes and swiftly lashed Holmes's hands behind his back, whilst I stood helplessly by. He thereupon treated me in like manner, going even further under Klein's command.

"Shove our good doctor into that chair and lash his ankles to its legs." Why Klein should have considered me a greater threat than Holmes, I did not understand. What courage I possess is thoroughly tempered, I fear, with a great desire to live out the years allotted me by the Almighty.

As his creature did his bidding, Klein turned on Holmes. "Did you think you could walk into my place undetected, Mr. Holmes?"

Replied Holmes, quietly, "I am curious to know how our entrance was discovered."

Klein laughed, a brutal sound. "One of my men had to roll some empty kegs out. Not spectacular, I grant you, Mr. Holmes. But I've got you just the same."

"Getting me, as you phrase it," said Holmes," and

keeping me, Klein, may be a steed of a different colour.''

It was evident to me that Holmes was attempting to gain time. But it was to no avail. Klein surveyed my bonds, found them to his liking, and said, ''You will come with me, Mr. Holmes. I shall deal with you in private. And if you expect help from below, you will be disappointed. I have cleared the place; it is closed and locked.''

The thug indicated Angela Osbourne with a worried glance. ''Is it safe leavin' this cull with 'er? She might loose 'im.''

''She would not dare,'' Klein laughed again. ''Not if she knows what's good for her. She still values her miserable life.''

This proved depressingly true. After Holmes and Michael Osbourne were dragged away, Angela Osbourne was impervious to all persuasion. I spoke with as urgent eloquence as I could command, but she only stared at me in despair, moaning, ''Oh, I dare not, I dare not.''

Thus passed several of the longest minutes of my life, as I struggled against my bonds, telling myself that Holmes would yet save the day.

Then came the most dreadful moment of all.

The door opened.

The chair in which I sat trussed was so situated that, when I heard the panel swing inwards, I was unable to see who stood there. Angela Osbourne, however, sat in view of the doorway. I could only look in her direction for a clew.

She arose from her chair. Somehow the veil slipped aside, and I saw that hideously-scarred face clearly. Every fibre of my being shrank at the unspeakable mutilation which Klein had visited upon her; but it was made even more repulsive by the wild expression with which she regarded the intruder in the doorway. Then she spoke. ''The Ripper! Oh, God in Heaven! It is Jack the Ripper!''

I confess with shame that my first reaction was relief. The man advanced within my sight, and when I
beheld the slim, aristocratic figure, clad in top-hat,
perfectly-fitting evening-clothes, and opera cape, I
cried thankfully, "Lord Carfax! You have come providentially!"

The ghastly truth dawned upon me an instant later,
when I espied the glittering knife in his hand. He
glanced my way, but only for a moment, and with no
sign of recognition. And I beheld the madness in that
noble face, a hungry, wild-beast's urge to destroy.

Angela Osbourne was incapable of further outcry.
She sat in frozen terror as the lordly Ripper rushed
upon her and in a trice tore away her upper clothing.
She could only mumble a prayer before Lord Carfax
plunged the weapon into her uncovered breast. His
clumsy efforts at dissection are best not described; suf-
fice it to say that they did not approach the skill of his
earlier mutilations, undoubtedly because he felt pressed
for time.

As the body of Angela Osbourne fell to the floor in
a welter of blood, the madman seized upon one of the
oil-lamps and extinguished the flame. Unscrewing the
wick-holder, he proceeded to pour out the oil. His in-
tent was all too clear. Around the room he dashed,
like some demon out of Hell, leaving oil in his wake;
and then out into the corridor, from whence he returned soon with an empty lamp, which he flung to the
floor in a shower of glass.

And then he seized the other lamp, and with it ig-
nited the pool of oil at his feet.

Strangely, he did not flee; even at that worst moment of my life, I wondered why. As it developed, his
maniacal ego proved my salvation and his destruction.
As the flames mounted, following the river of oil into
the corridor, he rushed at me. I closed my eyes and
consigned my soul to its Maker. To my stupefaction,
instead of slaying me, he slashed my bonds.

With dilated eyes, he hauled me upright and dragged

me through the flames towards the nearest window. I sought to struggle with him, but with his maniac's strength he threw me savagely against the window, and the glass shattered.

It was then that he uttered the cry that has echoed through my nightmares ever since.

"Carry the message, Dr. Watson!" he screamed. "Tell them that Lord Carfax is Jack the Ripper!"

With that, he thrust me through the window. Flames had caught my clothing; and I remember that, ludicrously, I slapped at them as I fell the one storey to the street. Then there was a stunning impact with the stones below, I thought I heard running footsteps, and unconsciousness mercifully gripped me.

I knew no more.

Chapter XII

The End of Jack the Ripper

The first face I beheld was that of Rudyard, the friend who had taken over my practice as locum tenens. I was in my room at Baker Street.

"A near thing, Watson," said he, as he felt my pulse.

Awareness came flooding back to me. "How long have I slept, Rudyard?"

"Some twelve hours. I gave you a sedative when they carried you here."

"My condition?"

"A most salutary one, under the circumstances. A broken ankle; a sprained wrist; burns no doubt painful, but superficial."

"Holmes. Where is he? Has he been—?"

Rudyard gestured. There was Holmes, seated grave-faced, at the opposite side of my bed. He was pale, but appeared otherwise unharmed. Thankfulness welled up in me.

"Well, I must be off," said Rudyard. To Holmes he said, "See that he doesn't talk too long, Mr. Holmes."

Rudyard departed, saying that he would be back to dress my burns, and warning me again not to tax my strength. But, even through my pain and discomfort, I could not restrain my curiosity. Holmes, I fear, was in no better case, despite his concern for my condition. So I soon found myself relating what had occurred in poor Angela Osbourne's room after Klein had forced him from it.

Holmes nodded, but I could see that he was struggling with a decision. Finally, he said to me, "I fear, old friend, that we have gone through our last adventure together."

"Why do you say that?" asked I, overwhelmed with dismay.

"Because your good wife will never again entrust your welfare to my bungling hands."

"Holmes!" cried I. "I am not a child!"

He shook his head. "You must go back to sleep."

"You know that cannot be until you tell me how you managed to escape from Klein. In a dream, after my sedation, I saw your mangled remains . . ."

I shuddered, and he placed his hand upon mine in a rare display of affection. "My opportunity arose when the staircase burst into flames," said Holmes. "Klein had glutted himself with gloating over me, and he was just raising his weapon when the flames swept down. He and his henchman died in the fire as the structure went up like tinder. The Angel and Crown is now a roofless ruin."

"But you, Holmes! How—?"

Holmes smiled, and shrugged his shoulders. "There was never a doubt but that I could slip my bonds," said he. "You know my dexterity. All that lacked was the chance, and the fire provided it. Unhappily, I was unable to save Michael Osbourne. He seemed to welcome death, poor fellow, and resisted my efforts to drag him out; indeed, he threw himself into the flames, and I was compelled to abandon his body to save my life."

"A blessing in disguise," I muttered. "And that infamous beast, Jack the Ripper?"

Holmes's grey eyes were clouded with sadness; his thoughts appeared to be elsewhere. "Lord Carfax died also. And also from choice, I am certain, like his brother."

"Naturally. He preferred death by fiery immolation to the hangman's noose."

Holmes seemed elsewhere still. In the gravest of voices, he murmured, "Watson, let us respect the decision of an honourable man."

"Honourable man! Surely you are jesting? Oh, I see. You refer to his lucid moments. And the Duke of Shires?"

Holmes's chin was sunken upon his chest. "I am a bearer of dire news about the Duke, too. He has taken his life."

"I see. He could not bear the awful revelation of his first son's crimes. How did you learn this, Holmes?"

"I proceeded directly from the fire to his Berkeley Square residence. Lestrade accompanied me. We were too late. He had already had the news of Lord Carfax. Whereupon he had fallen upon the sword he kept concealed in his stick."

"A true nobleman's death!"

I fancied Holmes nodded; it was the merest inclination of his head. He seemed deeply depressed.

"An unsatisfactory case, Watson, most unsatisfactory," said he. And he fell silent.

I sensed his wish to conclude the conversation, but I would not have it so. I had forgotten all about my broken ankle and the pain of my burns.

"I do not see why, Holmes. The Ripper is dead."

"Yes," said he. "Really, Watson, you must rest now." He made as if to rise.

"I cannot rest," said I, artfully, "until all the pieces are in place." He sank back with resignation. "Even I am able to follow the sequence of those last events that lead up to the fire. The maniacal Ripper, functioning from behind his philanthropic *façade* as Lord Carfax, did not know the identity or the whereabouts of Angela Osbourne or Max Klein. Am I correct?"

Holmes did not reply.

"When you found his lair," I pressed on, "I am sure you knew also who he was?"

Here Holmes nodded.

''Then we went to the hostel, and although we did not see him there, he saw and heard us—that, or he came shortly thereafter and learned of The Angel and Crown from Dr. Murray, who would have had no reason to withhold the information. Lord Carfax followed us and discovered the beer-keg entrance, as we did.''

''Lord Carfax preceded us,'' said Holmes, abruptly. ''You will recall that we found the hasp recently broken.''

''Amended. He must have been able to move through the foggy streets more surely than we. No doubt we interrupted his stalking of Angela Osbourne, who was slated to be his next victim. He must have been lying in wait in a corridor-doorway whilst we entered Mrs. Osbourne's room.''

Holmes did not contest this.

''Then, realising you had run him to earth, he determined to conclude his infamous career in the blaze of mad defiance that his monstrous ego dictated. His final words to me were, 'Carry the message, Dr. Watson! Tell them that Lord Carfax is Jack the Ripper!' Only an egomaniac would have said that.''

Holmes came to his feet with finality. ''At any rate, Watson, Jack the Ripper will prowl no more. And now we have defied your doctor's orders long enough. I insist that you sleep.''

With that, he left me.

Ellery Visits the Past

Ellery put the Watson manuscript down thoughtfully. He barely heard the click of the lock and the opening and closing of the front door.

He looked up to find his father standing in the study doorway.

'Dad!''

''Hi, son,'' said the Inspector with a defiant grin.

"I just couldn't stand it down there any more. So here I am."

"Welcome home."

"Then you're not sore?"

"You stayed longer than I expected."

The Inspector came in, scaled his hat to the sofa, and turned to regard his son with relief. It soon became concern.

"You look like hell. What's wrong, Ellery?"

Ellery did not reply.

"How do I look?" asked his father cunningly.

"A damsite better than when I packed you off."

"You're sure *you're* all right?"

"I'm fine."

"Don't give me that. Is your story still sour?"

"No, it's going fine. Everything's fine."

But the old man was not satisfied. He sat down on the sofa and crossed his legs and said, "Tell me all about it."

Ellery shrugged. "I should never have been born the son of a cop. All right, something's happened. An interlocking of events, past and present. The loosening of an old knot."

"Talk English."

"Grant Ames dropped in on me."

"You told me that."

"I got sucked into the manuscript. One thing led to another. And here I am."

"I don't get it."

Ellery sighed. "I suppose I'll have to tell you all about it."

And he talked for a long time.

"And that's where it stands, dad. She believes absolutely in his innocence. She's nursed it all her life. I suppose she didn't know what to do about it until, in her old age, she suddenly got this inspiration to drag me into it. Inspiration!"

"What are you going to do?"

"I'd just made up my mind to pay her a visit when you walked in on me."

"I should think so!" Inspector Queen got up and took the journal from Ellery's hand. "The way I see it, son, you've got absolutely no choice. After all, she's asked for it."

Ellery got to his feet. "Why don't you read the manuscript while I'm gone?"

"That's just what I'm going to do."

He drove north into Westchester, taking Route 22 until he came to Somers. He passed the wooden elephant at the main intersection, a reminder that Barnum & Bailey's Circus had once wintered there. In Putnam County he thought of the Revolutionary heroes, hoping they were all in a hero's heaven somewhere.

But these were surface thoughts. In depth he was thinking of the old lady he would find at the end of his journey. They were not pleasant thoughts.

He finally turned in at a trim little cottage with a doll's-house drive, got out, and reluctantly went up to the front door. It opened to his knock immediately, as if she had been lying in wait for him. He had half wished she would not be at home.

"Deborah Osbourne Spain," he said, looking down at her. "Hello."

She was very old, of course; she must be in her late 80s, according to his calculations. The manuscript had not given her age on the day Holmes and Watson visited Shires Castle, except in approximate figures. She could be 90.

Like so many very old ladies, especially the tiny plumpish ones, there was a slightly withered-apple look to her, with the bloom still touching her cheeks. Her bosom was large for her size, and fallen, as if tired of its weight. Only her eyes were young. They were bright, and direct, and they twinkled in spite of themselves.

"Do come in, Mr. Queen."

"Could you make it Ellery, Mrs. Spain?"

"It is something I have never quite become accustomed to," she said, ushering him into a cozy little parlor, as mid-Victorian as Victoria's bustle, Ellery thought. It was like stepping into 19th Century England. "I mean, the American habit of instant familiarity. However—take that Morris chair, Ellery—if you wish."

"I wish." He sat down and looked about. "I see you've kept the faith."

She seated herself in a ducal chair, in which she looked lost. 'What else does an ancient Englishwoman have?" she asked with a faint smile. "I know—I sound disgustingly Anglophilic. But it's so difficult to get away from one's beginnings. Actually, I'm quite comfortable here. And a visit to New Rochelle once in a while to see Rachel's roses rounds out my existence."

"Rachel *was* the one."

"Oh, yes. At my request."

"Miss Hager is related to you how, exactly?"

"My granddaughter. Shall we have tea?"

"Not just now, if you don't mind, Mrs. Spain," said Ellery. "I'm too chockful of questions. But first." He sat on the edge of the chair, avoiding the lace antimacassar. "You saw him. You met them both. Holmes. Watson. How I envy you!"

Deborah Osbourne Spain's eyes looked far into the past. "It was so very long ago. But of course I remember them. Mr. Holmes's glance, sharp as a sword. And so reserved. When I put my hand in his, I'm sure it disconcerted him. But he was very sweet. They were both such gentlemen. That above all. In those days, Ellery, being a gentleman was important. Of course, I was a little girl, and I recall them as giants, towering to the sky. As I suppose they were, in a way."

"May I ask how you came by the manuscript?"

"After Dr. Watson wrote it, the journal was turned over by Mr. Holmes to the Osbourne estate. It became the responsibility of the estate's solicitor, bless him!

He was so faithful to my interests. Then, after I was grown, and shortly before he died, he told me about the manuscript. I begged for it, and he sent it to me. His name was Dobbs, Alfred Dobbs. I think of him so often."

"Why did you wait so long, Mrs. Spain, before doing what you did?"

"Please. Everyone calls me Grandma Deborah. Won't you?"

"Grandma Deborah it shall be."

"I don't know why I waited so long," the old lady said. "The idea of asking an expert to verify my conviction never crystallized in my mind, although I am sure it has been there for a long time. Lately, a feeling that there is a need to hurry has come over me. How much longer can I live? And I should like to die in peace."

The implicit plea moved Ellery to her aid. "Your decision to send me the manuscript came from the manuscript itself, I take it?"

"Yes. Afterwards, Mr. Ames confided in Rachel about the hunt you sent him on."

"Grant's searching accomplished an end, though not the one I expected," Ellery smiled.

"Bless him! Bless them both. I know he gave you no help, Ellery. I also knew you would find me, just as Mr. Holmes had no difficulty in tracing the owner of the surgeon's kit. But I'm still curious as to how you did it."

"It was elementary, Grandma Deborah. It was obvious from the first that the sender had some personal interest in the case. So I put a call through to a friend of mine, a genealogist. He had no trouble tracing you from Shires Castle, as a child, to the custody of the San Francisco branch of the family. I had the names of Grant's four young ladies, and I was sure one of the names would pop up somewhere. From your marriage to Barney Spain in 1906 my expert got to the marriage of your daughter. And, lo and behold, the man your daughter married was named Hager. Q.E.D.'' His smile became a look of concern.

"You're tired. We can put this off for another time.''

"Oh, no! I'm fine.'' The young eyes pleaded. "He was a wonderful man, my father. Kind, gentle, He was not a monster. He was not!''

"You're sure you don't want to lie down?''

"No, no. Not until you've told me . . .''

"Then lie back in your chair, Grandma. Relax. And I'll talk.''

Ellery took the withered old hand in his, and he talked against the ticking of the grandfather clock in the corner, its pendulum, like a mechanical finger, wiping the seconds off the face of time.

The little frail hand in Ellery's squeezed at irregular intervals. Then it stopped squeezing, and lay in Ellery's hand like an autumn leaf.

After a while, there was a movement of the portieres at the archway to the parlor, and a middle-aged woman appeared, wearing a white housedress.

"She's fallen asleep,'' Ellery whispered.

He carefully laid the old hand on her breast and tiptoed from the room.

The woman accompanied him to the door. "I'm Susan Bates. I take care of her. She falls asleep like that more and more.''

Ellery nodded and left the cottage and got into his car and drove back to Manhattan, feeling very tired himself. Even old.

The Ripper Case Journal
Final Note
January 12, 1908

Holmes vexes me. I confess, because he was out of
England for an extended period, that I took it upon
myself, against his wish, to put my notes for the Jack
the Ripper case into narrative form. Twenty years
have now passed. For nine of these, a new heir, a
distant relation, has borne the Shires title. One, I
might add, who spends but a fraction of his time in
England, and cares little for either the title or its illustrious history.

I had come to feel, however, that it was high time
the world was informed of the truth about the Ripper
case, which held an equally illustrious place—if that
is the word!—in the history of crime, and about
Holmes's struggle to end the monster's bloody reign
in Whitechapel.

On Holmes's return from abroad, I broached this to
him, expressing myself in the most persuasive terms I
could muster. But he is adamant in his refusal.

"No, no, Watson, let the bones lie mouldering. The
world would be no richer from the publication of the
story."

"But, Holmes! All this work——"

"I am sorry, Watson. But that is my last word in
the matter."

"Then," said I, with ill-concealed annoyance, "allow me to present you with the manuscript. Perhaps
you will find use for the paper as pipe-lighters."

"I am honoured, Watson, and touched," said he,
most cheerfully. "In return, allow me to present you
with the details of a little matter I have just brought to
a successful conclusion. You may apply to it your un-
deniable *flair* for melodrama, and submit it to your

publishers without delay. It has to do with a South
American sailing-man, who came very close to duping
a European financial syndicate with a 'genuine' roc's-
egg. Perhaps *The Case of the Peruvian Sinbad* will in
some measure assuage your disappointment.''

And thus, matters now stand.

Ellery Explains

Ellery's arrival was timely. Inspector Queen had just
finished reading Dr. Watson's Ripper manuscript, and
he was staring at the journal with marked dissatisfac-
tion. He turned his stare of Ellery.

"Just as well it wasn't published. Holmes was
right.''

"I thought so, too.'' Ellery went to the bar. "Damn
Grant! I forgot to order scotch.''

"How did it turn out?''

"Better than I expected.'

"Then you lied like a gentleman. Good for you.''

"I didn't lie.''

"What?''

"I didn't lie. I told her the truth.''

"Then,'' said Inspector Queen coldly, "you're a
rat-fink. Deborah Osbourne loved and believed in her
father. She also believes in you. Your mind is certainly crooked enough to have twisted the truth a little.''

"I didn't have to twist the truth.''

"Why not? Tell me that! A little old lady—''

"Because, dad,'' said Ellery, sinking into his swivel
chair, "Lord Carfax wasn't Jack the Ripper. A lie
wasn't necessary. Deborah's father was no monster.
She was right about him all along. She knew it, I knew
it—''

"But—''

"And so did Sherlock Holmes.''

There was a silence of great length while *pater* tried to catch up with *filius* and failed.

"But it's all down here, Ellery!" protested the Inspector.

"Yes, it is."

"Richard Osbourne, this Lord Carfax, caught with the knife in his hand, butchering his last victim—why, Watson was an eyewitness!—wrote it all down!"

"Your point is, I take it, that Watson was an able reporter?"

"I'd say so. He also knew the evidence of his own eyes!"

Ellery got up and went over to his father, picked up the journal, and returned to his chair. "Watson was also human. He was oversubjective. He saw what Holmes wanted him to see. He reported what Holmes told him."

"Are you saying that Holmes was pulling a fast one?"

"You're damned right I am. The devious thing is that in this case every word from his lips was gospel. It's what he didn't say that counts."

"All *right*. What was it that he didn't say?"

"He didn't at any time, for instance, call Jack the Ripper by the name of Richard Osbourne or Lord Carfax."

"You're quibbling," snorted the Inspector.

Ellery riffled through the old journal. "Dad, didn't you spot the inconsistencies in the case? Certainly you weren't satisfied with the blackmail bit?"

"The blackmail? Let me see . . ."

"It went like this. Max Klein saw an opportunity for blackmail by conniving a marriage between Michael Osbourne and Angela, a prostitute. Considering the Duke of Shires' pride of name, that made sense from Klein's viewpoint. But it didn't work. The marriage became public knowledge."

"But Klein admitted to Angela that the plan had failed."

"Not exactly. He told her, after he'd brought the couple back to London, that the marriage was no longer important as a basis for blackmail. He'd found a better gimmick. Klein lost all interest in Michael and Angela after he discovered this new weapon, obviously a better one than the marriage."

"But the manuscript never said—"

"Dad, who was Klein? What was he? Holmes was aware from the start of his importance, even before the man was identified—when he was Holmes's missing link. And when Holmes confronted Angela, he pried a vital piece of information out of her. To quote her on the subject of Klein: 'Oh, yes, he was born here. He knows its every street and alley. He is greatly feared in this district. There are few who would dare cross him.' "

"So?"

"So what was the great secret Klein had discovered?"

"The identity of Jack the Ripper," said the Inspector slowly. "A man like that, who had an intimate knowledge of Whitechapel and its people—"

"Of course, dad. That's what it had to be. And with the knowledge of the Ripper's identity Klein got rich blackmailing—"

"Lord Carfax."

"No. You'll recall that Lord Carfax was trying desperately to locate Klein and Angela. Blackmailers confront their victims."

"Maybe Carfax knew all the time."

"Then why didn't he strike earlier? Because he only learned that night at the morgue that Klein and Angela were at The Angel and Crown!"

"But Carfax struck at Angela, not Klein."

"Further proof that he was not the blackmail victim. He mistakenly saw his brother's wife as the evil force in the Osbourne disaster. That's why he killed her."

"But none of that is enough to base—"

"Then let's find some more. Let's follow Holmes

and Watson that last night. You already know what *appeared* to happen. Let's see what really did. In the first place, there were two men on the trail of the Ripper that night—Sherlock Holmes *and* Lord Carfax. I'm sure Carfax already had his suspicions.''

"What indication is there that Carfax was on the Ripper's trail?"

"I'm glad you asked that question," Ellery said sententiously. "Acting on the tip he'd picked up in Madame Leona's whorehouse, Holmes set out on the last leg of his search. He and Watson arrived at the room in the Pacquin—"

"And Holmes said, 'If this was the lair of the Ripper, he has fled.' "

"Holmes didn't say that, Watson did. Holmes cried, 'Someone has been here before us!' There's a world of difference in the two statements. One was the observation of a romantic. The other, Holmes's, of a man trained to read a scene with photographic accuracy."

"You have a point," the older Queen admitted.

"A vital one. But there are others.'

"That both Holmes and Lord Carfax found the lair of Jack the Ripper at practically the same time?"

"Also that Carfax saw Holmes and Watson arrive at the Pacquin. He waited outside and followed them to the morgue. It had to be that way."

"Why?"

"In order for Carfax to act as he did, he needed two items of information—the identity of the Ripper, which he got at the Pacquin, and the place where he could find Angela and Klein, which he overheard at the morgue."

Inspector Queen got up and retrieved the journal. He searched and read: " 'And that infamous beast, Jack the Ripper?' Watson asked Holmes that question. Holmes answered, 'Lord Carfax died also—' "

"Hold it," Ellery said. "None of this out-of-context business. Give me all of it."

"Quote: 'Holmes's grey eyes were clouded with sadness; his thoughts appeared to be elsewhere. "Lord Carfax died also. And also from choice, I am certain, like his brother." ' "

"That's better. Now tell me, would Sherlock Holmes be sad over the death of Jack the Ripper?"

Inspector Queen shook his head and read on. " 'Naturally. He no doubt preferred death by fiery immolation to the hangman's noose.' "

"Watson's words, not Holmes's. What Holmes then said was, 'Let us respect the decision of an honourable man.' "

"To which Watson replied, 'Honourable man! Surely you are jesting? Oh, I see. You refer to his lucid moments. And the Duke of Shires?' "

"Watson drew an unwarranted inference from what Holmes had said. Let's quote Holmes again: 'I proceeded directly from the fire to his'—meaning the Duke's—Berkeley Square residence . . . He had already had the news of Lord Carfax. Whereupon he had fallen upon the sword he kept concealed in his stick.' "

"And Watson exclaimed, 'A true nobleman's death!' "

"Again Watson was fooled by his own preconceptions and his misunderstanding of Holmes's deliberate indirection. Look, dad. When Holmes reached the Duke of Shires' townhouse, he found the Duke dead. But 'he (the Duke) had already had the news of Lord Carfax.' I ask you, how could the Duke have 'already had the news of Lord Carfax' ? The implication is clear that the Duke had been at his Pacquin lair, where Lord Carfax confronted him, after which he went home and killed himself."

"Because the Duke was the Ripper! And his son, knowing it, took the blame on himself to save his father's reputation!"

'Now you've got it," said Ellery gently. "Remember again what Carfax said to Watson—to spread the word that *he* was Jack the Ripper. He wanted to make dead sure that the guilt fell on his shoulders, not his father's.''

"Then Holmes was right," murmured Inspector Queen. "He didn't want to give Lord Carfax's sacrifice away.''

"And Deborah's faith in her father has been vindicated after three-quarters of a century.''

"I'll be damned!"

Ellery took Dr. Watson's journal from his father's hand again and opened it to the "Final Note.''

"'*The Case of the Peruvian Sinbad,*'" he muttered. "Something about a roc's egg . . ." His eyes glinted. "Dad, do you suppose Holmes could have been pulling Watson's leg about that one, too?''

-EQ-

THE LODGER

by Mrs. Marie Belloc Lowndes

"There he is at last, and I'm glad of it, Ellen. 'Tain't a night you would wish a dog to be out in."

Mr. Bunting's voice was full of unmistakable relief. He was close to the fire, sitting back in a deep leather armchair—a clean-shaven, dapper man, still in outward appearance what he had been so long, and now no longer was—a self-respecting butler.

"You needn't feel so nervous about him; Mr. Sleuth can look out for himself, all right." Mrs. Bunting spoke in a dry, rather tart tone. She was less emotional, better balanced, than was her husband. On her the marks of past servitude were less apparent, but they were there all the same—especially in her neat black stuff dress and scrupulously clean, plain collar and cuffs. Mrs. Bunting, as a single woman, had been for long years what is known as a useful maid.

"I can't think why he wants to go out in such weather. He did it in last week's fog, too," Bunting went on complainingly.

"Well, it's none of your business—now, is it?"

"No; that's true enough. Still, 'twould be a very bad thing for us if anything happened to him. This lodger's the first bit of luck we've had for a very long time."

Mrs. Bunting made no answer to this remark. It was too obviously true to be worth answering. Also she was listening—following in imagination her lodger's quick, singularly quiet—"stealthy," she called it to

241

herself—progress through the dark, fog-filled hall and up the staircase.

"It isn't safe for decent folk to be out in such weather—not unless they have something to do that won't wait till tomorrow." Bunting had at last turned round. He was now looking straight into his wife's narrow, colorless face; he was an obstinate man, and liked to prove himself right. "I read you out the accidents in *Lloyd's* yesterday—shocking, they were, and all brought about by the fog! And then, that 'orrid monster at his work again—"

"Monster?" repeated Mrs. Bunting absently. She was trying to hear the lodger's footsteps overhead; but her husband went on as if there had been no interruption:

"It wouldn't be very pleasant to run up against such a party as that in the fog, eh?"

"What stuff you do talk!" she said sharply; and then she got up suddenly. Her husband's remark had disturbed her. She hated to think of such things as the terrible series of murders that were just then horrifying and exciting the nether world of London. Though she enjoyed pathos and sentiment,—Mrs. Bunting would listen with mild amusement to the details of a breach-of-promise action—she shrank from stories of either immorality or physical violence.

Mrs. Bunting got up from the straight-backed chair on which she had been sitting. It would soon be time for supper.

She moved abut the sitting-room, flecking off an imperceptible touch of dust here, straightening a piece of furniture there.

Bunting looked around once or twice. He would have liked to ask Ellen to leave off fidgeting, but he was mild and fond of peace, so he refrained. However, she soon gave over what irritated him of her own accord.

But even then Mrs. Bunting did not at once go down to the cold kitchen, where everything was in readiness for her simple cooking. Instead, she opened the door leading into the bedroom behind, and there, closing the door quietly, stepped back into the darkness and stood motionless, listening.

At first she heard nothing, but gradually there came the sound of some one moving about in the room just overhead; try as she might, however, it was impossible for her to guess what her lodger was doing. At last she heard him open the door leading out the landing. That meant that he would spend the rest of the evening in the rather cheerless room above the drawing-room floor—oddly enough, he liked sitting there best, though the only warmth obtainable was from a gas-stove fed by a shilling-in-the-slot arrangement.

It was indeed true that Mr. Sleuth had brought the Buntings luck, for at the time he had taken their rooms it had been touch and go with them.

After having each separately led the sheltered, impersonal, and, above all, the financially easy existence that is the compensation life offers to those men and women who deliberately take upon themselves the yoke of domestic service, these two, butler and useful maid, had suddenly, in middle age, determined to join their fortunes and savings.

Bunting was a widower; he had one pretty daughter, a girl of seventeen, who now lived, as had been the case ever since the death of her mother, with a prosperous aunt. His second wife had been reared in the Foundling Hospital, but she had gradually worked her way up into the higher ranks of the servant class and as useful maid she had saved quite a tidy sum of money.

Unluckily, misfortune had dogged Mr. and Mrs. Bunting from the very first. The seaside place where they had begun by taking a lodging-house became the scene of an epidemic. Then had followed a business experiment which had proved disastrous. But before going back into service, either together or separately, they had made up their minds to make one last effort, and, with the little money that remained to them, they had taken over the lease of a small house in the Marylebone Road.

Bunting, whose appearance was very good, had retained a connection with old employers and their friends, so he occasionally got a good job as waiter. During this last month his jobs had perceptibly increased in number and in profit; Mrs. Bunting was not superstitious, but it seemed that in this matter, as in everything else, Mr. Sleuth, their new lodger, had brought them luck.

As she stood there, still listening intently in the darkness of the bedroom, she told herself, not for the first time, what Mr. Sleuth's departure would mean to her and Bunting. It would almost certainly mean ruin.

Luckily, the lodger seemed entirely pleased both with the rooms and with his landlady. There was really no reason why he should ever leave such nice lodgings. Mrs. Bunting shook off her vague sense of apprehension and usease. She turned round, took a step forward, and, feeling for the handle of the door giving into the passage, she opened it, and went down with light, firm steps into the kitchen.

She lit the gas and put a frying-pan on the stove, and then once more her mind reverted, as if in spite of herself, to her lodger, and there came back to Mrs. Bunting, very vividly, the memory of all that had happened the day Mr. Sleuth had taken her rooms.

The date of this excellent lodger's coming had been the twenty-ninth of December, and the time late afternoon. She and Bunting had been sitting, gloomily enough, over their small banked-up fire. They had dined in the middle of the day—he on a couple of sausages, she on a little cold ham. They were utterly out of heart, each trying to pluck up courage to tell the other that it was no use trying any more. The two had also had a little tiff on that dreary afternoon. A newspaper-seller had come yelling down the Marylebone Road, shouting out, " 'Orrible murder in Whitechapel!'' and just because Bunting had an old uncle living in the East End he had gone and bought a paper, and at a time, too, when every penny, nay, every half-penny, had its full value! Mrs. Bunting remembered the circumstances because that murder in Whitechapel had been the first of these terrible crimes—there had been four since—which she would never allow Bunting to discuss in her presence, and yet which had of late begun to interest curiously, uncomfortably, even her refined mind.

But, to return to the lodger. It was then, on that dreary afternoon, that suddenly there had come to the front door a tremulous, uncertain double knock.

Bunting ought to have got up, but he had gone on reading the paper; and so Mrs. Bunting, with the woman's greater courage, had gone out into the passage, turned up the gas, and opened the door to see who it could be. She remembered, as if it were yesterday instead of nigh on a month ago, Mr. Sleuth's peculiar appearance. Tall, dark, lanky, an old-fashioned top hat concealing his high bald forehead, he had stood there, an odd figure of a man, blinking at her.

"I believe—is it not a fact that you let lodgings?" he had asked in a hesitating, whistling voice, a voice that she had known in a moment to be that of an educated man—of a gentleman. As he had stepped into the hall, she had noticed that in his right hand he held a narrow bag—a quite new bag of strong brown leather.

Everything had been settled in less than a quarter of an hour. Mr. Sleuth had at once "taken" to the drawing-room floor, and then, as Mrs. Bunting eagerly lit the gas in the front room above, he had looked around him and said, rubbing his hands with a nervous movement, "Capital—capital! This is just what I've been looking for!"

The sink had specially pleased him—the sink and the gas-stove. "This is quite first-rate!" he had exclaimed, "For I make all sorts of experiments. I am, you must understand, Mrs.—er—Bunting, a man of science." Then he had sat down—suddenly. "I'm very tired," he had said in a low tone, "very tired indeed! I have been walking about all day."

From the very first the lodger's manner had been odd, sometimes distant and abrupt, and then, for no reason at all that she could see, confidential and plaintively confiding. But Mrs. Bunting was aware that eccentricity has always been a perquisite, as it were the special luxury, of the well born and well educated. Scholars and such-like are never quite like other people.

And then, this particular gentleman had proved himself so eminently satisfactory as to the one thing that really matters to those who let lodgings. "My name is Sleuth," he said. "S-l-e-u-t-h. Think of a hound, Mrs. Bunting, and you'll never forget my name. I could give you references," he had added, giving her, as she now remembered, a funny sidewise look, "but I prefer to dispense with them. How much did you say? Twenty-three shillings a week, with attendance? Yes, that will suit me perfectly; and I'll begin by paying my first month's rent in advance. Now, four times twenty-three shillings is"—he looked at Mrs. Bunting, and for the first time he smiled, a queer, wry smile— "ninety-two shillings."

He had taken a handful of sovereigns out of his pocket and put them down on the table. "Look here," he had said, "there's five pounds; and you can keep the change, for I shall want you to do a little shopping for me tomorrow."

After he had been in the house about an hour, the bell had rung, and the new lodger had asked Mrs. Bunting if she could oblige him with the loan of a Bible. She brought up to him her best Bible, the one that had been given to her as a wedding present by a lady with whose mother she had lived for several years. This Bible and one other book, of which the odd name was Cruden's Concordance, formed Mr. Sleuth's only reading; he spent hours each day poring over the Old Testament and over the volume which Mrs. Bunting had at last decided to be a queer kind of index to the Book.

However, to return to the lodger's first arrival. He had had no luggage with him, barring the small brown bag, but very soon parcels had begun to arrive addressed to Mr. Sleuth, and it was then that Mrs. Bunting first became curious. These parcels were full of clothes; but it was quite clear to the landlady's feminine eye that none of those clothes had been made for Mr. Sleuth. They were, in fact, second-hand clothes, bought at good second-hand places, each marked, when marked at all, with a different name. And the really extraordinary thing was that occasionally a complete suit disappeared—became, as it were, obliterated from the lodger's wardrobe.

As for the bag he had brought with him, Mrs. Bunting had never caught sight of it again. And this also was certainly very strange.

Mrs. Bunting thought a great deal about that bag. She often wondered what had been in it; not a night-shirt and comb and brush, as she had at first supposed, for Mr. Sleuth had asked her to go out and buy him a brush and comb and tooth-brush the morning after his arrival. That fact was specially impressed on her memory, for at the little shop, a barber's, where she had purchased the brush and comb, the foreigner who had served her had insisted on telling her some of the horrible details of the murder that had taken place the day before in Whitechapel, and it had upset her very much.

As to where the bag was now, it was probably locked up in the lower part of a chiffonnier in the front sitting-room. Mr. Sleuth evidently always carried the key of the little cupboard on his person, for Mrs. Bunting, though she looked well for it, had never been able to find it.

And yet, never was there a more confiding or trusting gentleman. The first four days that he had been

with them he had allowed his money—the considerable
sum of one hundred and eighty-four pounds in gold—
to lie about wrapped up in pieces of paper on his
dressing-table. This was a very foolish, indeed a wrong
thing to do, as she had allowed herself respectfully to
point out to him; but as only answer he had laughed,
a loud, discordant shout of laughter.

Mr. Sleuth had many other odd ways; but Mrs.
Bunting, a true woman in spite of her prim manner
and love of order, had an infinite patience with masculine vagaries.

On the first morning of Mr. Sleuth's stay in the
Buntings' house, while Mrs. Bunting was out buying
things for him, the new lodger had turned most of the
pictures and photographs hanging in his sitting-room
with their faces to the wall! But this queer action on
Mr. Sleuth's part had not surprised Mrs. Bunting as
much as it might have done; it recalled an incident of
her long-past youth—something that had happened a
matter of twenty years ago, at a time when Mrs. Bunting, then the still youthful Ellen Cottrell, had been
maid to an old lady. The old lady had a favorite
nephew, a bright, jolly young gentleman who had been
learning to paint animals in Paris; and it was he who
had had the impudence, early one summer morning,
to turn to the wall six beautiful engravings of paintings
done by the famous Mr. Landseer! The old lady
thought the world of these pictures, but her nephew,
as only excuse for the extraordinary thing he had done,
had observed that "they put his eye out."

Mr. Sleuth's excuse had been much the same; for,
when Mrs. Bunting had come into his sitting-room and
found all her pictures, or at any rate all those of her
pictures that happened to be portraits of ladies, with
their faces to the wall, he had offered as only explanation, "Those women's eyes follow me about."

Mrs. Bunting had gradually become aware that Mr.
Sleuth had a fear and dislike of women. When she was
"doing" the staircase and landing, she often heard

him reading bits of the Bible aloud to himself, and in the majority of instances the texts he chose contained uncomplimentary reference to her own sex. Only to-day she had stopped and listened while he uttered threateningly the awful words, "A strange woman is a narrow pit. She also lieth in wait as for a prey, and increaseth the transgressors among men." There had been a pause, and then had come, in a high singsong, "Her house is the way to hell, going down to the chambers of death." It had made Mrs. Bunting feel quite queer.

The lodger's daily habits were also peculiar. He stayed in bed all the morning, and sometimes part of the afternoon, and he never went out before the street lamps were alight. Then, there was his dislike of an open fire; he generally sat in the top front room, and while there he always used the large gas-stove, not only for his experiments, which he carried on at night, but also in the daytime, for warmth.

But there! Where was the use of worrying about the lodger's funny ways? Of course, Mr. Sleuth was ec-centric; if he hadn't been "just a leetle 'touched' up-stairs"—as Bunting had once described it—he wouldn't be their lodger now; he would be living in a quite different sort of way with some of his relations, or with a friend of his own class.

Mrs. Bunting, while these thoughts galloped discon-nectedly through her brain, went on with her cooking, doing everything with a certain delicate and cleanly precision.

While in the middle of making the toast on which was to be poured some melted cheese, she suddenly heard a noise, or rather a series of noises. Shuffling, hesitating steps were creaking down the house above. She looked up and listened. Surely Mr. Sleuth was not going out again into the cold, foggy night? But no; for the sounds did not continue down the passage leading to the front door.

The heavy steps were coming slowly down the

kitchen stairs. Nearer and nearer came the thudding sounds, and Mrs. Bunting's heart began to beat as if in response. She put out the gas-stove, unheedful of the fact that the cheese would stiffen and spoil in the cold air; and then she turned and faced the door. There was a fumbling at the handle, and a moment later the door opened and revealed, as she had known it would, her lodger.

Mr. Sleuth was clad in a plaid dressing-gown, and in his hand was a candle. When he saw the lit-up kitchen, and the woman standing in it, he looked inexplicably taken aback, almost aghast.

"Yes, sir? What can I do for you, sir? I hope you didn't ring, sir?" Mrs. Bunting did not come forward to meet her lodger; instead, she held her ground in front of the stove. Mr. Sleuth had no business to come down like this into her kitchen.

"No, I—I didn't ring," he stammered; "I didn't know you were down here, Mrs. Bunting. Please excuse my costume. The truth is, my gas-stove has gone wrong, or, rather, that shilling-in-the-slot arrangement has done so. I came down to see if *you* had a gas-stove. I am going to ask leave to use it to-night for an experiment I want to make."

Mrs. Bunting felt troubled—oddly, unnaturally troubled. Why couldn't the lodger's experiment wait till tomorrow? "Oh, certainly, sir; but you will find it very cold down here." She looked round her dubiously.

"It seems most pleasantly warm," he observed, "warm and cozy after my cold room upstairs."

"Won't you let me make you a fire?" Mrs. Bunting's housewifely instincts were roused. "Do let me make you a fire in your bedroom, sir; I'm sure you ought to have one there these cold nights."

"By no means—I mean, I would prefer not. I do not like an open fire, Mrs. Bunting." He frowned, and still stood, a strange-looking figure, just inside the kitchen door.

"Do you want to use this stove now, sir? Is there anything I can do to help you?"

"No, not now—thank you all the same, Mrs. Bunting. I shall come down later, altogether later—probably after you and your husband have gone to bed. But I should be much obliged if you would see that the gas people come tomorrow and put my stove in order."

"Perhaps Bunting could put it right for you sir. I'll ask him to go up."

"No, no—I don't want anything of that sort done tonight. Besides, he couldn't put it right. The cause of the trouble is quite simple. The machine is choked up with shillings: a foolish plan, so I have always felt it to be."

Mr. Sleuth spoke very pettishly, with far more heat than he was wont to speak; but Mrs. Bunting sympathized with him. She had always suspected those slot-machines to be as dishonest as if they were human. It was dreadful, the way they swallowed up the shillings!

As if he were divining her thoughts, Mr. Sleuth, walking forward, stared up at the kitchen slot-machine. "Is it nearly full?" he asked abruptly. "I expect my experiment will take some time, Mrs. Bunting."

"Oh, no, sir; there's plenty of room for shillings there still. We don't use our stove as much as you do yours, sir. I'm never in the kitchen a minute longer than I can help this cold weather."

And then, with him preceding her, Mrs. Bunting and her lodger made a low progress to the ground floor. There Mr. Sleuth courteously bade his landlady good night, and proceeded upstairs to his own apartments.

Mrs. Bunting again went down into her kitchen, again she lit the stove, and again she cooked the toasted cheese. But she felt unnerved, afraid of she knew not what. The place seemed to her alive with alien presences, and once she caught herself listening, which was absurd, for of course she could not hope to hear what her lodger was doing two, if not three, flights upstairs. She had never been able to discover what Mr. Sleuth's experiments really were; all she knew was that they required a very high degree of heat.

The Buntings went to bed early that night. But Mrs. Bunting intended to stay awake. She wanted to know at what hour of the night her lodger would come down into the kitchen, and, above all, she was anxious as to how long he would stay there. But she had had a long day, and presently she fell asleep.

The church clock hard by struck two in the morning, and suddenly Mrs. Bunting awoke. She felt sharply annoyed with herself. How could she have dropped off like that? Mr. Sleuth must have been down and up again hours ago.

Then, gradually, she became aware of a faint acrid odor; elusive, almost intangible, it yet seemed to encompass her and the snoring man by her side almost as a vapor might have done.

Mrs. Bunting sat up in bed and sniffed; and then, in spite of the cold, she quietly crept out of the nice, warm bedclothes and crawled along to the bottom of the bed. There Mr. Sleuth's landlady did a very curious thing; she leaned over the brass rail and put her face close to the hinge of the door. Yes, it was from there that this strange, horrible odor was coming; the smell must be very strong in the passage. Mrs. Bunting thought she knew now what became of these suits of clothes of Mr. Sleuth's that disappeared.

As she crept back, shivering, under the bedclothes, she longed to give her sleeping husband a good shake, and in fancy she heard herself saying: "Bunting, get up! There is something strange going on downstairs that we ought to know about."

But Mr. Sleuth's landlady, as she lay by her husband's side, listening with painful intentness, knew very well that she would do nothing of the sort. The lodger had a right to destroy his clothes by burning if the fancy took him. What if he did make a certain amount of mess, a certain amount of smell, in her nice kitchen? Was he not—was he not such a good lodger! If they did anything to upset him, where could they ever hope to get another like him?

Three o'clock struck before Mrs. Bunting heard slow, heavy steps creaking up her kitchen stairs. But Mr. Sleuth did not go straight up to his own quarters, as she expected him to do. Instead, he went to the front door, and opening it, put it on the chain. At the end of ten minutes or so he closed the front door, and by that time Mrs. Bunting had divined why the lodger had behaved in this strange fashion—it must have been to get the strong acrid smell of burning wool out of the passage. But Mrs. Bunting felt as if she herself would never get rid of the horrible odor. She felt herself to be all smell.

At last the unhappy woman fell into a deep, troubled sleep; and then she dreamed a most terrible and unnatural dream; hoarse voices seemed to be shouting in her ear, " 'Orrible murder off the Edgeware Road!'' Then three words, indistinctly uttered, followed by ''—at his work again! Awful details!''

Even in her dream Mrs. Bunting felt angered and impatient; she knew so well why she was being disturbed by this horrid nightmare. It was because of Bunting—Bunting, who insisted on talking to her of those frightful murders, in which only morbid, vulgar-minded people took any interest. Why, even now, in her dream, she could hear her husband speaking to her about it.

"Ellen,"—so she heard Bunting say in her ear,—"Ellen, my dear, I am just going to get up to get a paper. It's after seven o'clock,"

Mrs. Bunting sat up in bed. The shouting, nay, worse, the sound of tramping, hurrying feet smote on her ears. It had been no nightmare, then, but something infinitely worse—reality. Why couldn't Bunting have lain quietly in bed awhile longer, and let his poor wife go on dreaming? The most awful dream would have been easier to bear than this awakening.

She heard her husband go to the front door, and, as he bought the paper, exchange a few excited words with the newspaper boy. Then he came back and began silently moving about the room.

"Well!" she cried. "Why don't you tell me about it?"

"I thought you'd rather not hear."

"Of course I like to know what happens close to our own front door!" she snapped out.

And then he read out a piece of the newspaper—only a few lines, after all—telling in brief, unemotional language that the body of woman, apparently done to death in a peculiarly atrocious fashion some hours before, had been found in a passage leading to a disused warehouse off the Marylebone Road.

"It serves that sort of hussy right!" was Mrs. Bunting's only comment.

When Mrs. Bunting went down into the kitchen, everything there looked just as she had left it, and there was no trace of the acrid smell she had expected to find there. Instead, the cavernous whitewashed room was full of fog, and she noticed that, though the shutters were bolted and barred as she had left them, the windows behind them had been widely opened to the air. She, of course, had left them shut.

She stooped and flung open the oven door of her gas-stove. Yes, it was as she had expected; a fierce heat had been generated there since she had last used the oven and a mass of black, gluey soot had fallen through to the stone floor below.

Mrs. Bunting took the ham and eggs that she had bought the previous day for her own and Bunting's breakfast, and broiled them over the gas-ring in their sitting-room. Her husband watched her in surprised silence. She had never done such a thing before.

"I couldn't stay down there," she said, "it was so

cold and foggy. I thought I'd make breakfast up here, just for to-day.''

''Yes,'' he said kindly; ''that's quite right, Ellen. I think you've done quite right, my dear.''

But, when it came to the point, his wife could not eat any of the nice breakfast she had got ready; she only had another cup of tea.

''Are you ill?'' Bunting asked solicitously.

''No,'' she said shortly; ''of course I'm not ill. Don't be silly! The thought of that horrible thing happening so close by has upset me. Just hark to them, now!

Through their closed windows penetrated the sound of scurrying feet and loud, ribald laughter. A crowd, nay, a mob, hastened to and from the scene of the murder.

Mrs. Bunting made her husband lock the front gate. ''I don't want any of those ghouls in here!'' she exclaimed angrily. And then, ''What a lot of idle people there must be in the world,'' she said.

The coming and going went on all day. Mrs. Bunting stayed indoors; Bunting went out. After all, the ex-butler was human—it was natural that he should feel thrilled and excited. All their neighbors were the same. His wife wasn't reasonable about such things. She quarreled with him when he didn't tell her anything, and yet he was sure she would have been angry with him if he had said very much about it.

The lodger's bell rang about two o'clock, and Mrs. Bunting prepared the simple luncheon that was also his breakfast. As she rested the tray a minute on the drawing-room floor landing, she heard Mr. Sleuth's high, quavering voice reading aloud the words:

''She saith to him, Stolen waters are sweet, and bread eaten in secret is pleasant. But he knoweth not that the dead are there; and that her guests are in the depths of hell.''

The landlady turned the handle of the door and walked in with the tray. Mr. Sleuth was sitting close by the window, and Mrs. Bunting's Bible lay open before him. As she came in he hastily closed the Bible and looked down at the crowd walking along the Marylebone Road.

"There seem a great many people out today," he observed, without looking round.

"Yes, sir, there do." Mrs. Bunting said nothing more, and offered no other explanation; and the lodger, as he at last turned to his landlady, smiled pleasantly. He had acquired a great liking and respect for this well-behaved, taciturn woman; she was the first person for whom he had felt any such feeling for many years past.

He took a half sovereign out of his waistcoat pocket; Mrs. Bunting noticed that it was not the same waistcoat Mr. Sleuth had been wearing the day before. "Will you please accept this half sovereign for the use of your kitchen last night?" he said. "I made as little mess as I could, but I was carrying on a rather elaborate experiment."

She held out her hand, hesitated, and then took the coin.

As she walked down the stairs, the winter sun, a yellow ball hanging in the smoky sky, glinted in on Mrs. Bunting, and lent blood-red gleams, or so it seemed to her, to the piece of gold she was holding in her hand.

It was a very cold night—so cold, so windy, so snowladen the atmosphere, that every one who could do so stayed indoors. Bunting, however, was on his way home from what had proved a very pleasant job; he had been acting as waiter at a young lady's birthday party, and a remarkable piece of luck had come his way. The young lady had come into a fortune that day, and she had had the gracious, the surprising thought of presenting each of the hired waiters with a sovereign.

This birthday treat had put him in mind of another

birthday. His daughter Daisy would be eighteen the following Saturday. Why shouldn't he send her a postal order for half a sovereign, so that she might come up and spend her birthday in London?

Having Daisy for three or four days would cheer up Ellen. Mr. Bunting, slackening his footsteps, began to think with puzzled concern of how queer his wife had seemed lately. She had become so nervous, so "jumpy," that he didn't know what to make of her sometimes. She had never been a really good-tempered woman,—your capable, self-respecting woman seldom is,—but she had never been like what she was now. Of late she sometimes got quite hysterical; he had let fall a sharp word to her the other day, and she had sat down on a chair, thrown her black apron over her face, and burst out sobbing violently.

During the last ten days Ellen had taken to talking in her sleep. "No, no, no!" she had cried out, only the night before. "It isn't true! I won't have it said! It's a lie!" And there had been a wail of horrible fear and revolt in her usually quiet, mincing voice. Yes, it would certainly be a good thing for her to have Daisy's company for a bit. Whew! It *was* cold; and Bunting had stupidly forgotten his gloves. He put his hands in his pockets to keep them warm.

Suddenly he became aware that Mr. Sleuth, the lodger who seemed to have "turned their luck," as it were, was walking along on the opposite side of the solitary street.

Mr. Sleuth's tall, thin figure was rather bowed, his head bent toward the ground. His right arm was thrust into his long Inverness cape; the other occasionally sawed the air, doubtless in order to help him keep warm. He was walking rather quickly. It was clear that he had not yet become aware of the proximity of his landlord.

Bunting felt pleased to see his lodger; it increased his feeling of general satisfaction. Strange, was it not, that that odd, peculiar-looking figure should have made all the difference to his (Bunting's) and Mrs. Bunting's happiness and comfort in life?

Naturally, Bunting saw far less of the lodger than did Mrs. Bunting. Their gentleman had made it very clear that he did not like either the husband or wife to come up to his rooms without being definitely asked to do so, and Bunting had been up there only once since Mr. Sleuth's arrival five weeks before. This seemed to be a good opportunity for a little genial conversation.

Bunting, still an active man for his years, crossed the road, and, stepping briskly forward, tried to overtake Mr. Sleuth; but the more he hurried, the more the other hastened, and that without even turning to see whose steps he heard echoing behind him on the now freezing pavement.

Mr. Sleuth's own footsteps were quite inaudible— an odd circumstance, when you came to think of it, as Bunting did think of it later, lying awake by Ellen's side in the pitch-darkness. What it meant was, of course, that the lodger had rubber soles on his shoes.

The two men, the pursued and the pursuer, at last turned into the Marylebone Road. They were now within a hundred yards of home; and so, plucking up courage, Bunting called out, his voice echoing freshly on the still air:

"Mr. Sleuth, sir! Mr. Sleuth!"

The lodger stopped and turned round. He had been walking so quickly, and he was in so poor a physical condition, that the sweat was pouring down his face.

"Ah! So it's you, Mr. Bunting? I heard footsteps behind me, and I hurried on. I wish I'd known that it was only you; there are so many queer characters about at night in London."

"Not on a night like this, sir. Only honest folk who have business out of doors would be out such a night as this. It *is* cold, sir!" And then into Bunting's slow and honest mind there suddenly crept the query as to what Mr. Sleuth's own business out could be on this cold, bitter night.

"Cold?" the lodger repeated. "I can't say that I find it cold, Mr. Bunting. When the snow falls the air always becomes milder."

"Yes, sir; but tonight there's such a sharp east wind. Why, it freezes the very marrow in one's bones!"

Bunting noticed that Mr. Sleuth kept his distance in a rather strange way: he walked at the edge of the pavement, leaving the rest of it, on the wall side, to his landlord.

"I lost my way," he said abruptly. "I've been over Primrose Hill to see a friend of mine, and then, coming back, I lost my way."

Bunting could well believe that, for when he had first noticed Mr. Sleuth he was coming from the east, and not, as he should have done if walking home from Primrose Hill, from the north.

They had now reached the little gate that gave on to the shabby, paved court in front of the house. Mr. Sleuth was walking up the flagged path, when, with a "By your leave, sir," the ex-butler, stepping aside, slipped in front of his lodger, in order to open the front door for him.

As he passed by Mr. Sleuth, the back of Bunting's bare left hand brushed lightly against the long Inverness cape the other man was wearing, and, to his surprise, the stretch of cloth against which his hand lay for a moment was not only damp, damp from the flakes of snow that had settled upon it, but wet—wet and gluey. Bunting thrust his left hand into his pocket; it was with the other that he placed the key in the lock of the door.

The two men passed into the hall together. The house seemed blackly dark in comparison with the lighted up road outside; and then, quite suddenly, there came over Bunting a feeling of mortal terror, an instinctive knowledge that some terrible and immediate danger was near him. A voice—the voice of his first wife, the long-dead girl to whom his mind so seldom reverted nowadays—uttered in his ear the words, ''Take care!''

''I'm afraid, Mr. Bunting, that you must have felt something dirty, foul, on my coat? It's too long a story to tell you now, but I brushed up against a dead animal—a dead rabbit lying across a bench on Primrose Hill.''

Mr. Sleuth spoke in a very quiet voice, almost in a whisper.

''No, sir; no, I didn't notice nothing. I scarcely touched you, sir.'' It seemed as if a power outside himself compelled Bunting to utter these lying words. ''And now, sir, I'll be saying good night to you,'' he added.

He waited until the lodger had gone upstairs, and then he turned into his own sitting-room. There he sat down, for he felt very queer. He did not draw his left hand out of his pocket till he heard the other man moving about in the room above. Then he lit the gas and held up his left hand; he put it close to his face. It was flecked, streaked with blood.

He took off his boots, and then, very quietly, he went into the room where his wife lay asleep. Stealthily he walked across to the toilet-table, and dipped his hand into the water-jug.

The next morning Mr. Sleuth's landlord awoke with a start; he felt curiously heavy about the limbs and tired about the eyes.

Drawing his watch from under his pillow, he saw that it was nearly nine o'clock. He and Ellen had overslept. Without waking her, he got out of bed and pulled up the blind. It was snowing heavily, and, as is the way when it snows, even in London, it was strangely, curiously still.

After he had dressed he went out into the passage. A newspaper and a letter were lying on the mat. Fancy having slept through the postman's knock! He picked them both up and went into the sitting-room; then he carefully shut the door behind him, and, tossing the letter aside, spread the newspaper wide open on the table and bent over it.

As Bunting at last looked up and straightened himself, a look of inexpressible relief shone upon his stolid face. The item of news he had felt certain would be there, printed in big type on the middle sheet, was not there.

He folded the paper and laid it on a chair, and then eagerly took up his letter.

> DEAR FATHER [it ran]: I hope this finds you as well as it leaves me. Mrs. Puddle's youngest child has got scarlet fever, and aunt thinks I had better come away at once, just to stay with you for a few days. Please tell Ellen I won't give her no trouble.
>> Your loving daughter,
>> DAISY.

Bunting felt amazingly light-hearted; and, as he walked into the next room, he smiled broadly.

"Ellen," he cried out, "here's news! Daisy's coming today. There's scarlet fever in their house, and Martha thinks she had better come away for a few days. She'll be here for her birthday!"

Mrs. Bunting listened in silence; she did not even open her eyes. "I can't have the girl here just now," she said shortly: "I've got just as much as I can manage to do."

But Bunting felt pugnacious, and so cheerful as to be almost light-headed. Deep down in his heart he looked back to last night with a feeling of shame and self-rebuke. Whatever had made such horrible thoughts and suspicions come into his head?

"Of course Daisy will come here," he said shortly. "If it comes to that, she'll be able to help you with the work, and she'll brisk us both up a bit."

Rather to his surprise, Mrs. Bunting said nothing in answer to this, and he changed the subject abruptly. "The lodger and me came in together last night, " he observed. "He's certainly a funny kind of gentleman. It wasn't the sort of night one would choose to go for a walk over Primrose Hill, and yet that was what he had been doing—so he said."

It stopped snowing about ten o'clock, and the morning wore itself away.

Just as twelve was striking, a four-wheeler drew up to the gate. It was Daisy—pink-cheeked, excited, laughing-eyed Daisy, a sight to gladden any father's heart. "Aunt said I was to have a cab if the weather was bad," she said.

There was a bit of a wrangle over the fare. King's Cross, as all the world knows, is nothing like two miles from the Marylebone Road, but the man clamored for one-and-sixpence, and hinted darkly that he had done the young lady a favor in bringing her at all.

While he and Bunting were having words, Daisy, leaving them to it, walked up the path to the door where her stepmother was awaiting her.

Suddenly there fell loud shouts on the still air. They sounded strangely eerie, breaking sharply across the muffled, snowy air.

"What's that?" said Bunting, with a look of startled fear. "Why, whatever's that?"

The cabman lowered his voice: "Them are crying out that 'orrible affair at King's Cross. He's done for two of 'em this time! That's what I meant when I said I might have got a better fare; I wouldn't say anything before Missy there, but folk 'ave been coming from all over London—like a fire; plenty of toffs, too. But there—there's nothing to see now!"

"What! Another woman murdered last night?" Bunting felt and looked convulsed with horror.

The cabman stared at him, surprised. "Two of 'em, I tell yer—within a few yards of one another. He 'ave got a nerve—"

"Have they caught him?" asked Bunting perfunctorily.

"Lord, no! They'll never catch 'im! It must 'ave happened hours and hours ago—they was both stonecold. One each end of an archway. That's why they didn't see 'em before."

The hoarse cries were coming nearer and nearer—two news-venders trying to outshout each other.

" 'Orrible discovery near King's Cross!" they yelled exultantly. And as Bunting, with his daughter's bag in his hand, hurried up the path and passed through his front door, the words pursued him like a dreadful threat.

Angrily he shut out the hoarse, insistent cries. No, he had no wish to buy a paper. That kind of crime wasn't fit reading for a young girl, such a girl as was his Daisy, brought up as carefully as if she had been a young lady by her strict Methody aunt.

As he stood in his little hall, trying to feel "all right" again, he could hear Daisy's voice—high, voluble, excited—giving her stepmother a long account of the scarlet-fever case to which she owed her presence in London. But, as Bunting pushed open the door of the sitting-room, there came a note of sharp alarm in his daughter's voice, and he heard her say: "Why Ellen! Whatever is the matter? You do look bad!" and his wife's muffled answer: "Open the window—do."

Rushing across the room, Bunting pushed up the sash. The newspaper-sellers were now just outside the house. "Horrible discovery near King's Cross—a clue to the murderer!" they yelled. And then, helplessly, Mrs. Bunting began to laugh. She laughed and laughed and laughed, rocking herself to and fro as if in an ecstasy of mirth.

"Why, father, whatever's the matter with her?" Daisy looked quite scared.

"She's in 'sterics—that's what it is," he said shortly. "I'll just get the water-jug. Wait a minute."

Bunting felt very put out, and yet glad, too, for this

queer seizure of Ellen's almost made him forget the
sick terror with which he had been possessed a moment before. That he and his wife should be obsessed
by the same fear, the same terror, never crossed his
simple, slow-working mind.

The lodger's bell rang. That, or the threat of the
water-jug, had a magical effect on Mrs. Bunting. She
rose to her feet, still trembling, but composed.

As Mrs. Bunting went upstairs she felt her legs
trembling under her, and put out a shaking hand to
clutch at the bannister for support. She waited a few
minutes on the landing, and then knocked at the door
of her lodger's parlor.

But Mr. Sleuth's voice answered her from the bedroom. "I'm not well," he called out querulously; "I
think I caught a chill going out to see a friend last
night. I'd be obliged if you'll bring me up a cup of tea
and put it outside my door, Mrs. Bunting."

"Very well, sir."

Mrs. Bunting went downstairs and made her lodger
a cup of tea over the gas-ring, Bunting watching her
the while in heavy silence.

During their midday dinner the husband and wife
had a little discussion as to where Daisy should sleep.
It had already been settled that a bed should be made
up for her in the sitting-room, but Bunting saw reason
to change this plan. As the two women were clearing
away the dishes, he looked up and said shortly: "I
think 'twould be better if Daisy were to sleep with
you, Ellen, and I were to sleep in the sitting-room."

Ellen acquiesced quietly.

Daisy was a good-natured girl; she liked London,
and wanted to make herself useful to her stepmother.
"I'll wash up; don't you bother to come downstairs,"
she said.

Bunting began to walk up and down the room. His
wife gave him a furtive glance; she wondered what he
was thinking about.

"Didn't you get a paper?" she said at last.

"There's the paper," he said crossly, "the paper we always do take in, the *Telegraph*." His look challenged her to a further question.

"I thought they was shouting something in the street—I mean just before I was took bad."

But he made no answer; instead, he went to the top of the staircase and called out sharply: "Daisy! Daisy, child, are you there?"

"Yes, father," she answered from below.

"Better come upstairs out of that cold kitchen."

He came back into the sitting-room again.

"Ellen, is the lodger in? I haven't heard him moving about. I don't want Daisy to be mixed up with him."

"Mr. Sleuth is not well today," his wife answered; "he is remaining in bed a bit. Daisy needn't have anything to do with him. She'll have her work cut out looking after things down here. That's where I want her to help me."

"Agreed," he said.

When it grew dark, Bunting went out and bought an evening paper. He read it out of doors in the biting cold, standing beneath a street lamp. He wanted to see what was the clue to the murderer.

The clue proved to be a very slender one—merely the imprint in the snowy slush of a half-worn rubber sole; and it was, of course, by no means certain that the sole belonged to the boot or shoe of the murderer of the two doomed women who had met so swift and awful a death in the arch near King's Cross station. The paper's special investigator pointed out that there were thousands of such soles being worn in London. Bunting found comfort in that obvious fact. He felt grateful to the special investigator for having stated it so clearly.

As he approached his house, he heard curious sounds coming from the inner side of the low wall that shut off the courtyard from the pavement. Under ordinary circumstances Bunting would have gone at once to drive whoever was there out into the roadway. Now he stayed outside, sick with suspense and anxiety. Was it possible that their place was being watched—already?

But it was only Mr. Sleuth. To Bunting's astonishment, the lodger suddenly stepped forward from behind the wall on to the flagged path. He was carrying a brown-paper parcel, and, as he walked along, the new boots he was wearing creaked and the tap-tap of wooden heels rang out on the stones.

Bunting, still hidden outside the gate, suddenly understood with his lodger had been doing the other side of the wall. Mr. Sleuth had been out to buy himself a pair of boots, and had gone inside the gate to put them on, placing his old footgear in the paper in which the new boots had been wrapped.

Bunting waited until Mr. Sleuth had let himself into the house; then he also walked up the flagged pathway, and put his latch-key in the door.

In the next three days each of Bunting's waking hours held its meed of aching fear and suspense. From his point of view, almost any alternative would be preferable to that which to most people would have seemed the only one open to him. He told himself that it would be ruin for him and for his Ellen to be mixed up publicly in such a terrible affair. It would track them to their dying day.

Bunting was also always debating within himself as to whether he should tell Ellen of his frightful suspicion. He could not believe that what had become so plain to himself could long be concealed from all the world, and yet he did not credit his wife with the same intelligence. He did not even notice that, although she waited on Mr. Sleuth as assiduously as ever, Mrs. Bunting never mentioned the lodger.

Mr. Sleuth, meanwhile, kept upstairs; he had given up going out altogether. He still felt, so he assured his landlady, far from well.

Daisy was another complication, the more so that the girl, whom her father longed to send away and whom he would hardly let out of his sight, showed herself inconveniently inquisitive concerning the lodger.

"Whatever does he do with himself all day?" she asked her stepmother.

"Well, just now he's reading the Bible," Mrs. Bunting had answered, very shortly and dryly.

"Well, I never! That's a funny thing for a gentleman to do!" Such had been Daisy's pert remark, and her stepmother had snubbed her well for it.

Daisy's eighteenth birthday dawned uneventfully. Her father gave her what he had always promised she should have on her eighteenth birthday—a watch. It was a pretty little silver watch, which Bunting had bought secondhand on the last day he had been happy; it seemed a long time ago now.

Mrs. Bunting thought a silver watch a very extravagant present, but she had always had the good sense not to interfere between her husband and his child. Besides, her mind was now full of other things. She was beginning to fear that Bunting suspected something, and she was filled with watchful anxiety and unease. What if he were to do anything silly—mix them up with the police, for instance? It certainly would be ruination to them both. But there—one never knew, with men! Her husband, however, kept his own counsel absolutely.

Daisy's birthday was on Saturday. In the middle of the morning Ellen and Daisy went down into the kitchen. Bunting didn't like the feeling that there was only one flight of stairs between Mr. Sleuth and himself, so he quietly slipped out of the house and went to buy himself an ounce of tobacco.

In the last four days Bunting had avoided his usual haunts. But today the unfortunate man had a curious longing for human companionship—companionship, that is, other than that of Ellen and Daisy. This feeling led him into a small, populous thoroughfare hard by the Edgeware Road. There were more people there than usual, for the housewives of the neighborhood were doing their marketing for Sunday.

Bunting passed the time of day with the tobacconist, and the two fell into desultory talk. To the ex-butler's surprise, the man said nothing at all to him on the subject of which all the neighborhood must still be talking.

And then, quite suddenly, while still standing by the counter, and before he had paid for the packet of tobacco he held in his hand, Bunting, through the open door, saw, with horrified surprise, that his wife was standing outside a green-grocer's shop just opposite. Muttering a word of apology, he rushed out of the shop and across the road.

"Ellen!" he gasped hoarsely. "You've never gone and left my little girl alone in the house?"

Mrs. Bunting's face went chalky white. "I thought you were indoors," she said. "You *were* indoors. Whatever made you come out for, without first making sure I was there?"

Bunting made no answer; but, as they stared at each other in exasperated silence, *each knew that the other knew*.

They turned and scurried down the street.

"Don't run," he said suddenly; "we shall get there just as quickly if we walk fast. People are noticing you, Ellen. Don't run."

He spoke breathlessly, but it was breathlessness induced by fear and excitement, not by the quick pace at which they were walking.

At last they reached their own gate. Bunting pushed past in front of his wife. After all, Daisy was his child—Ellen couldn't know how he was feeling. He made the path almost in one leap, and fumbled for a moment with his latch-key. The door opened.

"Daisy!" he called out in a wailing voice. "Daisy, my dear, where are you?"

"Here I am, father; what is it?"

"She's all right!" Bunting turned his gray face to his wife. "She's all right, Ellen!" Then he waited a moment, leaning against the wall of the passage. "It did give me a turn," he said; and then, warningly, "Don't frighten the girl, Ellen."

Daisy was standing before the fire in the sitting-room, admiring herself in the glass. "Oh, father," she said, without turning round, "I've seen the lodger! He's quite a nice gentleman—though, to be sure, he does look a cure! He came down to ask Ellen for something, and we had quite a nice little chat. I told him it was my birthday, and he asked me to go to Madame Tussaud's with him this afternoon." She laughed a little self-consciously. "Of course I could see he was 'centric, and then at first he spoke so funnily. 'And who be you?' he says, threatening-like. And I says to him, 'I'm Mr. Bunting's daughter, sir.' 'Then you're a very fortunate girl'—that's what he said, Ellen—'to 'ave such a nice stepmother as you've got. That's why,' he says, 'you look such a good innocent girl.' And then he quoted a bit of the prayer-book at me. 'Keep innocency,' he says, wagging his head at me. Lor'! It made me feel as if I was with aunt again."

"I won't have you going out with the lodger—that's flat." He was wiping his forehead with one hand, while with the other he mechanically squeezed the little packet of tobacco, for which, as he now remembered, he had forgotten to pay.

Daisy pouted. "Oh, father, I think you might let me have a treat on my birthday! I told him Saturday wasn't a very good day—at least, so I'd heard—for Madame Tussaud's. Then he said we could go early, while the fine folk are still having their dinners. He wants you to come, too." She turned to her stepmother, then giggled happily. "The lodger has a wonderful fancy for you, Ellen; if I was father, I'd feel quite jealous!"

Her last words were cut across by a loud knock on the door. Bunting and his wife looked at each other apprehensively.

Both felt a curious thrill of relief when they saw that it was only Mr. Sleuth—Mr. Sleuth dressed to go out: the tall hat he had worn when he first came to them was in his hand, and he was wearing a heavy overcoat.

"I saw you had come in,"—he addressed Mrs. Bunting in his high, whistling, hesitating voice,—"and so I've come down to ask if you and Miss Bunting will come to Madame Tussaud's now. I have never seen these famous waxworks, though I've heard of the place all my life."

As Bunting forced himself to look fixedly at his lodger, a sudden doubt, bringing with it a sense of immeasurable relief, came to him. Surely it was inconceivable that this gentle, mild-mannered gentleman could be the monster of cruelty and cunning that Bunting had but a moment ago believed him to be!

"You're very kind, sir, I'm sure." He tried to catch his wife's eye, but Mrs. Bunting was looking away, staring into vacancy. She still, of course, wore the bonnet and cloak in which she had just been out to do her marketing. Daisy was already putting on her hat and coat.

Madame Tussaud's had hitherto held pleasant memories for Mrs. Bunting. In the days when she and Bunting were courting they often spent part of their "afternoon out" there. The butler had an acquaintance, a man named Hopkins, who was one of the waxworks' staff, and this man had sometimes given him passes for "self and lady." But this was the first time Mrs. Bunting had been inside the place since she had come to live almost next door, as it were, to the big building.

The ill-sorted trio walked up the great staircase and into the first gallery; and there Mr. Sleuth suddenly stopped short. The presence of those curious, still figures, suggesting death in life, seemed to surprise and affright him.

Daisy took quick advantage of the lodger's hesitation and unease.

"Oh, Ellen," she cried, "do let us begin by going into the Chamber of Horrors! I've never been in there. Aunt made father promise he wouldn't take me, the only time I've ever been here. But now that I'm eighteen I can do just as I like; besides, aunt will never know!"

Mr. Sleuth looked down at her.

"Yes," he said, "let us go into the Chamber of Horrors; that's a good idea, Miss Bunting."

They turned into the great room in which the Napoleonic relics are kept, and which leads into the curious, vaultlike chamber where waxen effigies of dead criminals stand grouped in wooden docks. Mrs. Bunting was at once disturbed and relieved to see her husband's old acquaintance, Mr. Hopkins, in charge of the turnstile admitting the public to the Chamber of Horrors.

"Well, you *are* a stranger," the man observed genially. "I do believe this is the very first time I've seen you in here, Mrs. Bunting, since you married!"

"Yes," she said; "that is so. And this is my husband's daughter, Daisy; I expect you've heard of her, Mr. Hopkins. And this"—she hesitated a moment—"is our lodger, Mr. Sleuth."

But Mr. Sleuth frowned and shuffled away. Daisy, leaving her stepmother's side, joined him.

Mrs. Bunting put down three sixpences.

"Wait a minute," said Hopkins; "you can't go into the Chamber of Horrors just yet. But you won't have to wait more than four or five minutes, Mrs. Bunting. It's this way, you see; our boss is in there, showing a party round." He lowered his voice. "It's Sir John Burney—I suppose you know who Sir John Burney is?"

"No," she answered indifferently; "I don't know that I ever heard of him." She felt slightly—oh, very slightly—uneasy about Daisy. She would like her step-daughter to keep well within sight and sound. Mr. Sleuth was taking the girl to the other end of the room.

"Well, I hope you never *will* know him—not in any personal sense, Mrs. Bunting." The man chuckled. "He's the Head Commissioner of Police—that's what Sir John Burney is. One of the gentlemen he's showing round our place is the Paris Prefect of Police,whose job is on all fours, so to speak, with Sir John's. The Frenchy has brought his daughter with him, and there are several other ladies. Ladies always like 'orrors, Mrs. Bunting; that's our experience here. 'Oh, take me to the Chamber of 'Orrors!'—that's what they say the minute they gets into the building."

A group of people, all talking and laughing together; were advancing from within toward the turnstile.

Mrs. Bunting stared at them nervously. She wondered which of them was the gentleman with whom Mr. Hopkins had hoped she would never be brought into personal contact. She quickly picked him out. He was a tall, powerful, nice-looking gentleman with a commanding manner. Just now he was smiling down into the face of a young lady. "Monsieur Barberoux is quite right," he was saying; "the English law is too kind to the criminal, especially to the murderer. If we conducted our trials in the French fashion, the place we have just left would be very much fuller than it is today! A man of whose guilt we are absolutely assured is oftener than not acquitted, and then the public taunt us with 'another undiscovered crime'!"

"D'you mean, Sir John, that murderers sometimes escape scot-free? Take the man who has been committing all those awful murders this last month. Of course, I don't know much about it, for father won't let me read about it, but I can't help being interested!" Her girlish voice rang out, and Mrs. Bunting heard every word distinctly.

The party gathered round, listening eagerly to hear what the Head Commissioner would say next.

"Yes." He spoke very deliberately. "I think we may say—now, don't give me away to a newspaper fellow, Miss Rose—that we do know perfectly well who the murderer in question is—"

Several of those standing near by uttered expressions of surprise and incredulity.

"Then why don't you catch him?" cried the girl indignantly.

"I didn't say we know *where* he is; I only said we know *who* he is; or, rather, perhaps I ought to say that we have a very strong suspicion of his identity."

Sir John's French colleague looked up quickly. "The Hamburg and Liverpool man?" he said interrogatively.

The other nodded. "Yes; I suppose you've had the case turned up?"

Then, speaking very quickly, as if he wished to dismiss the subject from his own mind and from that of his auditors, he went on:

"Two murders of the kind were committed eight years ago—one in Hamburg, the other just afterward in Liverpool, and there were certain peculiarities connected with the crimes which made it clear they were committed by the same hand. The perpetrator was caught, fortunately for us red-handed, just as he was leaving the house of his victim, for in Liverpool the murder was committed in a house. I myself saw the unhappy man—I say unhappy, for there is no doubt at all that he was mad,"—he hesitated, and added in a lower tone—"suffering from an acute form of religious mania. I myself saw him, at some length. But now comes the really interesting point. Just a month ago this criminal lunatic, as we must regard him, made his escape from the asylum where he was confined. He arranged the whole thing with extraordinary cunning and intelligence, and we should probably have caught him long ago were it not that he managed, when on his way out of the place, to annex a considerable sum of money in gold with which the wages of the staff were about to be paid.''

The Frenchman again spoke. ''Why have you not circulated a description?'' he asked.

''We did that at once,''—Sir John Burney smiled a little grimly,—''but only among our own people. We dare not circulate the man's description among the general public. You see, we may be mistaken, after all.''

''That is not very probable!'' The Frenchman smiled a satirical little smile.

A moment later the party were walking in Indian file through the turnstile, Sir John Burney leading the way.

Mrs. Bunting looked straight before her. Even had she wished to do so, she had neither time nor power to warn her lodger of his danger.

Daisy and her companion were now coming down the room, bearing straight for the Head Commissioner of Police. In another moment Mr. Sleuth and Sir John Burney would be face to face.

Suddenly Mr. Sleuth swerved to one side. A terrible change came over his pale, narrow face; it became discomposed, livid with rage and terror.

But, to Mrs. Bunting's relief,—yes, to her inexpressible relief,—Sir John Burney and his friends swept on. They passed by Mr. Sleuth unconcernedly, unaware, or so it seemed to her, that there was anyone else in the room but themselves.

''Hurry up, Mrs. Bunting,'' said the turnstile-keeper; ''you and your friends will have the place all to yourselves.'' From an official he had become a man, and it was the man in Mr. Hopkins that gallantly addressed pretty Daisy Bunting. ''It seems strange that a young lady like you should want to go in and see all those 'orrible frights,'' he said jestingly.

''Mrs. Bunting, may I trouble you to come over here for a moment?'' The words were hissed rather than spoken by Mr. Sleuth's lips.

His landlady took a doubtful step forward.

"A last word with you, Mrs. Bunting." The lodger's face was still distorted with fear and passion. "Do you think to escape the consequences of your hideous treachery? I trusted you, Mrs. Bunting, and you betrayed me! But I am protected by a higher power, for I still have work to do. Your end will be bitter as wormwood and sharp as a two-edged sword. Your feet shall go down to death, and your steps take hold on hell." Even while Mr. Sleuth was uttering these strange, dreadful words, he was looking around, his eyes glancing this way and that, seeking a way of escape.

At last his eyes became fixed on a small placard placed about a curtain. "Emergency Exit" was written there. Leaving his landlady's side, he walked over to the turnstile. He fumbled in his pocket for a moment, and then touched the man on the arm. "I feel ill," he said, speaking very rapidly; "very ill indeed! It's the atmosphere of this place. I want you to let me out by the quickest way. It would be a pity for me to faint here—especially with ladies about." His left hand shot out and placed what he had been fumbling for in his pocket on the other's bare palm. "I see there's an emergency exit over there. Would it be possible for me to get out that way?"

"Well, yes, sir; I think so." The man hesitated; he felt a slight, a very slight, feeling of misgiving. He looked at Daisy, flushed and smiling, happy and unconcerned, and then at Mrs. Bunting. She was very pale; but surely her lodger's sudden seizure was enough to make her feel worried. Hopkins felt the half sovereign pleasantly tickling his palm. The Prefect of Police had given him only half a crown—mean, shabby foreigner!

"Yes, I can let you out that way," he said at last, "and perhaps when you're standing out in the air on the iron balcony you'll feel better. But then, you know, sir, you'll have to come round to the front if you want to come in again, for those emergency doors only open outward.''

''Yes, yes,'' said Mr. Sleuth hurriedly; ''I quite understand! If I feel better I'll come in by the front way, and pay another shilling—that's only fair.''

''You needn't do that if you'll just explain what happened here.''

The man went and pulled the curtain aside, and put his shoulder against the door. It burst open, and the light for a moment blinded Mr. Sleuth. He passed his hand over his eyes.

''Thank you,'' he said; ''thank you. I shall get all right here.''

Five days later Bunting identified the body of a man found drowned in the Regent's Canal as that of his late lodger; and, the morning following, a gardener working in the Regent's Park found a newspaper in which were wrapped, together with a half-worn pair of rubber-soled shoes, two surgical knives. This fact was not chronicled in any newspaper; but a very pretty and picturesque paragraph went the round of the press, about the same time, concerning a small box filled with sovereigns which had been forwarded anonymously to the Governor of the Foundling Hospital.

Mr. and Mrs. Bunting are now in the service of an old lady, by whom they are feared as well as respected, and whom they make very comfortable.

THE FINAL STONE
by William F. Nolan

They were from Indianapolis. Newly married. Dave and *stirring, flexing muscle, feeling power now . . . anger . . . a sudden driving thirst for* Alice Williamson, both in their late twenties, both excited about their trip to the West Coast. This would be their last night in Arizona. Tomorrow they planned to be in Palm Springs. To visit Dave's sister. But only one of them would make it to California. Dave, not Alice. *with the scalpel glittering*

Alice would die before midnight, her throat slashed cleanly across. *glittering, raised against the moon*

"Wait till you see what's here," Dave told her. "Gonna just be fantastic."

They were pulling their used Camaro into the parking lot at a tourist site in Lake Havasu City, Arizona. He wouldn't tell her where they were. It was late. The lot was wide and dark, with only two other cars parked there, one a service vehicle.

"What is this place?" Alice was tired and hungry. *hungry*

"You'll find out. Once you see it, you'll never forget it. That's what they say."

"I just want to eat," she said. *the blade eating flesh, drinking*

"First we'll have a look at it, then we'll eat," said Dave, *them getting out of the car, walking toward the gate* smiling at her, giving her a hug.

The tall iron gate, black pebbled iron, led into a picture-perfect Tudor Village. A bit of Olde England rising up from raw Arizona desert. A winged dragon looked down at them from the top of the gate.

"That's ugly," said Alice.

"It's historic," Dave told her. "That's the official Heraldic Dragon from the City of London."

"Is *that* what all this is—some sort of replica of London?"

"Much more than that. Heck, Ally, this was all built *around* it, to give it the proper atmosphere."

"I'm in no mood for atmosphere," she said. "We've been driving all day and I don't feel like playing games. I want to know what you—"

Dave cut into the flow of her words: "There it is!"

They both stared at it. Ten thousand tons of fitted stone. Over nine hundred feet of arched granite spanning the dark waters of the Colorado River. Tall and massive and magnificent.

"Christ!" murmured Dave. "Doesn't it just knock you out?" Imagine—all the way from England, from the Thames River . . . the by-God-for-real London Bridge!"

"It *is* amazing," Alice admitted. She smiled, kissed him on the cheek. "And I'm glad you didn't tell me . . . that you kept it for a surprise."

glittering cold steel

They moved along the concrete walkway beneath the Bridge, staring upward at the giant gray-black structure. Dave said: "When the British tore it down they numbered all the stones so our people would know where each one went. Thousands of stones. Like a jigsaw puzzle. Took three years to build it all over again here in Arizona." He gestured around them. "All this was just open desert when they started. After the Bridge was finished they diverted a section of the Colorado River to run under it. And built the village."

"Why did the British give us their bridge?"

"They were putting up a better one," said Dave. "But, hey, they didn't *give* this one to us. The guy that had it built here paid nearly two and a half million for it. Plus the cost of shipping all the stones over. Some rich guy named McCulloch. Died since then, I think.''

dead death dead dead death

''Well, we've seen it,'' said Alice. ''Let's eat now. C'mon, I'm really starving.''

''You don't want to *walk* on it?''

''Maybe after we eat,'' said Alice. *going inside the restaurant now . . . will wait . . . she's perfect . . . white throat, blue vein pulsing under the chin . . . long graceful neck . . .*

They ate at the City of London Arms in the Village. Late. Last couple in for dinner that evening. Last meal served.

''You folks should have come earlier,'' the waitress told them. ''Lots of excitement here today, putting in the final stone. I mean, with the Bridge dedication and all.''

''I thought it was dedicated in 1971,'' said Dave.

''Oh, it was. But there was this *one* stone missing. Everyone figured it had been lost on the trip over. But they found it last month in London. Had fallen into the water when they were taking the Bridge apart. Today, it got fitted back where it belonged.'' She smiled brightly. ''So London Bridge is *really* complete now!''

Alice set her empty wineglass on the tablecloth. ''All this Bridge talk is beginning to *bore* me,'' she said. ''I need another drink.''

''You've had enough,'' said Dave.

''Hell I have!'' To the waitress: ''Bring us another bottle of wine.''

''Sorry, but we're closing, I'm not allowed to—''

''I *said* bring another!''

''And she said they're closing,'' snapped Dave. ''Let's go.''

They paid the check, left. The doors were locked behind them.

The City of London Arms sign blinked off as they moved down the restaurant steps. *to me to me*

"You'll feel better when we get back to the motel," Dave said.

"I feel fine. Let's go walk on London Bridge. That's what you wanted, isn't it?"

"Now now, Ally," he said. "We can do that tomorrow, before we leave. Drive over from the motel."

"*You* go to the damn motel," she said tightly. "*I'm* walking on the damn Bridge!"

He stared at her. "You're *drunk!*"

She giggled. "So what? Can't drunk people walk on the damn Bridge?"

"Come on," said Dave, taking her arm. "We're going to the car."

"You go to the car," she snapped, pulling away. "I'm gonna walk on the damn Bridge."

"Fine," said Dave. "Then you can get a *taxi* to the motel."

And, dark-faced with anger, he walked away from her, back to their car. Got in. Drove off.

alone now for me . . . just for me

Alice Williamson walked toward London Bridge through the massed tree shadows along the dark river pathway. She reached the foot of the wide gray-granite Bridge steps, looked up.

At a tall figure in black. Slouch hat, dark cloak, boots.

She was looking at death.

She stumbled back, turned, poised to run—but the figure moved, glided, flowed *mine now mine* down the granite steps with horrific speed.

And the scalpel glitter-danced against the moon.

Two days later.

Evening, with the tour boat empty, heading for its home dock, Angie Shepherd at the wheel. Angie was the boat's owner. She lived beside the river, had all her life. Knew its currents, its moods, under moon and sun, knew it intimately. Thompson Bay . . . Copper Canyon . . . Cattail Cove . . . Red Rock . . . Black Meadow . . . Topock Gorge. Knew its eagles and hawks and mallards, its mud turtles and great horned owls. Knew the sound of its waters in calm and in storm.

Her home was a tall, weathered-wood building that once served as a general store. She lived alone here. Made a living with her boat, running scenic tours along the Colorado. Age twenty-eight. Never married, and no plans in that area.

Angie docked the boat, secured it, entered the tall wooden building she called Riverhouse. She fussed in the small kitchen, taking some wine, bread, and cheese out to the dock. It was late; the night was ripe with river sounds and the heart-pulse of crickets.

She sat at the dock's edge, legs dangling in the cool water. Nibbled cheese. Listened to a night bird crying over the river.

Something bumped her foot in the dark water. Something heavy, sodden. Drifting in the slow night current.

Something called Alice Williamson

Dan Gregory had no clues to the murder. The husband was a logical suspect (most murders are family-connected), but Gregory knew that Dave Williamson was not guilty. You develop an instinct about people, and he knew Williamson was no wife-killer. For one thing, the man's grief was deep and genuine; he seemed totally shattered by the murder—blamed himself, bitterly, for deserting Alice in the Village.

Gregory was tipped back in his desk chair, an unlit Marlboro in his mouth. (He was trying to give up smoking.) Williamson slouched in the office chair in front of him, looking broken and defeated. ''Your wife was drunk, you had an argument. You got pissed and drove off. Happens to people all the time. Don't blame yourself for this.''

''But if I'd stayed there, been there when—''

''Then you'd probably *both* be dead,'' said Gregory. ''You go back to the motel, take those pills the doc gave you and get some sleep. Then head for Palm Springs. We'll contact you at your sister's if we come up with anything.''

Williamson left the office. Gregory talked to Angie Shepherd next, about finding the body. She was shaken, but cooperative.

''I've never seen anyone dead before,'' she told him.

''No family funerals?''

''Sure. A couple. But I'd never walk past the open caskets. I didn't want to have to see people I'd love . . . *that* way.'' She shrugged. ''In your business I guess you see a lot of death.''

''Not actually,'' said Gregory. ''Your average Highway Patrol officer sees more of it in a month than I have in ten years. You don't get many murders in a town this size.''

''That how long you've been Chief of Police here, ten years?''

''Nope. Just over a year. Used to be a police lieutenant in Phoenix. Moved up to this job.'' He raised an eyebrow at her. ''How come you being a local, you don't know how long I've been Chief?''

''I never follow politics—*especially* small-town politics. Sorry about that.'' And she smiled.

Gregory was a square-faced man in his thirties with hard, ice-blue eyes, offset by a quick, warm way of grinning. Had never married; most women bored him. But he like Angie. And the attraction was mutual.

Alice Williamson's death had launched a relationship.

In August, four months after the first murder, there were two more. Both women. Both with throats cut.

Both found along the banks of the Colorado. One at Pilot Rock, the other near Whipple Bay.

Dan Gregory had no reason to believe the two August "River Killings" (as the local paper had dubbed them) had been committed near London Bridge. He told a reporter that the killer might be a transient, passing through the area, killing at random. The murders lacked motive; the three victims had nothing in common beyond being female. Maybe the murderer, suggested Gregory, was just someone who hates women.

The press had a field day. "Madman on Loose." . . . "Woman-Hating Killer Haunts Area" . . . "Chief of Police Admits No Clues to River Killings."

Reading the stories, Gregory muttered softly: "Assholes!"

Early September. A classroom at Lake Havasu City High School. Senior English. Lyn Esterly was finishing a lecture on William Faulkner's *Light in August*.

". . . therefore, Joe Christmas became the victim of his own twisted personality. He truly believed he was cursed by an outlaw strain of blood, a white man branded black by a racially bigoted society. Your assignment is to write a five-hundred-word essay on his inner conflicts."

After she'd dismissed the class, Lyn phoned her best friend, Angie Shepherd, for lunch. They had met when Lyn had almost drowned swimming near Castle Rock. Angie had saved her life.

"You're not running the boat today, and I need to talk to you, okay?"

"Sure . . . okay," agreed Angie. "Meet you in town. Tom's all right?"

"Tom's it is."

Trader Tom's was a seafood restaurant, specializing in fresh shrimp, an improbable business establishment in the middle of the Arizona desert. Angie, "the primitive," adored fresh shrimp, which had been introduced to her by Lyn, the "city animal," their joke names for one another.

Over broiled shrimp and sole amandine they relaxed into a familiar discussion: "I'll never be able to understand how you can live out there all alone on the river," said Lyn. "It's positively *spooky*—especially with a woman-killer running loose. Aren't you afraid?"

"No. I keep a gun with me in the house, and I know how to use it."

"*I'd* be terrified."

"That's because you're a victim of your own imagination," said Angie, dipping a huge shrimp into Tom's special Cajun sauce. "You and your fascination with murder."

"Lots of people are true-crime buffs," said Lyn. "In fact that's why I wanted to talk to you today. It's about the River Killings."

"You've got a theory about 'em, right?"

"This one's pretty wild."

"Aren't they all?" Angie smiled, unpeeling another shrimp. "I'm listening."

"The first murder, the Williamson woman, that one took place on the third of April."

"So?"

"The second murder was on the seventh of August, the third on the thirty-first. All three dates are a perfect match."

"For what?"

"For a series of killings, seven in all, committed in 1888 by Jack the Ripper. His first three were on exact matching dates."

Angie paused, a shrimp halfway to her mouth. "Wow! Okay . . . you *did* say wild."

"And there's more. Alice Williamson, we know, was attacked near London Bridge—which is where the Ripper finally disappeared in 1888. They had him trapped there, but the fog was really thick that night and when they closed in on him from both ends of the

Bridge he just . . . vanished. And he was never seen or heard of again.''

"Are you telling me that some nut is out there in the dark near London Bridge trying to duplicate the original Ripper murders? Is that your theory?''

"That's it.''

"But why *now?* What triggered the pattern?''

"I'm working on that angle.'' Lyn's eyes were intense. "I'm telling you this today for a vitally important reason.''

"I'm still listening.''

"You've become very friendly with Chief Gregory. He'll listen to you. He must be told that the fourth murder will take place *tonight,* the eighth of September, before midnight.''

But I . . .''

"You've got to warn him to post extra men near the Bridge tonight. And he should be there himself.''

"Because of your theory?''

"Of course! Because of my theory.''

Angie slowly shook her head. "Dan would think I was around the bend. He's a realist. He'd laugh at me.''

"Isn't it *worth* being laughed at to save a life?'' Lyn's eyes burned at her. "Honest, Angie, if you don't convince Gregory that I'm making sense, that I'm onto a real pattern here, then another woman is going to get her throat slashed open near London Bridge tonight.''

Angie pushed her plate away. "You sure do know how to spoil a terrific lunch.''

That afternoon, back at Riverhouse, Angie tried to make sense of Lyn's theory. The fact that these murders had fallen on the same dates as three murders a century earlier was interesting and curious, but not enough to set a hard-minded man like Gregory in motion.

It was crazy, but still Lyn *might* be onto something. At least she could phone Dan and suggest dinner in the Village. She could tell him what Lyn said—and then he *would* be there in the area, just in case something happened.

Dan said yes, they'd meet at the City of London Arms.

When Angie left for the Village that night she carried a pearl-handled .32-caliber automatic in her purse.

If. Just if.

Dan was late. On the phone he'd mentioned a meeting with the City Council, so maybe that was it. The Village was quiet, nearly empty of tourists.

Angie waited, seated on a park bench near the restaurant, nervous in spite of herself, thinking that *alone, her back to the trees, thick shadow trees, vulnerable* maybe she should wait inside, at the bar.

A tall figure, moving toward her. Behind her.

A thick-fingered hand reaching out for her. She flinched back eyes wide, fingers closing on the automatic inside her open purse.

"Didn't mean to scare you."

It was Dan. His grin made her relax. "I've . . . been a little nervous today."

"Over what?"

"Something Lyn Esterly told me." She took his arm. "I'll tell you all about it at dinner."

lost her . . . can't with him

And they went inside.

". . . so what do you think?" Angie asked. They were having an after-dinner drink. The booths around them were silent, unoccupied.

"I think your friend's imagination is working overtime."

Angie frowned. "I knew you'd say something like that."

Dan leaned forward, taking her hand. "You don't

really believe there's going to be another murder in this area tonight just because *she* says so, do you?''

''No, I guess I don't really believe that.''

And she guessed she didn't.

But . . .

There! Walking idly on the Bridge, looking down at the water, alone, young woman alone . . . her throat naked, skin naked and long-necked . . . open to me . . . blade sharp sharp . . . soft throat

A dark pulsing glide onto the Bridge, a swift reaching out, a small choked cry of shocked horror, a sudden drawn-across half-moon of bright crimson—and the body falling . . . falling into deep Colorado waters.

Although Dan Gregory was a skeptic, he was not a fool. He ordered the entire Village area closed to tourists and began a thorough search.

Which proved rewarding.

An object was found on the Bridge, wedged into an aperture between two stones below one of the main arches: a surgeon's scalpel with fresh blood on it. And with blackened stains on the handle and blade.

It was confirmed that the fresh blood matched that of the latest victim. The dark stains proved to be dried blood. But they did not match the blood types of the other three murder victims. It was old blood. Very old.

Lab tests revealed that the bloodstains had remained on the scalpel for approximately one hundred years.

Dating back to the 1880s.

''Are you Angela Shepherd?''

A quiet Sunday morning along the river. Angie was repairing a water-damaged section of dock, briskly hammering in fresh nails, and had not heard the woman walk up behind her. She put down the claw hammer, stood, pushing back her hair. ''Yes, I'm Angie Shepherd. Who are you?''

"Lenore Harper. I'm a journalist."

"What paper?"

"Free lance. could we talk?"

Angie gestured toward the house. Lenore was tall, trim-bodied, with penetrating green eyes.

"Want a Coke?" asked Angie. "Afraid it's all I've got. I wasn't expecting company."

"No, I'm fine," said Lenore, seating herself on the living-room couch and removing a small notepad from her purse.

"You're doing a story on the River Killings, right?"

Lenore nodded. "But I'm going after something different. That's why I came to you."

"Why me?"

"Well . . . you discovered the first body."

Angie sat down in a chair opposite the couch, ran a hand through her hair. "I didn't *discover* anything. When the body drifted downriver against the dock I happened to be there. That's all there is to it."

"Where you shocked . . . frightened?"

"Sickened is a better word. I don't enjoy seeing people with their throats cut."

"Of course. I understand, but . . ."

Angie stood up. "Look, there's really nothing more I can tell you. If you want facts on the case, talk to Chief Gregory at the police department."

"I'm more interested in ideas, emotions—in personal reactions to these killings. I'd like to know *your* ideas. *Your* theories."

"If you want to talk theory, go see Lyn Esterly. She's got some original ideas on the case. Lyn's a true-crime buff. She'll probably be anxious to help you."

"Sounds like a good lead. Where can I find her?"

"Lake Havasu High. She teaches English there."

"Great." Lenore put away her notepad, then shook Angie's hand. "You've been very kind. Appreciate your talking to me."

"No problem."

Angie looked deeply into Lenore Harper's green eyes. Something about her I like, she thought. Maybe I've made a new friend. Well . . . "Good luck with your story," she said.

Lenore's talk with Lyn Esterly bore colorful results. The following day's paper carried "an exclusive feature interview" by Lenore Harper:

"Is River Killer Another Jack the Ripper?" the headline asked. Then, below it, a subheading: "Havasu High Teacher Traces Century-Old Murder Pattern."

According to the story, if the killer continued to follow the original Ripper's pattern, he would strike again on the thirtieth of September. And not once, but twice. On the night of September 30, 1888, Jack the Ripper butchered *two* women in London's Whitechapel district—victims #5 and #6. Would these gruesome double murders be repeated here in Lake Havasu?

The story ended with a large question mark.

Angie, on the phone to Lyn: "Maybe I did the wrong thing, sending her to see you."

"Why? I like her. She really *listened* to me."

"I just get the feeling that her story makes you . . . well, a kind of target."

"I doubt that."

"The killer knows all about you now. Even your picture was there in the paper. He knows that you're doing all this special research, that you worked out the whole copycat-Ripper idea . . ."

"So what? I can't catch him. That's up to the police. He's not going to bother with me. Getting my theory into print was important. Now that his sick little game has been exposed, maybe he'll quit. Might not be fun for him anymore. These weirdos are like that. Angie, it could all be over."

"So you're not sore at me for sending her to you?"

"Are you kidding? For once, someone has taken a

theory of mine seriously enough to print it. Makes all this work mean something. Hell, I'm a celebrity now.''

''That's what worries me.''

And their conversation ended.

Angie had been correct in her hunch regarding Lenore Harper: the two women *did* become friends. As a free-lance journalist, Lenore had roved the world, while Angie had spent her entire life in Arizona. Europe seemed, to her, exotic and impossibly far away. She was fascinated with Lenore's tales of global travel and of her childhood and early schooling in London.

On the night of September 30, Lyn Esterly turned down Angie's invitation to spend the evening at Riverhouse.

''I'm into something *new,* something really exciting on this Ripper thing,'' Lyn told her. ''But I need to do more research. If what I think is true, then a lot of people are going to be surprised.''

''God,'' sighed Angie, ''how you love being mysterious!''

''Guilty as charged,'' admitted Lyn. ''Anyhow, I'll feel a lot safer working at the library in the middle of town than being out there on that desolate river with you.''

''Dan's taking your ideas seriously,'' Angie told her. ''He's still got the Village closed to tourists—and he's bringing in extra men tonight in case you're right about the possibility of a double murder.''

''I *want* to be wrong, Angie, honest to God I do. Maybe this creep has been scared off by all the publicity. Maybe tonight will prove that—but to be on the safe side, if I were you, I'd spend the night in town . . . not alone out there in that damn haunted castle of yours!''

'Okay, you've made your point. I'll take in a movie, then meet Dan later. Ought to be safe enough with the Chief of Police, eh?''

"Absolutely. And by tomorrow I may have a big surprise for you. This is like a puzzle that's finally coming together. It's exciting!"

"Call me in the morning?"

"That's a promise."

And they rang off.

Ten P.M. Lyn working alone in the reference room on the second floor of the city library. The building had been closed to the public for two hours. Even the staff had gone. But, as a teacher, Lyn had special privileges. And her own key.

A heavy night silence. Just the shuffling sound of her books and the faint scratch of her ballpoint pen, her own soft breathing.

When the outside door to the parking lot clicked open on the floor below her, Lyn didn't hear it.

The Ripper glided upward, a dark spider-shape on the stairs, *and she's there waiting to meet me, heart pumping blood for the blade* reached the second floor, moved down the silent hallway to the reference room, *pumping crimson* pushed open the door. *pumping*

To her. Behind her. Soundless.

Lyn's head was jerked violently back.

Death in her eyes—and the blade at her throat.

A single, swift movement.

pumping

And after this one, another before midnight.

Sherry, twenty-three, a graduate student from Chicago on vacation. Staying with a girlfriend. Out for a six-pack of Heineken, a quart of nonfat, and a Hershey's Big Bar.

She left the 7-Eleven with her bag of groceries, walked to her car parked behind the building. Somebody was in the back seat, but Sherry didn't know that.

She got in, fished for the ignition key in her purse,

and heard a sliding, rustling sound behind her. Twisted in sudden breathless panic.

Ripper.

Angie did not attend Lyn Esterly's funeral. She refused to see Dan or Lenore, canceled her tours, stocked her boat with food, and took it far upriver, living like a wounded animal. She allowed the river itself to soothe and comfort her, not speaking to anyone, drifting into tiny coves and inlets . . .

Until the wounds began to heal. Until she had regained sufficient emotional strength to return to Lake Havasu City.

She phoned Dan: "I'm back."

"I've been trying to trace you. Even ran a copter upriver, but I guess you didn't want to be found."

"I was all right."

"I *know* that, Angie. I wasn't worried about you. Especially after we caught him. That was what I wanted to find you for, to tell you the news. We *got* the bastard!"

"The River Killer?"

"Yeah. Calls himself 'Bloody Jack.' Says that he's the ghost of the Ripper."

"But how did you . . . ?"

"We spotted this guy prowling near the Bridge. 'Bout a week ago. He'd been living in a shack by the river, up near Mesquite Campground. One of my men followed him there. Walked right in and made the arrest."

"And he admitted he was the killer?"

"Bragged about it! Couldn't wait to get his picture in the papers."

"Dan . . . are you *sure* he's the right man?"

"Hell, we've got a ton of evidence. We found several weapons in the shack, including surgical knives. *Three* scalpels. And he had the newspaper stories on each of his murders tacked to the wall. He'd slashed the faces of all the women, their pictures, I mean. Deep knife cuts in each news photo."

"That's . . . *sick*," said Angie.

"And we have a witness who saw him go into that 7-Eleven on the night of the double murder—where the college girl was killed. He's the one, all right. A real psycho."

"Can I see you tonight? I *need* to be with you, Dan."

"I need you just as much. Meet you soon as I've finished here at the office. And, hey . . ."

"Yes?"

"I've *missed* you."

That night they made love in the moonlight, with the silken whisper of the river as erotic accompaniment. Lying naked in bed, side by side, they listened to the night crickets and touched each other gently, as if to make certain all of this was real for both of them.

"Murder is an awful way to meet somebody," said Angie, leaning close to him, her eyes shining in the darkness. "But I'm glad I met you. I never thought I could."

"Could what?"

"Find someone to love. To *really* love."

"Well, you've found me," he said quietly. "And *I've* found you."

She giggled. "You're . . ."

"I know." He grinned. "You do that to me."

And they made love again.

And the Colorado rippled its languorous night waters.

And from the dark woods a tall figure watched them. It wasn't over.

Another month passed.

With the self-confessed killer in jail, the English Village and Bridge site were once again open to tourists.

Angie had not seen Lenore for several weeks and
was anxious to tell her about the marriage plans she
and Dan had made. She wanted Lenore to be her maid
of honor at the wedding.

They met for a celebration dinner at the City of London Arms in the Village. But the mood was all wrong.

Angie noticed that Lenore's responses were brief,
muted. She ate slowly, picking at her food.

"You don't seem all that thrilled to see me getting
married," said Angie.

"Oh, but I *am.* Truly. And I know I've been a wet
blanket. I'm sorry."

"What's wrong?"

"I just . . . don't think it's over."

"What are you talking about?"

"The Ripper thing. The killings."

Angie stared at her. "But they've *got* him. He's in
jail right now. Dan is convinced that he . . ."

"He's not the one." Lenore said it flatly, softly. "I
just *know* he's not the one."

"You're nuts! All the evidence . . ."

". . . is circumstantial. Oh, I'm sure this kook
thinks he's the Ripper—but where is the *real* proof:
blood samples . . . fingerprints . . . the actual murder
weapons?"

"You're paranoid, Lenore! I had some doubts too,
in the beginning, but Dan's a good cop. He's done his
job. The killer's locked up."

Lenore's green eyes flashed. "Look, I asked you to
meet me down here in the Village tonight for a reason—and it had nothing to do with your wedding."
She drew in her breath. "I just didn't want to face this
alone."

"Face what?"

"The fear. It's November the ninth. *Tonight* is the
ninth!"

"So?"

"The date of the Ripper's seventh murder—back in
1888." Her tone was strained. "If that man in jail

really *is* the Ripper, then nothing will happen here tonight. But . . . if he *isn't* . . .''

"My God, you're really scared. One of *us* could become his seventh victim."

"Look," said Angie. "It's like they say to pilots after a crash. You've got to go right back up or you'll never fly again. Well, it's time for you to do some flying tonight."

"I don't understand."

"You can't let yourself get spooked by what isn't real. And this fear of yours just isn't *real*, Lenore. There's no killer in the Village tonight. And, to prove it, I'm going to walk you to that damn Bridge."

Lenore grew visibly pale. "No . . . no, that's . . . No, I won't go."

"Yes, you will." Angie nodded. She motioned for the check. Lenore stared at her numbly.

Outside, in the late night darkness, the Village was once more empty of tourists. The last of them had gone—and the wide parking lot was quiet and deserted beyond the gate.

"We're insane to be doing this," Lenore said. Her mouth was tightly set. "Why should *I* do this?"

"To prove that irrational fear must be faced and overcome. You're my friend now—my best friend— and I won't let you give in to irrationality."

"Okay, okay . . . if I agree to walk to the Bridge, then can we get the hell out of here?"

"Agreed."

And they began to walk.

moving toward the Bridge . . . mine now, mine

"I've been poking through Lyn's research papers," Lenore said, "and I think I know what her big surprise would have been."

"Tell me."

"Most scholars now agree on the true identity of the Ripper."

"Yes. A London doctor, a surgeon. Jonathan Bascum."

"Well, Lyn Esterly didn't believe he was the Ripper. And after what I've seen of her research, neither do I."

"Then who *was* he?" asked Angie.

"Jonathan had a twin sister, Jessica. She helped the poor in that area. They practically sainted her—called her 'the Angel of Whitechapel.' "

"I've heard of her."

"Did you know she was as medically skilled as her brother? . . . That Jonathan allowed her to use his medical books? Taught her. Jessica turned out to be a better surgeon than he was. And she *used* her medical knowledge in Whitechapel."

The stimulation of what she was revealing to Angie seemed to quell much of the fear in Lenore. Her voice was animated.

keep moving . . . closer

"No *licensed* doctors would practice among the poor in that area. No money to be made. So she doctored these people. All illegal, of course. And, at first, it seemed she *was* a kind of saint, working among the destitute. Until her compulsion asserted itself."

"Compulsion?"

"To kill. Between April third and November ninth, 1888, she butchered seven women—and yet, to this day, historians claim her *brother* was responsible for the murders."

Angie was amazed. "Are you telling me that the Angel of Whitechapel was really Jack the Ripper?"

"That was Lyn's conclusion," said Lenore. "And, when you think of it, why not? It explains how the Ripper always seemed to *vanish* after a kill. Why was it that no one ever *saw* him leave Whitechapel? Because 'he" was Jessica Bascum. She could move freely through the area without arousing suspicion. No one ever saw the Ripper's face . . . no one who *lived*, that is. To throw off the police, she sent notes to them signed 'Jack.' It was a *woman* they chased onto the Bridge that night in 1888.''

Lenore seemed unaware that they were approaching the Bridge now. It loomed ahead of them, a dark, stretched mass of waiting stone.

closer

''Lyn had been tracing the Bascum family history,'' explained Lenore. ''Jessica gave birth to a daughter in 1888, the same year she vanished on the Bridge. The line continued through her granddaughter, born in 1915, and her great-granddaughter, born in 1940. The last Bascum daughter was born in 1960.''

''Which means she'd be in her mid-twenties today,'' said Angie.

''That's right.'' Lenore nodded. ''Like you. *You're* in your mid-twenties, Angie.''

Angie's eyes flashed. She stopped walking. The line of her jaw tightened.

Bitch!

''Suppose she was drawn here,'' said Lenore, ''to London Bridge. Where her great-great-grandmother vanished a century ago. And suppose that, with the completion of the Bridge, with the placement of that final missing stone in April, Jessica's spirit entered her great-great-granddaughter. Suppose the six killings in the Lake Havasu area were done by *her*—that it was her cosmic destiny to commit them.

''Are you saying that you think *I* am a Bascum?'' Angie asked softly. They continued to walk toward the Bridge.

''I don't *think* anything. I have the facts.''

''And just what might those be?'' Angie's voice was tense.

''Lyn was very close to solving the Ripper case. When she researched the Bascum family history in England she traced some of the descendants here to America. She *knew*.''

''Knew what, Lenore?'' Her eyes glittered. ''You

do believe that I'm a Bascum.'' Harshly: *''Don't*
you?''

"No." Lenore shook her head. "I know you're
not.'' She looked intently at Angie. ''Because *I* am.''

They had reached the steps leading up to the main
part of the Bridge. In numb horror, Angie watched
Lenore slide back a panel in one of the large granite
blocks and remove the Ripper's hat, greatcoat, and
cape. And the medical bag.

"This came down to me from the family. It was *her*
surgical bag—the same one she used in Whitechapel.
I'd put it away—until April, when they placed the final
stone.'' Her eyes sparked. ''When I touched the stone
I felt *her* . . . Jessica's soul flowed into *me*, became
part of me. And I knew what I had to do.''

She removed a glittering scalpel, held it up. The
blade flashed in the reflected light of the lamps on the
Bridge. Lenore's smile was satanic. ''This is for you!''

Angie's heart trip-hammered; she was staring,
trancelike, into the eyes of the killer. Suddenly she
pivoted, began running.

Down the lonely, shadow-haunted, brick-and cobblestone streets, under the tall antique lamps, past the
clustered Tudor buildings of Old London.

And the Ripper followed. Relentlessly. Confident of
a seventh kill.

she'll taste the blade

Angie circled the main square, ran between buildings to find a narrow, dimly lit alleyway that led her
to the rear section of the City of London Arms. Phone
inside. Call Dan!

Picking up a rock from the alley, she smashed a rear
window, climbed inside, began running through the
dark interior, searching for a phone. One here somewhere . . . somewhere . . .

The Ripper followed her inside.

Phone! Angie fumbled in her purse, finding change
for the call. She also found . . .

The pearl-handled .32 automatic—the weapon she'd

been carrying for months, totally forgotten in her panic.

Now she could fight back. She knew how to use a gun.

She inserted the coins, got Dan's number at headquarters. Ringing . . . ringing . . . "Lake Havasu City Police Department."

"Dan . . . Chief Gregory . . . Emergency!"

"I'll get him on the line."

"Hurry!"

A pause. Angie's heart, hammering.

"This is Gregory. Who's. . . ?"

"Dan!" she broke in. "It's Angie. The Ripper's *here,* trying to kill me!"

"Where are you?"

A dry buzzing. The line was dead.

A clean, down-slicing move with the scalpel had severed the phone cord.

die now . . . time to die

Angie turned to face the killer.

And triggered the automatic.

At close range, a .32-caliber bullet smashed into Lenore Bascum's flesh. She staggered back, falling to one knee on the polished wood floor of the restaurant, blood flowing from the wound.

Angie ran back to the smashed window, crawled through it, moved quickly down the alley. A rise of ground led up to the parking lot. Her car was there.

She reached it, sobbing to herself, inserted the key.

A shadow flowed across the shining car body. Two blood-spattered hands closed around Angie's throat.

The Ripper's eyes were coals of green fire, burning into Angie. She tore at the clawed fingers, pounded her right fist into the demented face. But the hands tightened. Darkness swept through Angie's brain; she was blacking out.

die, bitch

She was dying.

Did she hear a siren? Was it real, or in her mind?

A second siren joined the first. Filling the night darkness.

bleeding . . . my blood . . . wrong, all wrong . . .

A dozen police cars roared into the lot, tires sliding on the night-damp tarmac.

Dan!

The Ripper's hands dropped away from Angie's throat. The tall figure turned, ran for the Bridge.

And was trapped there.

Police were closing in from both sides of the vast structure.

Angie and Dan were at the Bridge. "How did you know where to find me?"

"Silent alarm. Feeds right into headquarters. When you broke the window, the alarm was set off. I figured that's where you were."

"She's hit," Angie told him. "I shot her. She's dying."

In the middle of the span the Ripper fell to one knee. Then, a mortally wounded animal, she slipped over the side and plunged into the dark river beneath the Bridge.

Lights blazed on the water, picking out her body. She was sinking, unable to stay afloat. Blood gouted from her open mouth. "Damn you!" she screamed. "Damn all of you!"

She was gone.

The waters rippled over her grave.

Angie was convulsively gripping the automatic, the pearl handle cold against her fingers.

Cold.

JACK'S LITTLE FRIEND
by Ramsey Campbell

It's afternoon when you find the box. You're in the
marshes on the verge of the Thames below London.
Perhaps you live in the area, perhaps you're visiting,
on business or on holiday. You've been walking.
You've passed a power station and its expressionless
metallic chord, you've skirted a flat placid field of
cows above which black smoke pumps from factory
chimneys. Now reeds smear your legs with mud, and
you might be proposing to turn back when you see a
corner of metal protruding from the bearded mud.

You make your way toward it, squelching. It looks
chewed by time, and you wonder how long it's been
there. Perhaps it was dumped here recently; perhaps it
was thrown out by the river; possibly the Thames, be-
labouring and dragging the mud, uncovered the box.
As the water has built the box a niche of mud so it has
washed the lid, and you can make out dates scratched
on the metal. They are almost a century old. It's the
dates that provoke your curiosity, and perhaps also a
gesture against the dull landscape. You stoop and pick
up the box, which frees itself with a gasp of mud.

Although it's only a foot square the box is heavier
than you anticipated. You skid and regain your balance. You wouldn't be surprised if the box were made
of lead. If anyone had thrown it in the river they would
certainly have expected it to stay sunk. You wonder
why they would have bothered to carry it to the river
or to the marshes for disposal. It isn't distinguished,
except by the dates carved on the lid by an illiterate

301

or clumsy hand—just a plain box of heavy gray metal.
You read the dates:

   31/8/1888
    8/9/1888
   30/9/1888
    9/11/1888

There seems to be no pattern. It's as if someone had
been trying to work one out. But what kind of calcu-
lation would be resolved by throwing away a metal
box? Bewildered though you are, that's how you read
the clues. What was happening in 1888? You think
you read somewhere that expeditions were returning
from Egypt around that date. Have you discovered an
abandoned archaeological find? There's one way to
know. But your fingers slip off the box, which in any
case is no doubt locked beneath its coat of mud, and
the marsh is seeping into your shoes; so you leave off
your attempts to open the lid and stumble away, carrying the box.

By the time you reach the road your excitement has
drained somewhat. After all, someone could have
scratched the dates on the lid last week; it could even
be an understated practical joke. You don't want to
take a heavy box all the way home only to prise from
its depths a piece of paper saying APRIL FOOL. So
you leave the box in the grass at the side of the road
and search until you find a metal bar. Sorry if I'm
aborting the future of archaeology, you think, and begin to lever at the box.

But even now it's not as easy as you thought. You've
wedged the box and can devote all your energy to
shifting the lid, but it's fighting you. Once it yields an
inch or two and then snaps shut again. It's as if it were
being held shut, like the shell of a clam. A car passes
on the other side of the road and you begin to give in
to a sense of absurdity, to the sight of yourself struggling to jimmy open an old box. You begin to feel like
a tourist's glimpse. Another car, on your side this time,
and dust sweeps into you face. You blink and weep

and cough violently, for the dust seems to have been scooped into your mouth. Then the sensation of dry crawling in your mouth recedes, and only the skin beneath your tongue feels rough. You wipe your eyes and return to the box. And then you drop the bar, for the box is wide open.

And it's empty. The interior is as dull as the exterior. There's nothing, except on the bottom a thin glistening coat of what looks like saliva but must be marsh water. You slam the lid. You memorize the dates and walk away, rolling your tongue around the floor of your mouth, which still feels thick, and grinning wryly. Perhaps the hitch-hiker or whoever finds the box will conceive a use for it.

That night you're walking along a long dim street toward a woman. She seems to be backing away, and you can't see her face. Suddenly, as you rush toward her, her body opens like an anemone. You plunge deep into the wet red fronds.

The dream hoods your brain for days. Perhaps it's the pressure of work or of worry, but you find yourself becoming obsessive. In crowds you halt, thinking of the dates on the box. You've consulted such books as you have access to, but they didn't help. You stare at the asymmetrical faces of the crowd. Smoke rises from their mouths or their jaws work as they drive forward, pulled along by their set eyes. Imagine asking them to help. They wouldn't have touched the box, they would have shuffled on by, scattering their waste paper and condoms. You shake your head to dislodge the crawling thoughts. You aren't usually so misanthropic. You'll have to find out what those dates mean. Obviously your brain won't give you much peace until you do.

So you ask your friend, the one who knows something about history. And your friend says, "That's easy. They're the dates of Jack the Ripper," and tells you that the five murders everyone accepts as the Ripper's work were committed on those dates. You can't help smiling, because you've just had a flash of clarity: of course you must have recognized the dates subconsciously from having read them somewhere, and the recognition was the source of your dream. Then your friend says, "Why are you interested?"

You're about to answer, but your tongue sticks to the floor of your mouth for a moment, like the lid of the box. In that moment you think: why should your friend want to know anyway? They've no right to know, they aren't entitled to a fee for the consultation. You found the box, you'll conduct the inquiry. "I must have read the dates somewhere," you say, "They've been going round in my head and I couldn't remember why."

On the way home you play a game with yourself. No, that bus shelter's no good, too open. Yes, he could hide in that alley, there would be hardly any light where it bends in the middle. You stop, because the skin beneath your tongue is rough and sore, and hinders your thoughts. You explore the softness beneath your tongue with your finger, and as you do so the inflammation seems to draw into itself and spare you.

Later you ponder Jack the Ripper. You've read about him, but when you leaf through your knowledge you realize you're not so well informed. How did he become the Ripper? Why did he stop? But you know that these questions are only your speculations about the box, disguised.

It's inconvenient to go back to find the box, but you manage to clear yourself the time. When you do you think at first you've missed the place where you left the box. Eventually you find the bar, but the box has gone. Perhaps someone kicked it into the hedges. You search among the cramped roots and trapped crisp-bags until your mouth feels scraped dry. You could tell the local police, but then you would have to explain your interest, and they would take the credit for themselves. You don't need the box. Tomorrow you'll begin to research.

And so you do, though it's not as easy as you expected. Everyone's fascinated by the Ripper these days, and the library books are popular. You even have to buy a paperback of one of them, glancing sideways as you do so at the people browsing through the book. The sunlight glares in the cracks and pores and fleshy bags of their faces, giving them a sheen like wet wax: wax animated by simple morbid fascination. You shudder and hurry away. At least you have a reason, but these others haven't risen above the level of the mob that gloated squirming over reports of the Ripper's latest killing. You know how the police of the time must have felt.

You read the books. You spread them across the table, comparing accounts. You're not to be trapped into taking the first one you read as definitive. Your friends, and perhaps your spouse or lover as well, joke and gently rebuke you about your singlemindedness. No doubt they talk about it when you're not there. Let them. Most people seem content to relive, or elaborate, the second-hand. Not you.

You read. 31/8/1888: throat cut twice, head nearly severed, disembowelled twice. 8/9/1888: handkerchief wrapped around almost severed neck, womb missing, intestines cast over shoulder, relatively little blood in the yard where the corpse was found. 30/9/1888: two women, one with windpipe severed; the other, less than an hour later, with right eye damaged, earlobe cut off, intestines over shoulder, kidney and entrails missing. 9/11/1888: throat cut, ears and nose missing, also liver, and a mass of flesh and organs on the bedside table. There's a photograph of her in one book. You stare at it for a moment, then you slam the book and stare at your hands.

But your hands are less real than your thoughts. You think of the Ripper, cutting and feeling his way through the corpses, taking more time and going into more detail with each murder. The last one took two hours,

the books tell you. A question is beginning to insist
on an answer. What was he looking for?

You aren't sleeping well. You stare at the lights that
prick your eyeballs behind your lids and theorize until
you topple wakefully into sleep. Sometimes you seem
almost to have found a pattern, and you gasp in crowds
or with friends. They glance at you and you meet their
gaze coldly. They wouldn't be capable of your
thoughts, and you certainly don't intend to let them
hinder you. But even as their dull gaze falls away you
realize that you've lost the inspiration, if indeed it were
one.

So you confine yourself to your home. You're glad
to have an excuse to do so, for recently you've been
growing hypersensitive. When you're outside and the
sunlight intensifies it's as though someone were pumping up an already white-hot furnace, and the night set-
tles around you like water about a gasping fish. So you
draw the curtains and read the books again.

The more you read the stranger it seems. You feel
you could understand the man if a missing crucial detail were supplied. What can you make of his macabre
tenderness in wrapping a handkerchief around the
sliced throat of Annie Chapman, his second victim? A
numbed denial of his authorship of the crime, perhaps?
If there were relatively little blood in the yard then
surely the blood must have soaked into the Ripper's
clothes, but in that case how could he have walked
home in broad daylight? Did he cut the windpipe of
Elizabeth Stride because he was interrupted before he
was able to do more, or because she had seen too much
for him simply to leave her and seek a victim elsewhere? An hour later, was it his frustration that led
him to mutilate Catherine Eddowes more extensively
and inventively than her predecessors? And why did
he wait almost twice as long as hitherto before committing his final murder, that of Mary Kelly, and the
most detailed? Was this the exercise of a powerful will,
and did the frustration build up to an unprecedented

climax? But what frustration? What was he looking for?

You turn to the photograph of Mary Kelly again, and this time you're able to examine it dispassionately. Not that the Victorian camera was able to be particularly explicit. In fact, the picture looks like a piece of early adolescent pornography on a wall, an amateur blob for a face and a gaping darkness between the legs. You suck your tongue, whose underside feels rough and dry.

You read the Ripper's letters. The adolescent wit of the rhymes often gives way to the childish illiteracy of some of the letters. You can understand his feelings of superiority to the victims and to the police; they were undoubtedly at least as contemptible as the people you know. But that doesn't explain the regression of the letters, as if his mind were flinching back as far as possible from his actions. That's probably a common trait of psychopaths, you think: an attempt to reject the part of them that commits the crimes.

Your mind is still frowning. You read through the murders again. First murder, nothing removed. Second, the womb stolen. Third, kidney and entrails stolen. A portion of kidney which had been preserved in spirits was sent to the police, with a note saying that the writer had eaten the rest. Fourth, the liver removed and the ears and nose, but the womb and a three-month-old foetus untouched. Why? To state the hunger which motivated the killings, presumably, but what hunger was that? If cannibalism, surely he would never have controlled himself sufficiently to preserve a portion of his food with which to taunt the police? If not, what worse reality was he disguising from the police, and perhaps from himself, as cannibalism?

You swallow the saliva that's pooling under your tongue and try to grasp your theories. It's as if the hunger spat out the kidney. Not literally, of course. But it certainly seems as if the Ripper had been trying to sate his hunger by varying the delicacies, as if it

were a temperamental pet. Surely the death of Mary
Kelly couldn't have satisfied it for good, though.

Then you remember the box. If he had externalized
the hunger as something other than himself, could his
mind have persuaded him that the hunger was alive
independent of him and might be trapped? Could he
have used one of the portions of Mary Kelly as a lure?
Would that have seemed a solution in the grotesque
algebra of his mind? Might he have convinced himself
that he had locked away his hunger in time, and having
scratched the dates on the box to confirm his calculations have thrown it in the river? Perhaps the kidney
had been the first attempted lure, insufficiently tempt-
ing. And then—well, he could hardly have returned to
a normal life, if indeed he had left one, but he might
have turned to the socially acceptable destruction of
alcoholism and died unknown.

The more you consider your theory the more impressive it becomes. Perhaps you can write it up as an
article and sell it somewhere. Of course you'll need to
pursue your research first. You feel happy in a detached unreal way, and you even go to your companion willingly for the first time in, now you think about
it, a long while. But you feel apart from the moist
dilation of flesh and the hard dagger thrust, and are
glad when it's over. There's something at the back of
your mind you need to coax forward. When you've
dealt with that you'll be able to concentrate on other
things.

You walk toward her. The light is flickering and the
walls wobble like a fairground corridor. As you approach her, her dress peels apart and her body splits
open. From within the gap trails a web toward which
you're drawn. At the center of the web hangs a piece
of raw meat.

Your cry wakes you but not your companion. Her
body feels like burning rubber against you, and you
flinch away. After a minute you get out of bed. You
can't stand the sensation, and you want to shake off

the dream. You stare from the window; the darkness is paling, and a bird sings tentatively. Suddenly you gasp. You'll write that article now, because you've realized what you need. You can't hope to describe the Ripper or even to meet a psychopath for background. But there's one piece of first-hand research you can do that will help you to understand the Ripper. You don't know why you didn't read your dream that way at once.

Next day you begin searching. You read all the cards you can find in shop windows. They aren't as numerous or as obvious as you expected. You don't want to find yourself actually applying for a course of French lessons. You suppose there are magazines that would help you but you're not sure where to find them. At last, as the streets become grimmer, you notice a group of young men reading cards in a shop window. They nudge each other and point to several of the cards, then they confer and hurry toward a phone box. You're sure this time.

You choose one called Marie, because that was what Mary Kelly used to call herself. No particular reason, but the parallel seems promising. When you telephone her she sounds dubious. She asks what you want and you say, "Nothing special. Just the usual." Your voice may be disturbing her, because your tongue is sticking somehow to the floor of your mouth, which feels swollen and obstructive. She's silent for a moment, then she says, "All right. Come up in twenty minutes," and tells you where she is.

You hadn't realized it would be as swift as that. Probably it's a good thing, because if you had to wait much longer your unease might find you excuses for staying away. You emerge from the phone box and the sunlight thuds against your head. Your mouth is dry, and the flesh beneath your tongue is twitching as if an insect has lodged there. It must be the heat and the tension. You walk slowly toward your rendezvous, which is only a few streets away. You walk through a

maze of alleys to keep in the shade. On either side of
you empty clothes flap, children shout and barks run
along a chain of dogs.

You reach your destination on time. It's in a street
of drab shops: a boarded betting shop, a window full
of cardigans and wool, a Chinese take-away. The room
you want is above the latter. You skid on trodden chips
and shielding your face from the eyes of the queue
next door, ring the bell.

As you stare at the new orange paint on the door
you wonder what you're going to say. You have some
idea and surely enough money, but will she respond
to that? You understand some prostitutes refuse to talk
rather than act. You can hardly explain your interest
in the Ripper. You're still wondering when she opens
the door.

She must be in her thirties, but her face has aged
like an orange and she's tried to fill in the wrinkles,
probably while waiting for you. Her eyelashes are like
unwashed black paintbrushes. But she smiles slightly,
as if unsure whether you want her to, and then sticks
out her tongue at a head craning from next door. "You
rang before," she says, and you nod.

The door slams behind you. Your hand reaches
blindly for the latch; you can still leave, she'll never
be able to pursue you. Beneath your tongue a pulse is
going wild. If you don't go through with this now it
will be more difficult next time, and you'll never be
rid of the Ripper or of your dreams. You follow her
upstairs.

Seeing her from below you find it easy to forget her
smile. Her red dress pulls up and her knickers, covered with whorls of colour like the eye of a peacock's
tail, alternately bulge and crease. The hint of guilt you
were beginning to feel retreats: her job is to be on
show, an object, you need have no compunction. Then
you're at the top of the stairs and in her room.

There are thick red curtains, mauve walls, a crimson
bed and telephone, a color TV, a card from Ibiza and

one from Rhyl. Behind a partition you can see pans and knives hanging on hooks in the kitchen area. Then your gaze is wrenched back to her as she says, "Go on then, tell me your name, you know mine."

Of course you don't. You're not so stupid as to suppose she would display her real name in the window. You shake your head and try to smile. But the garish thick colors of the room are beginning to weigh on you, and the trapped heat makes your mouth feel dry, so that the smile comes out soured.

"Never mind, you don't have to," she says. "What do you want? Want me to wear anything?"

Now you have to speak or the encounter will turn into a grotesque misunderstanding. But your tongue feels as if it's glued down, while beneath it the flesh is throbbing painfully. You can feel your face prickling and reddening, and rotted in the discomfort behind your teeth a frustrated disgust with the whole situation is growing.

"Are you shy? There's no need to be," she says. "If you were really shy you wouldn't have come at all, would you?" She stares into the mute struggle within your eyes and smiling tentatively again, says, "Can't you talk?"

Yes, you can talk, it's only a temporary obstruction. And when you shift it you'll tell her that you've come to use her, because that's what she's for. An object, that's what she's made herself. Inside that crust of makeup there's nothing. No wonder the Ripper sought them out. You don't need compassion in a slaughterhouse. You try to control your raw tongue, but only the throbbing beneath it moves.

"I'm sorry, I'm only upsetting you. Never mind, love," she says. "Nerves are terrible, I know. You sit down and I'll get you a drink."

And that's when you have to act, because your mouth is filling with saliva as if a dam had burst, and your tongue's still straining to raise itself, and the turgid colors have insinuated themselves into your head like migraine, and tendrils of uneasiness are streaming up from your clogged mouth and matting your brain, and at the core of all this there's a writhing disgust and fury that this woman should presume to patronize you. You don't care if you never understand the Ripper so long as you can smash your way out of this trap. You move toward the door, but at the same time your hand is beckoning her, it seems quite independent of you. You haven't reached the door when she's in front of you, her mouth open and saying, "What?" And you do the only thing that seems, in your blind violent frustration, available to you.

You spit into her open mouth.

For a moment you feel free. Your mouth is clean and your tongue can move as you want it to. The colors have retreated, and she's just a well-meaning rather sad woman using her talents as best she can. Then you realize what you've done. Now your tongue's free you don't know what to say. You think perhaps you could explain that you sneezed. Perhaps she'll accept that, if you apologize. But by this time she's already begun to scream.

You were so nearly right most of the time. You realized that the stolen portions of Mary Kelly might have been placed in the box as a lure. If only you'd appreciated the implications of this: that the other mutilations were by no means the act of a maniac, but the attempts of a gradually less sane man to conceal the atrocities of what possessed him. Who knows, perhaps it had come from Egypt. He couldn't have been sure of its existence even when he lured it into the box. Perhaps you'll be luckier, if that's luck, although now you can only stand paralyzed as the woman screams and screams and falls inertly to the floor, and blood begins to seep from her abdomen. Perhaps you'll be able to catch it as it emerges, or at least to see your little friend.

YOURS TRULY, JACK THE RIPPER

by Robert Bloch

I looked at the stage Englishman. He looked at me.

"Sir Guy Hollis?" I asked.

"Indeed. Have I the pleasure of addressing John Carmody, the psychiatrist?"

I nodded. My eyes swept over the figure of my distinguished visitor. Tall, lean, sandy-haired—with the traditional tufted mustache. And the tweeds. I suspected a monocle concealed in a vest pocket, and wondered if he'd left his umbrella in the outer office.

But more than that, I wondered what the devil had impelled Sir Guy Hollis of the British Embassy to seek out a total stranger here in Chicago.

Sir Guy didn't help matters any as he sat down. He cleared his throat, glanced around nervously, tapped his pipe against the side of the desk. Then he opened his mouth.

"Mr. Carmody," he said, "have you ever heard of—Jack the Ripper?"

"The murderer?" I asked.

"Exactly. The greatest monster of them all. Worse than Springheel Jack or Crippen. Jack the Ripper. Red Jack."

"I've heard of him," I said.

"Do you know his history?"

"I don't think we'll get any place swapping old wives' tales about famous crimes of history."

He took a deep breath.

"This is no old wives' tale. It's a matter of life or death."

He was so wrapped up in his obsession he even talked that way. Well—I was willing to listen. We psychiatrists get paid for listening.

"Go ahead," I told him. "Let's have the story."

Sir Guy lit a cigarette and began to talk.

"London, 1888," he began. "Late summer and early fall. That was the time. Out of nowhere came the shadowy figure of Jack the Ripper—a stalking shadow with a knife, prowling through London's East End. Haunting the squalid dives of Whitechapel, Spitalfields. Where he came from no one knew. But he brought death. Death in a knife.

"Six times that knife descended to slash the throats and bodies of London's women. Drabs and alley sluts. August 7th was the date of the first butchery. They found her body lying there with thirty-nine stab wounds. A ghastly murder. On August 31st, another victim. The press became interested. The slum inhabitants were more deeply interested still.

"Who was this unknown killer who prowled in their midst and struck at will in the deserted alleyways of night-town? And what was more important—when would he strike again?

"September 8th was the date. Scotland Yard assigned special deputies. Rumors ran rampant. The atrocious nature of the slayings was the subject for shocking speculation.

"The killer used a knife—expertly. He cut throats and removed—certain portions—of the bodies after death. He chose victims and settings with a fiendish deliberation. No one saw him or heard him. But watchmen making their gray rounds in the dawn would stumble across the hacked and horrid thing that was the Ripper's handiwork.

"Who was he? What was he? A mad surgeon? A butcher? An insane scientist? A pathological degen-

erate escaped from an asylum? A deranged nobleman?
A member of the London police?

"Then the poem appeared in the newspaper. The
anonymous poem, designed to put a stop to speculations—but which only aroused public interest to a further frenzy. A mocking little stanza:

> I'm not a butcher, I'm not a Yid
> Nor yet a foreign skipper,
> But I'm your own true loving friend,
> Yours truly—Jack the Ripper.

"And on September 30th, two more throats were
slashed open. There was silence, then, in London for
a time. Silence, and a nameless fear. When would Red
Jack strike again? They waited through October. Every
figment of fog concealed his phantom presence. Concealed it well—for nothing was learned of the Ripper's
identity, or his purpose. The drabs of London shivered
in the raw wind of early November. Shivered, and
were thankful for the coming of each morning's sun.

"November 9th. They found her in her room. She
lay there very quietly, limbs neatly arranged. And beside her, with equal neatness, were laid her breasts and
heart. The Ripper had outdone himself in execution.

"Then, panic. But needless panic. For though press,
police, and populace alike waited in sick dread, Jack
the Ripper did not strike again.

"Months passed. A year. The immediate interest
died, but not the memory. They said Jack had skipped
to America. That he had committed suicide. They
said—and they wrote. They've written ever since.
Theories, hypotheses, arguments, treatises. But to this
day no one knows who Jack the Ripper was. Or why
he killed. Or why he stopped killing."

Sir Guy was silent. Obviously he expected some
comment from me.

"You tell the story well," I remarked. "Though
with a slight emotional bias."

''I suppose you want to know why I'm interested?'' he snapped.

''Yes. That's exactly what I'd like to know.''

''Because,'' said Sir Guy Hollis, ''I am on the trail of Jack the Ripper now. I think he's here—in Chicago!''

''Say that again.''

''Jack the Ripper is alive, in Chicago, and I'm out to find him.''

He wasn't smiling. It wasn't a joke.

''See here,'' I said. ''What was the date of these murders?''

''August to November, 1888.''

''1888? But if Jack the Ripper was an able-bodied man in 1888, he'd surely be dead today! Why look, man—if he were merely born in that year, he'd be fifty-seven years old today!''

''Would he? smiled Sir Guy Hollis. ''Or should I say, 'Would she?' Because Jack the Ripper may have been a woman. Or any number of things.''

''Sir Guy,'' I said. ''You came to the right person when you looked me up. You definitely need the services of a psychiatrist.''

''Perhaps. Tell me, Mr. Carmody, do you think I'm crazy?''

I looked at him and shrugged. But I had to give him a truthful answer.

''Frankly—no.''

''Then you might listen to the reasons I believe Jack the Ripper is alive today.''

''I might.''

''I've studied these cases for thirty years. Been over the actual ground. Talked to officials. Talked to friends and acquaintances of the poor drabs who were killed. Visited with men and women in the neighborhood. Collected an entire library of material touching on Jack the Ripper. Studied all the wild theories or crazy notions.

''I learned a little. Not much, but a little. I won't

bore you with my conclusions. But there was another branch of inquiry that yielded more fruitful return. I have studied unsolved crimes. Murders.

"I could show you clippings from the papers of half the world's greatest cities. San Francisco. Shanghai. Calcutta. Omsk. Paris. Berlin. Pretoria. Cairo. Milan. Adelaide.

"The trail is there, the pattern. Unsolved crimes. Slashed throats of women. With the peculiar disfigurations and removals. Yes, I've followed the trail of blood. From New York westward across the continent. Then to the Pacific. From there to Africa. During the World War of 1914–18 it was Europe. After that, South America. And since 1930, the United States again. Eighty-seven such murders—and to the trained criminologist, all bear the stigma of the Ripper's handiwork.

Recently there were the so-called Cleveland torso slayings. Remember? A shocking series. And finally, two recent deaths in Chicago. Within the past six months. One out on South Dearborn. The other somewhere up on Halsted. Same type of crime, same technique. I tell you, there are unmistakable indications in all these affairs—indications of the work of Jack the Ripper!"

"A very tight theory," I said. I'll not question your evidence at all, or the deductions you draw. You're the criminologist, and I'll take your word for it. Just one thing remains to be explained. A minor point, perhaps, but worth mentioning."

"And what it that?" asked Sir Guy.

"Just how could a man of, let us say, eighty-five years commit these crimes? For if Jack the Ripper was around thirty in 1888 and lived, he'd be eighty-five today."

"Suppose he didn't get any older?" whispered Sir Guy.

"What's that?"

"Suppose Jack the Ripper didn't grow old? Suppose he is still a young man today?"

"It's a crazy theory, I grant you," he said. "All the theories about the Ripper are crazy. The idea that he was a doctor. Or a maniac. Or a woman. The reasons advanced for such beliefs are flimsy enough. There's nothing to go by. So why should my notion be any worse?"

"Because people grow older," I reasoned with him. "Doctors, maniacs, and women alike."

"What about—*sorcerers?*"

"Sorcerers?"

"Necromancers. Wizards. Practicers of Black Magic?"

"What's the point?"

"I studied," said Sir Guy. "I studied everything. After a while I began to study the dates of the murders. The pattern those dates formed. The rhythm. The solar, lunar, stellar rhythm. The sidereal aspect. The astrological significance.

"Suppose Jack the Ripper didn't murder for murder's sake alone? Suppose he wanted to make—a sacrifice?"

"What kind of a sacrifice?"

Sir Guy shrugged. "It is said that if you offer blood to the dark gods they grant boons. Yes, if a blood offering is made at the proper time—when the moon and the stars are right—and with the proper ceremonies—they grant boons. Boons of youth. Eternal youth."

"But that's nonsense!"

"No. That's—Jack the Ripper."

I stood up. "A most interesting theory," I told him. "But why do you come here and tell it to me? I'm not an authority on witchcraft. I'm not a police official or criminologist. I'm a practicing psychiatrist. What's the connection?"

Sir Guy smiled.

"You are interested, then?"

"Well, yes. There must be some point."

"There is. But I wished to be assured of your interest first. Now I can tell you my plan."

"And just what is that plan?"

Sir Guy gave me a long look.

"John Carmody," he said, "you and I are going to capture Jack the Ripper."

2

That's the way it happened. I've given the gist of that first interview in all its intricate and somewhat boring detail, because I think it's important. It helps to throw some light on Sir Guy's character and attitude. And in view of what happened after that—

But I'm coming to those matters.

Sir Guy's thought was simple. It wasn't even a thought. Just a hunch.

"You know the people here," he told me. "I've inquired. That's why I came to you as the ideal man for my purpose. You number amongst your acquaintances many writers, painters, poets. The so-called intelligentsia. The lunatic fringe from the near north side.

"For certain reasons—never mind what they are—my clues lead me to infer that Jack the Ripper is a member of that element. He chooses to pose as an eccentric. I've a feeling that with you to take me around and introduce me to your set, I might hit upon the right person."

"It's all right with me," I said. "But just how are you going to look for him? As you say, he might be anybody, anywhere. And you have no idea what he looks like. He might be young or old. Jack the Ripper—a Jack of all trades? Rich man, poor man, beggar man, thief, doctor, lawyer—how will you know?"

"We shall see." Sir Guy sighed heavily. "But I must find him. At once."

"Why the hurry?"

Sir Guy sighed again. "Because in two days he will kill again."

"Are you sure?"

"Sure as the stars. I've plotted this chart, you see. All of the murders correspond to certain astrological rhythm patterns. If, as I suspect, he makes a blood sacrifice to renew his youth, he must murder within two days. Notice the pattern of his first crimes in London. August 7th. Then August 31st. September 8th. September 30th. November 9th. Intervals of 24 days, 9 days, 22 days—he killed two this time—and then 40 days. Of course there were crimes in between. There had to be. But they weren't discovered and pinned on him.

"At any rate, I've worked out a pattern for him, based on all my data. And I say that within the next two days he kills. So I must seek him out, somehow, before then."

"And I'm still asking you what you want me to do."

"Take me out," said Sir Guy. "Introduce me to your friends. Take me to parties."

"But where do I begin? As far as I know, my artistic friends, despite their eccentricities, are all normal people."

"So is the Ripper. Perfectly normal. Except on certain nights." Again that faraway look in Sir Guy's eyes. "Then he becomes an ageless pathological monster, crouching to kill."

"All right," I said. "All right. I'll take you."

We made our plans. And that evening I took him over to Lester Baston's studio.

As we ascended to the penthouse roof in the elevator I took the opportunity to warn Sir Guy.

"Baston's a real screwball," I cautioned him. "So are his guests. Be prepared for anything and everything."

"I am." Sir Guy Hollis was perfectly serious. He

put his hand in his trousers pocket and pulled out a gun.

"What the—" I began.

"If I see him I'll be ready," Sir Guy said. He didn't smile, either.

"But you can't go running around at a party with a loaded revolver in your pocket, man!"

"Don't worry, I won't behave foolishly."

I wondered. Sir Guy Hollis was not, to my way of thinking, a normal man.

We stepped out of the elevator, went toward Baston's apartment door.

"By the way," I murmured, "just how do you wish to be introduced? Shall I tell them who you are and what you are looking for?"

"I don't care. Perhaps it would be best to be frank."

"But don't you think that the Ripper—if by some miracle he or she is present—will immediately get the wind up and take cover?"

"I think the shock of the announcement that I am hunting the Ripper would provoke some kind of betraying gesture on his part," said Sir Guy.

"It's a fine theory. But I warn you, you're going to be in for a lot of ribbing. This is a wild bunch."

Sir Guy smiled.

"I'm ready," he announced. "I have a little plan of my own. Don't be shocked at anything I do."

I nodded and knocked on the door.

Baston opened it and poured out into the hall. His eyes were as red as the maraschino cherries in his Manhattan. He teetered back and forth regarding us very gravely. He squinted at my square-cut homburg hat and Sir Guy's mustache.

"Aha," he intoned. "The Walrus and the Carpenter."

I introduced Sir Guy.

"Welcome," said Baston, gesturing us inside with over-elaborate courtesy. He stumbled after us into the garish parlor.

I stared at the crowd that moved restlessly through the fog of cigarette smoke.

It was the shank of the evening for this mob. Every hand held a drink. Every face held a slightly hectic flush. Over in one corner the piano was going full blast, but the imperious strains of the *March* from *The Love for Three Oranges* couldn't drown out the profanity from the crap-game in the other corner.

Prokofieff had no chance against African polo, and one set of ivories rattled louder than the other.

Sir Guy got a monocle-full right away. He saw LaVerne Gonnister, the poetess, hit Hymie Kralik in the eye. He saw Hymie sit down on the floor and cry until Dick Pool accidentally stepped on his stomach as he walked through to the dining room for a drink.

He heard Nadia Vilinoff, the commercial artist, tell Johnny Odcutt that she thought his tattooing was in dreadful taste, and he saw Barclay Melton crawl under the dining room table with Johnny Odcutt's wife.

His zoological observations might have continued indefinitely if Lester Baston hadn't stepped to the center of the room and called for silence by dropping a vase on the floor.

"We have distinguished visitors in our midst," bawled Lester, waving his empty glass in our direction. "None other than the Walrus and the Carpenter. The Walrus is Sir Guy Hollis, a something-or-other from the British Embassy. The Carpenter, as you all know, is our own John Carmody, the prominent dispenser of libido liniment."

He turned and grabbed Sir Guy by the arm, dragging him to the middle of the carpet. For a moment I thought Hollis might object, but a quick wink reassured me. He was prepared for this.

"It is our custom, Sir Guy," said Baston, loudly, "to subject our new friends to a little cross-examination. Just a little formality at these very formal gatherings, you understand. Are you prepared to answer questions?"

Sir Guy nodded and grinned.

"Very well," Baston muttered. "Friends—I give you this bundle form Britain. Your witness.

Then the ribbing started. I meant to listen, but at that moment Lydia Dare saw me and dragged me off into the vestibule for one of those Darling-I-waited-for-your-call-all-day routines.

By the time I got rid of her and went back, the impromptu quiz session was in full swing. From the attitude of the crowd, I gathered that Sir Guy was doing all right for himself.

Then Baston himself interjected a question that upset the apple-cart.

"And what, may I ask, brings you to our midst tonight? What is your mission, oh Walrus?"

"I'm looking for Jack the Ripper."

Nobody laughed.

Perhaps it struck them all the way it did me. I glanced at my neighbors and began to *wonder*.

LaVerne Gonnister. Hymie Kralik. Harmless. Dick Poll, Nadia Vilinoff. Johnny Odcutt and his wife. Barclay Melton. Lydia Dare. All harmless.

But what a forced smile on Dick Pool's face! And that sly, self-conscious smirk that Barclay Melton wore!

Oh, it was absurd, I grant you. But for the first time I saw these people in a new light. I wondered about their lives—their secret lives beyond the scenes of parties.

How many of them were playing a part, concealing something?

Who here would worship Hecate and grant that horrid goddess the dark boon of blood?

Even Lester Baston might be masquerading.

The mood was upon us all, for a moment. I saw questions flicker in the circle of eyes around the room.

Sir Guy stood there, and I could swear he was fully conscious of the situation he'd created, and enjoyed it.

I wondered idly just what was *really* wrong with him. Why he had this odd fixation concerning Jack the Ripper. Maybe he was hiding secrets, too. . . .

Baston, as usual, broke the mood. He burlesqued it. "The Walrus isn't kidding, friends," he said. He slapped Sir Guy on the back and put his arm around him as he orated. "Our English cousin is really on the trail of the fabulous Jack the Ripper. You all remember Jack the Ripper, I presume? Quite a cut-up in the old days, as I recall. Really had some ripping good times when he went out on a tear.

"The Walrus has some idea that the Ripper is still alive, probably prowling around Chicago with a Boy Scout knife. In fact—" ' Baston paused impressively and shot it out in a rasping stage whisper—"in fact, he has reason to believe that Jack the Ripper might even be right here in our midst tonight."

There was the expected reaction of giggles and grins. Baston eyed Lydia Dare reprovingly. "You girls needn't laugh," he smirked. "Jack the Ripper might be a woman, too, you know. Sort of a Jill the Ripper."

"You mean you actually suspect one of us?" shrieked LaVerne Gonnister, simpering up to Sir Guy. "But that Jack the Ripper person disappeared ages ago, didn't he? In 1888?"

"Aha!" interrupted Baston. "How do you know so much about it, young lady? Sounds suspicious? Watch her, Sir Guy—she may not be as young as she appears. These lady poets have dark pasts."

The tension was gone, the mood was shattered, and the whole thing was beginning to degenerate into a trivial party joke. The man who had played the *March* was eyeing the piano with a *scherzo* gleam in his eye that augured ill for Prokofieff. Lydia Dare was glancing at the kitchen, waiting to make a break for another drink.

Then Baston caught it.

"Guess what?" he yelled. "The Walrus has a gun."

His embracing arm had slipped and encountered the hard outline of the gun in Sir Guy's pocket. He snatched it out before Hollis had the opportunity to protest.

I stared hard at Sir Guy, wondering if this thing had carried far enough. But he flicked a wink my way and I remembered he had told me not to be alarmed.

So I waited as Baston broached a drunken inspiration.

"Let's play fair with our friend the Walrus," he cried. "He came all the way from England to our party on this mission. If none of you is willing to confess, I suggest we give him a chance to find out—the hard way."

"What's up?" asked Johnny Odcutt.

"I'll turn out the lights for one minute. Sir Guy can stand here with his gun. If anyone in this room is the Ripper he can either run for it or take the opportunity to—well, eradicate his pursuer. Fair enough?"

It was even sillier than it sounds, but it caught the popular fancy. Sir Guy's protests went unheard in the ensuing babble. And before I could stride over and put in my two cents' worth, Lester Baston had reached the light switch.

"Don't anybody move," he announced, with fake solemnity. "For one minute we will remain in darkness—perhaps at the mercy of a killer. At the end of that time, I'll turn up the lights again and look for bodies. Choose your partners, ladies and gentlemen."

The lights went out.

Somebody giggled.

I heard footsteps in the darkness. Mutterings.

A hand brushed my face.

The watch on my wrist ticked violently. But even louder, rising above it, I heard another thumping. The beating of my heart.

Absurd. Standing in the dark with a group of tipsy fools. And yet there was real terror lurking here, rustling through the velvet blackness.

Jack the Ripper prowled in darkness like this. And Jack the Ripper had a knife. Jack the Ripper had a madman's brain and a madman's purpose.

But Jack the Ripper was dead, dead and dust these many years—by every human law.

Only there are no human laws when you feel yourself in the darkness, when the darkness hides and protects and the outer mask slips off your face and you feel something welling up within you, a brooding shapeless purpose that is brother to the blackness.

Sir Guy Hollis shrieked.

There was a grisly thud.

Baston put the lights on.

Everybody screamed.

Sir Guy Hollis lay sprawled on the floor in the center of the room. The gun was still clutched in his hand.

I glanced at the faces, marveling at the variety of expressions human beings can assume when confronting horror.

All the faces were present in the circle. Nobody had fled. And yet Sir Guy Hollis lay there.

LaVerne Gonnister was wailing and hiding her face.

"All right."

Sir Guy rolled over and jumped to his feet. He was smiling.

"Just an experiment, eh? If Jack the Ripper *were* among those present, and thought I had been murdered, he would have betrayed himself in some way when the lights went on and he saw me lying there.

"I am convinced of your individual and collective innocence. Just a gentle spoof, my friends.

Hollis stared at the goggling Baston and the rest of them crowding in behind him.

"Shall we leave, John?" he called to me. "It's getting late, I think."

Turning, he headed for the closet. I followed him. Nobody said a word.

It was a pretty dull party after that.

3

I met Sir Guy the following evening as we agreed, on the corner of 29th and South Halsted.

After what had happened the night before, I was prepared for almost anything. But Sir Guy seemed matter-of-fact enough as he stood huddled against a grimy doorway and waited for me to appear.

"Boo!" I said, jumping out suddenly. He smiled. Only the betraying gesture of his left hand indicated that he'd instinctively reached for his gun when I startled him.

"All ready for our wild-goose chase?" I asked.

"Yes." He nodded. "I'm glad that you agreed to meet me without asking questions," he told me. "It shows you trust my judgment." He took my arm and edged me along the street slowly.

"It's foggy tonight, John," said Sir Guy Hollis. "Like London."

I nodded.

"Cold, too, for November."

I nodded again and half-shivered my agreement.

"Curious," mused Sir Guy. "London fog and November. The place and the time of the Ripper murders."

I grinned through darkness. "Let me remind you, Sir Guy, that this isn't London, but Chicago. And it isn't November, 1888. It's over fifty years later."

Sir Guy returned my grin, but without mirth. "I'm not so sure, at that," he murmured. "Look about you. Those tangled alleys and twisted streets. They're like the East End. Mitre Square. And surely they are as ancient as fifty years, at least."

"You're in the black neighborhood of South Clark Street," I said shortly. "And why you dragged me down here I still don't know."

"It's a hunch," Sir Guy admitted. "Just a hunch on my part, John. I want to wander around down here.

There's the same geographical conformation in these streets as in those courts where the Ripper roamed and slew. That's where we'll find him, John. Not in the bright lights, but down here in the darkness. The darkness where he waits and crouches.''

''Isn't that why you brought a gun?'' I asked. I was unable to keep a trace of sarcastic nervousness from my voice. All this talk, this incessant obsession with Jack the Ripper, got on my nerves more than I cared to admit.

''We may need a gun,'' said Sir Guy, gravely. ''After all, tonight is the appointed night.''

I sighed. We wandered on through the foggy, deserted streets. Here and there a dim light burned above a gin-mill doorway. Otherwise, all was darkness and shadow. Deep, gaping alleyways loomed as we proceeded down a slanting side-street.

We crawled through that fog, alone and silent, like two tiny maggots floundering within a shroud.

''Can't you see there's not a soul around these streets?'' I said.

''He's bound to come,'' said Sir Guy. ''He'll be drawn here. This is what I've been looking for. A *genius loci*. An evil spot that attracts evil. Always, when he slays, it's the slums.''

''You see, that must be one of his weaknesses. He has a fascination for squalor. Besides, the women he needs for sacrifice are more easily found in the dives and stewpots of a great city.''

''Well, let's go into one of the dives or stewpots,'' I suggested. ''I'm cold. Need a drink. This damned fog gets into your bones. You Britishers can stand it, but I like warmth and dry heat.''

We emerged from our side street and stood upon the threshold of an alley.

Through the white clouds of mist ahead, I discerned a dim blue light, a naked bulb dangling from a beer sign above an alley tavern.

"Let's take a chance," I said. "I'm beginning to shiver."

"Lead the way," said Sir Guy. I led him down the alley passage. We halted before the door of the dive.

"What are you waiting for?" he asked.

"Just looking in," I told him. "This is a rough neighborhood, Sir Guy. Never know what you're liable to run into. And I'd prefer we didn't get into the wrong company. Some of these places resent white customers."

"Good idea, John."

I finished my inspection through the doorway. "Looks deserted," I murmured. "Let's try it."

We entered a dingy bar. A feeble light flickered above the counter and railing, but failed to penetrate the further gloom of the back booths.

A gigantic black lolled across the bar. He scarcely stirred as we came in, but his eyes flicked open quite suddenly and I knew he noted our presence and was judging us.

"Evening," I said.

He took his time before replying. Still sizing us up. Then, he grinned.

"Evening, gents. What's your pleasure?"

"Gin," I said. "Two gins. It's a cold night."

"That's right, gents."

He poured, I paid, and took the glasses over to one of the booths. We wasted no time in emptying them.

I went over to the bar and got the bottle. Sir Guy and I poured ourselves another drink. The big man went back into his doze, with one wary eye half-open against any sudden activity.

The clock over the bar ticked on. The wind was rising outside, tearing the shroud of fog to ragged shreds. Sir Guy and I sat in the warm booth and drank our gin.

He began to talk, and the shadows crept up about us to listen.

He rambled a great deal. He went over everything

he'd said in the office when I met him, just as though I hadn't heard it before. The poor devils with obsessions are like that.

I listened very patiently. I poured Sir Guy another drink. And another.

But the liquor only made him more talkative. How he did run on! About ritual killings and prolonging the life unnaturally—the whole fantastic tale came out again. And of course, he maintained his unyielding conviction that the Ripper was abroad tonight.

I suppose I was guilty of goading him.

"Very well," I said, unable to keep the impatience from my voice. "Let us say that your theory is correct—even though we must overlook every natural law and swallow a lot of superstition to give it any credence.

"But let us say, for the sake of argument, that you are right. Jack the Ripper was a man who discovered how to prolong his own life through making human sacrifices. He did travel around the world as you believe. He is in Chicago now and he is planning to kill. In other words, let us suppose that everything you claim is gospel truth. So what?"

"What do you mean, 'so what'?" said Sir Guy.

"I mean—so what?" I answered. "If all this is true, it still doesn't prove that by sitting down in a dingy ginmill on the South Side, Jack the Ripper is going to walk in here and let you kill him, or turn him over to the police. And come to think of it, I don't even know now just what you intend to *do* with him if you ever did find him."

Sir Guy gulped his gin. "I'd capture the bloody swine," he said. "Capture him and turn him over to the government, together with all the papers and documentary evidence I've collected against him over a period of many years. I've spent a fortune investigating this affair, I tell you, a fortune! His capture will mean the solution of hundreds of unsolved crimes, of that I am convinced."

In vino veritas. Or was all this babbling the result of too much gin? It didn't matter. Sir Guy Hollis had another. I sat there and wondered what to do with him. The man was rapidly working up to a climax of hysterical drunkenness.

"That's enough," I said, putting out my hand as Sir Guy reached for the half-emptied bottle again. "Let's call a cab and get out of here. It's getting late and it doesn't look as though your elusive friend is going to put in his appearance. Tomorrow, if I were you, I'd plan to turn all those papers and documents over to the F.B.I. If you're so convinced of the truth of your theory, they are competent to make a very thorough investigation, and find your man."

"No." Sir Guy was drunkenly obstinate. "No cab."

"But let's get out of here anyway," I said, glancing at my watch. "It's past midnight."

He sighed, shrugged, and rose unsteadily. As he started for the door, he tugged the gun free from his pocket.

"Here, give me that!" I whispered. "You can't walk around the street brandishing that thing."

I took the gun and slipped it inside my coat. Then I got hold of his right arm and steered him out of the door. The black man didn't look up as we departed.

We stood shivering in the alleyway. The fog had increased. I couldn't see either end of the alley from where we stood. It was cold. Damp. Dark. Fog or no fog, a little wind was whispering secrets to the shadows at our backs.

Sir Guy, despite his incapacity, still stared apprehensively at the alley, as though he expected to see a figure approaching.

Disgust got the better of me.

"Childish foolishness," I snorted. "Jack the Ripper, indeed! I call this carrying a hobby too far."

"Hobby?" He faced me. Through the fog I could see his distorted face. "You call this a hobby?"

"Well, what is it?" I grumbled. "Just why else are you so interested in tracking down this mythical killer?"

My arm held his. But his stare held me.

"In London," he whispered. "In 1888 . . . one of those nameless drabs the Ripper slew . . . was my mother."

"What?"

"Later I was recognized by my father, and legitimatized. We swore to give our lives to find the Ripper. My father was the first to search. He died in Hollywood in 1926—on the trail of the Ripper. They said he was stabbed by an unknown assailant in a brawl. But I knew who the assailant was.

"So I've taken up his work, do you see, John? I've carried on. And I will carry on until I do find him and kill him with my own hands."

I believed him then. He wouldn't give up. He wasn't just a drunken babbler anymore. He was as fanatical, as determined, as relentless as the Ripper himself.

Tomorrow he'd be sober. He'd continue the search. Perhaps he'd turn those papers over the the F.B.I. Sooner or later, with such persistence—and with his motive—he'd be successful. I'd always known he had a motive.

"Let's go," I said, steering him down the alley.

"Wait a minute," said Sir Guy. "Give me back my gun." He lurched a little. "I'd feel better with the gun on me."

He pressed me into the dark shadows of a little recess.

I tried to shrug him off, but he was insistent.

"Let me carry the gun, now, John," he mumbled.

"All right," I said.

I reached into my coat, brought my hand out.

"But that's not a gun," he protested. "That's a knife."

"I know."

I bore down on him swiftly.

"John!" he screamed.

"Never mind the 'John,'" I whispered, raising the knife. "Just call me . . . Jack."

DAW

Welcome to DAW's Gallery of Ghoulish Delights!

HOUSE SHUDDERS
Martin H. Greenberg and Charles G. Waugh, editors
  Fiendish tales about haunted houses!
☐ UE2223 $3.50

HUNGER FOR HORROR
Robert H. Adams, Martin H. Greenberg, and Pamela Crippen
Adams, editors
  A devilish stew of horror from the master terror chefs!
☐ UE2266 $3.50

RED JACK
Martin H. Greenberg, Charles G. Waugh, and Frank D.
McSherry, Jr., editors
  The 100th anniversary collection of Jack the Ripper tales!
☐ UE2315 $3.95

VAMPS
Martin H. Greenberg and Charles G. Waugh, editors
  A spine-tingling collection featuring those long-toothed ladies
  of the night—female vampires!
☐ UE2190 $3.50

THE YEAR'S BEST HORROR STORIES
Karl Edward Wagner, editor
  ☐ Series IX   UE2159—$2.95
  ☐ Series X   UE2160—$2.95
  ☐ Series XI   UE2161—$2.95
  ☐ Series XIV   UE2156—$3.50
  ☐ Series XV   UE2226—$3.50
  ☐ Series XVI   UE2300—$3.95

Attention:

DAW COLLECTORS

Many readers of DAW Books have written requesting information on early titles and book numbers to assist in the collection of DAW editions since the first of our titles appeared in April 1972.

We have prepared a several-pages-long list of all DAW titles, giving their sequence numbers, original and current order numbers, and ISBN numbers. And of course the authors and book titles, as well as reissues.

If you think that this list will be of help, you may have a copy by writing to the address below and enclosing one dollar in stamps or currency to cover the handling and postage costs.

DAW BOOKS, INC.
DEPT. C
1633 Broadway
New York, N.Y. 10019